BREATHLESS IN THE DARK

ALSO BY ELIZABETH COLE

Honor & Roses
Choose the Sky
Raven's Rise
Peregrine's Call

A Heartless Design
A Reckless Soul
A Shameless Angel
The Lady Dauntless
Beneath Sleepless Stars
A Mad and Mindless Night
A Most Relentless Gentleman

BREATHLESS IN THE DARK

ELIZABETH COLE

SKYSPARK BOOKS

PHILADELPHIA, PENNSYLVANIA

SkySpark Books
Philadelphia, Pennsylvania
skysparkbooks.com
inquiry@skysparkbooks.com

Publisher's Note: This is a work of fiction. Names, characters,
places, and incidents are a product of the author's imagination.
Locales and public names are sometimes used for atmospheric
purposes. Any resemblance to actual people, living or dead, or to
businesses, companies, events, institutions, or locales is completely coincidental.

Ordering Information:
Quantity sales. Special discounts are available on quantity pur-
chases by corporations, associations, and others. For details,
contact the "Special Sales Department" at the address above.

BREATHLESS IN THE DARK / Cole, Elizabeth. – 1st ed.
ISBN-13: 978-1-942316-42-8

℞

NOBODY EVER WALKED ACROSS THE bridge, not on a
night like this. Cold raindrops drove down like nails,
sharp and painful and unforgiving. In the city, the paved
streets grew slick, and the unpaved lanes turned into
muddy soup. But the bridge was worse, because there the
wind clawed over and under the thin stretch of stone, eager to pluck anyone foolish enough to be there straight
into the icy waters of the river below.

A solitary figure stood watching the swirling depths
beneath the span. His clothing was uniformly dark, and
made more so by the wet weather. Still, a sharp-eyed observer would have noticed the excellent cut of the greatcoat, and the craftsmanship of the leather boots. This was
a man of a class far better than this part of town usually
saw, since it lay so close to the depressing and derelict
slum of St Giles.

The man appeared not to care about his surroundings.
His attention was fully on the river. Earlier that night,
he'd talked about this bridge to a waterman, a worker who
knew the Thames like an old friend. The waterman said
that if an object were dropped off the south side right in
the middle, it would be swept out to sea before morning.

"Even a large, heavy object?" he'd asked. "Like a
body?"

The waterman scarcely blinked as he assured the questioner that anything disposed of from the top of Charlesway Bridge would disappear from all human knowledge. "The Devil himself couldn't fish it out, sir."

Pleased with the answer, the man paid for the information with a silver coin, and then walked off into the rain.

His greatcoat had fought valiantly against the damp, but the heavy wool was finally succumbing, and the chill settled against his skin. He didn't mind. He welcomed it, in fact. Even an unpleasant sensation was better than nothing.

A heaviness knocked against his leg, and he felt the gun under his greatcoat. The sensation reminded him of his duty.

He looked to the left, toward the other end of the bridge leading toward St Giles, a neighborhood chock full of dubious characters and slapdash housing, a mass of miserable humanity so desperate that they'd steal and lie to anyone for a bit of coin, and they'd kill for not much more.

Charming neighborhood.

But that was his destination tonight. There was a man in Catchpenny Lane he needed to find.

Royce Holmes was a lot of things. He was a son, he was a father, he was an earl, and he was a spy. For the past several years, he'd been one of a handful of agents working for a secretive organization called the Zodiac. The recruitment had been by happenstance, when a mysterious figure Royce later discovered was known only as the Astronomer had apparently noticed him and set the wheels in motion. Since Royce had not been an earl then, and had no expectations of becoming one, he'd leapt at the chance to leap into danger. He loved danger—it was one of the only things that made him feel alive.

He strode along the edge of the bridge, leaving the

darkest of his thoughts behind…for now. He had to get through tonight's assignment.

His task in this neighborhood was only part of a much larger operation. Royce had been tracking down a French agent who was deeply involved with the forgery of diplomatic documents. The forgeries had appeared in governmental agencies and even royal courts all through Europe. Catastrophe had narrowly been avoided so far, but soon there would be an incident due to these false papers, something that would hurt Britain in the war against Napoleon, or damage an important alliance with another country.

The miscreants had to be found. Through painstaking work, Royce traced one of the forged documents to a criminal named Swigg who controlled a large part of this neighborhood. Through the efforts of a number of informants, Royce built a list of locations where Swigg might be operating, based on rumors about who paid protection to him. He'd work through that list until he got his man.

"Evenin', handsome."

He looked over to the source of the sudden call.

From a shadowed doorway, a woman in a low-cut red dress leaned out, displaying her wares. "Fancy a tumble, my man?" she asked, crooking her finger to entice him closer. "Get out of the rain and into Molly's arms. I'll keep you warm all night…if you can pay."

As a trained agent, he instantly assessed whether this person could be a threat. But everything about Molly was genuine, and genuinely sad. She was older than the average prostitute, and used makeup to hide the fact. The rain was not kind to the cheap cosmetics available to a woman like Molly. Her dark hair frizzed out in the damp, and the red gown, once a fine creation for a lady far richer than Molly, was stained and tattered.

"Not tonight," Royce said. Just the thought of lying with her made his skin crawl. Possibly diseased, certainly covered in lice…not his dream woman. "But point me to Catchpenny Lane, if you don't mind."

"Two pence," she countered, ever the businesswoman.

Shrugging, he walked over and handed her a tanner. The larger coin lit her eyes right up.

"Walk up this street and turn right," she said, tucking the tanner away. "You'll see a tavern called the Frog & Frigate. That's in Catchpenny Lane."

Royce nodded thanks and turned to walk away. Then, on impulse, he said, "I could give you more. Enough to get out of here." He could give her all the money he had on his person. It would be a good act, to counter all the bad acts and worse thoughts in his life.

Molly blinked, not comprehending what he was offering. Then she understood…and laughed. "Bless you for a fool. Where'd I go? This is my home! And me mum and me kiddies can't scrape by without me."

The woman regarded him with pity, as if he were the one in trouble. "You're one of those crusading types, ain't you? Those swells who think that they can save everyone they meet. Can't save all of London, my man. But you can get out of the rain."

"You're sure?" he asked, still feeling the weight of unspent coins.

"Aye, I'm sure. Now, get on with you. I've got work to do." Molly gave him a mocking curtsey, and pointed him toward the slums.

Royce walked on, musing about the likely fate of Molly, who didn't care to be mistaken for some damsel in distress. Well, fair enough.

But perhaps he'd save the next damsel in distress who crossed his path.

♍

IN A COLD BOARDINGHOUSE, A woman hunched over the rickety desk in her rented room, a pen gripped in her right hand. She was known as Miss Tess Black, or Tess the Scribbler, among her current circle of acquaintances.

In truth, she was not a miss, and the names Tess and Black did not belong to her.

But that is a matter for later.

Outside, raindrops pelted against the shutters of the window, and wind whistled through a crack in the ancient wooden panels, allowing a band of icy mist to collect on the sill.

She shivered as one particularly strong gust grazed the bare skin of her shoulder. Unfortunately, her best (and indeed only) gown was drying in front of the tiny coal-fueled grate, and her shawl more resembled a sopping wet rag than an article of clothing.

Thus, she sat in only her damp shift. If anyone walked in, they'd see a most inappropriate sight: a barely clad woman with unbound hair, exposed calves and feet at one end, and far too much of her chest revealed at the other.

However, no one ever walked into this room uninvited. Miss Tess Black was quite adamant about privacy, and she had a latch on her door to enforce it. She needed to work uninterrupted. The slightest distraction could ruin a whole letter. And because Tess the Scribbler earned her living by writing other people's letters, among a vast array of other documents, this wish was grudgingly honored by the hard-faced landlady, Mrs Salinger.

Tess pinched the thin fabric of the shift, testing its saturation. Ugh, still disgustingly damp. For a moment, her mind shot back to the past, to a room full of silks and fine woolen fabric, and the modiste with her measuring tape and shrewd eye for fashion…

Mademoiselle must wear peach silk for her coming out. It is the color of her soul, ripening into the most beautiful season.

Ahh, the dream of that gown. She never got to wear it, and never would. No more silks for her.

She shook off the memory. The past was a dangerous place, and she had no business there.

She regarded the letter on her desk. "Focus, my girl," she told herself. "Get this done and then you can go to sleep." Her only escape was sleep…a few hours when she was not at the mercy of others' whims.

This letter was particularly challenging, considering the language was Italian—not one of Miss Tess Black's preferred languages, although she was certainly capable of transcribing the notes she'd been given to craft an artful document.

She was concentrating so hard on the paper in front of her that it took several moments for the voices from below to filter through her brain.

Granted, it was often loud. The boarders in this house worked strange hours, and half of the men were drunk when they stumbled home to bed. So shouts and curses, as well as the slamming of doors and heavy knocks against the walls were commonplace.

But these voices were different. A huge booming sound echoed up the stairwell.

"Where's the scribbler? Tell me which room she's holed up in, or we'll bust through them all!"

Miss Tess Black went still. A drop of ink splashed to the desk below, nearly ruining the effect of her careful penmanship.

"Coaker!" she whispered, dismayed. The man was well-known in this dangerous corner of London, and his arrival always heralded pain and misery. More ominously, he was Swigg's right-hand man.

Unwilling to sit around waiting for trouble, Tess grabbed the small leather case at the side of the desk, shoveling papers into it, leaving behind the one that she'd been working on. She lunged for her silver penknife, one of her few precious belongings. Then she dragged the still-wet gown over her head, grimacing at the pull of the fabric. A ripping sound suggested the outfit would never be the same after this.

Then she opened the shutters.

A sharp gust of wind greeted her, warning her that this was a foolish idea. Well, it was not the first time in her life that she'd been a fool.

Tess hauled the thin mattress from her bed to the window and shoved it through the opening. She climbed over the sill, then dropped the leather bag to the ground below near the mattress. She heard the pounding of footsteps in the hallway, took a deep breath, and then jumped.

The thin mattress cushioned her fall just enough to prevent grievous injury, though she felt the jarring of her bones when she hit the ground. The landlady would be furious at the misuse of this terrible mattress, but Mrs Salinger's ire was the least of her problems now.

Taking the leather case in hand, she darted out of the narrow alleyway toward the street. The men inside would know immediately how she escaped—her only hope was to get far enough away and out of sight that they might choose the wrong direction when the inevitable chase began.

Coaker's howl of rage sounded from the window she'd just escaped from.

"Tess, you moonling chit! Get back here!"

She skidded into the muddy strip of street called Catchpenny Lane, one knee dropping onto a cobblestone, which brought a gasp of pain to her lips. Tess struggled to a standing position again, and turned right down the first available street. She'd run across the bridge to the slightly better neighborhood on the other side of the river. This was Coaker's hunting ground, so the faster she got out, the better chance she'd have.

Shouts echoed behind her. She didn't have much time. What had gone wrong? Why was Coaker sent for her? And if she got caught, was there a chance in hell that she'd ever see daylight again?

Best not to find out. She kept running.

Rain ran down her bare head, the droplets getting into her eyes, forcing her to squint into the gloom.

"Just get across the river," she told herself, her words coming fast and breathy as she limped forward. "Move your feet, Tamsin!"

She reached the apex of the bridge. Ahead, a few lights glowed from the buildings in the neighborhood she was aiming for. Yes, she could make that distance. She'd gotten halfway there already.

Invigorated by the thought, she put on a burst of speed.

Then a huge hand slammed down onto her shoulder, stopping her short.

"Got you!" the gin-soaked voice of Coaker crowed behind her. "Come on, Tess. Swigg wants a word with you."

"Let me go!" Tamsin cried out. She turned around, trying to twist free of the man's grasp, but he only grinned, his yellowed teeth flashing.

"Swigg don't let anyone go. And I don't like having to chase you down." He raised his other arm, his giant hand splayed flat. "This'll knock that saucy attitude out of you," Coaker growled, starting to swing his arm downward.

Knowing that the open-handed blow would knock her off her feet, Tamsin squeezed her eyes shut to block out the horror of seeing it happen. She whimpered in anticipation, but the blow never came.

She looked up just as a shadow eclipsed the guttering torchlight. Before she could scream, a low voice cut through the night.

"Leave her alone."

A stranger stood there. He was tall, and even with the rain-soaked greatcoat obscuring the details, it was obvious the man was unusually strong. He'd grabbed Coaker's arm in midswing and pushed the thug away, putting himself between Coaker and Tamsin.

"It's not polite to strike a lady," he continued, his tone mild.

"She ain't no lady," Coaker responded, "and she sure as hell ain't your business!"

"I am making her my business." The stranger shoved Coaker hard, sending him stumbling a few steps back. "Leave her be."

Tamsin shrank from this new situation, from the intruding man who looked at least as dangerous as the one she was running from.

Coaker's blood was up, and he was in no mood to tolerate a stranger's observations. He lunged forward again. "Who in hell do you think you are? If I kill her in the gutter, it's none of your concern!" Coaker pulled a blade from its sheath in his big black boot. It was famous among residents of the neighborhood, known as Coaker's Calling Card for the blood it left behind.

He said, "If you ain't gone in two seconds, I'll carve your flesh off your bones."

The stranger actually laughed at that threat. Coaker growled, upset that the exchange was not going to plan.

That was when the stranger attacked.

It was swift, efficient, and brutal.

Tamsin missed the details, since she turned her face to the stone wall on the side of the bridge, trying to make herself as small a target as possible. She held the leather case in front of her body like a shield.

The hissing breaths and grunts from the fighters made her wince, but then a huge weight crashed to the stone surface, and she instinctively looked to see what happened.

Coaker lay on the slippery, cold surface, his eyes closed, only the sound of harsh breathing proving he was not yet dead.

She stared at the stranger, who hadn't so much as touched her with a finger.

"Bad night to be out," he commented, as if making an observation at a party. He reached into his greatcoat, and pulled out a pistol, the silver barrel glinting in the meager light.

Tamsin's heart dropped. Whatever trouble she was in, it was far worse than she'd thought.

She took a deep breath.

Then she jumped up and ran.

She got fewer than five paces before the stranger grabbed her, hooking his arm around her waist.

She spun around, arms out and her fists clenched, fear making her furious and wild. "Let me go! I don't know who you are but I won't go to Swigg or anyone else!"

"Steady, darling," he murmured, looking down at her face. "I'm not here to hurt you."

"You have a gun!"

"In case your friend over there wakes up," he said in a conciliatory tone.

Tess took a few quick breaths, realizing that she was pressed against him, and that she could feel the heat of his body through the greatcoat and her own scandalously disarrayed gown.

"Who do you work for?" she demanded, trying to keep her voice steady. Was she to be stolen for another criminal's petty empire, someone who could afford to hire muscle like this man?

The stranger shook his head. "That's an interesting question, but not one I'll answer."

"Then tell me why you're here!"

He shrugged. "Oh, I was in the neighborhood and saw the chase. I got curious, and followed you both, and it looks like a damn good thing for you that I did. If you tell me where you live, I'll see you home."

"Home?" she asked incredulously. The concept that this man didn't want to hurt her or steal her or kill her was frankly too much for her tired brain to deal with. Everyone had an angle. Was this hellishly handsome man supposed to be some guardian angel? She refused to believe it. "You think you can escort me *home*?"

"Night like this, you don't want to be out."

"Are you blind?" she asked. "I'm not out because I want to be. Coaker chased me out of my so-called home."

She turned and walked away as fast as she could from the hulking stranger. Once Coaker returned to action, she'd be in for it. She had to find a place to hide.

Footsteps sounded behind her. She glanced back and saw the stranger.

"I wasn't done talking to you," the man said.

"I don't want more trouble," Tess mumbled.

"I said I'm not going to hurt you."

"Thank you for the reassurance, but I often hear that just before it starts to hurt."

"Listen to me," he said, stopping her. "What is it with the women in this part of town that you all refuse aid? At least let me get you out of the rain."

"At what price?" she snapped back. She was well-acquainted with what most men expected as payment for earning a woman's gratitude.

"Price? Whatever price the inn charges, I suppose. There is a decent inn somewhere around here, isn't there? If I get any wetter, I'll have to start swimming down these streets. And I don't like swimming."

"And once we're to the inn?" she asked with narrowed eyes.

"Then we can get out of this damned rain. What do you say? You know where to go?"

Tamsin scrutinized the stranger's face, searching for some hint of nefarious intentions. In the poor light, his face was mostly shadows, his cheeks and forehead cut into planes of depth, hinting at an implacable personality. Stubble dusted his jaw and chin, shading his face with further detail.

And then there were his eyes. Deep-set and dark as ink. They might be blue or brown or black—she couldn't tell. But there was a strange warmth in them, the only warmth to be found on this dismal night.

"Well?" he prompted.

For some reason, she trusted those eyes. "Follow me."

♍

ROYCE ALLOWED THE WOMAN TO set her own pace, though he stayed right beside her. Part of him thought she'd bolt away at the first opportunity (and why should he care if she did?). Another part of him was too well-schooled to ever let a lady walk unescorted...even as dubious a lady as this one. She'd certainly been skittish with him, which made sense considering the situation.

He thought about the man he'd just fought. A brawler, made big with layers of thick fat over thicker muscle. He'd probably been a bully since he was a boy, and now he took pleasure in chasing after defenseless women on rainy nights.

Royce probably should have killed him, but he didn't want to deal with the mess. Besides, he didn't want to scare the woman even more than he had. The second he locked eyes with her, he knew in a flash that this woman didn't fit the scene. There was something about her bearing that was unusual.

Not to mention that the woman dropped Swigg's name back there on the bridge. Now *that* could be very useful to Royce.

The woman seemed remarkably composed for someone who'd just been chased and her life threatened. He admired that, even if she looked like something the rag collector would pass over.

Her outfit revealed a scandalous amount of skin, thanks to a long rip at the back of the bodice, and the fact that most of the buttons seemed to be missing. She wore a shift underneath, but it was soaked to the point of transparency. And her bare feet…

"Wait, where are your shoes?" he asked, suddenly shocked in a way that he hadn't been before. This part of London had a way of blunting normal human responses to misery.

"I told you, I left my room in a hurry," she responded.

"You've got to be freezing!"

"Yes," she said. "The first person who leads me to a fireplace will be a god to me."

What would her worship feel like?

The stirring of arousal surprised him. It had been a while since any woman caught his interest, and to think that this thin, half-drowned tatterdemalion was doing so was incredible to Royce. He realized her didn't even know her name.

What a damsel in distress to save, he thought wryly.

He took off his greatcoat. "Wear this," he said. Even as soaked as it was, it would cut the wind. She needed protection more than he did.

She looked at him with suspicion rather than gratitude as he put the coat around her shoulders. "Did you count your money first?" she asked.

"I never keep my money in my coat," he replied. "And you're welcome."

She sniffed, putting her nose in the air, and started walking again.

They trudged forward for perhaps half a mile, enough distance to allow the character of the neighborhood around them to change from hazardous to merely shabby.

"Here," she said, pointing to a sign swinging in the

wind. The Green Lion, it called itself, and a large cat's head on the sign illustrated the name for those who couldn't read.

He pushed the door open and led her inside. The innkeeper took one look at them and shook his head. "No rooms."

Royce put a short stack of coins on the counter, in no mood to be told off. "It states quite clearly on the sign that you do have rooms. Give me the best one."

The innkeeper raised an eyebrow at the coins, then produced a key. "Last door on the left-hand side. You'll be wanting supper delivered up there as well…sir?"

The innkeeper was frantically trying to place Royce's class, a task made difficult by his current sartorial condition, and the presence of a half-clad, barefoot woman on his arm.

"Naturally," Royce said shortly. "And give me a bottle of something to drink. Right now."

"You want whiskey or brandy?" A gentleman would expect brandy, but the innkeeper still couldn't be sure if this man was a gentleman, or merely a man with coin to spend.

Royce did not enlighten him. "I'll take one of each."

The innkeeper grinned and pulled two bottles out of a cabinet below the bar.

"Sealed bottles," the woman said suddenly. She leaned in close to the innkeeper. "I'll know if you give him the wood grain."

The innkeeper glared at her. Then he carefully shifted his arms before standing up again and slamming down two bottles on the counter. "Our *finest* brandy and whiskey, sir."

Royce grabbed the bottles. "Lead the way up, since you know so much," he muttered to his guide.

Upstairs, she took off the greatcoat and handed it to him. "Thank you for the loan of the coat. It was very kind of you." Her voice was still laced with wariness, as if kindness were an impossible feat.

Putting the bottles on a table, he asked, "What did you mean by wood grain?"

She examined the tops of the bottles with a cool professionalism. "These look all right. A lot of the bars around fill up empty bottles of better liquor with wood grain alcohol and colored syrup, then charge drunk swells ten times the cost. He thought he'd make a tidy little profit on you."

"And given me fake brandy! Ugh. Well, thank you."

"A pleasure to serve you, my lord." Her voice dripped with sarcasm. Then she paused. "You are a lord, aren't you."

He'd let his voice slip into its natural tone. He reverted to the accent he preferred to use while working. "Never mind what I am. What's your name?"

She hesitated before saying, "Tess Black."

He looked at her, hearing the catch in her voice, recognizing it for what it was—a lie.

"They call me Tess the Scribbler," she said before he could call her out. "I copy out letters and such for my living. Many folks in the area don't read or write, so they hire me to do it for them." She pointed to the leather satchel she'd carried. It did look more like a briefcase than a typical traveling case.

"Scribbler." He frowned. "You said your rooms were in Catchpenny Lane?"

She had said no such thing, but she didn't notice Royce's leading question, and merely nodded.

"Hmm. Interesting."

"Why is that interesting?"

Because that was where one of Swigg's subordinates was supposed to have been working out of. Then again, hundreds of scriveners worked in the city, and it was not surprising that two might live and work on the same street.

"Would you mind pouring me a drink?" he asked, offering her the brandy bottle.

She raised an eyebrow as she took the alcohol, but didn't press the matter of his interest in Catchpenny Lane.

Royce looked around. The room was surprisingly spacious and comfortable, with a sitting area by the fire, and a large bed on the other side of the room, with a heavy brocade curtain that could be pulled across to separate the space. No fire burned in the grate yet, but one was laid, and plenty of wood was stacked nearby. The bed linens and hangings looked clean, if faded. And the only smells were soap and woodsmoke. None of the grime and filth of the streets.

He bent to the floor in front of the fireplace, and was soon rewarded with a bright blaze from the tinder. Even the larger logs seemed dry, and he knew that the fire would burn steadily.

Royce turned and smiled at the woman. "Your fireplace, complete with fire."

The flames reflected in her eyes as she moved closer. "How divine," she breathed, stretching her hands toward the heat.

"Yes, you said you'd treat the person who brought you fire as a god," he noted.

"Rather, my own personal Prometheus," she said with a low chuckle. "Your brandy's on the table, by the way."

He went and got the drink, welcoming the tumble of heat down his throat. God, the weather was awful.

How does a woman who can't pay for shoes know who

Prometheus is? The thought woke Royce's mind up, stirring more curiosity about the woman. But he couldn't pepper her with questions. That would only alarm her. Fortunately, he'd been trained to get information out of people in many different ways.

"Will he find you here?" Royce asked. "That man who was after you? Coaker?"

"No." She sounded confident. "He'd never dream I'd be here. I can't afford this room." She looked him over, her expression turning cool and wary. "What do you want me to do?"

"Warm up. We'll see if the landlord actually delivers on that supper."

She sat in the wooden chair close to the fireplace, plucking at her sodden gown. She must be hellishly uncomfortable. He certainly was, and he wore both a coat and boots outside.

Thinking of that, he hung his greatcoat it on a wooden peg on the wall near the fire. His valet would yell at him later, since the peg would undoubtably pull the wool out of shape. Oh, well, such was the risk of spying in the rain.

His jacket was damp as well, so he took that off too, leaving him with only his shirt to cover his top half. If Miss Tess Black was raised like the ladies he associated with in his normal life, she'd shriek and faint at the transgression of a man wearing only his shirt in her presence.

However, she was entirely focused on the fire, stretching out her legs toward the flames, wiggling her bare toes in the heat. Her feet had lost the alarming blue tinge they'd had on the bridge, and were growing pink under the streaks of mud. Royce watched her for a moment, startled and rather charmed by her lack of self-consciousness. Also, her toes were cute.

He wondered if she was ticklish.

Stop it, he warned himself. Aloud, he asked, keeping his tone neutral, "Drying out now?"

"Somewhat," she replied. "My dress is going to take all night to dry, though, so I doubt I'll really get warm."

"I could pay the innkeeper to go find you a gown."

Looking alarmed, she shook her head. "No! That's the sort of thing that gets talked about, and Coaker will be listening—or someone will, and Coaker will hear it from them when he wakes up."

"Then what will you do?"

She looked down at her dress. "Do you mind if I strip naked, my lord?"

Royce blinked. "What?"

"To better dry my clothes," she clarified.

"I paid for the room, not for you." He took another sip from the glass. "But may I watch?"

"You may *not*," she retorted, her spirit evidently not as dampened as the rest of her. "But you can draw the curtain and then pull off the sheet from the bed and hand it over when I say."

"Going for the Greek goddess look, eh?" He stepped to the bed and drew the curtain that separated the areas, providing her privacy to strip.

And sparking his own curiosity about what he was missing.

He pulled the top sheet off the bed, noting that it was clean and without holes.

Then he heard a ripping sound, followed by Miss Black's muttered curse.

Royce smiled to himself. "All right over there?"

"No," she groused. "This fabric is possessed, and I think it's trying to strangle me."

"Do you require assistance?"

There was a long pause, and then she said, "Yes, I fear

so."

Royce slid the curtain aside to find Miss Black in the most charming and compromising position he'd ever seen.

The sopping wet skirt of the gown had somehow contrived to tangle itself up so that she couldn't disrobe without bending her spine at an impossible angle. Further, it looked as if her hair had also been attacked by the few remaining buttons near the neckline.

"You are a damsel in distress, aren't you," he murmured, trying not to be too obvious about his examination of her lower assets—long, sleekly muscled legs exposed up to her thighs.

Her lips pursed in irritation. "Again, I didn't choose to be out tonight, and if I owned a second gown that was dry, I'd…"

She trailed off as he reached for the gown, her eyes widening when the backs of his fingers grazed her still-damp skin.

"Never mind," she gasped out. "I shouldn't have asked. I'll deal with this myself!"

"Steady, Miss Black. You're not the first woman I've undressed, and something tells me that I'm not the first man to take your clothing off. Now stand still and let me help you."

She blinked, but didn't offer further objections.

Royce had to concentrate on the puzzle of her gown, which was ripped, sodden, and in such disarray that he doubted it could be saved. He freed her long hair from the buttons and peeled the bodice down, leaving only her shift to cover her breasts.

"You are," she mumbled, speaking more to the fire than to him.

"I am what?"

"The first man to actually take my clothing off."

Considering where and how he'd found her, it seemed like an unbelievable statement. And yet he believed her.

"I won't take off any more than you request me to," he assured her.

She sighed, the slope of her shoulders softening as some tension in her body loosened.

After that, it was easier. Royce managed to twist the dress back to where it was more or less supposed to be, though the wet fabric did cling to everything. He knelt to peel the dress away from the shift—she appeared to not have the benefit of a petticoat—and was treated to a tantalizing glimpse of her backside through the now nearly transparent cotton.

He finished with the dress in a circle around her feet, which were just as cute up close as they'd looked across the room. Suddenly feeling the need to see more of her, he looked up.

The expression on her face was one of intense interest. Probably, she'd never had a lord kneeling in front of her before. Her arms were crossed over her chest, an attempt to preserve modesty that only made her look more appealing.

Her mouth opened a little, and Royce wanted to hear her to tell him to go on, to rid her of the shift as well.

But her expression changed then, cooling to almost frosty. "Thank you, I'll manage from here," she said.

Royce got up slowly, and made his way back to the curtain, pulling it shut again behind him. Tess didn't move until he did so, and he heard the suddenly riveting sound of wet cotton being peeled off her skin. Then the patter of her feet across the floor.

"You may hand the sheet through now, please," Tess instructed, her voice startlingly near.

He did so, manfully avoiding the urge to peek through the gap in the curtain.

A moment later, she called, "I am done."

He waited, since his breeches were currently rather tight.

"My lord? Are you hiding?"

"Certainly not." Royce pushed the curtain aside and stepped through. In front of him, his damsel in distress had transformed into a classical beauty. She'd draped the white sheet around her body in a way that was modest yet beautiful. Her legs were now alas hidden, but her arms were left bare. Best of all, her hair still fell loose and wild around her face. The glow of the fire cast pink tones on the fabric and her skin.

He'd never seen a more alluring figure in his life.

♍

TAMSIN STOOD NERVOUSLY UNDER THE man's gaze. Had she made things worse by changing into this ridiculous outfit? "Will this be adequate for a few hours? Just until my gown dries."

"As far as I'm concerned, you can wear that until the end of time. Women's fashion has not improved since the Romans left Britain."

She blinked, the compliment taking a moment to filter into her fatigued brain.

But then a knock sounded at the door, saving her from making a reply.

He pointed her to the chair near the fire. "Sit. I'll deal with this."

He strode over and opened the door, accepting the offered tray from a skinny girl who curtseyed awkwardly.

"Supper, sir. If you need anything else, just shout for Gertie. Everyone does."

He nodded and closed the door. He carried the tray to a table near the fire. Tamsin was encouraged by the steam and appetizing smell.

"Beef. They were impressed by you," she said. She sat in front of the fire, leaning over to allow her long tresses to dry.

"Impressed by my money, more likely." He handed her a bowl and spoon.

She took a bite, and sighed with pleasure. "Ah, hot food may be the pinnacle of human civilization."

"I thought that was the fireplace."

"Both warm me," she said, smiling.

He took a bite, and nodded at the quality of the stew. "Not bad at all. Is hot food a novelty for you, Miss Black?"

"Sometimes." Tamsin ate a few more bites, then said, "I'm much better off than many in the city though. Well, I was." She frowned, recalling the events that brought them to this inn.

"You said you don't think you can go back to your rooms?"

"Even if Mrs Salinger took me back, which I doubt, since I destroyed a mattress to jump out the window—"

"You *jumped* out of a window?" he asked, incredulous.

"I had to. Coaker was coming up the stairs."

"And that's the man I met on the bridge. Why was he after you? You mentioned someone called Swigg."

Tamsin must have been half-mad when she was babbling on the bridge. "Did I?"

"You did." His eyes bored into hers. Eyes that were the darkest of blue, she saw now. Eyes that missed very little. The man obviously wasn't going to drop the matter, but Tamsin wasn't about to expose the extent of her links to the underworld around St Giles.

"Oh, it's really nothing. Swigg used my services as scrivener," she explained. It wasn't a lie, even if it was *barely* the truth. "I must have done something that displeased him as a customer." She finished her stew, and licked the spoon. Hot food really was marvelous.

"What could you possibly have done that caused him to send a thug like that after you?"

"Excellent question," Tess said. "With luck, I'll never find out. Swigg is not the most forgiving of men."

"He'll have to find a new scrivener, then. Is there another one in this part of town with your level of skill?"

"Definitely not. In fact, this may make things awkward," she said very softly. Considering the task Swigg hired her out for, and what Coaker's visit interrupted, Tamsin was going to irritate a lot of dangerous people. "I don't know what will happen when they find me."

She stared into the leaping flames, lost in the various futures presented to her. All looked bleak, and short. "I have to get away from here," she thought out loud.

"Miss Black," he said.

She didn't respond, not even hearing him.

"Miss Black. *Tess*."

That got her attention. "What?"

He'd leaned forward in his chair. "You don't respond to that name very well, darling. So tell me what your real name is."

"What purpose would that serve? If I wanted to tell the world who I am, I'd not have bothered to change my name."

"Ah, so you admit there's a real name you're hiding," he noted. He stood up and walked to the table where the bottles stood. He refilled his glass, but then downed his drink in one go.

"I do have a past," she admitted, watching him pour another drink.

He filled his glass again, and rejoined her at the fire. "So no name?"

"I'm afraid not. But I should thank you," she said, more sincerely. "It's a terrible night out. I am glad to be here."

"There's a little bit of truth," he said. "That's something. Are you really a scrivener?"

"Yes, of course. Who lies about that?"

He gestured to the leather case. "Would you show me your work?"

Tamsin nodded. "Bring it here, please."

He did so, handing her the case and then clearing the dishes from the little table. For a gentleman, he seemed quite comfortable doing tasks most men of his class would balk at.

Tess opened the case and paged through the collection of papers inside. There were some she didn't dare show him, and in fact she should set those on fire as soon as she reasonably could.

However, there were innocent pages inside as well. Tamsin pulled several out and laid them on the table.

"Here. You can see the sort of work my customers tend to ask for. A letter from a woman to her family in Cornwall. This one is a simple contract for the sale of a cow—they wanted to retain the calf should the cow prove to be pregnant at the time of sale. And this one is a will."

He raised an eyebrow, but his level of interest seemed to lessen at the sight of such mundane documents. "Isn't that a solicitor's business?"

"If one can afford a solicitor. There's a lot of business conducted in the city that does not have the full gloss of legality on it. But it suffices for the people involved. And anyway, I just write down the words people tell me. I am quite literally a hired hand."

Picking up a paper, he scanned it slowly. "It's well done indeed. I suspect you don't charge enough for your work."

"I charge what I can." She'd often been paid in vegetables and eggs, for that was what was available.

"Where did you learn?"

"Not in London," she said.

"So you'll be mysterious about that as well? I can guess that you had a tutor. Your handwriting is excellent, and there's no way a St Giles resident phrased their words this way. You improve what they give you."

"A little."

"I'm impressed, Miss Black. You've managed to carve out a niche in a very rough neighborhood."

He handed her the letter back. Tamsin sighed. Her niche was gone—Swigg and Coaker would see to that. If only she knew exactly what went wrong…and whether it had to do with Swigg's new partner. She shivered, remembering the man.

"Can you write in French as well?" he asked. Though his tone hadn't changed, Tamsin stiffened. The inquiry led too closely to the part of her job she wanted to forget.

"I can, though it's not something most of my customers care about," she said slowly. "Why?"

"Just asking. You seem highly skilled. You know your mythology, you write and speak well. You jump out of windows and wear bedsheets with style," he said. "I'm curious about you, considering how we met on that bridge."

"Why were you walking on the bridge tonight?" Tamsin asked. "It's no place for a gentleman of your class."

He looked wary. "What class is that?"

"Aristocracy. You try to hide it with that rougher way of speaking, but ever since you rescued me, you've dropped it. So out with it. Dazzle me with your titles and honor."

He tried to take a drink, but the glass was empty again. "Do you want the truth?"

"I would not have asked otherwise."

"Then I'll offer a deal. Truth for truth. In this room,

for tonight, we don't lie to each other."

"There are things I *cannot* tell you," Tamsin warned.

"Oh, there are things I can't ever tell you, darling. So with the caveat that we can refuse to reveal things when necessary, we will not lie. Fair?"

She nodded slowly. "Very well, my lord...if you are a lord."

"I am," he said with a wry smile. "My name is Royce Holmes, and I'm Lord Pelham. My father was an earl, and now he's dead, so the honor came to me."

"Oh." She hadn't been expecting that. *An earl.*

"Trust me," Royce said, evidently reading her mind, "no one else was expecting it either. Having two older brothers should have made the idea laughable. Alas, a riding accident and a nasty disease changed the odds."

"You have no other siblings?"

"No, I'm the last great hope of the line." He took another drink.

Then she asked, "Is your mother alive?"

"Oh, yes. I expect that she'll be here come Judgment Day. And she'll be judging everyone else until then."

"You love her," Tess said softly, smiling.

Royce paused. "Well, yes, I suppose I do. She's not easy to live with. But then, neither am I...so I am told."

"I suppose heart-stoppingly gorgeous gentlemen don't have to be easy to live with." Tamsin nearly bit her tongue after she blurted that out, but then again, it wasn't as if she'd ever see him again after tonight.

He smiled at her. "You said what?"

"You heard me," she mumbled.

"I *like* this kind of truth," he said. "And to be completely honest, I have to tell you that you're rather fetching yourself. I'd love to see you turned out in a ballgown...or nothing at all."

"That is quite enough of that line of talk." Tamsin suppressed a laugh, because this flirtatious exchange reminded her that she *had* heard of Royce Holmes, as he was known before he suddenly ascended to the earldom. He got mentioned in the gossip columns, and the stories connected to him were always outlandish and just this side of scandalous. He was reckless. Which reminded her…

"Why *were* you on the bridge? You never answered."

He shrugged. "I felt like walking, so I dismissed the carriage."

"On a night like this?" Tamsin asked. "I thought we agreed to tell the truth."

"All right." Royce took a breath, then looked her dead in the eyes. "I was pursuing an assignment given to me by my superior in the secret spy ring of which I am a part. In addition to being an earl, I am also a master of espionage."

Tess stared at him. Then she threw her head back and laughed. "I almost believed you!" she said, covering her mouth with her hand. It felt good to laugh at such an absurd joke. "Oh, my goodness."

Royce smiled back at her, his expression boyishly charming. "What's so funny about that?"

"Because you're an *earl*," she said, still laughing a little. "But honestly, please tell me."

"Tell you what?"

"Why were you on the bridge? I was so lucky you were, but I want to know what brought you there."

He paused, appraising her.

"All right, I'll tell you. But you won't like it."

♍

TESS LOOKED INTRIGUED AT HIS statement. "Try me."

He'd told the truth, and it hadn't sufficed—thank God. But Tess wanted some sort of truth she could understand. And Royce suddenly realized that he could tell her. Tonight, here with a woman he'd never see again, he could tell a truth he'd never told another living soul.

"I was walking on the bridge in dire weather," he said, "because I didn't want anyone else around when I got to the middle."

"What were you planning to…" She trailed off as understanding came.

Still, he spoke the words aloud. "I was thinking, very sincerely, of climbing the rail and jumping off."

Her eyes rounded in shock. "*Why?*"

"Because life has been dull lately."

"You're not serious."

"I'm making light of it, but not joking about what I intended." Maybe not at that exact moment, but it was certainly a thought that he'd had many, many times.

"You were going to drown yourself because your life was getting dull?"

"Did I say dull?" Royce shook his head. "That was not the right word."

Tess slid off her chair, moving toward him, ghostlike in her loose white garment. "Then what is the right word?"

"*Grey. Foggy. Dark.*" Royce gathered his thoughts, losing himself in the memories of so many evil thoughts. "It's a…sort of blinding blackness that waits for me to laugh, or think of the future…then it pulls me right back in, reminding me of everything I'll never be, whispering all the things people have said to me. And it makes it easy to consider…ending it."

Kneeling next to him, she reached out and took his hand. Royce almost didn't know what to do in response. When was the last time someone just held his hand? When was the last time he'd been with anyone who offered comfort with no underlying agenda?

"Life does get so dark sometimes," she whispered.

No platitudes, no attempt to pretend what he said earlier was anything but appalling. She just held his hand and acknowledged his words.

It was a singular experience.

"I've never told anyone this," he admitted. "Just you…Miss Tess Black."

"I'm not…I mean, you know my name isn't Tess Black."

"Then what's your real name?" he asked softly. "We did promise to tell each other the truth. And you now know much more about me than I know about you."

Her mouth dropped open a little, her lower lip temptingly soft.

"Just your given name, then?" he prompted. "What do your friends call you?"

"I have no friends. Not anymore."

He squeezed her fingers gently, reveling in the physical connection. "What do you call two people holding hands, if not friends?"

"Ours is a most sudden and odd friendship," she

pointed out.

"All the same, a friendship of sorts." He wasn't sure why he needed to know so badly, but he did.

"My name is Tamsin," she breathed.

"Tamsin," he repeated, feeling as if he'd won something precious. He liked the softness of the name. "It suits you."

Then, thinking that he was getting moonish over a name, he took another sip of his drink.

Tamsin looked over at him, saying, "You know, at the rate you're going, you'll need another bottle."

He grinned. "I can afford another bottle."

"Is my presence so distasteful that you need to drink yourself insensible? Every time you look at me, you take a drink."

He paused. "Believe me, I drink like this no matter who is around."

"Yes, I can tell."

Royce glared at her. He was a spy—he could put personalities on and off like coats. How could this woman divine anything about his personal habits?

"I know the signs," she went on. "I see them often enough. Buy two bottles when one will do. Flushed face. I'll bet your hand shakes in the mornings."

"What of it?" Royce flattened one hand against his thigh, as if it might start shaking at any moment.

"You'll kill yourself if you don't let up."

He looked at the empty glass. Then he refilled it. "As I mentioned before, it would not be the worst outcome."

"My God, you cannot be so nonchalant about life itself, which others must fight tooth and nail to keep!"

Tamsin snatched the glass away and hurled it into the fireplace. It smashed against the bricks, and the alcohol blazed up, the flames flickering red and purple and blue for an instant. It was unexpectedly beautiful, Royce thought, forgetting to be annoyed by this woman's censure.

"We only had the two glasses," he said finally, taking refuge in another flippant comment.

"I don't wish to drink any more," Tamsin snapped back. "You're doing quite well enough for the both of us."

"I'm not a violent drunk," he said, guessing at her worry.

"How wonderful to hear." Tamsin's own skills at sarcasm were impressive. She'd be a hit at some *ton* parties, where fast and witty repartee was the coin of the realm.

Royce pondered the outline of her face as she stared into the fire. There was a delicacy there, a refinement that suggested noble birth. Or perhaps he was reading into it, based on the fact that Tamsin clearly wasn't born in this part of London.

"Where *are* you from?" he asked, curious. "I can't place your accent to save my life."

Her lip quirked. "My accent is unique. No one else has it, and I'd never wish any other woman to develop it."

"What happened to bring you to London?"

She glanced at him, but only said, in her dry tone, "I was looking for employment."

"As a scrivener?"

"Not initially." She laughed without humor. "But thank God I found a way to make a living with my hands, rather than other parts of my body."

A huge number of young women in the city ended up prostituting themselves in order to stay fed. It said something about Tamsin's stubbornness that she didn't choose that option. Particularly considering her natural assets. Royce became aware once again of a long-dormant sexual urge, spurred by Tamsin's odd but appealing manner.

"We agreed to tell each other the truth," he said.

"We also agreed that certain things would not be shared." Tamsin steadfastly refused to look Royce in the eye. "Leave my past alone, my lord. That's what I did."

He suspected that, like the man on the bridge, there was someone else in Tamsin's life who ought to be taught a lesson. Royce nearly offered to do the teaching. The truth was that he liked fighting—he was good at it, due to a youth full of poor decisions, spent far away from the refining influences of polite society. Truly, he was woefully unprepared to become an earl. Earls weren't encouraged to get into brawls.

Furthermore, Tamsin clearly didn't want to revisit her past, so that meant Royce couldn't either. The two of them sat quietly in front of the fire for a quarter hour. Royce missed his brandy, but perhaps he did have enough for the night.

He glanced at his companion, wondering what she was thinking of.

Tamsin's eyelids had fluttered down, and her head nodded until she suddenly snapped it up. The woman was exhausted, done in by a terrifying chase, the cold rain, and the strain of hiding here with Royce.

He stood, and walked to her chair. He scooped her up, toga and all.

"What are you doing?" She struggled to free herself, only getting tangled in the voluminous sheet. Royce didn't bother to point out that he was both taller and stronger than her, easily able to carry her as far as he liked.

"Calm down. I'm taking you to bed," he told her. "You can't even keep your eyes open."

"No! I'll sleep in the chair. Or on the floor."

"You will not. The bed is paid for and you will sleep

in it. And so will I because I'm not that self-sacrificing. But I promise not to ravish you."

"Ravish? Are we trapped in *Otranto*?"

"No, London." He laid her on the bed, and since he'd committed to full honesty for a night, he added, "I wouldn't mind ravishing you…if you wanted me to."

"Certainly not." Tamsin grasped the sheet, pulling it tighter to her body, and in the process only emphasized the shape underneath, from the swell of the breasts to the very nice curve of one hip. She glared at him. "How about this for truth? If you don't touch me, I won't scratch your eyes out."

"I wish all ladies were as straightforward as you are."

"I'm not a lady," she insisted.

"You *were* a lady, were you not?"

"In name," she admitted. "I lacked the income to match my lineage."

That was a common problem for daughters of the gentry. Too many children, not enough money to support them. Over a few generations, well, it was no surprise that some women had to make very hard choices about their future.

Royce stretched out along the bed on the other side, carefully maintaining a sizable gap between them.

"I don't know how you expect me to sleep," she said.

"Well, I'm going to sleep. You may stay awake, but please don't ravish me…unless you wake me first."

Tamsin's eyes widened, but Royce just put his arms behind his head and took a deep breath. The woman was quite safe from him. He'd be lucky to stay awake five minutes.

As it happened, Tamsin fell asleep first, proving that her exhaustion was extreme. Royce dozed, woke long enough to get up and throw one more log on the fire, and then dozed again.

A plan was hatching in his mind. The luck of finding someone who knew Swigg…Royce could use Tamsin to get more information, perhaps even an entry to Swigg's headquarters. He'd already discarded the most obvious option—trading Tamsin herself to Swigg in exchange for more information about the forgeries. It would be direct, but Royce had little faith that Swigg would tell him the truth. And he wouldn't want to frighten Tamsin by bringing her into that situation, or she'd clam up forever afterward. In Royce's experience as a spy, it was more effective to persuade people than to scare them.

So he'd persuade Miss Black by giving her exactly what she needed: an escape. He'd take her to the safest place he could think of. His home was miles and miles away from the city. Royce could take her there, leave her, and continue working on the assignment knowing that he had an extra asset. He just needed a reason to convince her that his offer was legitimate, or she'd run the moment he turned his back.

Unfortunately, there were not many positions a man could legitimately hire a woman for. His household didn't require a governess, nor a chaperone of any sort.

At that moment, Tamsin turned in her sleep, stretching one hand outward. He noticed the black stains on her fingers, the side effect of her work. He smiled then, because an idea popped into his head. A silly idea…an idea one would only expect from the madcap Earl of Pelham.

He slept again. The evening stretched into night, and he woke once more in near darkness. The fire had died to embers, and in the cold air of the room, he'd unconsciously pulled Tamsin close.

She was now tucked against him, and he couldn't pretend to be sad that he could feel the soft curves of her body through the sheet she wore. Royce knew he ought to let her go, but then again, perhaps keeping her warm was a form of chivalry.

Then Tamsin woke up, obviously startled.

"Relax," he told her. "I didn't take advantage of the situation."

She took a few deep breaths, then said, more calmly, "I know that. I was just…I didn't remember where I was."

"You're here at the Green Lion, in bed with a melancholic earl who drinks too much."

"Ah, yes. My typical Tuesday night. How could I forget?"

He chuckled. "I like you, Tamsin."

"I rather like you too, my lord," she said after a moment's hesitation.

He looked down into her eyes, and caught the interest there. Perhaps Tamsin's words of warning were for herself as much as him.

He ran one finger along Tamsin's lower lip, daring her to object. Instead, her mouth fell open on a gasp, and his own body reacted predictably.

"If I kiss you once, will you scratch my eyes out?" he asked.

"Not…immediately," Tamsin replied in a breathy tone.

With that guarantee, Royce kissed her.

Tamsin's lips were delicious, perfectly full and touched with the lingering sweetness of brandy. He ran his tongue along hers, loving the way she opened her mouth wider and then slid her hands over his shoulders, pulling him toward her.

He sensed the deep desire in her response, which was enough to make him wish that he'd bargained for a lot more than one kiss. But he also detected her inexperience, and he knew it would be wrong to push her further.

Catching her lower lip between his teeth, he finished off the kiss.

Tamsin looked dazed for a moment, an expression that he enjoyed immensely.

Then her eyebrows drew together in a little frown. "You really stopped at a kiss," she said wonderingly.

"One thing I've learned at the card table is to quit when I'm ahead. Besides, we had an agreement."

"I don't understand you at all, Royce Holmes," she declared.

"You don't have to understand me, you just have to tolerate me for the rest of the night."

"That I can do." Tamsin smiled then, a smile as warm as the red embers in the fireplace.

Royce would have to be careful to not get burned.

"Sleep, Tamsin," he advised. "You need it."

She nodded, hiding a yawn as she snuggled down amid the covers. This time, she turned toward Royce.

♍

THE NEXT MORNING, TAMSIN AWOKE in Royce's arms. She was well-fed, warm, and delightfully comfortable. She couldn't recall the last time all three of those things happened to her within the span of a day.

She remained still, enjoying the sensation of heat in her toes, and the pleasant feeling of Royce's chest rising and falling against her cheek. She supposed she should be irritated by the man's closeness, the tickle of the hair on his chest, or the way he'd pulled her into his embrace while they were sleeping.

But the truth was she didn't mind it. Royce's arms were as solid as oak, contoured with muscle. His broad shoulders made a perfect resting spot for her head, and Tamsin even liked the way he smelled, half-rainwater, half-spice. She glanced upward, and saw a shadow of stubble along his jaw and chin.

"Are you awake?" she asked.

He nodded, not opening his eyes. "Yes, but that can be remedied."

"You ought to wake up. *I* ought to wake up. My lord, are you listening? It's tomorrow."

"They won't kick us out. Besides, you said no one would look for you here."

"Eventually, Coaker will look everywhere for me."

"Then we'd better find a way to hide you." Opening

his eyes, he looked at her hair and ran his fingers through it. "Auburn. It looked darker before."

Tamsin didn't pull away, instead looking into those dark blue eyes, wondering what was going on in the mind behind them. Royce was the most puzzling man she'd ever encountered.

"Tell me something," he said suddenly. "If you had all the blunt you ever needed, and no one could take it from you, where would you live?"

"A Persian palace, surrounded by spice trees and swarming with peacocks."

"Really?"

"No, not really," she said with a little laugh. "For one thing, I don't speak a word of Persian. I'd like to live by the sea, I think. Or a lake. Somewhere far away from others. Not a town." She paused. "I don't much care for people."

"A cottage by the sea," he mused. "That's a fine dream. I have a house by the sea."

"Of course you do. Is it lovely?"

"I suppose. It's mostly empty." He paused. "Would you like to join me there?"

She frowned. "As what?"

"As my secretary. You said you're a scrivener."

She pulled away abruptly. "You can't be serious."

"It's unusual, I grant you, to hire a woman as a personal secretary. But I've not had the best luck with my previous hires—they all seem incompetent or leave after a few months. You could stay at the house, answer my damned correspondence from the comfort of a desk, and not have to deal with the polite society you so despise."

"And there would be no catch?" she asked.

"If I hired you as a mistress the interview would go quite differently, I assure you."

"So you would not have asked to watch me strip naked?"

He smiled, and the expression made her stomach flip. "All right, you've got me there. But it was a singular evening, and I promise it won't be repeated. Ever. I would treat you just the same as any of my household staff. Which is to say, I would not take advantage of you."

Tamsin closed her eyes, remembering things from her past that she'd rather forget.

"You've shown your work to me," he went on, more practically. "You write a fine hand. I paid the last man twenty-five pounds quarterly. Does that sound fair?"

She suppressed a gasp. One hundred pounds a year, *fair*? It sounded extravagant.

"And you need a place to hide," he pointed out. "Mr Coaker, or Mr Swigg, or whoever, will never find you at my estate."

"Where is your estate?" she asked.

"Norfolk."

"Oh." She relaxed on hearing a location very far from the ones she knew. "That would be all right."

"So do we have a deal?"

Tamsin bit her lip. It was an offer too good to be true. She'd be a fool to accept it.

She held out her hand. "Very well, my lord. Consider me hired."

After that bargain was struck, Royce seemed to come fully awake all at once. He dressed quickly and called for Gertie to bring up something to eat.

"I've got a few matters to attend to," he said. "You stay here in this room, and I'll come back with the carriage when I've done. We'll leave for Seabourne—that's my home—directly from here."

That sounded unlikely to Tamsin. "Very well, my lord.

It has been an interesting evening. And I do thank you for helping me."

He stopped moving, and regarded her with narrowed eyes. "Are you accusing me of lying? Do you think I won't return?"

"I think you'll think better of your offer once you're on your own, without my distracting presence," she said.

Royce pulled a ring off his finger and handed it to her. "My surety, then. Please don't lose it. It belonged to several grandfathers."

"How do you know I won't steal it?" Tamsin examined the signet ring, which was a heavy, solid gold object that most pawnbrokers would drool over.

"I trust you."

He left shortly after, leaving her alone with the tray that Gertie brought, the one holding a pot of piping hot tea and a half a loaf of crusty bread with butter. He'd not eaten a bite.

So she waited. Tamsin spent most of her time sitting in front of the fire, relishing the warmth. She slid the giant signet ring onto various fingers, though it was too large for any of them. She examined the intricate design etched into the center stone, and noted the fine goldwork of the heavy band.

"He really is Lord Pelham," she said wonderingly. The newspapers said he was mercurial and reckless. Possibly he was gullible too—Tamsin could take this ring and pawn it for a tidy sum, more than enough to get her some cheap gown and a seat on a mail coach.

She rolled the ring in her palm. Royce had been serious about coming back, and he trusted her to be here when he did. It had been a long, long time since Tamsin dealt with any sort of credit. In her world, you paid up front or you didn't get anything.

The afternoon light was turning cloudy when Royce returned. "Well," he said. "You were right. I heard a few rumors while I was out. People are looking for Tess the Scribbler."

Her stomach clenched. "Who said that?"

"Does it matter? You'll be away from here in less than an hour. A carriage will arrive shortly to take us to Norfolk. Now get dressed. A Greek goddess would be a little too conspicuous for London streets." He handed her a large traveling case made of heavy canvas. "Everything you need should be in there."

Tamsin opened the bag to find an entire wardrobe neatly packed. A wool gown. A new petticoat. A shift. Shoes. Stockings and garters. Stays. Royce must have gone to some establishment and asked for a shopgirl to select every necessary item.

The bag even included four different types of footwear.

"No employee of mine is going barefoot," he declared as Tamsin pulled a pair of low-cut traveling boots from the bag.

She walked around in the boots, pleased by the warmth in her toes. "I assume the cost will be deducted from my wages." Her extravagant, just-as-much-as-a-man's wages!

He waved the suggestion away. "That requires more accounting than I've got the patience for."

Once she was dressed respectably, there was nothing more to keep her in the room. Royce and Tamsin walked down the stairs to the ground floor. Royce had forgotten to ask for a cloak for her, so he offered his own greatcoat, which was miraculously dry.

Tamsin smiled as she let him drape it around her shoulders. "Is this my clever disguise?" she murmured.

He'd only thought of keeping her warm, but he nodded. "It gives you twice the bulk, so if you keep your head down, no one should recognize you unless they got very close."

On the ground floor, the innkeeper looked up from where he was mopping a stain on the floor.

"You're leaving?" asked the innkeeper. "Together?"

"We came in together, didn't we?" Royce asked.

The proprietor shrugged. "I seen many a man and woman come in together, sir. I don't see them leaving together quite so often." He returned to mopping, having imparted all the wisdom he cared to in that moment.

Royce turned his attention to her. "Button up. It's cold out."

"Yes, but the rain has stopped." She smiled at him. "Are you ready to go?"

Together, they stepped out into the world.

♍

THE JOURNEY TO SEABOURNE, LORD Pelham's estate in Norfolk, took two days, but the moment Tamsin lost the view of London behind them, she felt as if she'd flown into a new land. Tension drained from her body when she realized that for the first time in years, she was free of Swigg's shadow, that she was out of the city's invisible web of underground influence. No one would find her in her new place because it was utterly unconnected to anyone or anything she knew.

"Why are you smiling?" Royce asked. He was seated across from her, perfectly attired. His fine blue wool coat probably cost as much as the entire wardrobe she'd received that morning.

"I was thinking that it's been a long time since I've enjoyed a visit to the country," she said, amused at her own whimsy.

"How long?"

"Years, I'm afraid. I forgot a world outside London existed."

"I hope you like Seabourne."

Tamsin bit her lip, recalling the strangeness of the situation. "It will be a vast improvement over my room in Catchpenny Lane, my lord. But I do not need to like a place to work there. I ask only to be tolerated."

"You should be more than tolerated, Tam—Miss

Black, that is." He made a gesture to indicate that he misspoke. "I promise I will not be familiar with you at Seabourne. Our evening at the inn was an anomaly."

"Quite," she agreed dryly.

He chuckled. "You must have been a popular name on the guest lists, Miss Black."

Tamsin went cool. "No, my lord." She'd never been on any guest lists, and now she never would be. Odd how that world of Society parties and vapid courtship suddenly seemed appealing. She wondered if her little sister, Georgina, ever got to have a coming out. Probably not. The whole family's lives had been changed the day they came to take her father away.

He recognized her shift in mood and said, "Well, take heart. There are no opportunities for social interaction at Seabourne, and I generally avoid attending other people's events as well."

"Yes, you're legendary by your absence at the biggest parties hosted by the *ton*."

"How would you know that, Miss Black, when you yourself don't appear on guest lists?" he asked, one eyebrow arching.

It was no great feat on her part. Tamsin knew the name of Royce Holmes because she read newspapers regularly, and his exploits featured in them over and over again. Tamsin scoured the papers to look for news of her family…and of certain people she wanted to avoid. But the result was that she learned a lot of other news as well, including the gossip and whispered secrets of London that made it to the printed page.

So she knew that the new Lord Pelham had a wild, outsized reputation. He frequented gambling hells and raced horses and carriages in places they ought not to be raced. He was invited to the grandest parties but rarely attended any of them. It was a coup for any hostess who managed to get him to her crush.

He was also an extremely eligible bachelor. He was wealthy, handsome, and young. According to the gossip columns, mothers among the *ton* stalked him like a tigress stalks a gazelle; except he wouldn't be eaten, he'd be trussed up and delivered to the altar to make some lucky young lady into the next Countess of Pelham.

She recalled another piece of news. "You nearly killed the Duke of Weddley when you raced a carriage through Hyde Park on Easter Sunday."

"Well, he should have been in church," Royce said with a smile. Of course, he also should have been in church, but a man with his reputation didn't worry about little things like salvation. He was looked after by the Devil himself...according to one of the more alarmist reporters.

"How do you know about that carriage race?" Royce asked.

"It was widely reported, my lord," Tamsin explained. "One paper even had an illustrator draw his version of what the race looked like. Quite exciting."

"It was stupid. The result of a bet I made when I'd been drinking all night."

"You won, did you not?"

He smiled slightly. "Of course I did."

She laughed at his quiet arrogance. To be fair, she could not recall a single instance where Pelham didn't come out on top. Whether it was a dare, a challenge at the card table, or some young lady's heart, he always seemed to win.

She looked out the window of the carriage, pondering the life ahead of her. She must not allow herself to hope, though. Hope was a dangerous feeling.

"What is it?" Royce asked. "You just sighed as if you got word of a death."

"No, no." Tamsin pasted on a smile. "I was merely thinking that it will be wonderful to get away from the city. I look forward to a complete lack of social rounds."

Royce dusted an offending speck of dust off his coat. "You've got nothing to worry about. You're a world apart from your old life. There's no crossover. No one exists in both."

How did he identify her real fear? Tamsin said only, "You did."

"For one night. Believe me, no one would ever think to connect Miss Black of Seabourne with some scrivener in Catchpenny Lane."

That was her plan. And surely there could be no safer place than a grand estate in Norfolk...far from the city, and far from Tamsin's roots in Somerset.

They reached Seabourne on the second day.

The estate was both grand and gloomy. Grey stone walls brooded over a hilly landscape, with the sea churning in the background. The wind whipped Tamsin's hood off as she alighted from the carriage.

"My goodness," she said, taking in the sight of the house. "Now we really are in *Otranto*."

His lip quirked in a smile at her reference to Walpole. "It's rather dreadfully gothic, isn't it? Alas, I didn't choose my inheritance. I'll get used to the place eventually."

"What do you mean?" she asked. "Why do *you* have to get used to it? Is it not your family home?"

"I lived most of my life in London," he said. "This house is almost as strange to me as it is to you. But the fireplaces work very well. You'll never be cold, Miss Black."

It was an optimistic thought, but one that did not come to pass…at least not immediately.

When Royce introduced her to the housekeeper, Mrs Arnott, as the new personal secretary, Tamsin got a look that was distinctly frigid.

"Secretary," the woman repeated, in a tone that implied utter disbelief.

Royce didn't appear to notice. "Make up Mr Fletcher's room for her. The last secretary was named Fletcher, wasn't he?"

"Yes, my lord."

"Miss Black will begin her duties tomorrow morning. Until then," he said, looking at Tamsin, "get yourself settled. Mrs Arnott will show you everything you need to know."

"Yes, my lord," Tamsin replied with a little curtsey as Royce headed off, looking very much like an earl, leaving Tamsin feeling very much like a leftover.

"Follow me, miss," the housekeeper said. She strode down the hallway in the opposite direction that Royce had taken. "Mr Fletcher's room was in the east wing, which I suppose you'll find inconvenient."

"Oh?" Tamsin asked, hurrying to keep up. "Is it not near the other servants' quarters?"

"It is not, for secretaries are not domestics," Mrs Arnott snapped. "And I'd certainly not put *you* near my maidservants!"

Tamsin was about to ask why not, but held her tongue. The housekeeper was obviously out of sorts.

"I am sorry that you had no notice of my arrival," she said. "It must be an additional burden to make up another room with no warning."

"This house has forty-seven rooms and all would pass muster whatever the hour! The late Lord Pelham never complained of my work."

"Oh, I'm sure not," Tamsin murmured, at a loss.

At the end of the long corridor, Mrs Arnott flung open a door. "Here is Mr Fletcher's room. I'll send a maid with water and coals before evening. Supper will be served at seven."

"Shall I join the other servants in the kitchen?"

"Nancy will bring a tray," the housekeeper replied, then abruptly pulled the door shut.

Tamsin stared at the door, then took stock of her surroundings. It was a plain room, but quite comfortable. A small grate would provide heat when lit—the coal shuttle was mostly full, and Tamsin took a few moments to light the fire, anticipating the coming warmth. A simple wooden chair had been placed nearby, and the narrow bed was neatly made and smelled reassuringly fresh. All good signs.

It took less than ten minutes for Tamsin to unpack her things. She put away the new clothes in the small chest of drawers and lined up her four—four!—pairs of footwear near the door. Then she pulled the papers from her leather case and laid them out on the little desk in the corner.

The dreadful rain on the night she ran away took its toll on her paper, half of which was curled and stained from the damp. But several pieces of foolscap survived, and she also had three quills, her pen knife, and a bottle of black ink still half full. It would do.

With no task at hand, and no invitation to do anything else, Tamsin spent a lonely evening in her room. The meal delivered to her at suppertime was perfectly adequate, consisting of mutton, potatoes, and a heavy brown gravy. But the maid spoke only the bare minimum, and after she admitted her name was Nancy, she refused to answer even the most general questions, asked in Tamsin's friendliest tone.

What a strange household. The housekeeper had been cold, but Tamsin chalked it up to a harried nature and the unpleasant surprise of a new employee she'd been given no warning about. But Nancy had no such excuse. Perhaps she was tired, and irritated to be serving yet another meal before she could eat her own.

Tamsin ate the meal slowly, knowing that once it was done, she'd need to distract herself till bedtime. There was a Bible on the nightstand, but no other books. If only she knew where the library was, or had the courage to seek it out tonight. But Tamsin had learned one lesson very well while living in Catchpenny Lane: it was better to go unnoticed than risk the wrath of others. For whatever reason, Mrs Arnott seemed to be annoyed with her. Tamsin could definitely wait until morning to see the rest of the house. Perhaps by then the general mood would lift.

She went to bed early, stifling a feeling of homesickness. This house was not like her own growing up, but there was something in the air that generated a host of memories of her home and her family. Especially her father.

Tamsin's father was a good man, if a little too doting. However, he was not good with money. His wife was perhaps a little better, but since she only managed her own pin money, it didn't make much difference in the end.

Thomas Latimer borrowed more than he ought to for years, but only at the end did the debt become truly crushing and the extent of the problem known to his family. Tamsin remembered being surprised at the news. How could her father have money problems? They lived in a beautiful house. They all had lovely gowns to wear. The girls took music lessons and art lessons and had a French tutor. All the ladies of the house received fine jewels on

New Year's Day. The supper table was always full of the richest, most wonderful foods. Surely this was what it meant to be rich?

Of course, she quickly learned that all these trappings of wealth were hiding the awful truth that the Latimers were destitute. No, worse, because all the fine things they had weren't even theirs. They were owned by someone else. And those people who made the loans now wanted their money back.

So Thomas sold the jewels. He sold the horses. He sold his art. Shockingly, he sold a parcel of land. The tutors left, the servants were reduced from six to two. Tamsin was nearly to her coming out, and she nobly announced that she'd accept the richest man who offered for her in the coming Season, no matter how old or ugly. She knew what the role of a daughter was.

But it was too late for that. The Latimers could not afford to go to London for the Season, and in fact, Tamsin's and Gina's dowries were gone...taken by the creditors.

What was left for the family? Work. Tamsin was pretty and well-educated. She'd make a fine governess or teacher at a girls' school. When her mother summoned her to the parlour (the cold, bare parlour) she told Tamsin that she had been offered a position as governess at the Englefield home nearby, because Mr Englefield knew her father and sympathized with the family's plight. Tamsin numbly accepted the job. What choice did she have?

She packed the few serviceable gowns she had and rode in a coach to the Englefield home. There, she took charge of two children and did quite well at it. Their father, Hector, who had lost his wife during the birth of the younger child, seemed pleased with Tamsin.

Tamsin was rather intimidated by him, for he was tall

and very handsome, with thick blond hair. He dressed fashionably and cut a fine figure while riding across the estate. He always seemed to be in a good mood, for whenever he saw Tamsin, he smiled.

One evening, he summoned her to give a report on the children's progress. He offered her a glass of wine, which she accepted, not wishing to be rude. One glass of wine became two. Then three. Then Hector pushed her back onto the couch and kissed her, and Tamsin was far too addled by wine to resist.

After that, he found reasons to touch her when no one else saw. He'd pull her into a corner and kiss her. Tamsin was scared but flattered, and the kisses grew bolder. More passionate.

Then he came to her room one night, and pressed her onto her bed and pulled up her skirts and pulled down his falls. Tamsin knew it was wrong, but again, she didn't know how to tell the master of the house she didn't agree. And perhaps it was not wrong if he said it was all right?

It hurt at first, but he told her that he was so big that he couldn't help it. She'd learn to accommodate his girth. He told her that she was just what he needed, and that made her keep silent. He came to her room again the next night. It still hurt, but there was less shock. And he kissed her all over.

Hector bought her a pearl pendant, telling her it was a special gift just for her, and to not tell anyone else in the house. He put it around her neck, and the pearl fell just between her breasts. She felt deliciously mature to have the secret love of the master, and a secret pearl to wear. Surely that meant something?

Three months after their affair began, Tamsin realized that she'd missed her courses. She was not an idiot, and when she started to feel sick every morning, she knew she was carrying Hector's baby.

She waited until that night to tell him. Surely he'd be happy to learn that Tamsin would have his next child. But after she announced that she was with child, Hector sneered and said, "So soon? That's a pity. I wanted to keep you around."

Instead of doing the honorable thing, he announced that she was no longer fit to see his children, and told her to keep to her room till he arranged for her to be taken away.

"Home?" Tamsin asked, shocked into dullness.

"As if your family would accept you back, ruined as you are. No, there's a place in the neighboring parish that takes in unmarried girls till their time. I don't want you giving birth in my parish…there are enough of the poor here already."

So that was the end of the affair, and the end of Tamsin's innocence.

When she'd demanded her wages from Hector, he just laughed. "Wages? You're working off your father's debt. Or did you not know that? How did you think you got this position? It wasn't for your teaching skills. It was because I wanted to see your tits bounce in bed."

The night before the cart came to take her away, Tamsin packed her belongings and snuck out of the house. In a noble rage, she left behind the pearl necklace, to show Hector what she thought of his gifts.

Idiocy. That pearl could have paid for many meals in London. Instead, Tamsin nearly starved before she found some small employment and a place to sleep. As it was, she miscarried a few weeks later—an irony that was not lost on Tamsin.

It was several more months until she landed in Catchpenny Lane.

Hector had been the first and last man to use Tamsin like that. In London, her naiveté died a swift death, and she never let faith in other people lead her into another disastrous encounter.

Not until Royce found her, and she let her guard slip, indulging in that one kiss.

Well. A mistake was understandable. She'd been quite overwhelmed.

But there would be no more mishaps or misunderstandings. She and Royce—that is, Lord Pelham—would have a strictly professional relationship founded on her skills and his need for an employee.

It did not matter that he was scandalously attractive, sly and witty, and unexpectedly kind and gentle.

Tamsin was too hardened to be swayed by those qualities, or his deep, deep blue eyes.

She drifted to sleep dreaming of those eyes, which (had she been awake) she'd have dismissed as another minor mistake.

♍

TAMSIN WOKE EARLY THE NEXT day, her maudlin thoughts banished to the recesses of her mind. She possessed an inborn sense of practicality that kept her from dwelling on things she could not change. That trait was probably what kept her alive.

She added coals and stoked the fire herself to take the worst chill from the room. She rang the bell for breakfast. Then she dressed, still reveling in the newness of her wardrobe. She ran her hands over the soft cotton of her shift, which was blindingly white and featured a delicate lace edging on the bottom hem and the edges of the short sleeves. A lady's stays were difficult to tighten without help, but after years of living on her own, Tamsin had learned the knack for it. Then a petticoat in a heavier cotton, also white. Finally, she pulled on the wool gown, anticipating chilliness throughout this massive house. She smiled, thinking of how nice it was to have a gown clean enough to go visiting in—not that she had anywhere to go. But there was a simple pleasure in well-made things.

Tamsin had no jewelry, since she'd long ago sold the few items she owned in exchange for food in the darkest days when she first moved to London. But there was extra blue ribbon tucked into her case, the same type as the ribbon she used to garter her stockings. Tamsin tied it around the base of her neck, adjusting the little bow to sit exactly at the back. There, she looked quite respectable.

She rang the bell again, and waited a few more minutes. Since no one seemed to be responding to her summons, Tamsin concluded that she ought to go to the kitchen to find her breakfast. Perhaps the household staff was quite busy in the mornings. Though in a stately house containing exactly one earl, she wasn't sure what they could be busy doing.

Arriving in the kitchens, Tamsin managed to secure a cup of tea and a hunk of buttered bread. The cook and scullion ignored her, and the maids only sent fleeting glances her way.

She finished her meal and saw a young man in livery examining her.

"Excuse me," she said to the footman. "Do you happen to know the way to the lord's study? Or wherever it is that his previous secretaries worked?"

"Aye," the young man said. He gave her a long, appraising look that she recognized all too well. "I'll show ye."

Tamsin stayed several paces back, not liking the man's attitude in the slightest. They walked down a grand, gloomy, shadowed hallway. Though it was morning, the light barely filtered into this interior corridor, and no candles were lit now—only after dark would they be used.

Finally, the footman stopped at a pair of oak doors. He didn't open them, which was odd considering his role as footman. Instead, he turned to Tamsin. "This is the library, but the lord probably isn't here yet."

"I do not mind waiting." She expected him to move, so she could enter the room, but the oaf just stood there, leering at her.

"I've got a mind to wait with ye." He put a meaty hand on her shoulder, obviously intending to touch what he'd previously only viewed.

Tamsin's spine went ramrod straight. She grabbed his wrist and twisted it away. "How dare you. If you touch me again, I'll report your behavior to the lord himself," she warned in a low voice.

The footman winced slightly, rubbing his wrist. "You're a frosty one," he complained.

"And you're impertinent. You may go now." Tamsin glared at him, in the imperious manner she'd used every day in her long-ago life as a lady. How easily it returned! She blamed the grandness of her surroundings.

Once the footman left in a huff, she opened the library doors herself and walked in, shutting them behind her.

She leaned against the oak panels, taking in the library in all its glory.

Tamsin loved books because she loved writing and she loved words. Growing up, her family's home had a pretty room with a whole wall devoted to books. Her father's favorite books took up most of it, but there were other shelves with bound journals from the Royal Society, interesting picture books with the hand-painted images of lions and camels and glorious elephants, and several Bibles all printed with different type and different translations. As a child, Tamsin would trace the complex filigree of the words, trying to see how someone could make a simple *A* or *M* into a miniature work of art. On winter nights, her father would read stories while Tamsin and her sister lay by the fire, playing with the cat.

To her, libraries were magical places.

And the Seabourne library was the most magical of all.

Bookcases lined every wall, and nearly all the shelves were full. Above the fireplace, a large mirror with an ornate frame hung, creating the illusion of yet more books beyond. Tamsin spent what seemed like hours peering at the spines of the books, trying to discern what sort of literature the earl preferred.

She found law books and religious treatises. She found books in German and French. She found an atlas, tall and thin and flat, but containing worlds within. She sighed with happiness when she encountered a copy of *Le Morte d'Arthur*. She ran her hands over the red leather book containing some of her most beloved stories.

On one shelf, she saw a book with letters she knew to be some language from India, though she couldn't read a word. She pulled it out and opened it, finding an illustration of a man and a woman clearly engaging in sexual congress, smiles on their faces. She quickly flipped to the next page...and saw yet another act depicted. Tamsin paged through the book, finding a dizzying array of sensual, often improbable (according to her limited experience) positions. But the most shocking thing was that the couple shown was always the same couple, and they showed neither shame nor shyness.

Hearing a sound from the hallway, Tamsin quickly put the book back on the shelf and darted toward the window, looking out blindly over the landscape.

The doors swung open as Royce strode in. He looked very dashing in his dark blue breeches and jacket, with the white-as-snow shirt and cravat underneath.

She realized she was staring, and swung back to the window. "Good day, my lord."

"Morning, Miss Black."

The formality should have reassured her; instead she felt the urge to giggle. Tamping it down, she asked, "Is there a usual hour I should be prepared to begin my work, sir? We never discussed the particulars of my duties."

"We didn't," he agreed, joining her at the window. "It

occurs to me that I failed to discuss particulars with all my previous secretaries as well. Perhaps that's why I was so dissatisfied with them."

"Well, I don't want to join their number," Tamsin said. "So we could talk about it now."

"Let me show you the library first," he countered, "since this is where you'll be working. I've been told I ought to have an office and just have this room dedicated to reading, in case there are guests. But there are never guests."

What would this man do once he got married? Tamsin wondered. His countess would surely entertain.

"My desk is there," he said, indicating a massive piece of cherry furniture absolutely covered with books and papers. "Yours will be that one."

Tamsin looked to a smaller but much less messy desk about twenty feet away.

"What sort of work do you need done, my lord?" she asked curiously, taking in the quantities of correspondence.

"Oh, the usual," he answered vaguely. "Replies to invitations, help with scheduling, some...organization." He looked at his own desk with an expression of surprise. "It does seem to have got a bit out of hand."

"Yes, my lord," she agreed.

"I've been in London most of the time," he defended himself. "My duties have taken me very far from here, and I haven't got time to...*file* things when I've got..." He trailed off, leaving Tamsin unenlightened as to what specific duties he had. What did a newly minted earl need to do in London when it wasn't the Season?

"Anyhow, I'm sure you'll figure it all out. You're probably ten times more intelligent than the previous secretaries. Not that it is a high bar."

"Thank you, my lord." With praise like that, no wonder he couldn't keep an employee around very long.

Royce gave her a half smile. "You are free to read or borrow any of the books that catch your fancy. Just write down the titles in the ledger over there, so no one thinks the books got stolen." He gestured to a slim red volume placed on a table near the door.

"Thank you, my lord," she said again, this time sincerely. "There were a few books I'd like to read."

"Oh? Which ones were you looking at?"

Tamsin blushed as she contemplated the embarrassment of mentioning the erotic tome she'd seen before. She'd never have the guts to borrow that one. She covered by mentioning a few poets she liked, including Milton.

"I do have Milton," he said. "I'm reading *Paradise Lost* again, but the book is in my bedroom."

Tamsin blinked. Was he going to bribe her with Milton to get her in his bed? What happened to their agreement that their relationship was going to be entirely professional?

After a moment, she said in a tight voice, keeping her disappointment in check, "I do not need to read about the Fall so much that I'll fall again myself."

Royce looked at her in confusion, then in anger. "Excuse me, Miss Black. What the hell did you think I was implying? I'm offended that you would even hint that I'd go back on my word the very day after I give it."

"I misinterpreted your intention, my lord. Please forgive me."

He opened his mouth, and she expected a blast of invective, but all he did was exhale, and turn away.

"Never mind," he said. "I can see how that could have sounded. But honestly, I didn't mean anything untoward."

Tamsin nodded. "Of course not. It was my own sensibility to blame. Now, I think I can spend the rest of my morning tidying up before I get to the real task of organization. If you have any specific requests, I am ready to address them."

Stiffly, Tamsin walked to her own desk. She'd hoped to get off on a good foot with Lord Pelham, and until the last few moments, it had been going well. She glanced over at him, and saw that he was still in front of the window, one arm stretched out to grasp the frame. With the light streaming in, his silhouette was sharp, and she could see once again that he was a very well-made man. Tall, with strong shoulders and a slim torso, with no hint of lazy living that turned many wealthy men into pudding-like specimens. *Do not look at your employer like that,* she warned herself.

The simple work of clearing away the mess occupied her mind for the next few hours. She set up the top of the desk to her preference, with the inkwell on the right side, and her silver penknife at the top of the felt blotter, secure in its leather sheath. She got that penknife on her fourteenth birthday, and she'd used it nearly every day since, in her lessons and later in her work…and once in a dark street to ward off a drunk who mistook her for an easy mark.

Royce said nothing as he sat at his own desk, absorbed in whatever he was doing. Shortly before noon, a footman hurried in and whispered to Royce, whose expression grew stormy. "Fine, let's go," he muttered.

Tamsin had paused in her work, and Royce noticed. "Miss Black, take some lunch. I shouldn't be more than an hour."

She nodded as he rushed past with the footman. For a man who wanted a secretary to handle personal matters, he was very closed-mouthed about what those matters were.

Upon finding that her luncheon was apparently meant to be taken cold (for that was what arrived on the tray), Tamsin ate quickly and joylessly, then walked outside to escape the suddenly oppressive walls of Seabourne.

After lunch, Tamsin walked back to the library and stopped short on seeing a young man standing near one of the bookcases.

"Oh, I'm sorry! I didn't realize anyone was here," she said.

He turned, the alarm on his face turning to curiosity. "You're new."

"I'm Tamsin Black," she said, after a moment. She'd remembered rather abruptly that the protocol of formal introductions no longer applied to her. "I'm Lord Pelham's new personal secretary. Yes, I know it's odd."

"*Odd* is one word for it," the young man said. "But then, what isn't odd about all of us here? I'm Laurent Suchet."

He walked toward her with a hand extended. His smile was friendly, but held a trace of bitterness in it.

She shook his hand, reveling in the new practice, unknown to ladies. "How do you do, Mr Suchet. Are you a friend of Lord Pelham's?"

"Not remotely. I'm his son."

Tamsin blinked in surprise, but then the disparate features of the young man's face came to her, matched with Royce's. The eyes especially were strikingly similar. Now she saw that he was even younger than she'd first thought. He was likely no more than sixteen or seventeen.

"I didn't know he had children," she said, feeling silly. She knew he wasn't married when he became earl (all of the female gentry paid attention to that sort of thing, and thus the papers were up-to-date), but perhaps he'd once been?

"Only one, and I'm a mere bastard," Laurent replied, the bitterness now more evident. "A mistake he cannot ever correct."

"Does he wish to correct it? You're here, after all." Bastards weren't uncommon in the aristocracy, and many noblemen refused to even acknowledge their illegitimate offspring, let alone provide for them, a fact Tamsin knew all too well.

"Oh, my lord has a strong sense of duty. When he found out about me, he had me sent for to be raised like a proper boy. He thinks it his role to rescue the unfortunates he finds in the streets. *Noblesse oblige* and all that."

Tamsin felt a sinking in her stomach. It made perfect sense. What was she but an unfortunate that Royce came across in the streets?

"So, you're the new secretary," Laurent was saying. "They don't last long around here. Pelham's hell to work for. Not the household servants," he clarified. "They've all been here longer than him. They've been here since the Conqueror, probably. Have you met Mrs Arnott? She's got to be eight hundred years old at least. But secretaries and solicitors and estate managers and all of those types…he's never satisfied. Though perhaps he'll be satisfied with *you*."

The implication was plain, and Tamsin snapped back, "If he finds my penmanship or filing skills lacking, I shall of course move on. That is all I am here for."

But that was not true. Tamsin didn't have the freedom of movement that a man of her age did—she was at the mercy of expectations and assumptions for women. Not to mention that she had no money to her name until Royce paid her at the usual quarterly date. Or that Swigg and Coaker still wanted to find her….

"Good luck to you, then," Laurent said. "My father's a difficult man to judge, and subject to whims. He'll disappear for weeks without telling anyone—no wonder his past secretaries despaired."

"I've held more unpleasant posts," Tamsin said quietly, thinking of Swigg and his strange, secretive demands. "I can only do my best."

Royce appeared in the doorway. "Miss Black, I'd like to discuss— Laurent, where the hell have you been? I've been looking for you all over."

"My lord," Laurent said with a mocking bow. "I've just met your new secretary. Charming."

"It's not Miss Black's job to be charming," Royce said shortly. "And if you bother her or keep her from her work, I'll be extremely annoyed with you. More annoyed than I am already, after you wasted my time this morning."

"I tremble in fear, my lord," said Laurent. He turned to her, and said, far more politely, "Good afternoon, Miss Black." Then he grabbed a stack of books from the desk and stalked out of the library.

Tamsin and Royce stood in awkward silence for a moment. What does one say to a lord about his bastard son? Tamsin pointed to the paper in Royce's hand. "You had a question, my lord?"

"Ah, yes... That is..." he said, looking toward the door. Doubtless he wanted to go after the young man and talk with him.

"Go, my lord," she said quietly. "Family is important. My tasks can wait."

He flashed her a grateful look, and said, "Tomorrow, we'll get to the real work. Bright and early."

Before Tamsin could reply, he was gone.

♍

ROYCE LEFT THE LIBRARY, DETERMINED to chase down Laurent and have a serious discussion with the boy. It wasn't difficult to find him, since Laurent had merely ambled down the hallway, already reading one of the books he'd taken.

As a spy, Royce knew how to move fast and silently, and when he swept up behind Laurent, the young man whirled in surprise.

"God, don't do that!" he yelped. "It's uncanny, you sneaking around like a cat when you're the size of a horse."

"We need to chat," Royce replied, taking Laurent by the arm and propelling him up the staircase to the floor above.

"Ugh, why? Where are we going?"

"Your room, unless you want the entire house to hear what I've got to say."

Laurent scowled but didn't try to protest, which Royce regarded as a first-round victory. In Laurent's room, he shut the door firmly and turned to face his son.

"I set certain expectations when you first moved here," he began.

"You dragged me here!" Laurent countered, flinging himself into a chair in the corner. "I didn't ask to come."

"Would you have preferred to scrounge in the streets?

Not many books in the gutters," Royce noted, pointing at the stack Laurent just put down. "Nor food or clean beds or servants to attend you."

"But there's freedom," Laurent muttered.

"Oh, yes, freedom to die horribly, whether of disease or violence or starvation. Your mother—"

"Don't talk about my mother! I told you to never talk about her! You abandoned her."

Royce inhaled slowly, trying to keep his frustration in check. "That is not true, and you know it."

Laurent didn't answer, and he didn't look at Royce. "There must have been a reason why she did what she did."

If there was, they'd never know. The fact was that Royce had no idea he'd fathered a child until three years ago, when he received a letter from one of Dominique's associates in Paris. The woman wrote to him to tell him of Dominique Suchet's death...and the existence of a son that Dominique told her was the result of her passionate affair with the Honorable Royce Holmes during her stint in London. The woman wrote that she would not have presumed to tell Royce anything, except for the fact that Dominique died destitute and with no relatives who might take in the child.

The implication was clear, but Royce did not need any persuading to travel to Paris and retrieve his son. If he'd known earlier, he'd have taken charge of the boy earlier... a fact that Dominique surely knew, hence her silence on the matter.

He never questioned the truth of it—the boy's date of birth matched exactly to the period of time that Royce and Dominique were together. And his eyes were Royce's eyes.

The boy was named Laurent, and he'd inherited his

father's coloring but his mother's temperament. In short, he was a holy terror. Raised among actors and artists in the less-reputable areas of Paris, he had little of the education found at Eton or Harrow, but a wealth of knowledge about things no boy should know.

Royce took him home under protest, and immediately set about finding a proper boarding school to make up for lost time.

Laurent managed to get booted from no less than three schools, and by the time Royce received the title, he'd already resigned himself to paying for private tutors for the boy.

At Seabourne, Laurent was just as sullen, but got into slightly less mischief...the isolated location made getting into trouble much more difficult.

The most vexing thing about raising Laurent was seeing how much potential the boy had. He was wildly intelligent, naturally charming, and possessed an aptitude for languages. The household staff liked him, and his tutors all said that he grasped ideas instantly (though he often resisted studying). Only to Royce was he rude and petulant, flinging uniquely personal barbs with cruel precision. Often, he used his illegitimacy to taunt Royce for his failures.

But none of that changed the fact that he was Royce's son. So Royce said, as he'd said many times before, "I can't tell you what your mother was thinking when she chose to keep your birth secret from me. But I can tell you that if I'd known, your life would have been very different from the outset. For God's sake, I'm trying to help you."

"You never should have brought me back from Paris! I was happy there!"

"A thirteen-year-old boy doesn't know what happiness is."

"I hate you!" Laurent burst out, sounding very much like the boy Royce first encountered.

"Yes, I know," he replied. "But nevertheless, I did bring you back, and that's the reality you have to face."

Laurent suddenly looked over at him with narrowed eyes. "And this woman you brought back from London? What's your explanation of that?"

Royce ground out, "I do not give explanations."

"I suppose you don't have to. She's the most attractive amanuensis I've ever seen," Laurent needled.

"Miss Black was hired as a secretary and that's all she is. Her looks have nothing to do with it."

Laurent snorted. "As if you'd have hired her if she weren't beautiful."

True, Tamsin's attractiveness was making it a little difficult for Royce to think of her solely as an asset, a way to get to his real target of Swigg. But he couldn't say that out loud.

"You know nothing of the situation," Royce said. "And it's none of your concern. All I want from you is polite and proper behavior toward her. In her way, she's had as much difficulty in her life as you have. I brought her here to remove her from some of it."

"The house will get crowded with all your little rescues," Laurent noted. "When you do find a wife, I imagine we'll all have to be removed for her peace of mind. Perhaps then Miss Black and I can go into business together! I'll be a secretary's secretary, won't that be fitting? I wonder if she's a by-blow too. There's something blue-blooded about her, isn't there?"

"I didn't pry." But he noted Laurent's appraisal and approved of the boy's perception. "It's rude to ask that."

"Oh, I know you didn't ask her directly," Laurent said. "Always awkward, talking about whose parents were properly married when their lust got out of hand and produced a baby. The other lads at my schools never knew whether to ask more questions or ignore me entirely."

"Who could ignore you?" Royce asked dryly.

Laurent gave him a sudden smile. "I do have some skills."

"I never doubted that," Royce said. "Now, please remember to be polite to Miss Black."

"Fear not, Papa. I do know the rules."

"Then follow them. For God's sake, Laurent, must everything be a fight with you?"

His son shrugged. "Evidently the apple didn't fall far from the tree. Ma mère did tell me you fought like cornered cats half the time. Said she had to flee back across the Channel to get a little peace."

"Sounds like something she'd say," Royce agreed. "Your mother always knew how to make an entrance… and an exit."

In fact, she'd probably orchestrated the reveal of Laurent's parentage from her deathbed…a final performance for an audience of one.

Royce left his son sulking in the room. He was never sure whether their conversations resulted in any progress whatsoever. Certainly, Laurent still hated him. Royce thought he understood the source of the boy's resentment—what child wouldn't hate a parent they believed didn't care for them?—but even after nearly three years, Laurent's attitude hadn't changed, despite all Royce's attempts to reach him.

Granted, Royce wasn't able to step fully into the role of father. He had his work with the Zodiac, which pulled him from home over and over again. Even when he was physically present, his mind was often far away, puzzling over the assignments he had to solve.

The current one was the worst of all. Royce remembered when Aries, the code name of Julian Neville, who ran the operations of the Zodiac, brought him in to discuss the assignment.

"Something's come up, and it's rather troubling," Aries had said, in that deceptively mild tone he always used. If an earthquake caused half of Europe to sink into the sea, Aries would say "Something's come up, and it's rather troubling."

As it turned out, the assignment Aries gave him was more than troubling, it was poisonous. The British government was a bureaucracy, and bureaucracies ran on paper. Documents passed from hand to hand, departments wrote statements, diplomats wrote letters. Many times, those papers were quite mundane. It wouldn't matter if a newspaper reprinted them on the front page. But sometimes, those papers had to be kept secret from the world. In the wrong hands, they could destroy a man's career and reputation. They could spur murders. They could change the course of a war.

And an agent on Napoleon's side was working diligently to use the British government's own papers to wreak havoc.

Aries handed Royce a letter. "Read this."

Royce read it. "Seems ordinary. A naval captain's orders were updated. He was first told to sail to Faro, and now he's been instructed to sail to Porto instead."

"Seems ordinary," Aries agreed. "Except that no such orders were ever given. This letter is fake."

"Someone forged an official order?" Royce asked.

"And did it very well. The paper is authentic, so is the seal. By God, the ink is what that officer uses every day. He attested to that when interviewed. He said the signature looks just like his, but he swore he never wrote it."

"So I'm to hunt down the forger?"

"You're to identify whoever is involved in this scheme. There's more than one person. A nest of vipers."

"How so?" Royce asked.

Julian's constant assistant, Miss Chattan, chimed in then. "The quality of the forgery. It's highly unlikely one person could infiltrate a government department to steal the right stationery, note the right ink, get samples of the captain's real handwriting and signature, and also be a skilled forger, and also track the ship movements and orders well enough to be able to write a false order that sounds plausible. My guess is a minimum of three people, and possibly several more."

Though Miss Chattan's role in the Zodiac was supposedly administrative (she did not have a Sign like the agents did), Royce suspected the woman was somehow connected to the very heart of the Crown in some way. She simply knew far too much…about *everything*.

Royce frowned. "More agents means more potential for a leak, or for something to go wrong. Do you really think that there are multiple foreign agents in England working on this specific task?"

"I do. This letter is not the only example we uncovered, once we started looking. Whatever is going on, it's orchestrated. It's detailed."

"You've got to find out who's at the head of it and eliminate them," Aries concluded. "Or him. Or her. Whoever is responsible, just find them."

So Royce began tracking down this nest of vipers. It was a nightmare. He followed cold leads, went down false alleys, and in general drove himself mad in an effort to learn anything about the malefactors.

Over the course of a few months, Royce grew frustrated and despondent at his lack of progress. Everything was made worse because he was now Earl of Pelham, with more duties and expectations thrust on his shoulders. He couldn't put all his obligations off, or it would become evident that he was up to something. The Zodiac succeeded as an organization because it was small and highly secretive. Only twelve agents operated at any one time. They were hand-selected, often by unconventional means. They were all adept at concealing their espionage work from everyone in their ordinary lives. It was the only way to keep themselves and those they loved safe.

But the work was wearing Royce down, and it was beginning to affect his day-to-day life. In fact, choosing Royce to join the Zodiac was a mistake from the beginning. He was certain of it.

The only question was when his superiors would realize it.

♍

THE NEXT MORNING, TAMSIN WOKE early again (her cold room did not encourage loafing around in bed), and hurried to the library to begin working, since Royce had promised a bright and early start.

Along the way, she encountered the maid Ellen, and mentioned the lack of fuel.

Ellen gave her a sidelong glance. "Apologies, miss. I'll bring up more wood."

"Soon, if you please. The room will not get any warmer tonight."

The maid walked off, and Tamsin heaved an exasperated sigh. What was the matter with everyone? Laurent mentioned that the household staff had been at the estate long before Royce became earl. However, that did not explain why they all seemed to forget their jobs when it came to Tamsin. Her fire was not laid in the evening, nor cleaned in the morning. They forgot to bring up a pitcher of water for Tamsin's washing.

At least the chamber pot got emptied. Tamsin laughed to herself. *See, my girl? Things can always be worse.*

In the library she waited for Royce, but he failed to appear. She straightened her own desk, and tidied the rest of the library. Soon the only mess left was that which Royce lived with—the stacks and stacks of envelopes, papers, old newspaper clippings, and stuffed ledgers that populated his corner of the room. Just looking at it made Tamsin feel anxious. That was how invitations got overlooked and important documents got lost. She'd hate to have to dig through all that to find one thing from half a year ago.

Perhaps that was what the unfortunate Mr Fletcher had been asked to do, and that was why he quit in despair.

Well, she'd been hired as a secretary. She might as well do something to earn the title, even if her employer wasn't there to give her the express order. Surely he'd want her to organize his papers, since that's what secretaries did. Tamsin approached the nearest pile of papers and began to sort through it, hoping to bring some system to this chaos.

It was far worse than she'd guessed. Papers were thrown on top of each other with no regard for subject or date. Invitations to dinners sat atop quarterly earnings statements from tenants at various locations owned by the Earl of Pelham. Tamsin made several piles to corral the mess: social correspondence (mostly far out of date), estate business, and personal. The personal items she tried to ignore entirely, after determining they *were* personal. At least some of the letters were obviously from a lover— distinctly feminine handwriting from a London location, often sent daily for stretches of time.

She put aside yet another letter from the mysterious woman, hoping that it was not jealousy blossoming in her heart. Tamsin didn't love Royce! She hardly knew him, and discounting the bizarre night at the Green Lion— where he did nothing more than kiss her—they'd scarcely touched.

But it was a good kiss, she had to admit. The memory of it came to mind very quickly, and with a vividness that left her flushed.

"What is going on here?"

She looked up, seeing Royce just inside the doorway, all six feet of him enraged.

"Are you going through my papers?" he demanded.

"Of course, that's what a secretary does. They are a fire hazard at the very least." Tamsin let another letter from the London lady flutter to the top of the personal pile.

Royce followed its movement with his eyes and then rushed over to Tamsin, pushing her away from the papers.

"You cannot do this. I forbid it. You are not to touch any of these papers!"

She frowned. "My lord, they need to be sorted. It's the most basic task in an office, and one you were clearly neglecting."

"I was not."

"You were! Mountains of papers are not an organizational system. You and your former short-lived secretaries did neglect this work, and if you will not let me do it, I will resign!"

"You just got here!"

"Perhaps I should leave again!"

"And go where?"

"I don't know." Tamsin looked at the floor, upset at Royce's bizarre reaction to her work and her own inability to carry out her threat. Instead, she scooped up the items in the personal pile. "Here. Do something with your love letters. I may be a personal secretary, but I don't care to be *that* personal."

Royce went still, confusion on his face. "My what?"

"All of…these," she said, indicating the letters. "I can see a woman wrote them."

He took the box, glancing at the letters. Then, without

warning, he started to laugh, quietly at first but then louder.

"You needn't make fun of me," Tamsin said, rather stiffly.

"I'm not at all. You've just misunderstood. The woman who sent these is…well, she so far from a lover I can't begin to explain."

"Is it not personal, then? Should I file them among the business papers?" Tamsin reached for the box, but he stood and walked to the fireplace. Without a word, he hurled the letters in.

"What are you doing?" she gasped.

"What I should have done long before," Royce said with a sigh.

As the letters smoked in the depths of the fireplace, Tamsin moved next to him, grabbing the poker nearby. She prodded at the mass of letters, stirring them about.

Royce clearly thought she was going to fish them out, desperate to save them, but she smiled when the flames rose as the papers finally caught.

"There. If you're going to do something, do it properly. That's what my nursemaid used to say." She turned to him, seeing the orange flickering reflecting in his eyes. "I don't understand you at all. You keep all these letters for weeks and months, but the moment I suggest dealing with the matter, you immolate them. I don't wonder that you drove your previous secretaries away."

Royce didn't reply. He was watching Tamsin, his expression impossible to read. He said softly, "It's adorable that you get so impassioned about paperwork."

He laid his hand against her face, his thumb stroking along the cheekbone. Tamsin went still, too surprised to object, and frankly too taken by the tenderness in the gesture.

It was all well and good to agree that there would be no sexual relations between them. However, their logical, forward-thinking deal couldn't stop Tamsin from dreaming about such a relationship. Worse, it was clear that Royce thought of it too. Raw attraction crackled between them, immune to her better sense.

And why not? Royce was a sinfully attractive man, all the more because he didn't work to appear so. He lacked classically balanced features. His eyes were probably a little too deeply set, and his nose was a tiny bit crooked, and his mouth too wide, with full lips suggesting a frankly uncivilized amount of sensuality. His hair needed to be cut, for it grew too long, the dark waves swinging over his eyes when he bent over at the desk. Tamsin found herself with a strong urge to push his hair back, tangling her fingers in it.

In fact, she found herself with a strong urge to do all sorts of things with Royce that would be highly inappropriate for his own wife to do, if he had one. Ladies were not supposed to even have such impulses, let alone act upon them.

But how could she not have such impulses, having actually lain in a bed with him for one strange and unrepeatable night? And as a woman who'd only experienced unsatisfying intercourse, conducted in haste and in secret, she longed to know what she might be missing.

Royce leaned closer, his breath teasing her skin. In the next moment, he would kiss her. Tamsin ought to pull away, or say something. But just one kiss....

A knock at the door hurled them apart. Tamsin jumped five feet away, turning her back from him as she grabbed for some papers on her desk in an attempt to look innocently busy.

Royce sank into a crouch in front of the fire, grabbing

the poker to prod the logs and smoldering letters.

Tamsin called for whoever it was to enter, and some-how—miraculously—managed to sound collected and calm as she accepted the daily post and then told the maid that morning tea in a half hour would be appreciated.

"And bring extra sandwiches for Lord Pelham. As you can see, we're quite determined to plow through the worst of this mess, so we cannot be distracted."

She laid extra emphasis on the last words, an emphasis she hoped Royce understood.

After the maid left, Tamsin said in a low voice, "I suggest we get back to the task at hand."

She looked over at him, and was startled to see him standing at his full height, holding the poker and looking utterly cool and collected. As if he barely knew Tamsin.

"Excellent," Royce said in a crisp tone. "It's about time."

* * * *

Over the course of the next several days, a routine was already taking hold. Tamsin woke early, dressed and ate without benefit of any help or interest from the servants, and headed to the library.

As always, the curtains were still drawn and the fire unlit. She pulled the heavy fabric aside, letting in the bright morning. The earl claimed to be an early riser, but thus far she'd been first to the room. Tamsin lit the fire herself, unwilling to wait for the lord to arrive before getting the room to a livable temperature.

Each day, Tamsin made herself quite useful for the whole morning, because there was a truly staggering amount of papers and correspondence that Royce had not handled at all. When she asked about the previous secretaries, including the unfortunate Mr Fletcher, the maid Ellen told her that Fletcher left a month ago, but he'd only been employed for two months before that.

"His lordship wasn't even here for most of that time, or when he was, he was locked in his room, in one of his moods, you know."

Tamsin did not know, but she nodded. "So that made it difficult for Mr Fletcher to do his job."

"I suppose, miss. All I know is that since his lordship became earl here, he's had five secretaries and none of them for more than four months. Don't know how long you'll last," Ellen added, with an arch note to her words.

"Time will tell," Tamsin murmured. Even a month would be a victory—then Royce would have to pay her for the work she'd done and Tamsin could leave, choosing a direction as far from London as possible. She wondered if Edinburgh had need of scriveners. Surely Swigg's influence didn't extend beyond England's borders.

After Ellen left, she turned back to the work at hand, which was sorting through dozens of invitations for events in the nearby area. Many of them were already over and done with, rendering an RSVP moot. For those that had not yet occurred, Tamsin wrote polite refusals on Royce's behalf.

She used a more masculine style of handwriting than she preferred for her own writing. But Royce was correct—a male secretary was expected, and she didn't want to make her gender obvious. So she eschewed the fine nib and extra loops that her own tutor had shown her and Georgina while they were learning.

Whenever it was necessary to note her name on a document, she used "T. Black" in the hopes that people would ignore it altogether. Yes, it was better to not be noticed at all.

That was the situation at Seabourne, in fact. Tamsin was essentially alone. She worked with Royce in the library, but they kept to topics relating to the business at hand. Tamsin told herself that the earl had not really meant anything by his previous advances. It must be difficult for him, she reasoned, to picture a woman in a professional role like this one, even though he himself had proposed the idea. Tamsin's mother once told her that men were hardly capable of restraining their savage, animalistic nature. It was up to women to put a stop to any scandal that a man might start. After her one encounter with a man, Tamsin happened to agree.

So she spoke to Royce only in the library, and then excused herself well before the dinner hour. Happily, he usually put himself to work with a minimum of fuss. To his credit, he appreciated the mess he'd inadvertently created. He often ordered lunch and tea to be served in the library, delivered on trays and eaten quickly, without regard for the quality of the meal.

And in Tamsin's opinion, the quality left something to be desired. One day, when tea was delivered, Tamsin touched the side of the pot, which was barely more than lukewarm. Ugh, more tepid tea. Then she noticed the steam rising from the teapot on Royce's desk. Steam!

Of course, she thought. The servants were not bad— they were being selectively ineffective. Irked but unwilling to start a scene, Tamsin grabbed her teacup, rose, and walked to Royce's desk. She poured herself tea from his pot, and strolled back to her own desk feeling like she'd cheated the devil.

At the doorway, she caught sight of Nancy, who was staring at her in chagrin. Tamsin nodded to her as she took a sip. The tea was scalding, but Tamsin wasn't going to give the maid the satisfaction of seeing the reaction on her face. Through it all, Royce hadn't noticed a thing, being entirely consumed in reading whatever paper he was holding in his hands.

Another time, she discovered that her blue gown had a long tear in the skirt after being returned from the laundry. At first, she felt a deep pain on seeing the damage to the item, her first new gown for three years. But it wasn't as if fabric could be untorn. Sighing, Tamsin threaded a needle and mended the tear within a few minutes. As if she'd trust anyone below-stairs to sew anything for her at this point. In fact, she was certain that the gown was damaged deliberately. Laundresses did not typically use knives in the wash!

Life was rather lonely for Tamsin, especially after she divined that the household staff had launched this campaign against her from the very first day. The injustice rankled, but it was a familiar feeling—Tamsin told herself that she would endure it as she'd endured all the previous injustices in her life.

At least she had a safe place to sleep and eat. That was enough.

But wouldn't it be nice to have more, a little voice asked in her head, the voice that knew so much of the world was being denied to Tamsin.

"I am content," Tamsin said out loud. Content would have to do.

So she worked, day after day, with that mask of placid contentment to keep her going. One day, however, lunch came and went, but still Royce never appeared.

Needing some instruction for what to tackle next, Tamsin at last pulled the bell. After a very long time, Mrs Arnott herself came.

"What is it, miss?"

"Has Lord Pelham gone out for the day? I have not

seen him, but I need to know what tasks he has for me."

The housekeeper raised an eyebrow. "Well, I'm sure I shouldn't know that, miss."

Tamsin repressed a sigh. "Yes, that's why I wanted to locate him. Can you show me to where he is?"

"Still in his suite, miss."

She bit her lip, but then said, "Then show me there. I cannot waste his time and money by sitting around."

Looking as if she'd swallowed a lemon, Mrs Arnott turned around and began stalking down the hallway. Tamsin hurried after.

Upstairs, a separate wing housed the master's suite. Huge portraits of bygone earls and countesses gazed at passersby. One lady in a blue satin gown was particularly spectacular, but Tamsin had no time to appreciate the art, since the housekeeper was still pacing forward.

"Here," she said, stopping abruptly. "His lordship's suite. You may disturb him if you wish, but I will not! Good day."

She left, bustling away with great purpose.

Tamsin waited until the housekeeper descended the stairs, and then she knocked on the solid oak door.

There was no answer.

She knocked again. "My lord? It's me, Miss Black. May I speak to you?"

Again, there was no response, but she heard something from the room beyond, perhaps footsteps.

"My lord?" she called.

"Go away!"

Tamsin blinked at the rude response, but then wondered if he wasn't feeling well.

"It will only take a moment, my lord. I just need—"

"I said go away!" Royce roared, obviously in full health, to judge by the energy in that yell. "Get the hell out, and while you're at it, tell everyone that the next person to bother me will be thrown off the cliff."

She took a deep breath, stepping away from the door. "Well," she said under her breath, "at least it's an order."

Tamsin walked back downstairs, finding the maid Nancy dusting in the foyer. She bid her a polite good morning, and then added, "Lord Pelham has left instructions not to be disturbed."

"Aye," Nancy said, unaffected and uncaring.

"I'll be outside until dinner. I intend to walk the estate, since I haven't seen much of it at all."

"Aye." Nancy dusted a marble statue of Pan with particular disdain.

Tamsin nodded to herself. "All right, then."

She retrieved her pelisse and pulled on her gloves, then left the house, feeling more alone than ever.

♍

WALKING THROUGH THE GARDENS DIDN'T take long—the season for greenery and flowers was over, and the formal gardens were not that extensive. She was drawn to the home's main attraction: the cliffside lawn that offered a stunning view of the sea.

Today was cloudy, and the water was an even darker grey, reflecting her mood.

The simple truth was that she was lonely at Seabourne. Royce was usually polite and often kind, when he wasn't in one of his moods. But he was now careful to avoid any intimacy with Tamsin, and this precluded otherwise innocent gestures of companionship. She could not dine with him, she could not ride or walk with him, and besides the hours spent in the library—with the doors deliberately kept open—they did not remain in the same room together for more than a few moments.

She understood all this, and certainly appreciated Royce's commitment to treating her like an employee. But that didn't mean the long, empty hours didn't feel oppressive.

Tamsin turned toward a wooded section of the grounds, seeing a path leading toward a gap in the trees.

It was a pleasant walk, even in this treeless season. The woods were quiet except for the sounds of birds and the faint hiss of the wind past the branches. Tamsin

walked mindlessly, allowing the peaceful setting to replace the stir of emotions in her gut.

The path continued for some time, then all of a sudden, she came upon a young man dressed in the simple,
rugged clothing of a gameskeeper. Next to him was a dog.
He had tied the dog to a tree and was slowly loading a
gun. A shovel leaned against a nearby tree. The implication was clear enough to Tamsin.

"What do you think you're doing?" she demanded.

The young man looked up, alarm on his features. "Oh,
miss! You startled me. Why are you on Weston land?"

"The path started on Pelham's land," she said.

The dog, who had already noticed her, was sniffing
the air experimentally. He yelped once, straining at the
leash in an attempt to reach Tamsin.

She walked toward the creature and knelt down to pet
him. His brown and white fur was long and silky, and his
ears especially so. "Why is this dog tied up?"

"My orders are to kill him, miss," the young man said,
misery in his voice. "My master says he's a bad hunter,
and he's not worth it to feed. Nor does he want to risk the
bloodline getting tainted."

"What makes him a bad hunter? He looks healthy!"

"Oh, there's nothing wrong with him, except that the
training didn't take. He'll flush out the birds, but he won't
bring them back. He's lazy and unreliable."

"You cannot kill him," Tamsin said. "Let me go to
your master and I'll explain."

The young man shook his head vigorously. "No,
ma'am. Lord Weston is never moved once he makes up
his mind, and he never listens to ladies. Begging your
pardon."

"Then give the dog to me," she pleaded. "I'll take him
and you can say you buried him out here in the woods.

That was your plan, wasn't it? Who would know the difference?"

The man looked doubtful. "The master would recognize him if there was a hunting party. All the gentlemen hunt together, you know."

"I'll find some way to keep the dog separate from the hunting dogs." To be honest, Tamsin didn't even know where the earl kept his hunters. "What's his name?" Tamsin asked, gazing into the liquid brown of the dog's eyes.

"Jasper," the man replied. "He'll probably go with you. He's gentle enough. Too gentle for proper hunting."

"Good. For I'm not a hunter either."

"Do you know how to care for an animal like him? What to feed him and what not to?"

"I don't," she admitted. "But I could ask the stable-hands. They've got some dogs who live with the horses."

"Curs to catch rats and keep away the foxes," the young man said dismissively. "None of them are proper bred like this one."

He gave her some instruction as to what to feed the dog, and how often to exercise him, and where he ought to sleep. After promising that she'd keep the creature far from the border of the two properties, which fell more or less halfway through the woods, Tamsin took the leash and walked back toward Seabourne, Jasper prancing happily at her side. He seemed delighted by everything, jumping toward squirrels and barking at an especially loud crow. Tamsin smiled just to see him.

She'd hoped to bring the dog to the stables and ask the workers how to best house the dog. But she stopped short upon seeing Royce and Laurent there. Dressed in riding gear, Laurent was standing next to a massive black stallion who looked far too challenging for the young man to ride. Laurent was a decidedly slender person who ought to be on a horse a few hands shorter.

This was Royce's opinion as well—Tamsin knew that because he was yelling loud enough for the whole parish to hear.

"You do not have permission to ride Sentinel! What did you tell them to convince them to even saddle him? That I would be riding?"

Laurent's expression went icy. "As if anyone would believe we'd ride out together!"

A stablehand hovered nearby. "I'm sorry, my lord! It's…it's my fault."

Royce cut off any further explanation with a look. "If there's fault, it lies with my son. Laurent, get away from that horse."

"You ride him all the time."

"Because *I* can handle him!"

Laurent was about to retort when he suddenly noticed Tamsin and the dog. His eyes widened as he detected a distraction.

Royce turned too. "What sort of creature is that?"

"It's a dog," she said, feeling like a child. Anyone could see it was a dog.

"Whose dog?" he pressed.

"Um, mine?"

"Nonsense. That's a hunting spaniel."

"Well, I'm not going to take him hunting," she said. "He's just going to be my companion."

"Where did you find him in the first place?"

Tamsin explained, and watched as Royce shook his head. "These old men and their obsession with hunting. To think of shooting a dog for not being bloodthirsty enough." His sigh seemed more depressed than warranted by the situation, though he'd clearly been despondent and angry all day. But this was the lowest she'd seen him with her own eyes.

"Is that why you don't hunt?" she asked, mostly to keep him talking about normal things. "You don't like the violence?"

"I don't hunt because I don't care to," Royce said shortly. His mood wasn't improving much. "And I'm rather busy."

"Doing what?" Tamsin still didn't understand exactly what occupied Royce's attention all day and all night. Several people had mentioned that he often went away for days or weeks at a time. He certainly was doing something, to judge by the massive amount of materials coming to his study, and the few but seemingly important letters he sent out. "What does an earl do all day?"

"I haven't the foggiest," he retorted. "My father must have been bored stiff. Laurent, don't sneak away! I'm not done with you yet."

"You sounded *quite* done with me." Laurent looked curiously at the dog. "What's his name?"

"Jasper," Tamsin said.

Laurent knelt down to greet the dog. All the wary smugness he normally wore slid off as he petted the creature in front of him. "Who's a good boy? Is it you?" Both Laurent and the dog grinned happily at each other.

Royce looked astonished at his son's sudden shift in behavior, but he quickly covered his reaction. "Laurent, you may not ride any horse for a week, and anyone who saddles a horse for you—hell, a mule—will be sacked. You need to go inside the house and apply yourself to your studies. I heard from your tutor that you have not been keeping up."

Then Royce turned to Tamsin. "Miss Black, I'm afraid that I've been rather behind schedule today." She noticed that he made no mention of yelling at her from behind his bedroom door earlier. "Would you come to the library when you've figured out what to do with your pet? He can't run around loose while you work."

"Oh, I'll watch him!" Laurent said, looking eagerly at Tamsin. "I'm very good with animals."

"I'd appreciate that, Laurent. Um, don't take him anywhere near the Weston lands, please."

Laurent raised an eyebrow but didn't protest. "Yes, Miss Black."

"Well," Royce said, "better that than sulking and hiding in your room."

That evening, Tamsin actually ate her supper in the kitchen with the rest of the servants, solely because she'd come with Jasper to find food that was suitable for the dog to eat.

As it turned out, he was delighted to eat the scraps of meat and vegetables from that day's cooking. And Jasper's big brown eyes melted the hearts of everyone, to the point that even Mrs Arnott pointed Tamsin to a corner of the table when it came time to eat.

"You may as well take your meal here tonight," she'd said grudgingly. "Save Ellen the trip with the tray."

Tamsin ate quietly and quickly, noting that the soup was hot and the bread fresh, with lots of creamy butter for spreading. Jasper's nose twitched constantly, but he looked at Tamsin with adoration, and lay down at her feet after he finished his meal.

When it came time to go to bed, Tamsin found that she could not abandon her new friend to sleep in the stables with the others. And to be fair, he didn't show the slightest interest in leaving her.

Tamsin stood up, and the dog did too.

"You'll put that beast outside yourself, will you?" Nancy asked.

"Certainly," Tamsin lied without compunction.

She took the dog out for a final walk, letting him run over to a few posts and tree trunks that he'd decided were in need of his attention. But then she smuggled him back inside and down the lonely corridor to her room. At last, there was an advantage to being located so far from everyone else!

"Now, you can't bark, understand? They'll come and take you away if they know you're here." Tamsin laid out the extra blanket near the fireplace, and patted it. "Here you go. This is your bed."

The dog understood immediately and curled up on the blanket, wuffling softly when Tamsin stroked the soft fur on the top of his head.

She climbed into bed and blew out the light. The mere presence of the dog was incredibly reassuring to Tamsin, who generally only fell asleep after exhaustion overtook her. Tonight, she drifted off quickly, thinking of the many walks she'd take Jasper on while she lived here.

In the middle of the night, Tamsin awoke for the unusual reason of being too warm. Then she realized that the dog had climbed onto the bed, and was lying on her feet.

"Oh, Jasper," she said. She should immediately send the dog back to its bed by the fire (which had gone out). But she didn't. She reached down and petted the dog's head, earning a sleepy woof and a big lick.

She smiled, and went back to sleep.

♍

ROYCE WAS BEGINNING TO DOUBT the wisdom of bringing Tamsin to Seabourne. The plan made sense in the abstract. Get the girl out of immediate danger, then soften her up to persuade her to tell what she knew of Swigg, which was clearly a lot more than she pretended. And he couldn't have left her where he found her…so he decided to keep her within arm's reach. But arm's reach was a dangerous distance, because Royce increasingly wanted to stretch out and grab her every time he saw her.

He couldn't recall ever being so entranced by a woman. The only possible contender was Dominique, and that had been less about enchantment and more about raw lust. Royce had to admit that his younger self wasn't too discerning. A beautiful body and a willing spirit had been quite enough to keep him entertained for months. In bed, at least. He and Dominique barely got on when outside the bedroom. They fought nearly every day—which allowed for some incredible, dramatic declarations of hate and love. But it wasn't exactly ideal.

Tamsin was entirely different. Quiet, wary, restrained…until she let loose with a well-chosen comment, proving that her mind was as sharp as her body was gorgeous. She was a woman with secrets, and Royce was compelled to expose secrets. That's why he'd been selected for the Zodiac, and why he kept pursuing this assignment.

A footman entered, carrying a silver tray. He set it down on a clear spot on the corner of Royce's desk. "The morning's post, sir. And the London papers from Monday."

Royce nodded, thinking that until recently, that spot had been covered with papers, and no one would have been able to put anything there. Tamsin had worked wonders.

She seemed intent on working more wonders, because she'd gotten up from her chair and was making directly for the letter tray.

Royce put his hand out and took all the letters.

"I'll go through them first," he said.

"Sorting correspondence is literally what you hired me for," Tamsin said.

"Not these."

She huffed and returned to her desk, casting a narrowed-eyed look at him when she sat down. Tamsin clearly knew that something odd was going on, but Royce was certain that she was still on the "secret mistress" theory rather than the "official spy" theory.

Royce had pounced on the letters because the top one was recognizable as being from Miss Chattan, a fact that Tamsin would know, since she compiled all the old ones before he burned them. Chattan's letters all looked the same—folded into a tidy square, contained in an envelope made of especially thick paper. It was impossible to hold it up to the light to read through it. The wax seal and the edges dipped in wax also meant that the contents couldn't be read by anyone but the recipient. It would be evident right away.

Royce broke the seal and pulled out the letter. He skimmed it, and sighed. No good news from the Zodiac.

The few overseas contacts they'd hoped to learn from had either not responded or knew nothing.

He wrote out his reply, informing Chattan, and by extension Aries, that he had found a contact of Swigg's who he thought he could persuade to cooperate. He just needed time. Royce had to utilize the code the Zodiac employed to keep messages secret, and that also kept his explanation much shorter than it would otherwise be. He didn't mention Tamsin's name or where he found her—that could all wait till later.

After sealing the letter to Chattan, he flung it into the tray for outgoing post. Tamsin raised her eyebrow, but he didn't bother to make an excuse.

He opened another note, this one much less formal looking. He read that letter more thoroughly, often muttering the words out loud—the poor spelling suddenly made sense when spoken. But at the end, he was no wiser.

"God damn it." All of Royce's contacts were coming up with nothing. He'd sent a few reliable people to track down more of the names on his list of likely forgers in London. But not a single person seemed to fit. Either they didn't have the skills, or the timing was off, or a half a dozen other reasons why they could not be the man Royce was hunting for.

He slammed his hand down the desk, eliciting a started gasp from Tamsin.

"Sorry," he growled.

With wide eyes, she asked, "Is this a bad time to discuss your social calendar, my lord?"

"Is there ever a good time? Go on." He needed a distraction.

She held up a paper. "There's an invitation from Lord Weston for a hunting party next week. I assume you'll want to send your regrets."

Royce just made a face. "Indeed. I understand a man's need to hunt for food. I allow the tenants to go small game hunting on my own lands, and my estate manager turns a blind eye to most poaching, provided it's not too boldly done. But all the trappings of a fox hunt with horses and hounds and a whole day wasted...I see nothing interesting in it. For God's sake, the hounds do all the work and deserve the credit. What are you smiling at?"

Tamsin quickly shook her head. "Nothing. I did not expect such an extensive answer. I shall send Lord Weston your regrets."

"Do that. My father loved the hunt, and he and Lord Weston were always planning the next outing. Shooting pheasants, hunting fox...it seemed every season offered an opportunity to leave the house and ride through the woods, getting twigs in your hair and pebbles in your boots."

"I thought you said you didn't go."

"When I was young, I had to attend. My father expected it, and I wanted to like what he liked. But I never did, and by the time I was fifteen or so, I stopped going altogether. I'm sure I disappointed him." He frowned. "It would have been nice to have a sister. My older brothers were like my father—they both loved a hunt. No wonder they said I sulked and hid in my room."

"You said that to Laurent," Tamsin noted, then looked up, her expression stricken. "Forgive me, my lord. It's certainly not my place to...never mind." Tamsin stood up, anxious under Royce's gaze. "Excuse me. I'll leave..."

"Leave me to sulk?"

"That's not what I meant."

"I know what everyone says," Royce went on. "They're right. I've got moods. I'm irritable. I'll brood for weeks on end and who can stop me?"

"It is still an improvement over my last situation," she said coolly. "Speaking of which, you might offer to speak to your son in a less...combative way. He's unhappy, and to be yelled at will not improve things."

"You know nothing of it."

"I don't have to, my lord. All I am saying is that you ought to try. Laurent is quite a fine young man under all that misery. And you may have the power to alleviate his pain if you try."

"This conversation is over," Royce said, throwing all the weight of his position behind it.

Tamsin shut her mouth, but didn't leave.

Why not? Oh, yes. He was the earl, and he had not dismissed her.

"Get the hell out," he said in a low voice.

Without a word, she walked to the door, her spine straight and her manner icily correct.

Royce closed his eyes after Tamsin fled the room. God, what was the matter with him? It seemed like his mind could never be still, until his thoughts crashed head-long into a cliff, and then he felt like his mind could never stir again. He'd just lie in bed, wishing he was anywhere else but lacking the drive to do anything about it.

A pathetic excuse for an earl. His mother should have tried for more children, until another survived. Then Royce could walk off a cliff and leave the title to someone who knew how to behave in Society.

Tamsin's arrival at Seabourne only emphasized how inept he was, as an earl and as a spy. His moods were longer and darker than they used to be. He should never have allowed secret letters from the Zodiac to be found by another person. True, the letters were always written in careful and often coded language, but it was still a breach of security.

They should get rid of you. They can't trust you to do the simplest things. They can't rely on you for the job you're on now. The familiar thought surfaced, and immediately took hold. It sounded so sensible, so logical.

He picked up the newspaper that arrived with the letters. His gaze went immediately to a column headlined with NAVAL DEFEAT NEAR PORTO—NAPOLEON ADVANCES.

"Bloody fucking hell." The mention of Porto made his hands clench up. Royce knew his quarry had something to do with the defeat. The British Navy outclassed the French by nearly every measure. A defeat could only be traced to poor intelligence…or a clever trick.

If Royce had located the enemy by now, maybe that defeat wouldn't have happened.

Unable to focus on any task, Royce tossed Chattan's latest letter into the fire. Then he left the library and went up to his own suite. Whenever his mood grew too dark, he hid there, where he could do the least damage.

Up in his room, Royce stoked the fire and sat in front of the flames. Annoyingly, the scene put him in mind of Tamsin…again. He thought of the night they met, how she'd sat in front of the fire in her bedsheet-gown, looking quite at home.

Damn it, the woman got into his blood. He should be grateful that she clearly wanted to avoid any romantic relationships at all, because currently, Tamsin's resistance to the attraction between them was the only thing keeping them apart. It certainly wasn't Royce's doing—he'd never been good at resisting temptation, and Tamsin was the most tempting woman he could ever remember meeting.

He was attracted to her looks, with her wild auburn hair and her half smile and her sweetly curving body. He dreamed about her more than once, waking up either rock hard, or already spent.

A soft knock on the door startled him. He glanced at the clock on the mantel, and was appalled to see that it was nearly midnight.

He'd lost time again...brooding instead of working.

You're not the man for this job...or any job.

He shoved the thought away and moved to the door. Probably a maidservant with a tray—the staff knew to bring up food to keep their employer alive.

But when he opened the door, it wasn't a servant at all.

Tamsin stood there, clad in a dressing gown. It was proper...technically. That is, it would be proper for him to see her wearing it in, say, the dining room while she took her breakfast, or in a sitting room on a day when no callers were expected.

It was not proper to see her standing in front of his door before bed.

"Yes?" he asked, internally debating whether to place a wager on what she'd ask for.

Ask for me, he thought.

"My lord," Tamsin said, her eyes locked on the floor. In anticipation of bed, her hair was only tied back with a ribbon, a look that softened her appearance considerably. He liked it. "The first day I came here, you mentioned that you had *Paradise Lost*, but it wasn't in the library...."

Talk about a fall.

"I've got it in here," Royce said. "Just a moment."

Tamsin hovered at the door while he walked to retrieve the book in question. He could feel her curiosity like a physical thing.

What was the lord's room like, this lair where he hid and sulked so often?

Not very appealing, actually. Royce didn't much care

for his suite, since it had been decorated to his father's taste nearly forty years ago and never changed. Royce always meant to…but it was hard to prioritize the decor when he had to chase a spy or simply survive the black moods that so often took him over.

The walls featured silk hangings in an ochre color he never liked. The furniture was dark-stained oak, heavy and old-fashioned. In an effort to bring some openness, he had removed a number of smaller items, including chairs and little tables and a host of random knickknacks. But the result was just that the room looked oddly incomplete, with strange open areas where something obviously used to be—in fact, Royce pushed a lot of the remaining furniture against the walls so he could pace uninterrupted. Nothing was balanced.

The bookcase was between the bed and the fireplace, and it was loaded with titles, some jammed in horizontally above the others. A few were open, the pages flapping in the hot draft of the fire.

"It's here, I just need to find it," he called.

"Let me help." Tamsin's reply was soft, but he jumped, not realizing she'd followed him to the bookcase.

"It's got a blue cover," he said unwillingly. He ought to know where it was, but just like his professional life, his personal life was a mess.

Tamsin began to skim the shelves, running one finger over the spines of the books as she searched, her mouth slightly open while she absorbed the titles.

He shouldn't be aroused by a woman looking for a book…but he was.

And then he spotted *Paradise Lost* on a shelf above Tamsin's head. He reached over for it, just as she saw it and reached up too.

His hand closed over hers, feeling an almost palpable

shock as skin slid against skin.

Tamsin went still, but didn't pull her hand back. Royce stepped closer, moving his body behind hers so she was between him and the bookcase.

"Let me," he told her.

She slowly drew her hand down and spun so she faced Royce. He pulled the book from the shelf and handed it to her. The moment she took it, their fingers touched again, and that time he saw the desire in her expression.

The air was thick with words unspoken. They both knew that some things were too dangerous to ever say out loud.

"I have to leave," Tamsin whispered, looking dazed, her eyes fixed on his.

"Not yet," he said, unwisely.

His suggestion may as well have been a direct proposition.

She inhaled, as if coming awake from a dream. Then she managed to duck under his arm and dash twenty steps away before he could turn around.

"How the hell do you move that fast, Miss Black?" he demanded, more surprised than irritated.

"A skill learned in my previous life," she retorted from the doorway, once again her composed, slightly sardonic self. "If you don't move fast near Catchpenny Lane, you soon won't be moving at all."

"You are wasted as a secretary."

She smiled, a little wicked light coming into her eyes. "Oh, that reminds me. You're going to dinner on Tuesday, at Newbury House. The dowager has invited you."

"What? I'm not going to any dinner."

"I've already sent your response this afternoon, and you're delighted to attend," Tamsin said sweetly. "Do enjoy the evening, my lord."

"This is revenge," he guessed, quite accurately. "Look, I'm sorry I lost my head earlier today, but I can *not* sit around a whole evening with some dire crowd who only want to talk about the wool trade."

"I'm sure they'll talk about the sheep as well, my lord." She tilted her chin up. "Look, the dowager is a neighbor, and she deserves some reward for so faithfully inviting you to events over the past two years, despite your lack of response. And it's clear you need to be more social than you are now. You'll forget all your manners if you're not forced to use them occasionally."

He glared at her. "I should make you come with me."

"Ha! I'd almost go, just to see the expressions as they realize a fallen woman is enjoying the soup course."

"Don't say that," Royce told her. "It's not what you are."

Tamsin shrugged. "You know how gossip works in the country."

"I thought I made it quite clear to all that you're no more or less than a personal secretary. It's not as if I'm hauling you off to my bedroom at night."

And yet, they were both in his bedroom, and the bed was so very close by.

She swallowed nervously and ducked her head. "I don't think the truth matters."

"I've made things worse, haven't I? You should have stayed in London."

"If I stayed in London, I'd be dead now," Tamsin said bluntly. "It's just a matter of perspective. I'll be all right. Gossip is nothing new."

She clasped the book to her chest, saying in a polite, formal way, "Thank you for the loan, my lord. I'll be sure to return it to the library when I'm finished."

"Tamsin…" He didn't want to be formal with her. He

wanted a whole lot less formality, in fact. Nudity would be a good starting point.

"Good night, my lord. I'm sorry that I disturbed you." Tamsin pulled the door shut, leaving him alone, highly disturbed, and in no state for sleep.

But, he could say honestly, his mood definitely improved.

♍

TAMSIN ENJOYED SEEING ROYCE THE next day, largely because he mostly avoided catching her eye, and he was scrupulously polite.

"If I offend you, you'll accept more invitations on my behalf," he explained midmorning. "I now know how a rabbit feels when a wolf is near."

"My lord," Tamsin replied, "no one would mistake me for a wolf, and certainly not you for a rabbit!"

She laughed at the image of the six-foot-tall earl as a helpless creature. There was nothing soft or fluffy about him.

As it happened, she did not accept any more invitations for him, because none arrived. The new Earl of Pelham's reputation for refusals was finally making its way around the county. Plus, it was not really the time of year for grand entertainments. The next large event in this area of the country was not likely to be until Yuletide. And soon after that, Royce would probably head back to London for the Season. An earl must find a bride, after all.

Tamsin tried not to think about that too much. She retired early to her room, eating alone and then reading her hard-won copy of *Paradise Lost*.

Unfortunately, she finished reading the book well before her bedtime. "Drat," she said aloud. She needed another book, which meant leaving the warm nest of her bed, where Jasper lay sleeping at her feet, and throwing on her dressing robe to scuttle like a mouse through the dark halls to get to the library.

It was an unappealing notion. But worse than that was the prospect of having no books to read. So Tamsin slid out of bed, put her slippers on before her feet could touch the icy cold floor, and tugged her dressing gown on over her shift.

Jasper snored loudly, and she hoped he wouldn't be alarmed if he woke and found her gone. She'd only be a quarter hour at most anyway.

She picked up her candlestick and made her way through the long, drafty passages of Seabourne. Shadows leapt and writhed around her as she went, and faces of long-ago lords and ladies blinked in and out of her vision like ghosts, briefly illuminated by Tamsin's candlelight before they were plunged into darkness once again.

On seeing the library doors, Tamsin paused. There was light emanating from within. It was too late for any servants to be at work cleaning or dusting, and this was the one night Royce couldn't be here, since he'd grudgingly accepted the supper party invitation from the dowager. He wouldn't be back until midnight at the earliest.

So who was now in the library, and what were they doing there? Remembering Royce's initial rage when he discovered Tamsin "snooping" through his papers, she wondered if someone else was doing just that. Clearly, Royce had some sort of confidential business, and if a servant was paid to steal some papers, tonight was a perfect time to try.

Tamsin extinguished her own candle and crept toward the doors. She peeked inside, catching the silhouette of a woman bending over Royce's desk, a paper in her hands.

"Stop that right now!" Tamsin ordered in her most

authoritative voice as she stepped into the room.

The figure whirled around, gasping in dismay. With a start, Tamsin recognized her as the maidservant Ellen.

"What are you doing here, Ellen?" Tamsin demanded. "It is very late!" Not to mention that the maid had no reason to be in the library at all.

"Begging your pardon, miss!" Ellen gasped, clutching a paper to her chest. "I'll go."

"One moment. What is that you're holding?"

"Nothing, miss!"

"Let me see." Earlier, Royce had nearly taken Tamsin's head off when he thought she'd moved some of his papers. What if they really were going missing, and one of the servants was stealing them? "Hand it over."

"No, miss!" Ellen turned away violently, hiding the paper as she whirled to face the desk. "It's none of your business."

"Is it *your* business?" Tamsin asked. "If that is one of Lord Pelham's documents, you have no right to take—"

"The lordship's? No, miss! I'd never take such a thing. This letter is mine!"

"Then let me see it so I can verify the fact." Tamsin was blocking the only way out of the room, and she doubted the maid would put up much of a fuss for long.

Indeed, Ellen glanced over her shoulder with guilt all over her face. "It *is* mine," she repeated. "It's a letter."

"From who?"

"My sweetheart." She said that word so shyly that Tamsin could scarcely hear it.

"And what does your sweetheart have to say?"

"I…I'm not sure. He knows his letters and I told him to write, but the truth is that I don't read very well. I came here to go over his letter in the light, and to get away from Nancy—she shares the room, you see. And she'd never stand for me keeping the candle burning while I worked at reading."

"Would you like me to read it aloud to you?" Tamsin offered.

Ellen's face lit up. "Oh, would you, miss?"

"Certainly. But I need to see it in order to read it."

Now the maid handed the letter over eagerly. Tamsin unfolded it and held it toward the lamp.

"He says: Dear Ellen, I write from London. It is cold and dreary here in the city, and I miss Norfolk. But I miss you more. Nights here are so lonely. The days are long and tiring, but the work keeps me from worrying. At night, I think only of my family, and of you. As soon as I make enough, I'll come home and we'll marry. I shall not send for you to come here—that plan is over. London is no place for a woman like you, dearest. It's dirty and loud and busy and there are no end of horrors to assault a simple lady's eyes. No, I have decided that I alone shall endure it, and only until I have made enough to pay off the loan and return home. Promise me in your reply that you'll wait for me. It is the only thought that propels me forward. Forever yours, Adam."

Tamsin handed the letter back to Ellen, whose eyes were glassy with unshed tears. "He sounds like a dedicated young man, and very devoted to you."

"Oh, my dear Adam. What he must be going through in that vile place! Oh, I shall wait for him, but I hope it's not too long!"

"He'll be grateful to hear from you, I'm sure. A note from home is a powerful thing, especially to a person who is lonely." There were nights when Tamsin would have given her soul for a letter from her sister, Gina, or her mother and father.

The maid nodded, but said, "Miss Black. My handwriting is not…that is…it takes me a long time to get the words down on paper, and I am already sneaking out…"

Tamsin understood the issue before it was plainly stated. "Sit down, Ellen. You shall dictate your words and I will write them for you."

In her element, Tamsin moved to the desk and sat. She took her favorite pen from its holder and dipped it in the inkwell.

"Come," she ordered Ellen. "We haven't got all night."

Ellen sank to the opposite chair as a breathy sigh escaped her. "Oh, miss, you're too kind."

Yes, Tamsin was being rather too kind. Neither of them should be in this room at this hour, and she should not be making free with Royce's supplies and materials to pen a letter for a housemaid! But she couldn't think about that now.

Ellen haltingly spoke her reply, the phrasing stilted and formal compared to her mode of speech. Tamsin hid a smile and made only a *few* adjustments to the text as dictated—an added service she'd often performed as a scrivener.

When she finished, she handed Ellen the pen and instructed her to make her mark at the conclusion of the text.

"Oh, your handwriting is ever so beautiful. Adam will know it's not me who wrote it!"

"I have added a line at the bottom," Tamsin said, pointing. "Here: *from Ellen Smythe, as spoken to T. Black, scrivener*. Very common in London, to hire a scrivener. He'll think you quite sophisticated."

"Oh, I hope not, miss!" Ellen looked horrified.

"It's not a bad word," Tamsin told her, striving to keep the laughter out of her voice.

"Isn't it?"

"It means someone who is aware of the styles of the time."

"Are you sophisticated?"

Tamsin gave a little laugh. "I once thought so—pretty gowns, a gold chain around my neck—but that was a long time ago. Now I am just grateful for what I have."

"You really are his lordship's secretary, aren't you?" Ellen looked at the handwriting on the letter again. "That's all he asks of you?"

"What else?"

"Well, they all said you're his mist—" Ellen broke off.

"Who says I'm his mistress?" Tamsin demanded. "Do I dress like a mistress? Do I act like a mistress? Does *he* act like I'm his mistress? No, no, and no. I don't know that much about what a mistress does all day, but it doesn't involve sorting correspondence and keeping the lord's calendar and being ordered about and getting my fingers black with ink! I scarcely see the lord other than when he's in his office, and during that time, the door is open and others come and go. If he expected me to come to his bed, I'd never have taken the job!"

Tamsin stopped, her uncharacteristic outburst having left her winded and tired.

"Oh, miss. I'm so sorry. It's just rumors."

"Rumors that result in cold tea and ripped laundry and dusty floors in my bedroom." She caught Ellen's guilty look. "The message was clear enough. I'm not welcome here."

"Mrs Arnott told us how to treat you."

"Many lords keep mistresses. What will she do when he inevitably *does* have one?" Tamsin spoke the words a little bitterly. Men were always allowed to indulge their desires. Royce would have no difficulty finding a mistress delighted to warm his bed.

"Mistresses are all well and good," Ellen agreed. "His lordship may do what he likes. But it's not proper to bring them home and install them in among God-fearing folk."

"He *didn't*. I'm a secretary."

"I think Mrs Arnott doesn't believe that," Ellen said meekly.

"But you do?"

"Oh, yes, miss. I do now."

"Well, I thank you for clarifying the issue. Now, it is very late, and we must both go to our own beds."

Following the exchange with Ellen, Tamsin found that she had an ally among the servants. So long as Ellen was in charge of cleaning her room and sending up food, Tamsin would be assured that the firewood was plentiful and the meals actually hot.

It did not change the fact that she dined alone in her room—she was still in the awkward and lonely position of being not-quite-guest-not-quite-help. If only Royce had young children, because then she could eat with the governess. Laurent was too old for such attention. Tutors came to the house on certain days, but none stayed there. And in any case, all of Laurent's tutors were men, and Tamsin wouldn't have dined alone with a man anyway.

Oh, well. She bit into the crusty top of a shepherd's pie, relishing the warmth of the meal on this windy night. Better to dine alone than not eat at all. There were nights in London when Tamsin went hungry, unable to afford even a meager supper.

Jasper's nose appeared at the corner of the table, and Tamsin laughed out loud.

"I'm not entirely alone," she reminded herself, giving the dog a piece of the crust, which disappeared into his gullet.

But she couldn't banish the image of another dining companion. Royce, dressed in his most aristocratic style, escorting her into supper in his dining room—just the two of them, and a splendid meal, and then him leaning over, telling her that nothing was as special as that beef stew at the Green Lion...

Tamsin laughed again, more cynically. "Stop mooning over impossibilities, girl," she told herself. "You live in the same house, but in different worlds. No good can come from his attention."

How many times would she have to learn that lesson? Once should be enough.

♍

TAMSIN HELD A MYSTERIOUS LETTER in her hands.

She was in the library again that morning, and Royce had not yet appeared when the footman brought in the post and the paper on the tray, as he did every day.

So she'd taken the liberty of sorting through it all, and then found another of those letters Royce guarded so fiercely…and then set afire after reading.

She didn't dare open it. Whatever it contained, it must be very private. But she studied the handwriting (obviously a woman's) and the paper (extremely high quality). The seal was nothing remarkable (a star pressed into a blot of blue wax), but the letter had also been dipped into blue wax along the edge, so that if it were somehow opened, the transgression would be obvious.

"Who are you?" Tamsin asked aloud, as though the letter might answer. It *had* to be a lover. Who else wrote with such secrecy and devotion?

He'd want to open this straightaway. Tamsin sighed, and took the newspaper under her arm before she pulled the bell.

The same footman appeared shortly after. "Yes, miss?" he asked.

"Is the earl still in his rooms? This letter should go to him immediately. And he does seem to want the paper quickly as well."

"Ah…his lordship isn't there." The footman looked slightly alarmed as he spoke.

"Where did he go?" Tamsin had charge of Royce's sparse social schedule. She would have known if he were expected at an event of any kind. "Is he riding?"

"Not that we know of."

"What? How can the household not know where he is?"

"Well, his lordship just goes off sometimes, around the estate, you know."

"On foot?" If the carriage or a horse were missing, the household would be up in arms.

"Yes. It's not our place to disturb him, miss. The lord would be most displeased."

Tamsin rolled her eyes, but then remembered Royce's confession on the first night they met…his impulse to jump off the Charlesway Bridge into the cold waters below. The ocean outside might offer a similar lure. She shivered.

"I'll go find him," she announced.

"Miss, that's not a good idea."

"The worst he can do is sack me, just like all his other secretaries."

Tamsin left the library to retrieve Jasper, who was sleeping in her room, and to put on her sturdy walking boots, since it might take a while to find Royce.

She led the dog to the kitchens, hoping to grab a hunk of bread before leaving out the door to the vegetable garden. When the cook asked what she was about, Tamsin explained her errand.

"Oh, miss," a groundskeeper interjected from his place at the long table. "He could be anywhere. Do you know how big this estate is?"

"Jasper will help me."

The groundskeeper looked skeptical. "He's not a bloodhound."

"No, but any dog's nose is better than mine. And Jasper will want a walk anyway." Tamsin slid the mysterious letter into her pocket, put on her pelisse, and marched out of the house.

She and Jasper trod several paths in search of her wayward employer. Luckily, Tamsin worked up enough energy and warmth to offset the biting wind coming in off the sea.

Finally, Jasper started tugging in a particular direction, and Tamsin followed, willing to let the dog lead.

At the end of that path, they found him.

Royce was sitting on a fallen tree, staring out over the cliff to the grey waters beyond. The scene was desolate, with the waves crashing hollowly on the shores, echoing up the stone face of the cliff. A strong wind whipped the few remaining leaves, sending many of them over the cliff to a watery grave.

Tamsin approached quietly, afraid to disturb him, but aware that something was terribly wrong.

"My lord? Sir?" she asked. "Royce?"

His shoulders jerked in response to his personal name, and he looked back, his expression as forbidding as the ocean. "What is it?"

"No one could find you. Your household is worried."

"Let them worry. I'll be back in my own time." He turned to face the water again.

A wiser woman would let him brood. He was the master here, and no one had any authority over him. However, Tamsin was drawn to Royce in a way she couldn't explain. She walked forward and sat beside him on the fallen tree. Wind rustled the bottom of her skirts, chilling her ankles.

"What, are you here to babysit me?" Royce asked, his tone bitter.

"No, I'm quite done with hiring out as a governess. You're old enough to watch over yourself."

"Then why are you intruding on my solitude?"

"Your solitude looked very lonely," she said. "How long have you been sitting here?"

"I don't know. I lose track of time when I get in a mood."

Tamsin nodded. It seemed that Royce was often subject to these *moods*…a long period of brooding in which he ignored all the rules of Society and snarled at the staff and made life difficult for everyone around him. An earl in a mood was a challenging thing to face.

Tamsin did turn to face him, perhaps because she was also used to ignoring the rules of Society. "It is very cold, my lord. And you can brood just as well in the comfort of your own suite, can you not?"

"Go to hell."

"Perhaps I'll end up there eventually, but for now our destination is the house."

"I don't want to move. There's no point."

"It's freezing!"

"Let it freeze."

Tamsin frowned, putting facts together. She asked, "That's what it is, isn't it? The night we met, you wanted to start a brawl with Coaker because you needed to get your blood up. You saved me because it made you feel something, got you unfrozen. And you kept me around because I was a novelty. But I'm no longer a novelty, am I? And now you're bored again."

"It's not boredom," he protested.

"Ennui? Melancholy?"

"I can't describe it. Every time I try to explain it to

another person, I fail." He sent her a narrowed-eyed glance. "What's it matter? Why do you care what I do?"

"Well, first because you are my employer and it's difficult to work while one's employer is not available to tell one what to work on. And second, because I would like to think we are still…forgive me for my presumption… friends of a sort."

"Friends?" His eyes went dark, with an unnameable emotion in them.

"Yes." She grew hesitant. "You said it that first night, when we spent time together in a way that Society would never understand—a man and woman spending the whole night alone, just talking. I understand that I am now merely one of your many subordinates, but—"

"I do not think of you as subordinate."

Tamsin leaned toward him, drawn to him in way she couldn't explain. Then the sharp corner on the folded letter jabbed her thigh through the fabric of her shift.

Tamsin pulled back, remembering the impossibility of this situation.

"My lord, you asked why I came to find you. A letter arrived. I thought you would want to see it." She pulled the letter from her pocket.

"You didn't open it," he said. It was a simple statement, not an accusation.

"It's not my place," said Tamsin. "But even if you won't tell me anything about the sender, she's obviously important to you."

Royce held the letter lightly in his hand. "Thank you for bringing it. And not opening it. There aren't many people in this world I can trust. But you seem to be one of them, Tamsin." His expression tightened. "Or should I say Miss Black?"

"That would be best," Tamsin admitted, wishing it

were otherwise.

"Very well." He stood up, offering his hand to help her stand as well. "Let's go back to the house, Miss Black. Then I'll open this letter and apply myself to all the things I've been avoiding."

"If you told me what those things were, perhaps I could assist you," she offered.

Royce suddenly smiled, and it was if the clouds broke apart and sunlight flooded the world. "Be careful what you wish for, Miss Black."

Tamsin had long ago learned not to wish for anything, but now, she wished that she could be of some help to Royce, because whatever he was up to, it seemed like more than one person could handle.

His gaze swept over her, making her wish for a lot of things she'd never get. Then, dropping his hand down, he touched her gown, and ran a finger over the mended tear on her skirt. "Isn't this outfit new? Are you especially accident-prone?" He answered the question before she could. "No. You're too careful for that. What happened?"

Tamsin took a breath. "Well, the truth is that my clothing fares very poorly in the laundry here at Seabourne."

"Is that so? I've never noticed an issue."

"That's because you're the master," she said dryly. "I am not so respected."

"What do you mean?"

So Tamsin explained the whole situation. The cold tea, the ripped clothes, the uncleaned room…even the fact that Ellen was the sole servant who was on Tamsin's side.

By the end, Royce's mouth was set in a thin line.

"That is completely unacceptable. I'll deal with the matter," was all he said.

Tamsin didn't know precisely what that meant, but she would never want to be the object of the earl's displeasure.

"Please don't make a fuss on my account."

"Tamsin, you are worth a fuss." He leaned toward her slightly, and once again, she felt he was about to kiss her —

Then Jasper barked, breaking the mood. He dashed off in pursuit of some invisible quarry, and Royce offered an elbow to escort Tamsin back along the path.

All very proper, and very safe.

Except for the way her heart thudded when she got close to him.

♍

THE NEXT DAY, AFTER WORKING in the library for hours, mostly writing out copies of documents until her hand cramped up, Tamsin returned to her room at about three. She had a long, dreary afternoon and evening before her. Despite the weather, she thought she'd go for a walk, an idea that Jasper, who'd lain obediently at her feet for hours, approved of. It was always better to be out in the world than hermitted in her chamber, waiting for supper to be delivered, and then reading until she could no longer bear the candlelight.

When she and Jasper reached her door, however, it was open. Sounds emanated from inside, and Tamsin hurried to see what was the matter.

She discovered Ellen and two other maids hard at work, scrubbing the floor, cleaning the grime off the window, and changing the bed linen.

"Begging your pardon, miss," Ellen said. "We'll be done in a quarter hour. Didn't expect the task to be quite so hard as it was."

Tamsin raised an eyebrow, but didn't make the obvious comment that if the housekeeper instructed the maids to clean regularly, there'd be no need for a small army now.

"I'll wait." She sat in the ladder back chair near the door. Evidently, Royce had discussed things with Mrs

Arnott, and the result was this rigorously cleaned room.

"Would you like to take tea in the kitchens with the servants?" Ellen asked when they were finally done. "It's rather warmer in there, isn't it? I'll be sure to tell Alvin to bring more coal for your room tonight too."

"Yes, tea in the kitchen would be fine," Tamsin agreed.

Thus she had perfectly hot and delicious tea that day, along with a generous supply of bread and berry jam, and crackers with potted ham, and a cup of creamy soup, and even cinnamon-dusted biscuits to finish. It was a change from her usual, but the greater change was the sound of other people laughing and talking around her. The maids mended things in between bites, and the footmen all tried to feed Jasper scraps, until Tamsin forbade it lest the dog get sick on all the treats.

The housekeeper sat on the opposite end of the table, presiding over the biggest teapot like a queen. Every time she looked at Tamsin, her expression soured, but she said not a single word objecting to her presence.

In fact, Tamsin found that life at Seabourne became quite pleasant once the servants stopped their campaign against her. She suspected that Ellen had a lot to do with the turn, because not only did the other servants treat her decently, some went out of their way to be extra attentive. Her breakfast tray featured a small vase with a late-blooming wild rosebud. Her room was suddenly immaculate, and everyone now greeted her in the halls.

She normally avoided optimism, but she decided that living here and working for Lord Pelham was perhaps the best thing to ever happen to her. She had a safe place to sleep, worthy and respectable work, and a dog for a companion. Considering that she had shortly before been sought by an underworld criminal and likely to be killed, she was tremendously lucky.

And if her employer was moody, well, moody was better than murderous.

And if her employer was also undeniably attractive, well, she wouldn't deny it. But she certainly wouldn't allow herself to fall for him.

* * * *

A few days later, Tamsin was in her room, searching for her walking boot under the bed, where Jasper enjoyed dragging all her shoes.

A knock at the door startled her, and she looked over her shoulder to see Ellen.

The maid carried a large, flat box into the room. "Delivery for you, miss."

"I am not expecting anything," Tamsin protested. What could she even purchase? Her total savings equaled seventeen pennies, and a shilling that she'd hidden in a book.

"Well, it's addressed to Miss Black, and there's only one Miss Black here." Smiling, Ellen left, already thinking about her next task.

Curious, Tamsin opened the box. It contained two new woolen gowns—one in blue and the other in a soft grey. Everything was just slightly higher quality than what she had before.

A note read: *To replace what was damaged.* There was no signature, but none was needed. Only Royce would have or could have done this.

At the bottom of the box, another item was wrapped in a length of muslin. Tamsin peeled away the muslin and touched silk. Silk!

She shook out the item, and the silk tumbled all the

way down to her feet. It was a shift—but not anything like her plain cotton shift. This was a *lady's* garment, luxuriously fine and smooth against her skin.

Tamsin flushed. This was above and beyond what any employer did to make amends for an error. Did he expect her to pay him back by going to him at night, with only this shift on?

No. Royce had ample opportunity to demand that the last time she'd wandered into his bedroom, and he hadn't. Despite a few lapses in restraint—and really, those were just as much her fault as his—he'd been quite circumspect. Chances were he just gave a general direction for some quality clothing, and a shopkeeper took advantage of the earl's spending power to add an expensive item to the bill.

She stashed the fancy garment in the lower shelf of the clothes press, strangely shy about it. After trying one of the new gowns, and loving it, Tamsin hunted for her slippers, since they were the correct footwear if she were to wear this gown indoors.

She finally found the slipper under her bed. It was between Jasper's teeth, half-destroyed as the dog chewed at it.

"Oh, no," she said, upset. "How could you? That's my only pair of slippers, Jasper!"

The dog sensed her distress, looking at her with big, soulful eyes. Tamsin considered yanking the slipper out of his jaws, but the damage was done. "All right, I guess that's your toy now."

She'd not tell Royce about this incident. The last thing she needed was a steady supply of gifts from the lord arriving in her room.

Deciding that the gnawed slipper meant that Jasper needed more exercise, she took the dog for an extra-long walk through the woods on the north side of Pelham's estate. Though the leaves were now gone and the trees bare, it was still a pretty path. The sounds of the sea reached even here, and Jasper found no end of interesting smells to investigate.

Tamsin smiled to herself. Yes, things had worked out after all. Coming to Seabourne had been a leap of faith… not in the sense of religion, but in the hope that her life might improve after her astounding first encounter with Royce.

All of a sudden, the woods filled with the thunder of hoofbeats and the unmistakable sounds of a hunt. Tamsin gasped in alarm, and then remembered all at once that Lord Weston had sent an invitation to Royce for this very day. She hurried to the side of the path, praying that the swiftly approaching hunters would be smart enough, or at least sober enough, to avoid shooting *her.*

The ruckus increased and then a party of riders emerged from the trees. The horses were excited, and the riders even more so. One of the men fired a shot into the air out of sheer exuberance.

Jasper yelped and whined at the report, hiding behind Tamsin.

Several riders stormed past, their faces and outfits obscured by the speed of the horses. The only thing she could say for certain was that all were gentry, decked out and disregarding anything in the world that wasn't the direct object of their pursuit.

It seemed no one even saw a grown woman walking on the path. As the party advanced, Tamsin pressed herself against the trunk of a huge sycamore, praying it would block any collision.

Even so, one horse nearly ran into Tamsin, veering away at the last moment.

She choked on a scream, certain her life was about to end. Then Tamsin yelled at the backs of the party, fear making her voice ten times louder. "Watch out! You could have killed someone!"

The riders naturally did not react, since they'd gone by so quickly and probably didn't even hear her scream or Jasper's angry bark.

But one rider did turn in his seat, and then drew his horse up sharply.

He rode back, his attention locked on Tamsin.

Her heart dropped down into her feet. No, it could not be.

It could not *possibly* be.

But it was.

"Hector Englefield," she whispered, watching as the man who'd haunted her nightmares now loomed above her in broad daylight.

Beside her, Jasper pressed close to her skirts. A low growl bubbled in his throat.

"Well, well, well. If it isn't Thomasina Latimer. What the hell are *you* doing here, of all places?" Hector asked, as if this were an ordinary conversation.

"I am walking my dog," she replied tightly.

"I can see that." He laughed, and made as if to dismount.

Jasper's growl suddenly increased in volume, and the horse nickered nervously.

Hector paused, and then elected to remain astride.

"What are you doing in Norfolk?" he asked. Tamsin felt his gaze on her, and her skin crawled in response. The memory of his hands on her body was nearly enough to make her gag right there.

"Well, Thomasina? What *are* you doing here?"

"That is none of your business," she said.

He gave her an appraising look that was somehow worse than the leer it replaced. What was happening in that selfish, cruel mind of his? He said, "Considering how close we once were, I think it is my business."

"You are wrong," she retorted. She tried to back away and retreat to the narrower paths of the woods, but Hector maneuvered his horse to prevent it.

"Now, now, Thomasina. That's no way to treat an old friend."

She didn't bother to choke back the ugly laugh that erupted from her throat. "That is not the word I'd use to describe you, sir. Now, kindly let me leave, or I will set my dog on you."

Though Tamsin had never taught Jasper to do any such thing, the dog was already straining at his leash, and the threat was quite believable.

Hector's expression went cold and calculating. "Miss Latimer," he said quietly. "I'd assumed you were long dead."

"If I had died, the blame could be laid directly at your feet. Good day, sir."

"Not so fast," he said, riding forward to block her way. "If you're not dead, what the hell have you been up to? You're not staying in Lord Weston's house, because I would have definitely noticed. His land borders…Pelham's, isn't it? But Pelham is an old man to have such a doxy as you. He was seventy years if a day last I met him."

Tamsin bit her lip to avoid correcting Hector about the changes in the line of Pelham. The idiot clearly hadn't kept up with the news. Royce had been earl for months and months now. If it had been an unmarried countess, Hector would have been first in line with congratulations.

"I cannot see that it should matter to you," she said.

"Good *day*, sir."

Jasper barked in angry agreement, the sound echoing through the woods.

"Well, shall I give you a head start?" Hector asked, unmoved. "That would be sporting, would it not?"

"You have confused me with the object of your hunt, sir."

"I don't think I have. Rather, I've just discovered a far more interesting hunt to pursue. Having found you by fate, don't think I'll let you go again, Thomasina," he said, his tone light and mocking, yet filled with a menace that chilled her spine. Laughing, Hector rode away on the chestnut-colored horse, looking as powerful and triumphant as ever.

And all the hate she thought she'd buried rose up again, twining about her limbs like ropes, keeping her from running for her life.

♍

TAMSIN'S LIMBS FELT LIKE JELLY after the encounter with Hector. She came to this place because it seemed so far out of the way of her old home and from London. Surely no one would find her here.

But the world of the *ton* was small, and the island of Britain was not nearly so large as it seemed. Of course the gentlemen who adored the hunt would find each other and then visit each other's estates for their stupid hunting parties. And of course these same men would not care that the dogs ran pell-mell over the boundaries of the neighbors' properties and of course Hector would be there.

"I would sell my soul for the chance to bring about Hector Englefield's humiliation!" she screamed into the cold air of the leafless glade. Beside her, Jasper growled in sympathy.

She waited for some response from heaven or hell. If an angel appeared, she'd take it to task for not watching over her when it was most needed. If a devil did, she'd sign a contract in her blood, and laugh while doing so.

However, there was no evidence that a world beyond her own took note of her words, and Tamsin sighed. In her darkest, most despairing moments, this dreadful silence confirmed her deepest cynicism about faith and hope. There was nothing there.

She was on her own.

Tamsin sighed, but then felt the cold nose of Jasper nudging her hand. Wordlessly, the dog refuted her conclusion. Though he may not be an angel or a god or a being of any great power, he was there, and he refused to leave.

"All right, Jasper. I take your point." Tamsin petted the dog's soft head, and absently picked a burr off his ear, smoothing the silky fur.

She walked back to the house, casting glances over her shoulder far too often, half expecting Hector to come galloping after her. Then she worried that he would ride directly to Seabourne and speak to Lord Pelham, revealing the shameful details of Tamsin's past. She doubted Royce would keep her on after that. It was too much scandal for a new lord with enough scandals brewing in his life.

When she returned to the house, she found the servants in an uproar, but not due to anything she did.

"His lordship travels to London," Ellen told her breathlessly, hurrying past with an armload of clothing. "He gave us less than an hour to prepare. Something's got him in a mood!"

"Oh, dear," Tamsin murmured. But she was actually elated. This was perfect. Royce would leave, thus depriving Hector of a chance to speak to him about Tamsin. And she could leave along with Royce, thus escaping the house that had become a prison.

She hurried up the stairs to Royce's suite.

There, she saw his valet and a footman working together to pack such things as the earl would need for his journey. They barely spared her a glance.

Royce, however, noticed her immediately. He stopped what he was doing, which was shuffling papers near his leather case. "Miss Black, there you are. I have to go to London."

She nodded. "Yes, I heard. That's grand. I can have my things ready in twenty minutes."

"What? No! You're not coming along."

"You can't leave me here," she said aghast. "I can't stay at this house!"

"My business in town does not require a secretary," he said, and then lowered his voice slightly so the other servants wouldn't overhear. "And anyway, the whole point of bringing you here was to keep you *out* of London."

"Things have changed! Please let me go back with you. You don't even need to keep me on as secretary. Pay me my wages so far and I'll vanish into the city. I promise you'll never see me again."

Royce frowned at her. "What's changed?"

"Nothing!" she said, realizing her mistake. "That is, I've…had time to think. And running away was very childish of me and I'll manage in London and I've taken far too much advantage of your good nature—"

"Stop." Royce strode over to her in three steps, his frame blocking the light from the lamp behind him. "I've never heard you sound so ridiculously flustered. I liked you better when you didn't lie, you just refused to talk. That at least showed some respect for my intelligence."

"My lord—"

Just then, another footman opened the door. "Carriage is ready, my lord."

"Good. I'll be only a few more moments. Did Mrs Arnott pack a hamper? I don't want to stop for meals."

"Oh, I'll check, my lord." The footman vanished.

Royce dragged a hand through his hair. "God damn it, I don't have time for this, Tamsin. We'll talk when I get back."

"What sort of business are you on? Is someone ill?" Tamsin wouldn't have been surprised if he rushed to his mother's bedside, but Royce told her she lived in Bath, not London.

"No," he said shortly.

"Well, at least let me help you pack your attaché case. I can see from here that the papers are in disarray, and I'm better at organizing than you'll ever be."

She bent to pick up the papers, automatically glancing over the text so she could sort them properly.

Then she stopped in shock on seeing one particular letter, written in Italian with bold black ink. Her fingers trembled as she read over words she could recite from memory.

"Oh, my God," she whispered.

Royce took the letter from her. "You're not supposed to see that, Miss Black. It's confidential. Look, the truth is that I do some work on behalf of the government, and this document is part of it. You can't know what's contained in this letter. I'm sorry."

"It's too late," Tamsin said, feeling faint. "I already know all about it."

"You do?"

"It's a letter from the Italian ambassador suggesting that a secret deal can be done with Napoleon's people to get the Portuguese court out of Brazil and to safety in Italy."

His eyebrow rose at what he assumed was a lightning-quick reading of the text. "Yes, it's from the ambassador and it's a disaster for British interests."

"It is not."

"Tamsin, you've got no idea of the intricacies of international politics during wartime—"

"I meant that it's not a letter from the Italian ambassador."

"What? Of course it is. His signature is right there."

Royce jabbed the offending mark, inked in heavy black with a ridiculous curlicue underneath.

"That is Signore Gianbattista's signature," she said quietly. "but he did not sign it and he never saw that letter."

"How could you possibly know that?"

Tamsin took a deep breath. "Because *I'm* the one who wrote it."

♍

ROYCE STARED AT HER IN shock, sure he'd misheard Tamsin's words. "You."

"Yes."

"You were the one who drafted a letter in Italian and forged the ambassador's signature…amazingly well, I might add."

She nodded.

Royce took one look at the men packing his things and yelled at them to get out. This interrogation required far more confidentiality. Then he pointed to a chair near the window. "Sit."

She did so, and he noticed at last how flushed her cheeks were, and how shakily her breath came to her lips. But he couldn't ask after her health after a revelation like that.

"Explain what you mean," he said. "You wrote this?"

"The night we met. I left that letter behind in my room in an attempt to distract Coaker—he must have gone back for it," Tamsin said. "I went through a dozen sheets of paper just to get the signature correct. Who would have thought that my years of learning calligraphy in the schoolroom would be put to such a use?"

"Tamsin, why?"

"Because that's what I was told to do. That's the price I paid to live more or less unmolested and unknown in

London. I told you that Swigg sometimes used my services, or hired my services out to others. But it wasn't just basic tasks. I was his forger. And for the last several months, he hired me out to a particular gentleman who wanted some very specific documents created."

A particular gentleman... Royce's guts went cold. Had Tamsin worked for the very spies he'd been chasing? Why had he not thought about the possibility that a foreign agent would have *hired out* the detail work of his plan to an otherwise innocuous person? Royce had assumed that the forger would be a full partner in the scheme.

"What's this gentleman's name?" he asked. "Who were his associates?"

"I don't think he had associates. I never learned his real name, and I was smart enough not to ask. Swigg addressed him as Yves, which is surely as false as Tess."

"Undoubtedly. You knew that he was asking you to do something highly illegal."

Tamsin's lips quirked. "*Everything* associated with Swigg is highly illegal. I was not in a position to take the moral high ground."

He was troubled by just how untroubled Tamsin sounded when she said it. How had she grown so callous in such a short time? Then he remembered the neighborhood he'd found her in. People there didn't have the luxury of softness. You grew a hard shell or you'd be eaten alive.

"Can you describe this man Yves?"

She nodded. "I had many opportunities to watch him. He spoke English most of the time, but he's French. He's older than you—I'm not sure how many years. But there's silver in his hair, and it's the result of age. Otherwise, the hair is almost black, and rather wavy. He had blue eyes, and a long face—flat, thin lips and a narrow nose, but a significant jaw. It's more noticeable because he wears no beard. He's always looked as if he'd just walked away from the shaving bowl."

Royce nodded, absorbing the description she gave, and somehow getting a picture that was even more complete than her bare words offered. A fastidious man, precise in his appearance and his movements, and no doubt precise about the orders he gave Tamsin.

"Did this man ever object to your work, or was he surprised Swigg offered the services of a woman?"

"If he did, he never said so to me. But then, Swigg probably showed him some samples beforehand. I'd often forged documents for Swigg's own business. False statements from witnesses, deeds that listed Swigg as owner, that sort of thing."

"So this man came to you for forgery work…how often?"

"At first it was once or twice a month. But toward the end, it was more. Possibly four or five documents in a week. It was hard to keep up. I had to put hours in on each, and they were all different styles and in different languages."

"How did you know what to practice?"

"The man brought me samples of the handwriting to copy, and templates for what the finished document should look like." She tapped the letter in Royce's hand. "For this one, I had several real letters to learn the ambassador's handwriting and signature, and I even knew what sort of paper and inks I'd need to use to make the forgery believable. The Italian Embassy would never use British paper! If it hasn't got a Florentine watermark, you may as well throw it in the fire."

"How did you get Florentine paper?"

Tamsin shrugged. "I just told the gentleman what was needed, and he provided it. No expense was spared to make the forgeries as realistic as possible."

"Did you understand the content of what you were forging?"

Finally, Tamsin paused. "I understood more than I let on. Forgeries aren't just mimicking the lines you see before you. You need to know what's being forged, and know whose voice you're trying to imitate. If not…well, you might fool a casual viewer, but you'd never convince those who understand the document." Tamsin's tone warmed as she spoke. "So it was an advantage that I know some French and Italian and German. It's an added benefit that I studied my history and I know why our boys are down on the Penninsula and why another emperor is a bad idea. Not that I said as much! All I said was *yes sir* and *no sir.*"

Royce pondered the revelation. After the initial shock, all that lingered was a strange feeling of rightness. Of course Tamsin was the forger he was seeking. Of course he should run into her while walking toward Catchpenny Lane that night. That was her base of operations.

"Wait a moment," he said. "You finished the letter, but you still ran away that night. Why?"

"Coaker was looking for me, and he's not a subtle man. He busted into Mrs Salinger's boardinghouse, screaming for me. Swigg doesn't send him as messenger unless things have gone very badly indeed. I was already feeling that the work I was doing for the French gentleman was suspect, and I chose not to linger. I knew too much, so I'd be a liability just as soon as my usefulness passed. Swigg probably charged the gentleman a lot for my services. Enough that he'd not mourn my death afterward."

"So you don't know what specifically might have set Swigg off."

"No." She looked at him shrewdly. "Do you?"

"Possibly. I've been working for months to discover the source of some very odd documents. Private letters and official army orders and government communications that looked authentic but couldn't possibly be real. But I was far behind, only able to identify the forged items weeks after they'd been sent, after the damage had been done. A few days before I met you, though, I had a stroke of luck. A letter addressed to a Commodore Landers was accidentally opened by his wife instead, as it got put with her personal correspondence."

Her eyes widened in recognition of the name.

"I knew addressing it to his home was a mistake!" Tamsin burst out. "It would have made sense to send it to the offices he worked at during the day, but my employer wanted it to be read as soon as possible."

Royce actually laughed. "That mistake must have been the turning point. The wife knew it was peculiar, and she wasn't part of the usual chain of workers who push things through in the name of efficiency. I was able to identify the letter as a fake before anyone could take the action it suggested. And it gave me a few more days to pursue the list of scriveners in London, including Catch-penny Lane."

"Where you found me right after I'd exited my old haunt. Well." Tamsin smiled. "At the time, I thought you were merely another thug out to get me. I am glad to be wrong."

Royce took her hand. "Tamsin, you must know that the things you wrote…they had dire consequences."

She looked away. "If I'd refused, the consequences for me would have been just as dire. Should I have been bold and heroic and taken a stand? Should I have felt triumphant like Joan of Arc while Swigg executed me? That's what would have happened, you know."

He recognized the truth, and the damning situation Tamsin had been in.

Tamsin pulled her hand away. "You're going to lecture me, aren't you? I see it in your eyes. You going to tell me that I ought to have done the right thing. That I should have chosen the morally upright path, instead of choosing my personal survival."

"I wasn't going to say that."

"You didn't have to…it's in your whole bearing. Ah, to be a man in charge of your own destiny. You never have to be at the mercy of another. You never have to choose between dignity and hunger."

"Tamsin."

She stood up, her spine brittle and her expression stony. "Are we done, my lord? I wish to be excused, and I expect that as of this moment, I'm no longer employed. I'll leave Seabourne in the morning."

He moved quickly to stop her exit. "You will do no such thing. I need more answers from you."

"I told you everything I know. Get out of my way."

Instead of listening, he put both arms out to the wall, confining her against it. "God damn it, Tamsin. Just listen to me. This doesn't have to be a fight."

"Then what is it?" She looked up, her eyes bright with anger and unshed tears. "Stop hinting at things and just tell me outright what you're thinking. Tell me what you want!"

What he wanted….

Without saying a further word, he leaned forward and kissed her.

Tamsin went still for a moment, but then her arms

slipped around his shoulders and drew him closer, responding to the kiss with a desperation that told him he wasn't the only one who'd been finding the last few weeks difficult.

God, her mouth was perfect. So soft and so ripe. Tamsin's tongue darted against his, and sparked an instant fire in his groin. He pushed her into the wall with his body, angling his hips against hers.

She gave a little whimpering moan when he deepened the kiss, fueling his need.

They fed off each other, each clinging like they'd never encountered desire before. Royce was ready and willing to pick her up and walk straight to the bed, to hell with what anyone thought.

"My lord?" Tamsin asked, impatience in her tone. "Why will you not tell me what you want?"

Royce came out of his fantasy with a jolt. There she was, far too close, but the kiss he'd just felt in his bones was a mere imagining.

But she must have sensed some of his thoughts, because she gazed at him and unwittingly licked her lower lip. "Royce," she whispered. "If you want to ask me something…I'm listening."

The invitation was there, the permission to kiss her. But Royce pulled back.

"Pack your things," he told her abruptly. "We're going to London."

♍

FASTER THAN TAMSIN WOULD HAVE credited, she found
herself in Royce's private coach again, this time speeding
back toward London. Royce sat across from her, his eyes
boring into her very soul…or at least that was how it felt
to Tamsin.

"Can you please stop staring at me," she said at last.
"It's most uncomfortable."

"So is discovering that one's employee is hiding a
multitude of secrets."

"Oh, is that what troubles you, my lord?" Tamsin had
just about enough of this. "What about *your* secrets? I
have not spent much time among the aristocracy, but I
know that earls are generally not called upon to search
through the worst neighborhoods in London to find total
strangers."

"I told you that I did some work for our government."

"And I'd like to know exactly what that means."

"Remember when we met? I told you that there are
things I could never tell you."

"You also promised to tell the truth."

"I did." His eyes flashed with something like guilt.

Suddenly, Tamsin recalled the absurd thing he had
shared with her, the thing that made her laugh out loud.
"You told me that in addition to being an earl, you were
also a master of espionage. You *were* telling the truth!"

"Yes."

"But lords aren't spies," she said. "It's…ungentleman-ly to engage in such activities."

"That is a commonly held belief," he agreed. "One that does make my work easier."

"Before I tell you anything more about *my* work, then," said Tamsin, "I want to know about yours."

"I'll do better than tell you, Miss Black. When we get to London, I'll introduce you to my superior. And if you think I've got questions, just wait 'til you hear his."

"I don't wish to be involved in any of this."

"Too late for that, Tamsin." His voice softened. "But your life won't be in danger this time. The organization I'm a part of has many resources. You're an asset, and you've been one since the moment I found you on the bridge. You'll be protected."

"Just as a prison cell protects a criminal," she said.

"Not like that. I won't let anyone harm you."

She sighed. "Tell me more about this organization I'm entrusting with my life."

Royce looked out the window for a moment, then said, "When I was younger, I was rather reckless in my behavior. But I was also smart, and lucky. Together, those things drew the attention of someone who was looking for smart, lucky, reckless people."

"To be spies?" she asked.

"Yes. I joined an elite group that is dedicated to pro-tecting British interests and the British crown. With the war on the Continent, our work has become rather more urgent. Months ago, I was tasked with finding the source of several falsified documents…all different in form, but all highly damaging to Britain. I gathered all the informa-tion I could, and decided that if I found the person respon-sible for creating the documents, I'd soon find the nest of vipers who commissioned them. Except that it now seems to be only one man. The Viper, if you will."

"And you did find the person responsible. Me."

"By purest accident."

"Not really," Tamsin corrected. "After all, you found me very close to where I was working and living. If I hadn't run out that night, you'd probably have come to the boarding house yourself. You might even have prevented me from finishing the forged letter from the Italian ambassador...the one Coaker took."

"And used."

"That will be the last one they can use," Tamsin vowed. "At least, the last one I'll ever write."

"I hope so," he said quietly.

"Trust me, I already hate myself for what I did. You needn't spend any more hate on me...it would be gilding an extremely rotten lily."

"I don't hate you."

She turned her face to the window, afraid to confront the person able to say such words with honesty in his tone.

Royce must be an *excellent* spy.

After a few moments with nothing but the rattling of the coach wheels to fill the silence, Tamsin asked, "So you didn't know what I was that first night? You didn't grab me to get me off the street and away from Yves or Swigg?"

"You were just a very soaked siren," he said, now smiling at the memory. "I thought I could do a little bit of good. I ran into another woman just before you, actually, and she was not interested in being helped at all. Laughed in my face."

"It's not a trusting neighborhood."

"You trusted me," he said, and when their eyes met,

Tamsin felt that warmth in her belly again, that connection with him.

"I'm glad I did," she whispered. The tension grew thick between them, and Tamsin remembered all the things they'd shared during that one night of wild honesty. She admitted how attracted she was to him, he admitted some of the darkest thoughts she'd ever heard someone speak out loud. They'd lain together on a bed all night long, strangers and companions at the same time.

Royce stretched out one leg and nudged her foot, breaking the mood. "Enough reminiscing. You told me once that you don't live in the past. Good advice, Miss Black."

"I'm not sure the future is much more promising," she said.

"Oh, it is now," he replied, smiling. "I can sense it. Maybe not the way I expected to move forward with this assignment, but better than wallowing at Seabourne. It's time to get back to work!"

After that exchange, Tamsin felt much better. Their former rapport was back—that odd version of friendship they had discovered the night Royce rescued her. She could face a lot of things knowing that Royce would be there to help her face them, and she did want to help him as much as she could.

That night, they stayed at a well-kept inn. Royce insisted that Tamsin have her own room, but he told her that if for any reason she felt uneasy, she should knock on his door.

"I wouldn't want to wake you," she protested, though the idea of a half-dressed Royce Holmes opening the door to her was undeniably appealing.

"Too much on my mind to sleep much," he said. "And not to worry...I won't take advantage of a lovely woman coming to me in the middle of the night." His words were both reassuring and a little disappointing.

"Well, I'll promise this. If I get scared, I'll scream loud enough for you to hear."

"Good girl," Royce said, smiling.

Tamsin couldn't help feeling pleased at his words, a reaction that annoyed her no end, because she really did try to ignore her desire for him, and she just wasn't very good at it.

The next day, they resumed the journey. Though private coach represented the most expensive and prestigious mode of travel, it was still torturous to endure a long trip in one. Tamsin's back and shoulders ached from the constant jolting as the wheels rolled over pitted tracks.

"You know, my father refused to travel more than ten miles from Seabourne," Royce said, rubbing his neck after a bad bump. "Every time I go to London I think of him, and wish I could follow the same whim."

"How much longer today?" she asked, hoping it didn't sound too petulant.

"Three hours, maybe four."

"Oh, Lord deliver me."

He chuckled. "We will survive."

Just then, one of the wheels dipped, tilting the seat and sending Tamsin slamming into the side of the carriage. Straightening up again, she winced at the pain. "That was not a hole in the track. That was a gateway to Hell."

"Does it hurt?" he asked, looking her over in concern.

"It will be quite sore in the morning, I think."

"Can't have that." He moved across to her seat, and reached for her shoulders. Tamsin sighed when he began to knead the muscles in her neck and shoulder with one hand, holding her steady with the other.

"Just relax," he told her. "I know what I'm doing."

"Where does an earl learn massage?" she asked, realizing too late the obvious answer.

Indeed, he chuckled. "Nowhere I could take you, Tamsin. You'd be scandalized."

"You underestimate my capacity for scandal."

"Tell me more."

Oddly, she wanted to tell him more. It felt natural to want to share something of her life. "When I first came to London, I had very little to my name. Even the cheapest respectable boarding houses were far too costly for me. If they'd known my cond—" Tamsin stopped speaking abruptly. "You know, my past is not that fascinating. Suffice to say that I saw many scenes that would have horrified me only a year previously. I quickly got used to them."

"It must have been an ordeal," he said. Royce slid his fingers along her neck, kneading away the worst of the stiffness and discomfort. She reveled in his touch. There was something so tender in the way he stroked her skin, so…loving.

"Not as horrific as riding in a coach," she quipped, trying to distract herself from the way her thoughts were drifting.

"Is this helping at all?" he asked, rolling his palm into her shoulder blade.

She melted into pliancy wherever he touched her. "You know it is."

"Good. It's an easy enough favor, and I have an interest in keeping your writing arm intact."

She stifled a giggle. "Ah, so this is just part of your assignment."

"Whatever is necessary," he replied, his tone low and teasing.

Tamsin closed her eyes, deciding to enjoy these few

minutes.

She didn't know when she dozed, but she woke up to find herself leaning into Royce's chest, her head on his shoulder.

Tamsin stiffened up. "Oh, I shouldn't have let myself fall asleep. This is an inappropriate position."

"Comfortable, though," he said, his voice low and mesmerizing. "I don't mind at all. It's improving my experience of coach travel an untold amount. You're exquisitely soft, you know."

She ought to sit up and slide to the furthest corner of the seat she could find…and yet, she didn't move.

"Reminds me of our night at the Green Lion," he went on. "I think that just having you near me, being able to hold you in bed all night…that might rate as one of my most delightful evenings."

"It does?" she asked, her mouth going dry. Because it made her think about all the things they didn't do in that bed. And how much she'd thought about doing them with Royce ever since.

Royce said something she didn't catch. She lifted her head to ask him to repeat it, and her lips grazed his neck. Rather than pull back as she ought to, Tamsin instead opened her mouth, inhaling his scent as she kissed him there.

Instantly, his hands tightened around her waist, and he said, "Tamsin," in a low rasp.

If that was meant to be a warning, she ignored it, too entranced by the texture of his skin under her tongue, the faint pulse below the surface, and the musky, warm smell of his body beneath the clothes. There was the hint of spice that he always had, but mostly it was him, and she discovered that the scent fascinated her. She breathed in, and sighed.

"I like the way you smell," she confessed, expecting a laugh.

He wasn't laughing. He gazed at her like she was something dangerous. "All right, this has gone too far. I would never let anything bad happen to you, Tamsin."

"The worst already has happened," she confessed, then inhaled as she realized what she said.

Royce looked at her, his gaze dark but his voice tender. "What happened? You've been hiding the whole story from me since we met. Just tell me, and you won't have to hide it anymore."

She looked away. "It's not a pleasant tale. Nor an interesting one."

"Everything about you interests me." Royce ran his fingers along her cheek, soothing rather than arousing.

"Please, Royce. Don't make me tell you." A prickling in her eyes told her she was near tears. *Please don't let me be so weak in front of him*, she prayed. *He'll use it against me.*

But then Royce pulled her closer, into an embrace that felt like home.

"No, you don't have to tell me," he said, his voice low and raw in her ear.

"Thank you," she breathed. Oh, she would like to be held like this forever. Something in her was so drawn to him. Against all her better judgment, she wanted to be close to him, to touch him in deeply improper ways, and to know what he was thinking when he went quiet and his eyes got that faraway, brooding quality.

Oh, this man would bring her pain. Tamsin warned herself of it, and yet couldn't summon the alarm she should feel. All she felt was the deep joy of being held in his arms, able to hide her face from the world for just a little while. To feel a bit of peace.

These were feelings she'd never experienced around Hector. Even when she was in his favor, there was always an element of fear. If only Tamsin had been able to recognize it earlier. But aside from the first five minutes of their acquaintance, Royce never scared her. Something about Royce drew her to him, yes, but that was also new. She'd never been drawn to Hector. He'd pushed every aspect of their relationship…to disastrous consequences.

And just now, Royce very firmly stopped himself from pushing further, even though they both wanted to indulge each other.

Paradoxically, it just made Tamsin want him more. She shifted enough to bring her face to his. And then she kissed him.

Tamsin had never pursued pleasure before, but the feel of his lips on hers was enough to make her realize what she'd missed. She was not just hungry, but starving for the sensations sparking throughout her body now.

"We just said…" Royce got out between her frantic kisses.

"…that you won't let anything bad happen to me," Tamsin said, her breath fast. "And I know that you won't. *Please*, Royce. I can't explain why I need this now, but I do."

After an agonizing moment of stillness, he leaned forward to meet her mouth again, and this time, he didn't hold his own desire back.

Tamsin followed her instincts, and they led her to press herself against Royce, and run her hands over him, or at least what she could feel of him beneath the expensive clothing that hid his body from her curious touch.

His eyes took her in, and everywhere he looked, he kissed the same spot a second later. Her lips, her cheeks, her neck. He stripped off her gloves and laid his mouth on her palms, then kissed her fingertips, ink and all.

She mirrored some of his moves, but also tested some of her own theories. For instance, she thought his collar looked tight, and so she loosened it, revealing more skin that she had to taste. He let her, leaning his head back to allow it.

Then he abruptly put his hands on her waist and pulled her onto his lap. She slid her leg over his, angling so she faced him, her hair falling over her shoulders and down the front of her gown.

"Stay like this," he said. This scandalous, compromising position, straddled over him, his hands slipping around her hips to her backside. "Nothing more than this, I promise. I just need...to feel you."

He rocked her against him, and she realized exactly how aroused he was, and that the promise suggested that he wanted to do far more than merely hold her like this. In this possessive, unseemly way.

Let things get a little unseemly, she thought. Tamsin reached up to shake the last of the pins from her hair, earning a growl from Royce. Her body sang with the need to be close to this man.

He pulled her very close indeed. There was enough fabric between them that she felt no danger. In fact, she rather liked the gentle pressure, even letting out a little gasp every time their bodies grew close.

He leaned against the seat again, tilting his head back and closing his eyes. Tamsin stared at him, fascinated by his minute reactions to the repeated contact of her body against his. The bulge beneath the fabric of his falls grew harder, and she hesitantly reached to one button, expecting that he'd want her to pleasure him more directly.

But the moment she began to tug on the button, he moved his hand to stop her. "No, Tamsin."

"I don't mind," she said.

"That's the problem. I don't get much pleasure from a woman who doesn't mind. I want her to want to do it as much as I do."

"Oh." That was...novel.

"But I do like to listen to you," he said, opening his eyes. He ran his hand up her torso, grazing one breast before touching her lips with his fingers. "All your little gasps and moans."

He pressed her harder against him, drawing a sharper gasp.

"There." He smiled. "I think you like that, Tamsin."

In answer, she sucked his finger into her mouth. Royce's eyes went dark. He increased the rhythm of their rocking, his big hand gripping her bottom.

Tamsin felt a stirring in her belly, a need to be close to this man, to give herself up to the mysterious pleasure he was creating between them.

The carriage hit a bump, slamming Tamsin into Royce. He moaned, and held her tightly to him. "Christ," he growled, his expression suddenly changing to blissful. His breathing slowed, though he still held her to him. "That's what I get for playing with you in a carriage."

She whispered, "I'm sorry. I didn't mean to..."

"It wasn't you, it was the damn roadway and my own randiness. Christ, when was the last time I was so ready for a woman that I couldn't get my clothing off first."

"You wouldn't let me," she said, tapping the button with one finger.

He kissed her suddenly. "If we'd removed any clothes, I would have done something I shouldn't have. You made it plain enough that you don't want intercourse."

"It's not that I don't want it," she confessed. "It's just that it's not worth it."

"Oh, Tamsin." Royce put his arms around her, pulling her against him in an enveloping embrace. "You break all the rules, you know that?"

"What rule did I just break now?"

"The rule that says ladies are shy and retiring and don't know their own minds."

"Well, whoever came up with that rule is an idiot."

He laughed. "Indeed. You never say what I expect you to, but I can't wait to hear what you'll come up with next."

"My mind is a blank right now. Did you want to, um, release me?"

"I don't. I want to hold you all the way to London. You're really delightfully soft."

"Thank you?"

He chuckled. "You're not eager to accept a compliment, are you?"

"I suppose I haven't have much practice lately."

"Well, let me remedy that, at least. You have beautiful eyes. They're expressive and reveal how intelligent you are."

Tamsin inhaled, truly surprised that a man who'd just used her body for his pleasure would bother to notice her eyes.

"Say thank you," he prompted.

"Thank you."

"Good. Your hair I've complimented before, but it's worth it to mention again. It's the sort of hair a siren would have. Long and wavy and the only thing maintaining her modesty, lying over her bare breasts while she entices men to their doom."

"Are you quite certain that is a compliment?" she asked.

He smiled, gathering some of her hair in his hand,

then brushing it over her shoulder. "Are you insulted?"

"No, but I must say I'm no siren. And I don't need my hair to hide my breasts from the gaze of hungry sailors, as my gown is quite enough."

"Hmm." Royce trailed his finger along the neckline of her gown. "It's not that much of a barrier." He tugged at the gown and the petticoat beneath, exposing her stays.

"See?" she said smugly. "I remain hidden by my feminine armor."

"Not for long." Royce leaned forward and caught the front lacings in his teeth. Pulling back, he dragged the ribbon with him, undoing the tie. He slipped his hand between the stays and her chemise, his thumb rubbing across her breast until the nipple grew hard under his touch.

"Let me touch you like this, Tamsin," he said. "I want you to enjoy this ride as much as I did."

She closed her eyes, reveling in the caresses he was giving her. Then she felt his mouth on the top of her breast, where it rose above the neckline of the chemise, and she moaned.

"Yes," Royce growled. He pushed the stays and the fabric roughly to the side, then kissed his way across her breast. When he reached her nipple, his lips encompassed it, and he licked the hardened bud.

Tamsin nearly melted in his arms. She leaned into him, begging for more with words that made little sense to either her or him. But fortunately, Royce knew what she wanted, and gave it to her, in slow, steady doses that left her breathless and hot.

This was divine. His lips and tongue created swirls of pleasure in her body, spreading from her chest down to her stomach and her hips, urging her to lose herself in the primal need summoned by his touch.

She realized that he shifted his position so she strad-dled just one of his legs, and his thigh pressed hard against her center. Shamelessly, Tamsin rocked while he teased her breasts with his mouth.

Then she dug her nails into his shoulders, stifling a cry. She finally found her release, the very first time that had happened with…well, another person. Her body trembled as the feeling raced through all her limbs and settled in her belly.

"Oh," she whispered, still reeling.

Royce sucked hard at one nipple, drawing out a gasp. Then he leaned back, pulling her with him. "There," he said quietly. "We are equally contented…though I can still think of many other diversions I'd like to teach you."

"Please don't," she told him. "In fact, it would be bet-ter if you ignore me from now on."

"Not likely."

"Royce," she said firmly, sitting up to separate herself from him. "Just because a man and woman are attracted to another doesn't mean they should act upon it. We were just…idle, and the closeness of the carriage made it easy to forget propriety."

"I didn't forget it, I just didn't care about it," he said harshly.

"That's my point. You can afford not to care."

Royce put his hand on her shoulders, and his gaze grew fierce. "Someday, Tamsin, you're going to tell me who hurt you."

"Why?" she whispered.

"So I can hurt him."

The statement hung between them. Tamsin wanted to believe it, wanted to believe that Royce cared that much.

But when it came to it, gentlemen always ended up on the same side. There was no way Royce would ever harm a man of his class on some penniless girl's account. Tamsin had seen too much to believe tripe like that.

Looking away, she started to slide off of him, but he tightened his grip. "Oh, no, siren. I promise to be less compelling when we reach London. Until we leave this carriage, I get to hold you."

"Why should you want to?" He'd already gotten the satisfaction he craved, though not in the form he probably preferred.

"It's simple." He leaned close to her ear, looking very serious. He murmured, "If the carriage overturns, at least I'll land on something soft."

She laughed once, then tucked her head on his shoulder. "You're terrible."

"Yes, I know. Now settle in. We've got a couple of hours."

Tamsin nestled against him, relaxing as the carriage continued along. After a little while, she was certain Royce fell asleep, though his grip on her remained firm.

And thus, entwined in an earl's arms, Tamsin Black returned to London.

♍

IT WAS GROWING DARK WHEN the carriage drove through the streets of London. Royce wanted nothing more than to go directly to his own home, but it was long past time to present Tamsin to the Zodiac.

Part of him resisted doing so. He wasn't sure why, other than because once he did reveal Tamsin to the Zodiac, they might well decide to take her into deeper hiding, squirreling her away in some secret, remote spot that even he wouldn't know.

And Royce was not ready to lose Tamsin.

He regarded her as she dozed against him on the seat. Only a few hours ago, her position on the seat had been even more scandalous, and the feeling of her body pressed against his was going to be etched into his memory. So would the image of her face when she announced that what happened was just the result of his boredom on a long carriage ride.

Like hell it was.

He told himself that his attachment to her was purely due to her knowledge of his assignment. The scraps of information she'd provided him so far would be immeasurably helpful. Royce was going to be able to leap ahead in this assignment, perhaps bringing the French agent down within days. After months of tracking the mysterious spy, Royce wanted to stop all the sniffing and be loosed on his quarry's trail, like a hunting dog straining at his leash.

But even though he did very much want to complete this assignment, Royce also knew that a large part of his interest in Tamsin had nothing to do with her forgery skills, and everything to do with the woman herself.

She fascinated him. The more he learned about her, the more he wanted to know.

Just then, the carriage rolled to a stop.

"Gate and Adams," his driver called down.

Tamsin stirred, blinking the sleep out of her eyes.

"Where are we?" Tamsin asked, peeking out the window at the buildings, which were very different from the residences she'd been expecting to see. "You can't live here."

"Come along, and it will become clear. And in case this isn't obvious, you can never tell a living soul that you were here. If you mention anything about this place or the people you meet…"

Tamsin nodded in comprehension before he could finish the warning. "One more secret won't kill me," she said.

He hoped that was true.

After ordering his driver to wait, Royce led Tamsin into the building, practically deserted at this hour. She allowed herself to be escorted, bemused at her surroundings.

It looked like an office building, and most of the offices within were perfectly legitimate. She read off the names of the various businesses that had offices in the building. "Circle Trading. London-Delhi Christian Publishing. Harolds and Sons Shipping. Is your dark secret that you're a spy, or that you've gone into trade?"

He laughed, but didn't reply. On the fifth floor, he

knocked on a plain unmarked door, then waited.

"It's late," Tamsin said. "Are you sure we shouldn't come back tomorrow?"

But just then the door opened. A woman with ash-blonde hair regarded them both, then said to Royce, "I suppose you'd better come in."

"Not the warmest welcome, Miss Chattan," he noted. Royce gestured for Tamsin to precede him inside.

He kept his attention on Tamsin as she took in the sur-roundings, trying to see it with her eyes. A plain, almost shabby office, with a large desk at one side, backed by a wall of cabinets dedicated to papers and files.

Another door led to an inner office, and Chattan was already leading them there. "Aries is going to have ques-tions," she warned. "We don't like surprise visitors."

"You'll both like this one," he promised.

The inner office was dimly lit by a lamp on the desk. A man with sand-colored hair was sitting there, reading some papers which he put aside the moment the door opened.

"Virgo," he said to Royce. Then he looked at Tamsin. "Who is this?"

Royce replied, "Our forger."

Miss Chattan's jaw dropped, and Aries pushed himself away from the desk, standing up to confront Royce. "I know you've got a reputation as a joker to maintain, Pel-ham, but this is a serious matter."

"I'm aware of that," Royce said dryly. "A while ago, I discovered Miss Black in Catchpenny Lane near St Giles, where she had rooms and hired out as a scrivener for the locals. But she also had connections to the underworld, and that's the connection that concerns us. She wrote sev-eral of the documents that the Viper managed to substitute for the real ones."

"The Viper?" Chattan asked, surprised at the moniker.

"According to Miss Black, there's only one agent. So we're giving him the nickname. Napoleon would probably love it."

Then Royce turned to Tamsin. "He's been making life difficult for our side. And for the last six months, it's been my assignment to track him down and stop him in whatever way I could."

"Do you mean kill him?"

"If it comes to that. But I'll also be content with compromising his cover and his identity so that he cannot work effectively in Britain. The problem is that he's damnably comfortable over here. Like he's almost at home."

Tamsin frowned. "As if…he were an emigre?"

Royce nodded. "For a while, I was convinced he must be one, come over after the Revolution, but keeping his loyalty to the man who would be emperor."

"But now…"

"I'm not sure, but I spent long enough poking around the emigre communities of London. If the man were part of them, he'd have likely found a way to kill me by now for being far too curious."

"You'd get killed for asking questions?"

"If they're the wrong questions, yes," Royce said. "You know that well enough, don't you, Miss Black?"

"Miss Black, is it?" Neville looked at her in a considering way. "Have a seat, please. How exactly did you start doing business with the Viper?"

"Most unwillingly," Tamsin replied, her manner polite and restrained. Only Royce saw how her fingers were clenched into a fist below the desk.

Her head held high, Tamsin then offered an edited but factual account of how she ended up in Catchpenny Lane, and how Swigg's grip on the neighborhood forced Tamsin into working for the mysterious Viper as a sort of professional-on-loan.

"If you ask around the neighborhood, you'll learn about Tess the Scribbler. That's me. Anyone can describe my appearance."

No doubt. She was the prettiest scrivener in London, and the prettiest forger too.

Aries continued his interrogation, using that mild tone that worked far better than any threat. "So under the assumed name of Tess Black, you fell under the purview of Mr Swigg, and he offered your services to the Viper, who called himself Yves. Do you happen to know how Swigg and he first met?"

Tamsin shook her head. "I was not informed of anything beyond what I needed to know to create the documents."

"But you're an educated lady," Miss Chattan interjected. "You must have gleaned more than what those men told you."

Tamsin looked at her with alarm, and Royce guessed that the term *lady* was the sticking point. So far, the woman had been scrupulous in avoiding any details of her former life. Royce didn't even know what shire she hailed from, let alone her real name or her family's exact place in Society.

"Yes," he interjected, hoping to keep Tamsin talking. "Tell them what you can about the Viper. You gave me a description earlier, but any hints as to personality or character can help me catch him."

Tamsin's eyes grew distant. "He scared me," she said at last.

On the face of it, the statement didn't sound like much. But Royce knew Tamsin fairly well at this point, enough to know that she wasn't the type to scare easily.

"He was very charming," she said, clearly assembling her thoughts. "Far more urbane than the usual riffraff Swigg associates with."

Aries leaned forward, intent on building a mental picture of this man. "Did he ever flirt with you? Try to seduce you?"

"Oh, yes," Tamsin said, though without any emotional reaction. "But most men do, so I didn't think much of it. He complimented me, told me how pretty I was…that sort of thing." Now there was a bitterness in her voice. "But I've heard all that before, and I knew it didn't mean anything."

How did she know that? Royce wondered. *Who had told her these things before?* It had to be connected to whatever event forced her to leave her former life and go to London, and the man who Tamsin refused to name.

"Yves—I was told to call him Yves, for he never gave a last name—gave up any attempt to seduce me fairly quickly. I think he actually rather appreciated not having to play the role of lover."

"Is he that repugnant?"

"Oh, no. He's really very handsome. And charming, as I said. His eyes are the sort of eyes that seem to be very soulful, even though there's nothing in his soul at all. I think Yves might be the coldest, cruelest gentleman I've ever encountered. And that takes some doing."

"Did he hurt you or threaten you?" Aries asked.

"He didn't have to." Tamsin looked over at him. "You're a man, and a powerful man at that. You've probably never felt like someone else could hold your life in their hand. Yves never had to threaten me because I knew from the start that if I ever displeased him, he'd kill me, and no one would ever know or care what happened."

Chattan sighed in sympathy, then said, "I'd better make more tea."

After she got up, Aries said, "I'd like a demonstration of your skills, Miss Black." He handed her a sheet of paper that looked like an official letter of some sort. "Can you make a copy of this?"

Tamsin took the paper and studied it carefully. "I could...but I'd like to see another document with this signature. And I'll need several sheets of paper with this same watermark. And I'll need ink of the same quality. And of course a pen."

Aries raised his eyebrow at the list. "Naturally, Miss Black. You may use the desk in the outer office. Take all the time you need."

When Tamsin left for the outer office, Julian pulled the door shut, then looked to Royce. "How much do you trust this woman?"

Royce once lay asleep beside her and she hadn't killed him—not that he could offer that as proof. "Everything she told you tonight matches what I've seen. She is educated, very skilled at writing, and she's absolutely capable of creating the documents we discovered."

"If she's so smart, why did this Swigg and the Viper let her live?" Julian asked, evaluating Tamsin the way a criminal or spy would—as an asset, not as a person.

"They didn't intend to let her live. I found her being chased down by Swigg's goon. He meant to take her to Swigg...probably to forge the last few documents before she was to be killed and dumped in the river."

"So you intercepted her...and then left for the country." Julian raised an eyebrow. "How romantic."

Royce suppressed the urge to deny it, because that would reveal his true feelings all too obviously. "She was very adamant that if she remained in London, Swigg would track her down. She lacked the means to escape the city on her own, and I thought it might be useful to keep her where the Zodiac could find her."

"At your house."

"I hired her as a private secretary. She has reorganized all my files," Royce added. "I can see the surface of my desk now. She's worth every penny."

"Surely it would have been less conspicuous to let everyone think she's your mistress. You know how servants talk."

"Well, as it turns out, that's what everyone assumed anyway. Miss Black was rather upset, but I managed to sort things out with the housekeeper."

Julian rolled his eyes. "Christ. Well, now that you've got her, your orders are to keep her within arm's reach until this assignment is concluded. Do whatever you must to get her to cooperate."

"She's already cooperating," he pointed out. "I believe she wishes to do the right thing."

"And *I* believe that she could be hiding any number of motives behind that pretty face. Be careful, Virgo. This assignment is too important. The Zodiac must not fail."

Royce's gut tightened at the mere thought of failure, and the moment he pictured such an outcome, a part of his mind began coloring in details, making it seem as inevitable and stark as any reality.

But he knew what he had to say. "I won't fail."

"Of course not," Julian returned. "That's why you're here."

Royce nodded, and then they were interrupted by Chattan, bearing two cups of tea. Royce drank his down immediately. The brew was dark and strong, just what he needed after a full day of travel.

"Miss Black says she won't be long," Chattan informed them.

And indeed, she wasn't. Only a quarter hour later, Tamsin returned with Chattan at her heels. She handed Julian a piece of paper.

He surveyed it, then frowned. "Wait, I want to see your copy, not the original I gave you."

"That is the copy," Tamsin said with just a hint of pride in her tone.

"Nonsense. This paper is stained in the corner."

"Just like the original was. I dipped it in some tea—you'll notice it's still a bit damp."

Chattan then produced another sheet. "Here's the original. Miss Black requested that I hold it while she put the finishing touches on her copy."

Julian looked at the two letters side by side. "Amazing," he said finally. "I'd never know this second one was a forgery."

"It was an easy document to copy," Tamsin said. "Short, simple, and in English. Furthermore, there were no seals or other marks to duplicate. That complicates things."

Julian handed the letters to Royce, who had to agree that he couldn't tell the new from the old. His estimation of Tamsin went up again.

Julian fretted, "If you can forge documents so well, there are surely others who are working to do the same. How can British officials trust the documents they receive if it's known so many false ones got through?"

"Trust," Tamsin said quietly. "That's exactly it."

"What do you mean?"

"When correspondents know each other and trust each other, forgeries are much more difficult to carry off. It's no fluke that the document that tripped me up with Swigg and Yves—the Viper, that is—was the one that the wife intercepted and showed to her husband. So he knew something was wrong about that letter even though he couldn't point to anything on the paper itself. I could mimic the handwriting, but not the personal knowledge."

"Unfortunately, we can't promise that all the materials are sent to and from friends."

"Of course not. But you can provide proof of trust, such as a minor key."

"Are we talking about music?"

"No." Tamsin smiled. "I mean that people who will be receiving important communications are provided with a crucial piece of information. They are told that all real and trusted letters will include a word or phrase in the text. Something innocuous, but not something so common that it will be used otherwise. Say, the word *sister* or *bell*. You can incorporate the word *sister* in a lot of personal correspondence without people noticing anything out of the ordinary. *I must end this letter, my sister has arrived.* Or, *According to my sister…*"

"But the writer does not have a sister. And the intended receiver knows that, but anyone intercepting the letter would not."

"Exactly. And someone creating a false document in a similar style wouldn't know which word is the key, so they won't know to retain it."

"That's a possibility," Chattan mused, looking intrigued.

"It's not perfect, but it could work. The key would need to be changed regularly, of course, to protect the security of the letters."

"Did the Viper tell you that?" Royce asked.

"No, it's just something I thought about while I was creating all those false documents. What would I do to ensure that I couldn't be tricked that way? I like a key word, or a deliberate mistake. Say, the writer always makes sure to cross out the last word in the first sentence. Or they make a sign, like a doodle or sketch in the corner—a rosebud, for example."

"Most impressive, Miss Black." Julian smiled at her, a spymaster's smile that looked friendly but hid a world of calculation. "You'll understand that for your protection, you'll need to stay close to Virgo, that is, Pelham."

"I'd assumed," Tamsin said dryly.

"Please take her to a safe place," Julian ordered Royce. "Verify all the earlier forged documents with her as soon as possible."

"I'll take care of it," Royce assured him. "I've got them in my safe."

"Good. And take care of Miss Black. She is the key to catching one of the most dangerous spies working today…present company excepted."

♍

AFTER LEAVING THE ZODIAC'S SECRET headquarters (she'd never look at a plain brick building the same way again), Tamsin craved nothing more than sleep. As the carriage clattered over rough pavers, Royce leaned over to her. "You impressed Aries."

"Did I?" Tamsin shrugged, trying not to react to his nearness. "That was not my aim."

"What was your aim? Because he was about to recruit you for clandestine service."

"No, thank you! I wish to be left alone."

"All alone?" He took her hand.

Tamsin sighed, tilting her head back. "Royce," she murmured. "You shouldn't do this."

"Do what?"

"Pretend that I'm anything other than a…fugitive. Look, I'm grateful that you've kept me alive. And I'm happy to hide wherever you intend to stash me…"

"Tamsin, I'm not *stashing* you anywhere. You're staying at my townhouse, with me, and the whole thing will be perfectly civilized. You won't need to scurry around like a mouse in an attic. For Christ's sake, I'm an earl. If I can't provide you protection, what's the point of being an earl?"

He kissed her hand then, leading Tamsin to forget what would surely have been a witty rejoinder…except that when she noticed his eyes, she got a very upsetting flutter in her stomach.

Just then, the carriage lurched to a halt, and she pulled her hand back sharply. "Oh! Are we stuck in the road?"

Royce lifted the corner of the shade. "No, we're home."

Naturally, his townhouse was in Grosvenor Square. It stood in one corner, thus securing a larger-than-usual yard and some more privacy from the neighbors. The cream brick building was four stories tall, and even at this time of year, the evergreen plantings in the front were full and lush-looking.

The large front door was painted green, and the moment Royce stepped onto the gravel walk, the door opened.

A man stepped out—very nearly bald, but straight-backed and keen-eyed. He gave a little bow as Royce reached him.

"Welcome home, my lord. We received word of your arrival and you'll find everything is ready."

"Excellent, Marlow. This is Miss Black, who is acting as my personal secretary."

The butler turned to her and gave another precise bow. "Welcome, Miss Black. A room has been prepared for you. It does not look onto the square, but you'll find it all the more quiet and peaceful because of that. Wendy will show you up."

"Thank you," Tamsin murmured. The difference between her reception here and Seabourne was night and day.

Wendy, a bright-eyed girl of about fourteen years, pointed up the staircase, with its heavy oak bannister. "This way, miss. Your luggage will be brought up in a jiffy."

"Actually, I'll show Miss Black the way myself," Royce said, and the maid bobbed a curtsey.

Royce led Tamsin up the stairs. "I'm going up anyway," he explained. "And why shouldn't I give the tour? This is where I spend most of my life."

"Why do you prefer the townhouse? Most people among Society can't wait to escape the city...until it's time for the Season, that is." Thankfully, the Season was still several weeks away. Not that it mattered to Tamsin, since she would never again attend any parties or spend an afternoon calling upon influential ladies of the *ton*. But the Season meant more crowds in the city, and Tamsin detested crowds, especially when they were composed of people who might possibly recognize her. "To be fair, it's a lovely house."

"It's my real home," Royce said. "I've spent more time here than anywhere else since I was a child. I've been able to make it so this place suits me."

It was not fashionable, in the sense that the rooms Tamsin passed through were not decorated in the latest style or presented in a way to encourage guests. The parlour was more of a library, and the dining room contained a beautiful mahogany table, but only eight chairs, a pointedly low number for a member of the aristocracy who would normally be expected to entertain his peers regularly.

The walls were painted rather than papered, which made the rooms seem calm. Royce also exiled all the usual portraits of ancestors to his country estate, and here hung landscapes and interesting, odd still-lifes.

"Do you know many artists?" she asked, before thinking that an earl was not likely to know any at all. But then, Royce was an unusual earl.

"I know a few," he conceded. "In the past, my work

brought me into contact with a circle of French emigres, all artists who fled the country after the Revolution. I bought several works to support them, but also because I liked the art. The more modern and strange, the better." He touched the frame of one landscape, a winter beach scene that was desolate and bare, the canvas mostly occupied by cloudy skies. "My mother invariably hates my taste in art."

"So you keep it here, where she won't see it?"

"No one sees it. I don't like visitors."

"Oh."

He glanced at her. "You're not a visitor, Tamsin. Ah, here's your room. And if I'm not mistaken, your luggage is practically chasing us down the hall." He grinned. His mood seemed immeasurably better in London.

Tamsin's room proved to be charming, with walls painted in a pale pink the color of the sky just before dawn. The bed was a massive four poster probably carved during Queen Anne's reign, though the soft white bedding looked as new as yesterday. Tamsin wanted to collapse in the middle of the bed and pull the pink velvet curtain closed to keep out the world, but alas, she could not.

Shortly after, Tamsin left her room dressed in a fresh gown. The traveling costume had been bundled and whisked away by Wendy, who declared that she could smell "a little too much country road" on the hem.

Seeing Marlow, she asked the way to where Royce kept his office in the townhouse, and was pointed to a door on that same floor. "Just through there, miss. His lordship is within, reading."

"Thank you."

"Wendy will call you for supper," he added as he walked away.

Tamsin nodded, once again appreciating that these

servants seemed to treat her as a full human. It would be nice to get back to her room and find a *warm* meal waiting.

She knocked on the door of the office. "My lord?"

"Yes, come in," Royce responded.

She entered to find an enchanting space. It was much smaller than the great library at Seabourne, of course. But it was warmer, and filled with curiosities in addition to books.

A set of glass-fronted cabinets displayed seashells, ancient artifacts, interestingly colored rocks, and the occasional stuffed bird with startlingly bright plumage.

"The birds are all from India. My father collected them. He always wanted to see the jungles and the mountains there."

"But it was more than ten miles from Seabourne," Tamsin said, remembering Royce's comment from earlier.

"True," he agreed. "But he could buy what other men brought back. And so he did. I only kept these few specimens though. I much prefer living here, but I can't house a whole menagerie."

"My lord, you have mentioned some other papers—"

But just then, a knock sounded at the door, and Tamsin shut her mouth, knowing it wasn't safe to speak about spies and forgeries in front of the servants. Wendy stepped in to announce supper.

"Good, I'm famished," Royce said, standing up. He offered an arm to Tamsin, a gesture so common for a gentleman escorting a lady to a meal that Tamsin took it before realizing that she'd be heading in a different direction once outside the door.

"Where are you going?" he asked, when Tamsin stepped toward her room. "Did you forget your wrap?"

"No, my lord," Tamsin replied. "I just...won't my

meal be served in my room, as always?"

"Not here," he said firmly. "Come along, and quickly. Cook gets quite difficult when we throw off her serving schedule, and we've already done that by arriving so late."

With little choice, she allowed herself to be escorted to the dining room, which had been set for two. Mercifully, they'd not been seated at opposite ends of the table, but rather on adjoining sides. Tamsin was glad she would not have to peer through the dense jungle of the centerpiece to see Royce's head.

The meal was plain enough for an everyday supper, but the food was expertly prepared and Tamsin's stomach appreciated every bite.

"Cook's made her gingerbread, sir," Wendy said with a smile after she cleared the last of the dishes from the main meal.

After she left, Tamsin looked inquiringly at him.

"I'm very fond of gingerbread."

"Really." Was this the man who nearly beat a man to death on a freezing bridge to save Tamsin's life one night? Gingerbread was far too wholesome to be associated with Lord Pelham, aristocrat, spy, and champion brooder.

"You'll see."

And just then, Wendy reentered with a tray. She put the plates down in front of them. On each was a generous square of gingerbread, four inches high and redolent with spices. Not just ginger, but cloves, cinnamon, pepper, nutmeg…. She inhaled deeply. "This smells like Christmas."

It even looked like Christmas, since the plate had been dusted with fine white sugar suggesting snow.

Wendy poured two small cups of coffee for them, and left the room.

Royce picked up his fork. "Well? What are you waiting for?" He took a bite and chewed, looking utterly blissful.

Tamsin didn't need more encouragement. She nibbled away, savoring the warming flavors of the ginger and the sweetness of the bread...really more like cake. She was glad Wendy served such ridiculously oversized portions. She intended to eat it all.

It paired well with the strong coffee. Together, it was the perfect treat for an autumn night.

She put her coffee cup down. "I can see why you prefer living here."

Royce chuckled. "Just one of the many benefits."

"It's almost a shame that no one gets to eat this but you. You said you dislike visitors, and I assume you don't host parties of any kind."

He winced. "Not if I can help it. And I'm perfectly happy to hoard all of Cook's treats for myself. No one else in London deserves them...other than you, obviously."

Tamsin shook her head. "I certainly do not deserve such a luxury. I haven't tasted ginger for years and years."

The truth was that a treat like this was well beyond Tamsin's reach while she lived on her own in Catchpenny Lane.

The gingerbread appeared simple, and even humble. But it required substantial amounts of expensive spices, the sort locked away by the housekeeper's cupboard, along with the tea and coffee and sugar. The cook would need to ask permission to get the items—no one but the housekeeper even had keys for that cabinet. All for gingerbread!

Royce leaned back in his chair, sipping his coffee slowly while he regarded her. "You've been coy about your past. How many years since you tasted ginger?"

"More than five and less than ten."

He looked surprised that she offered that much detail. Then he said, "Do you want to go home? Your home, I mean?"

Tamsin swallowed past the sudden lump in her throat, thinking of her family's old house in Somerset. "I cannot, my lord. Even if I wanted to...the home I knew no longer exists."

"What makes you so sure? You said that you lost contact with your family."

"I know enough of what happened." She picked up her coffee cup, found it sadly empty, and put it down again. "Can we speak of something else?"

"Of course. Should I choose a topic suitable for post-prandial discussion, or will you?"

"How about forgeries? Your mysterious superior said I was to verify some documents."

"They're in my study, locked in the safe. It can easily wait until tomorrow. If you like, I'll walk you to your room. You must be tired."

Tamsin shook her head, trying to clear it of the sudden image of Royce laying her down in that decadent four poster bed and doing all sorts of things to her that would make her lose her breath. "Please, my lord. I think it best if we get to the matter at hand...you have me here. You ought to make use of me."

Her cheeks went hot when she heard her words out loud, for a very different meaning came to mind.

Royce's half smile suggested he thought of it too, and was laughing at her discomfort.

But then he rose to his feet. "If you'll join me in the study, Miss Black."

Upstairs again, Tamsin waited while Royce unlocked

a safe—hidden behind a framed seascape—and pulled out a leather pouch of the type that clerks used. He gestured to the settee near the fire. "Sit there, it's got the best light."

He opened the pouch and pulled out several pieces of paper, laying them on the low table in front of where Tamsin sat.

He said, "I have spent the last three months pursuing the source of these forgeries. Aries assigned me to the matter after a naval officer turned in a letter containing orders that he knew could not be right. He risked his career to circumvent the normal chain of command, and thank God he did. We discovered that the letter was a fake."

Tamsin ran her hands over the paper. "Yes, I wrote this. I remember how many times I had to practice the signature for Commodore Landers. Evidently I did not practice it enough."

"Oh, it looked real, even to the officer. He was only suspicious because the written document directed the officer to do exactly the opposite of what the commodore had told him *personally* to do just before he sailed. In this case, the camaraderie of those two men was unusual. And the officer trusted what he heard from his superior more than an official letter. Any other officer was unlikely to have spoken to a commander and got those orders verbally."

She sighed. "And this was it, wasn't it? The document that put your department on alert."

"It's not a department, but yes. There were a few other instances previously that piqued the Zodiac's interest. I'll show them to you. But the short version is that several items never made it to their intended destinations."

"Good." Tamsin had to cover her mouth to hide an

unladylike yawn. The coffee at dinner wasn't enough to keep her going after a full day. "I'm glad it never made it. That means Yves didn't succeed at everything he made me help him do."

Royce put his hand over Tamsin's. "You couldn't have known."

"I should have guessed that the outcome of my work would only result in pain," she said bitterly. "It doesn't take a genius to understand that war is a dangerous business, and meddling in it will get people hurt."

"Tamsin, you've already said that you had no choice. That if you refused, you'd have been killed."

"Then I should have let him kill me," Tamsin said, despair flowing into her heart. "My whole adult life has been one weak moment after another. I am the duchess of poor choices, falling lower with each one."

"How can that be true? You survived, didn't you?"

"But at what cost?"

"Tamsin, stop it. You are not the only person in the world to make a bad decision. Lord knows I've made plenty. But I'll tell you one decision that I'll never regret, and that's the moment I asked you to come with me, to leave London and start fresh."

"I can never start again. No matter how I change my name, I'll always know the sort of person I am. The sort of person who…writes things like this…"

Tamsin blinked, wondering why the words looked so fuzzy. Then the paper slid from her grasp as her eyes slid closed and sleep overtook her.

♍

"Tamsin?" Royce asked, unsure what to do.

One moment she was talking normally, and the next she'd slid down upon a few pillows, clearly deeply asleep.

He certainly didn't want to wake her—she deserved the rest. But in general, a gentleman shouldn't keep a lady helpless and alone in a room.

Then again, Tamsin was an unusual lady.

Royce regarded the woman sleeping on the long couch. Her head lay on the deep green silk of the cushions, and her auburn hair caught extra red tones from the fire burning in the hearth. The rather plain gown she wore now draped her body in a way that made her hip's outline prominent, and it was a curve dramatic enough to send Royce's thoughts to dangerous places.

In retrospect, he should have known she was special. The way Tamsin plowed through his office and arranged literally all his documents told him what he needed to know: she was a person with exacting standards and little tolerance for sloppiness. Lord, the last few years living in Catchpenny Lane must have been torture for her.

Royce remembered Tamsin's harshly spoken words from the carriage ride: *the worst has already happened.* What was the worst thing that could happen to a young lady? The clear implication was that she'd been pregnant at the time. She'd also begun to say something else: *if they'd known my condition…* A boarding house would not rent a room to an unmarried woman carrying a child.

Which raised the fascinating question of where her child was.

Well, it was no business of Royce's. He had managed to misplace his own child for thirteen years, after all. And now the boy hated him. The less he intervened with other people's children, the better for everyone.

On the couch, Tamsin gave a little sigh and eased further into the cushions, lost to the world.

Royce smiled. Tamsin Black, forger extraordinaire. He'd spent all his time looking for a man, and then fate had thrown Tamsin across his path. He remembered the terror on her face when she'd first seen him on the bridge, when she thought he was one of the many criminals out to exploit her. He'd prevent any of those characters from hurting Tamsin now. Stooping to pick up the letter Tamsin had dropped, he knelt beside her. She sighed in her sleep, and he caught cinnamon and coffee in her breath.

"Tamsin," he said softly, leaning over her. "You need to wake up." He took her by the shoulder and squeezed lightly.

Her eyes fluttered open, and she stared at him in confusion. "Royce?"

The use of his given name unlocked something in his consciousness, a need for closeness that only she could satisfy.

She knew exactly what he intended, and from the way she instinctively licked her lower lip, she wanted it too.

He'd kissed her before, but this was the first time he'd tasted cinnamon and ginger and coffee on her tongue, and the intoxicating scents combined with the softness of her mouth sent his rationality over a cliff.

With a little moan, she deepened the kiss. Her fingers

pressed into his shoulders and back, dragging him closer. Not that he needed the encouragement.

Tamsin's breath came hot against his skin as she broke the kiss. "Royce, I shouldn't have—"

"Stop it," he growled. "I wanted to kiss you, and you wanted to kiss me. Leave it at that."

"Can *you* leave it at that?" she whispered.

Not if she kept teasing him with such coy questions. If it were up to him, he'd move this discussion to his bedroom as soon as humanly possible.

Tamsin watched him with wide eyes, and then she suddenly pushed herself back into the couch, breaking the mood. "I must have nodded off. Inexcusable of me. Where were we? I was looking at some documents."

"They can wait until you're fully alert," he said, accepting that the moment was over, and she'd found her own way out of this very uncomfortable conversation. "Perhaps you'd just tell me more about how you worked for Swigg. I want to understand how you came into all this. The details."

Tamsin nodded. "I'll tell you everything I can...but only you. And you can't tell anyone else my identity. If it got out that Tess Black was alive and helping the government, well…"

"I shall not tell anyone but my direct superior," Royce said. "And you already can guess after meeting him, he's a man who knows how to keep secrets."

She took a breath, then said, "Very well. I told you that I worked for Swigg, and that he occasionally hired me out, but only when it was worth his while. About five months ago he sent for me and I went, because one doesn't say no to Swigg. He has a sort of headquarters in St Giles, and he's like a king holding audiences there."

"Does he have guards with him?"

Tamsin laughed. "Everyone in there is essentially a guard for him, from the barkeeper to the scullion. But yes, he's always got muscle with him. Often Coaker, but others as well."

"And the night he summoned you, what happened?"

"He told me that I had some important scribbling to do, and he walked me back to his private office. There he introduced me to a man he called Yves, who you call the Viper."

He took her hand in his. "How did Yves find Swigg?"

"I don't know. Perhaps it was just luck. Maybe he was looking for a quality forger and Swigg's ears twitched when he heard the rumors. In any case, the price was right, because Swigg was delighted to offer my services. And I am a good scrivener," she added.

"That doesn't necessarily mean you'd be a good forger."

"Oh, but Swigg already knew that I was. When creating a product that must be exact," she said, "one must be exacting in all the steps. A small mistake will be evident in the final document, and reveal it to be a forgery."

"What gave you the idea to become a forger?"

"Oh, that part was happenstance. Really, most of my time was spent on perfectly legal work for clients. So many people in London do not read or write well enough to do it on their own. I was looking for a boarding house and while I was at one prospect, the landlady mentioned that she had to go find a scrivener to write a letter for her —the old man she used before had recently died. I told her I could do all her letters in exchange for lower rent. I went out and purchased paper and cheap ink with the last of my money, but it was a good investment. I took the room and started doing piecework for those who needed writing."

"And that paid your way?"

"It covered my expenses, if I was careful. I didn't have to resort to occasional prostitution, or beg. Of course, I'd have had more money if Swigg didn't take a cut."

"Yes, tell me about Swigg."

She shrugged. "What's to tell? He's the local head of the criminals in that area. Shortly after I set up in Catchpenny Lane, he came to the house and had me summoned to the parlour. There, he told me that he was fine with another scrivener setting up on his turf, and that for a reasonable fee, I'd be safe from ruffians and from the threat of another scrivener going into business too close by."

"How much?"

"Twenty percent of everything I made…more or less. Because Swigg could see that I was very good at what I did, he never made too much of a fuss about the exact payment. He used my services for free when he had need, and he was the one who suggested that I start forging documents he wanted to have. It was little things at first. A land deed. An IOU that had somehow got lost…petty things."

"And you never thought about running away?"

"Where should I have gone? I had a room, a job, and some measure of protection. It wasn't as if I could flee to a friend and thrown myself on their mercy. None of the people I once called friends would dare look at me in my current state. I may as well not exist to Society."

"What happened, Tamsin? You never explained the details."

She shook her head. "There's little to explain. My father ran into debt. A rather shocking amount of debt. And he couldn't pay it. It's a common story."

"But you…your family. You have a family. You mentioned it."

"I have a younger sister, who was taken in by a cousin." She looked upset. "I don't want to talk about her, my lord. In fact, it is high time for me to go to my own room."

Royce had struck a nerve there, and he had to tread carefully to keep Tamsin's good graces. He stood and offered his hand to help her up. "Yes, I've asked far too much of you tonight."

Tamsin stood, and for a moment they were face to face. This time, Royce stepped back. "Good night, Tamsin."

She looked uncertain for a moment, then nodded. "Yes, my lord."

"Royce. Please."

"Good night, Royce," she said quietly. When she reached the door, she glanced back. "Sleep well."

He smiled, but he didn't think he would. Not with the memory of Tamsin's cinnamon-flavored lips to keep him awake.

♍

FOR TAMSIN, THE MOST SIGNIFICANT difference of the townhouse from Seabourne was that it was far less populated. The estate employed a dozen servants in the house, with even more for the grounds and the wider property. There was an army of maids, footmen, gardeners, stable-hands, groundskeepers, and others all with specific domains. It had been impossible to walk down a hallway without encountering at least three people.

By contrast, the townhouse required only a handful of people to keep it running, and luckily the Marlow family fit the bill perfectly. They all seemed capable of performing several positions at once. Marlow, the older man who greeted them initially, acted as butler...and valet while Royce was in town. His wife, Mrs Marlow, served as both housekeeper and cook. It was funny to Tamsin when she was called Mrs Marlow when discussing household accounts, but Cook when it came to preparing meals. Wendy Marlow was the daughter, and she also worked twice as hard, as the household's maid, both upstairs and down. The son, Errol, was a few years older than Wendy, and he was footman, ostler, driver, gardener, and whatever else Marlow dictated. The tight-knit family made the house feel quite cozy, considering that it officially was a bachelor's home.

Furthermore, as far as Tamsin could tell, the servants

were attached to Royce personally, unlike the servants at Seabourne, who were more invested in the notion of the Pelham name and title. Royce mentioned to her that he'd found Marlow several years ago, and found himself hiring the whole family in due time. They accepted the explanation of Tamsin's presence without protest or surprise, and she found their service absolutely faultless.

On the second day, Tamsin was working in the sitting room designated for her use. As twilight fell, Wendy brought in tea for Tamsin and set the tray down carefully. She then poured the first cup and waited for Tamsin to taste it.

She did, delighted by the aroma, which was grassy with faint notes of jasmine. This was clearly an excellent blend. Not to mention that the tea was suitably hot.

"Ah," Tamsin said, delighted. "I needed this."

"Yes, miss. Do you require anything else?"

"No, Wendy. And I'll likely work late tonight, so I'll put the lamp out myself when I go up to bed."

Wendy stepped back, but then paused. "May I ask a question, miss?"

Tamsin looked up, wondering what was coming. "Go on."

"How did you become a secretary? Is it difficult? I…I don't want to be a maid my whole life. Mama says I can work up to lady's maid, but I'd rather try something else."

Tamsin put the teacup down, thinking through her reply. "Well, Wendy, the fact is that I rather stumbled into this position. I had the qualifications, though. Which is to say that I write very well, both in terms of my penmanship but also my diction. I speak not only English, but French fluently. And I have some understanding of Italian and German too."

Wendy's face fell at this listing of accomplishments.

"Oh. You must have gone to a school and done wonderful there, miss. I can read and write, but I'd take no prizes for either."

"Well, as I say, a female secretary is not exactly a position much in demand. The real question is: what do you *want* to do, Wendy?"

"Oh, miss, there's so much. I want to…*go* places. I've never been out of London. I want to be on board a ship, but what if I get sick? Errol did that once and he said he couldn't eat for a week. Then I see all the fine ladies in the park, with their gowns and hats so pretty, and I think I'd like to make such things. But my friend Carla is a milliner's assistant and she says it's hard work too, especially when everyone comes for the Season and they all want things done straightway… Excuse me, miss! I'm prattling on."

"It sounds as if you've a very active mind, Wendy. Perhaps you could ask your father to seek permission from the earl to use the library. You could borrow some books and learn about new things and places. Then you might get a better idea of what you'd like to do. Though," she added judiciously, "there is a lot to be said for a place as a household servant." In fact, it was one of the more respected and stable positions a woman could have. And as long as Wendy stayed in Lord Pelham's employ, she'd be protected from the greatest dangers maids faced—the unwelcome attention of men in the house.

Wendy bobbed her head. "Yes, miss. I don't mean to sound ungrateful."

"You don't at all," Tamsin assured her.

A few minutes after Wendy left, Errol came in. "A letter arrived for you in the last post, miss."

Tamsin's chest tightened. "For me? No one knows I'm here!" Indeed, Royce had instructed his servants to avoid mentioning Tamsin's presence, even in casual gossip. He didn't say why, but they had nodded as if this were a perfectly normal request, which it was assuredly not.

"It was posted from Norfolk," he added helpfully, lowering the tray with the letter to her.

She took it as if it were coated in poison. Had Hector dared to torment her in this way?

But upon opening it, she saw that the letter was from Laurent, and she laughed in relief. Errol left the door open as he left, and her laugh probably echoed down the hall.

She read the letter, still smiling.

Dear Miss Black,

Forgive my presumption. I am writing of behalf of Jasper, who would write himself, but cannot because he is a dog. Since you had to depart so quickly from Seabourne, without Jasper, I knew you'd want to know how he is faring. He is doing excellently, and we walk every day, though never in the forbidden area. He surely misses you (he chews one of your slippers as a memento), but he's a good sport and plays fetch with me until he can scarcely stay awake. He is also excellent at finding rabbits. He sniffs out their nests and curls up around them to protect them from the stablehands' other dogs.

He awaits your return to Seabourne. I am grateful for the loan of him, though it will be pleasant to see you again as well. This assumes that you are still Pelham's secretary, and have not quit in exasperation. I still don't know why he dashes off to London without warning, or why he should take a secretary but not his son.

Respectfully, L and...

There was a paw print in ink at the bottom of the paper. Tamsin giggled, but caught the envy in Laurent's words. Of course Royce could not bring his son along if he was working on secret assignments for the Crown, but the boy did not know the real reason, and saw only that his father left him behind in the country instead of allowing him to enjoy the city, as so many young men wished to do.

"What are you reading?" Royce asked, entering the room. "I heard you laugh."

"Laurent sent a letter with news of Jasper," she said, holding it up to show the paw print. "That was a very sweet thought, wasn't it?"

"Hmm. Astonishingly mature, actually."

"He is an intelligent young man," Tamsin said. "He notices a lot more than you think."

"Such as?"

"Such as when you go to London and don't take him."

"I wouldn't know what to do with him here. We don't get along at all, and every time we're in the same room, we fight. He's far too stubborn."

"Well, he's his father's son in that respect."

"The only respect." Royce sighed, falling into a chair opposite. "How are you getting on here?"

"Very well, my lord, thank you."

"I've been thinking. You must have forged more documents for Yves—the Viper—whatever we're calling him now—than the government intercepted."

"I'm afraid so," she admitted.

"Can you create a list of the sender, the receiver, and the subject of the document for each one? Or at least all those you can remember."

"Certainly. I should have done that right off, I suppose." Tamsin cursed herself for not thinking of such a basic step.

"You've had a lot on your mind," Royce said dryly.

"I'll do it tonight, my lord."

"After dinner," he said. "You've been cooped up in this room all day. Don't think I haven't noticed. One hour, Miss Black. And then you can return to your salt mine." The smile he gave her was annoyingly attractive.

Dinner proved to be the break she needed. The meal was once again delicious, consisting of foods that she'd not enjoyed in years. Tender lamb with mint sauce, a pineapple salad, a little partridge pie, and for dessert, a chocolate-laced pudding that tasted like temptation in a cup. She appreciated the meal without realizing that Royce had given explicit orders to his cook for what to serve in the coming days (and quite shocking her with the expected costs). In fact, he'd thought of all the flavors Tamsin might miss, and wanted to remedy the situation.

She put down her coffee cup at last. "You said I could go back to my salt mines, but I'm so full I might have to go directly to bed."

"Whatever you desire," he said, regarding her from across the table. He looked totally at ease, his eyes heavy lidded and his mouth touched with a faint smile. She caught his gaze and suddenly felt her heart flutter. The mention of *bed* and *desire* was not helping her maintain her professional demeanor.

She pushed her chair away from the table and stood. "No, I'll complete the work now. It's too important to waste time."

Royce had stood up too, as required of gentlemen whenever a lady stood. Unfortunately, that meant she was suddenly reminded of his height and physique because his clothes were distressingly well-tailored.

She swallowed nervously. "Excuse me, my lord. I'll see you tomorrow."

Tamsin fled to her sitting room. Why must she be so

nervous around him? Surely she'd learned by now that physical attraction was a danger to be avoided, not a pleasure she could indulge in.

The thought of what pleasures he could provide her made Tamsin feel a little light-headed. After all, the carriage ride down to London proved how seductive he was, and how weak she turned out to be.

"Oh, stop," she told herself in a low voice. "It meant nothing."

Nothing except that Tamsin wanted more of it. She wanted more of Royce's kisses, and his words in her ear, telling her he wanted her to enjoy it all as much as he did…

Tamsin pinched her arm to distract herself from the memories.

She sat down and devoted herself to listing all the items she'd worked on at Yves's orders. Most of them came easily to her mind, since she'd spent so much time practicing the names and double checking the dates and addresses to make her forgeries appear as real as possible.

In the morning, she presented the list to Royce. "This is as complete as I could make it. There may be few items I can't recall."

Royce took the list and scanned it. "That's all right. What I'm really looking for is a common element. Why did Yves have you work on these particular documents?"

Tamsin shrugged helplessly. "I've wondered that myself. But I suspect it's purely the result of opportunity. Yves or his comrades were able to get hold of particular documents and materials, and therefore I could make a forgery based on what was there. You'll see that I worked on letters in English, French, Spanish, and Italian. There are items pertaining to naval matters, taxes in Paris, something in Brazil…as I say, I think Yves simply wanted to sow discord wherever he could, and I was the instrument."

"Perhaps." Royce sounded distracted, his attention locked on the paper.

"If you need anything," she began, but she recognized the look of concentration on his face. She felt it herself all too often.

Quietly, she backed out of the room and closed the door softly. Clearly, the people who selected Royce to be a secret agent of the Crown knew exactly what they were doing.

* * * *

That evening, Royce sat in the chair by the window, allowing Marlow to shave him—a task Royce often put aside until it was absolutely necessary, since he hated the scrape of a blade against his skin. Fortunately, the bald man was skillful with a razor, which was one of the reasons Royce had hired him in the first place. The other reason was that Marlow saved his life during a Zodiac assignment gone awry.

Marlow wiped the blade off in between passes. He commented, "Don't mind my saying, sir, that we were a bit surprised to learn that there'd be a guest with you this time."

"Miss Black is an employee, not a guest. And no, she's not my mistress either." Though he'd make her his mistress in a heartbeat if he thought she'd accept a carte blanche.

"Oh, didn't think she was, sir. She's not got the look. And if she were, you'd have told us to make up the adjoining bedchamber, wouldn't you?"

"Very true." Royce liked that Marlow and his family

all thought logically. Perhaps he ought to send Mrs Arnott over here for training. "I must remind you not to mention her presence, though, not to the neighboring houses or in the markets. Miss Black prefers to keep a low profile."

"Her name's not actually Black, is it?" Marlow asked.

"No, though what her real name is I could not say. She used to have dealings with some underworld characters in town, and she would not like to have any more dealings with them."

"Aye, sir. That's just good sense. She say who?"

"The name Swigg came up."

Marlow pulled the razor away from Royce's throat abruptly. "Swigg?"

"Yes. He's got a subordinate named Coaker."

"Oh, aye. That's the one. Rough character, from what I've heard. Thankfully, I retired from my old profession well before Swigg became well-known in his."

Marlow's past was a checkered one. He'd been a thief, a smuggler, and possibly worse in his younger days. A chance encounter during an assignment showed Royce that a man's quality did not depend on his bloodline or his profession. Marlow the thief was a far better ally than many aristocrats he knew.

When he mentioned Marlow to Aries, the man had smiled. "And you'd like to help him out, is that it? Give him a chance for a new life?"

Then Aries revealed that the Zodiac had begun to work with a group of people with similar backgrounds: former criminals who now worked as reliable domestic servants while helping the agents of the Zodiac on various matters. They were known as the Disreputables.

Aries refused to say more, but in short order, Royce was able to get Marlow and his whole family out of the dangerous London underworld and into his townhouse as servants. He never regretted it.

When Marlow declared Royce done with his shave, he said, "I put out the new blue jacket and the striped waist-coat for tonight, sir. Will that serve?"

"I'm sure it will," Royce said indifferently. He'd agreed to go to a party tonight since it was hosted by a friend, who'd pleaded, "If you don't come, it will be a year until I see you again! The mysterious Lord Pelham must go to at least one event...if only to prove he's still among the living!"

Dressed in the outfit laid out for him, Royce looked in the mirror and wished he could stay home instead. A quiet evening with Tamsin was a thousand times more appealing than chatting idly with other members of the *ton* and all the people who wanted to say they'd met an earl.

Worse, his mind was still turning over the matter of the letters Tamsin forged. There had to be link between them all, and Royce felt like he *almost* had it...but then it drifted apart like smoke.

On the ride to the party, Royce considered the issue. During the party, he danced with two young ladies whose names he could not recall a half hour later, and considered the issue. He conversed with some gentlemen about life in the country versus life in the city (one of the men knew where Seabourne was and thought the hunting very fine) and considered the issue. He spoke to his host about the quality of the light supper provided, and considered the issue. In short, he did the bare minimum of what was required of him socially, all while turning over the matter of Tamsin's many forgeries, teasing out the essential nature of them, the thing that made the Viper risk life and limb to get them made.

On the ride home, he was still mulling it over. Letters in Spanish, documents in French, naval orders in English.

A direction to move ships from a harbor in Portugal. A letter from an ambassador to his mistress in Lisbon. Supply lines adjusted in Spain...bound for Portugal.

Royce had been tapping his hand against his leg, and he suddenly stopped.

Tamsin had assumed that the Viper used her to send random letters, chosen based on what documents he managed to steal from British officials. To her, it must have appeared quite scattershot. One letter from a Navy officer to a lower-ranking man. A letter from a diplomat to an embassy in Rome. A short, casual note from an ambassador to his lover.

But what if the forgeries weren't just opportunistic? What if the Viper stole specific items to forge new versions, to send out with the intention of shaping one future event?

What did all the forgeries have in common?

"Portugal," he muttered.

That was where the Navy captain was supposed to sail. That was where the diplomat had mentioned refugees should not go. That was where the British official had been stationed until the lover's identity forced him out of the position, leaving the post open.

The Viper's work all aimed at weakening the military and diplomatic strength of strategically important places in Portugal. Why? To allow Napoleon's forces to take it with an unusually small force. Probably a force that wouldn't attract notice as it moved into place on land and sea. A few battalions here, a few ships there, sailing to nearby ports. It was a chess game with Europe as the board, and the Emperor was very good at playing.

He leaned out and shouted new directions to his driver, who was forced to wheel the horses around in response.

A quarter-hour later, Royce was bounding up the twisting stairs to the offices of the Zodiac. He burst in, finding Chattan at her desk, staring at him in shock.

"Virgo!" she whispered.

"I know what he's doing," Royce announced grandly. Then he amended, "Well, I think I know."

"Go on," Julian said, having appeared in the doorway to his inner office.

"It's Portugal. That was the subject of nearly everything Miss Black forged." He saw Chattan's confused look, and said, "Not directly! But think about the results the altered documents had—or would have had if they'd not been identified as false. In each case, the effect was to weaken the defenses of Portugal's most important cities in some way. Sometimes in a very direct way, such as diverting those supplies to a different city. Sometimes in a more subtle way—like smearing the most important diplomat and forcing him to resign and return to England, leaving the post empty. That's a vital intelligence link severed due to the *appearance* of the man's unreliability. But what's more unreliable than getting no reports, because there is no replacement to send them?"

"Our government will get someone there soon," Julian said, though in the tone of voice he used when he was thinking fast.

"And it will take that man time to get settled and understand the situation," Royce said. "I think that Napoleon is planning an attack on the city of Lisbon, and that attack is intended to take place within weeks. Maybe days. The Viper's work is meant to soften up the target before the actual attack."

"If this is true," Julian said, "we need some sort of test to confirm it."

"Like what?" Chattan asked, putting her hands to her

forehead. "What can we do now that will somehow prove that previous documents were faked?"

"Well, there bloody well must be *some*thing we can think of," Julian retorted, his normally calm demeanor snapping under the tension he'd been hiding. Then he sighed. "I didn't mean to shout. We've all been worried about this assignment."

"It's my assignment," Royce said. "I should be able to think of what play will tangle up his plans."

"Then go home and ponder it until a solution comes to you. Perhaps Miss Black can help."

"She'd rather stay out of it. And I'd rather she stayed out of it too."

Chattan shook her head sadly. "That may not be an option. She was the key to his work—he'll be looking for her so he can complete it."

"He'll have to get though me first," Royce nearly growled. Then he jammed his hat back on. "I'm going. I'll send word the moment I've got something useful."

Charged with angry energy, Royce left in a hurry, stalking down the hall. Then he thought of something else and hurried back to the door. But before he could open it, he heard his code name spoken beyond, and paused to listen.

"He's growing more erratic," came the voice of Miss Chattan, cool and detached. "Communications were always difficult, but it's worse now. How can I be sure if he's just ignoring my messages or if he's dead?"

"None of our agents are perfect. Virgo's delivered results when it mattered, and his loyalty is unquestionable."

"I'm not questioning his loyalty, Julian! I'm asking if we can dare *rely* on him anymore. This current chase with the Viper…and this woman he managed to find… Perhaps we're asking too much of him."

"Who else do we ask, then?" Julian responded wearily. "This matter with France is growing more deadly every day. People know we're at war, but they've got no idea what that really means. We have a tiny number of agents and they are all stretched to their limits. Do I tell one to stop working and then tell another to pick up the slack and do the work of two agents? Do I wait to train more, and all the while the Viper and France's other spies continue to wreak havoc and destroy more of our troops and intelligence and material?"

"I didn't suggest that, Julian."

"Then what do you suggest?"

"I don't know." She sighed. "All I know is that if we fail, if the Zodiac fails, then the whole population of these isles will be in more danger than ever. And it will be on my conscience."

There was a long silence, so long that Royce thought it was high time to sneak away.

He walked blindly, stung by the words that echoed the worst of his own fears. The conversation chilled him, not just because he understood the reasons for Chattan's doubts, but because he also finally felt the weight on her shoulders and Julian's shoulders and his own shoulders—the pressure to preserve not just the Zodiac or a single life, but all that was British. Chattan was correct...the stakes were as high as they could possibly be, and Royce had let this assignment dog him too long. He wallowed in self-pity while the Viper played more tricks. He spent months chasing shadows while Tamsin had been stuck in a dark room in London, forced to create false documents or be killed for refusing.

He was unreliable. He shouldn't be an agent.

Part of Royce wanted to slink home to Norfolk and

never return to this building.

But who else could pick up the threads now? He knew more about the Viper and the forged documents than any other agent. He had to finish this.

And when it was done, *then* he'd be out.

So he had to get the Viper, no matter the cost.

♍

TAMSIN HAD SPENT A QUIET evening in the small library, curled up next to the fireplace with a few of the books from the shelves to keep her company. Royce had apologized for the need to attend a party, and Tamsin reminded him that she herself had set it in his agenda. "You're the Earl of Pelham. Your job is to go to parties…and enjoy them."

"I'll concede to the first part, not to the second," he'd replied, looking put out. Privately, Tamsin thought he would be the highlight of the evening for many guests, especially the young ladies. He was well turned out in a subdued dark blue jacket that was cut so close to his form that she could see the outline of his muscles under the fabric. Freshly shaved, but with that slightly-too-long hair, he looked decidedly rakish.

For half a second, she wished she could dance with him that night. To reach out across the floor and see such a man reaching back…she bit back a little gasp.

But fortunately, Lord Pelham hadn't noticed her mooning about, and he left, telling her that he'd see her tomorrow.

In the morning, she woke later than usual, lulled into a doze by the warm blankets and the crisp sheets, simple pleasures that now felt like paradise to her.

After eating a light breakfast of tea and a hot buttered

muffin, she put on her pelisse and hat, and stepped into the back garden. She'd quickly made a habit of a few brisk turns around the small yard. Tamsin didn't like to be cooped up, and though she had no wish to be seen in public, she yearned for blue sky and fresh air. She missed her long rambles with Jasper.

On the fourth circuit, she heard an odd sound from the shed in the back corner, a sturdy building that housed most of the tools Errol used in the yard, as well as a stall for a couple of goats who were kept for their milk. Tamsin worried that something was bothering them, so she walked over to investigate.

No sooner did she push open the door than a hand closed about her wrist, and someone yanked her inside. Before she could scream, a hand covered her mouth.

"No need to shriek, Thomasina. I've been waiting for you."

She gasped at the voice. Wrestling free, she whirled around to see the man who tormented her by his mere existence, his face triumphant in the dim light of the shed. Too late, she remembered that there was also a door that opened to a narrow alley behind the houses.

"What are you doing here?" she demanded, moving as far as she dared toward the open door without being seen from the house.

"I came to see you," he said. "After I discovered you on Pelham's estate that day, it was easy enough to chat with a few servants to learn what was going on. Mrs Arnott does not care for you."

The feeling was mutual. "What did she tell you?"

"She told me that you were the earl's secretary," he said, obviously not believing it to be possible. "Told me that the earl himself was adamant of the title, though she had her own opinion for why the man returned from London with a penniless doxy in tow. Your skills in the bed-room must have improved considerably since I initiated you. To enchant an earl so much that he brings you to his home! And then packs you up and takes you along to London when he goes. I'm impressed."

"None of that explains why you are *here*," she ground out. "Why aren't you still in Norfolk, shooting pheasants out of the sky and getting drunk with your cronies?"

"Pheasants are flushed up from the ground, dear girl," he said, shaking his head at the idiocy of non-hunters. "That's why the beaters are hired."

"I do not care about your hunting practices, Mr Engle-field. Tell me what you want."

Hector merely stood there, one leg crossed over the other as he tapped the riding whip against his boot. "You've grown much more snappish and bitter."

"Alas. You must prefer women to be sweet as treacle and just as stupid."

He grinned, his eyes squinting into a piggish appear-ance. She may have grown bitter, but he'd grown softer. His attractiveness had been thanks to youth. A young no-bleman who is well-fed and well-raised on country air is inherently attractive to some degree…particularly to an innocent young lady.

But in only a few years, that youthful charm had fad-ed. Hector, though still wide-shouldered and trim, looked somehow less defined, less vital, as if painted by an indif-ferent artist.

"I quite liked you before," he said, "but I think I may also like you now. A bit of bite can be amusing."

"I am not here to amuse you. Tell me the purpose of your arrival here, and how soon you're leaving. It is cold out."

"And you'd like to rush back inside, where you can

enjoy the delights a mistress is accustomed to."

"That is not my title," Tamsin ground out. She was sick to death of defending her position.

"Oh, I know. You are supposedly a personal secretary. A woman! It's absurd on its face. But the earl stuck to that story when I spoke to him, so the game must amuse him as well."

"What?" she asked, feeling the cold hit her and seep into the pit of her stomach. "When did you speak to him?"

"Last night, at a party he attended. We had a pleasant conversation—well, it pleased me, because now I can claim acquaintance, and I may even call upon his lordship, as it behooves new friends to do."

She dug her nails into her palms to keep from rushing at him and pushing him into the goats' stall. Hector, coming to the townhouse though the front door? Finding ways to associate with Royce, to invite himself to dinner, or who knew what. It was unbearable to think of. "You can't come to this house."

"I can do whatever I want, Thomasina," he said with simple, infuriating truth. "But as it happens, it's not the lordship's favor I'm looking for. It's yours."

Tamsin backed away.

"Hmm, not like that." Hector's leer widened. "Though I enjoyed tupping you, and breaking in your sweet soft cunt, I don't need Pelham's leftovers."

She choked back a curse, remembering just in time that pleading her innocence with Royce was not going to save her here.

"By the way," he said then. "Was it a boy or a girl?"

"What?" she asked, bewildered by the sudden change in topic.

"The child I put in your belly, was it a boy or a girl?"

"I never bore a child," she whispered. "I grew very

sick a month after leaving your house. It was a miscarriage."

He looked at her, and then started to chuckle. "Oh, that's just grand. If you'd only kept your head about you and kept your mouth shut, nature would have solved our little problem for us!"

"What do want from me?" she asked. "Just to come back and bring up a past I never want to think about again?"

"No, what I want from you, dear girl, is one hundred pounds."

"Excuse me?" She was certain she misheard.

"One hundred pounds, or I'll tell Pelham exactly what you are...a slut who spread her legs at the first opportunity." He moved to go past her, toward the back doorway to the house.

"You will not go to Pelham!" Tamsin blocked Hector's way. She'd rather die than have Royce learn about her mistakes. "You *cannot*!"

"And how will you stop me? Offer me your body to keep me silent?"

She slapped him straight across the jaw. "I wouldn't let you touch me."

"You did before." He grinned, unmoved by her strike.

"I was young and stupid then, with much lower standards." And with the benefit of hindsight, she now knew that Hector had relentlessly maneuvered her into a sexual relationship from the start. He'd taken advantage of her ignorance and his position.

Now Hector's mouth twisted into something ugly. "I won't stand here and be insulted by some diseased woman. If you want to keep me from revealing the truth to your precious Lord Pelham, it will cost you one hundred pounds."

Entering any sort of arrangement was a mistake, but what choice did she have? Hector would provide her life story to Royce, and it would be the most despicable telling imaginable. Tamsin took a deep breath, hoping to reason with him. "Your blackmail scheme can't work, sir, because I have no money."

"But Pelham has plenty. You'll figure out some way to lay your hands on some of it...steal some silver and sell it. He won't even notice! Get one hundred pounds to me, and I'll keep our little secret. And don't protest that theft is beneath you, because we both know you'll do it in the end."

"I need time," she said, her mind spinning with the enormity of the task. One hundred pounds! It was preposterous.

"I want the money within a week," he said bluntly. "Check the personal column of the *Pall Mall Advertiser* for an entry starting with Quill. I'll tell you how and where to meet me with the money."

"I may not even be in London in a week."

"Then Pelham will be reading a full, detailed, exhaustive account of our love affair on Friday." Hector's leer grew. "In fact, I'll start writing it tonight, just in case. As a memoir, it may prove very amusing."

"Go to hell."

"Go to the newsstand, Thomasina. And then wait for my instructions." Hector opened the other door and strolled away toward the street, leaving Tamsin in near tears and shaking with rage.

After all these years, after hiding, after losing her identity and building a new one, this man waltzed back into her life and threatened to ruin the few good things left to her.

God damn all men, she thought.

She took several moments to recover her wits. Then she marched over to the alleyway door, intent on relatching it so Hector couldn't return that way. She discovered that the whole latch had been destroyed or removed, leaving only a splinted edge of the door. She stepped back, unsettled by the violence of the act. Hector would stoop very low to get to her.

A shadow darkened the already dim shed. Tamsin turned and gave a little scream, unable to deal with yet another threat.

"Lord have mercy!" Errol shouted. Then he gasped. "It's you, Miss Black? I thought you were a ghost! What are you doing in the shed, miss?"

"The door..." She gestured helplessly toward the latch. "I...I heard something and came in...and I found the door like this."

"What mischief happened here?" Errol frowned as he examined the door. "The lock's been pulled clean off. Someone's out to rob this house. *This* house!" He repeated in astonishment, as if it were unthinkable.

"Can you fix it?" she asked.

"Can and will, Miss Black. Don't you fret." He pulled a long board from a corner and wedged it against the door, preventing anyone from opening it from the alley. "You get back in the house now, miss. Leave this all to me. When I'm done, no thief will be able to set a foot on this property."

Tamsin left, hearing Errol mutter, "The earl will hear about this."

She returned to the house and told Wendy about the door. Wendy was polishing a silver teapot, and she was reminded of Hector's suggestion of petty theft to pay his blackmail.

"You all right, miss?" Wendy asked. "You look a

shade pale."

"I'm fine," she said absently. "I'll be in my room."

Upstairs, she went to her room and shut the door and paced while she tried to find a way out of this maze. Hector knew where she was. He knew that she was vulnerable. And he knew that she dared not seek any help. Certainly not from Royce.

♍

To SAY THAT ROYCE WAS upset by the news of the broken door latch would be an understatement. "You're saying that anyone could have gotten to the house at any time last night?"

"Seems to be that way, sir," Errol said, when he reported the situation a little while later. "I closed and latched the door at nine o'clock last night. So it must have happened after that. Luckily, Miss Black noticed the issue this morning. I suspect that some thieves were planning a big heist, thinking you were a fat mark being an earl and all. They got things ready last night and were going to come back late tonight, hoping to catch us all sleeping."

Royce's jaw twitched at the thought of anyone entering a house where Tamsin lay helplessly asleep. "Fix the door," he ordered.

"M'father's already on it, sir. He knows all the ways to break into a house, so he knows all the ways to stop someone breaking in too."

"I want someone to stay awake tonight. You can take shifts, but we need a watch."

"Yes, m'lord," Errol replied. "We could send for a couple more Disreputables too. They could take up places in the yard in back and the park in front."

"Excellent idea," he approved. "And when Marlow is done with the door, send him to me. I have a few items to discuss." Royce's identity as an agent of the Zodiac was a secret, so he never bothered to secure his townhome more than any other man of means did. But the timing of this event couldn't be coincidence. As soon as he started getting closer to the Viper, and as soon as he brought Tamsin to this house, someone tried to break in.

He might not value his own life very highly, but he'd be damned if anything happened to her.

The news brought by Errol spurred him to think of a test, a way to trap the Viper. He wanted to use the fact that he had access to the best forger in the city. What sort of document could he have Tamsin create in order to catch the attention of the Viper and flush him out? Something simple, but noticeable to a man who was clearly paying close attention to all the news regarding Portugal.

As Royce thought, he shuffled through the few items on his desk, including ones that Tamsin had placed there the day before. Among the papers were a few invitations to parties. Tamsin had put them in their own large envelope with the note: "Refuse as usual?"

He looked through them, expecting to tell her yes. But then one invitation caught his eye. A party at Lady Mathering's. He happened to know something about Lady Mathering's social circle, and something sparked…an audacious, even insane idea. Luckily, the Earl of Pelham was known for those.

After turning over several ideas in his mind, one in particular seemed workable. He summoned Tamsin to his study.

"Yes, my lord?" Tamsin asked when she appeared. She was dressed in a modest grey gown, and her hair was pulled back in a simple knot. She looked serene, except for a tightness around her eyes.

A couple weeks earlier, Royce wouldn't have been

able to detect the subtle signs. But now he knew some-thing was bothering Tamsin. However, he also knew that the woman would deny any troubles until the end of time.

So he merely said, "Yes, have a seat. I've got an idea to bring the Viper out into the open. And you're the key to testing it."

She paled. "You can't! I will not contact Swigg *or* Yves. If I walked into a meeting with either of them, I'd never walk out."

"Tamsin! I suggested no such thing." Did she really think he'd use her as bait?

She slowly sank back into her chair. "It's the most direct way for you to find your Viper."

"It's also far too dangerous. I'd never ask you to risk yourself that way."

Tamsin's expression was one of disbelief. "You're a spy. I'm an asset."

"You are under my protection," he reminded her. "And you're much too valuable for me to consider sending you into a...a..."

"...pit of vipers?" she asked wryly.

"I was trying to avoid that analogy." But he smiled to see her regain a bit of her spirit. "No, my plan is to have you forge a document that will get the Viper's attention. If we choose the document and the time of the reveal care-fully, I can then get one step ahead of the Viper and see what he does next. Then I'll know where and when he acts. I can catch him at that point."

After a moment, she nodded. "I can do that. What am I going to write?"

"That's not quite settled yet. Give me a few days to consult with the Zodiac and discover what materials you'll need. How fast can you write out a letter, if you haven't seen the writing before?"

She pursed her lips in thought. "Hmm, depends on the handwriting and the length of the letter. I suppose the very quickest I might do it is a half hour, but it might take longer."

"All right, I'll try to find something short and sweet."

"Why will time be a factor?" she asked. "Wouldn't you just bring the materials here?"

"No more questions, Tamsin. You have to trust me."

"You can't simply tell me?"

"That's the hell of being a master of espionage," he said. "There are a lot things I can never tell you. But one thing is always true. I'll never send you into danger alone. Understand?"

"Yes, my lord."

She rose from her chair. "I'll get back to work, then. Do you have those invitations? I'll reply to them all with your regrets."

He handed her the envelope, minus the one invitation that he kept. He'd reply to that one himself, accepting with pleasure for him and his guest.

Later that day, Marlow helped Royce dress for dinner. Royce had grown to love the hour he spent with Tamsin over the meal. He enjoyed seeing her react to foods that she'd been denied for years because of the poverty in which she'd lived. He enjoyed seeing her without papers and ink in front of her, and he wished he could justify ordering her a slew of evening gowns, instead of the single one he'd managed to include in her wardrobe.

Royce glanced in the mirror and nodded at his reflection. The best anyone could do with him, he supposed.

"That will be all, Marlow. Tell the other Disreputables to continue the watch on the house tonight. I'm still not easy about the possibility of a break-in."

Marlow nodded, but didn't leave.

"What is it?" Royce asked. "You're not usually one to keep quiet when you've got something to say."

"Well, my lord…it's like this. Wendy has been chatty today, and Miss Black happened to learn about my past."

Royce steeled himself for unpleasantness. Perhaps despite Tamsin's seeming openness, she would look upon Marlow's criminal experience with disdain. "Did she say something rude?"

"Oh, no, my lord. Far from it." Marlow smiled. "Told Wendy that sending a man to prison for a crime punished everyone around him too—family and friends who rely upon him are often forced into the very kind of activities that Society is so quick to condemn. Very kind young lady, she is."

He relaxed, and then realized how disappointed he'd have been if Tamsin had reacted the way a typical member of the *ton* undoubtedly would have.

"It's just this, my lord," Marlow continued. "Miss Black then asked me if I still knew any folk who might have access to Fleet Prison. There was someone she wanted to find there, or if he was no longer there, learn what happened to him."

Him. Jealousy rushed through Royce. "Who's this man she wanted to find?"

"The name is Thomas Latimer."

♍

THE NEXT DAY, TAMSIN STEELED herself for a visitor. Royce had mentioned casually at dinner last night that he thought Tamsin should have more than one evening dress.

Tamsin had looked at him with narrowed eyes. "Why should I need that? I thought we agreed that I'd stay here at the house and no one would ever see me."

"I see you," he countered. "And if I say I'd like you to have more gowns, what's the harm in indulging me?"

"The cost, for one."

"The cost means nothing to me." Royce smiled. "Honestly, women are supposed to jump at the chance for gifts."

"Such things are rarely *gifts*," she pointed out. "They come with strings attached." Strings that led to intimate and dangerous places. "I must remind you that I am your secretary."

"And I must remind you that I am a high-handed, moody earl who likes to get his own way. So it's not pure altruism, I admit it. I'll be able to enjoy the sight of you. Is that so wrong?"

"You are a difficult man to deal with, my lord."

"I'll take that to mean I win. A dressmaker is coming tomorrow to see about measurements. Do be nice to her— she's expensive."

In fact, she was one of the most sought-after modistes

in London. Madame Lucille was a French expatriate who fled to England following the Revolution, and she maintained an exclusive salon on an exclusive street where ladies begged for exclusive appointments. And yet, she was coming to Royce's home!

Tamsin was waiting for her, and with a shock, she realized she'd met the woman before. It was the same modiste who designed her coming out gown! Back then, Tamsin had been too young and countrified to understand that her father paid for such extravagance. No wonder the man ran into debt.

The modiste looked her over with a practiced eye. If she recognized Tamsin as the same person she designed a gown for years ago, she gave no indication of it. However, once she frowned at Tamsin, saying, "I look at you and I could swear I know you, mademoiselle."

"I've never hired you," Tamsin promised. And she was not lying—technically, her parents did, and then Royce did.

"No? An oversight on your part, for I am the best. And your figure, your coloring...yes, I can work with this."

The modiste was at least sixty, with silver hair in corkscrew curls. Her lips were pursed into a tiny pout, and she did most of her talking with expressive eyebrows as she circled Tamsin, hmm-ing and sighing to herself.

At last she declared, "Yes, I will do it. There is a princess inside you to bring out."

"Oh, please, don't go overboard on my behalf. I know Lord Pelham requested me to have a few evening gowns, but they can be quite plain. Something modest. Perhaps in grey? I don't mind grey."

"Plain. Modest. *Grey*." The modiste repeated the words with a look of one who has been shocked and deeply offended. "I am an artist, mademoiselle! I do not aspire to make my creations *plain.*"

"It's just that I'd much prefer no one look at me," Tamsin said in a rush. "Make me something you think fits my needs, and you can then concentrate your powers on other ladies' gowns."

The older lady regarded her with an appraising eyebrow that practically lifted into the heavens. "What gown will fit mademoiselle's needs? I have an idea. Yes, there is something in it."

"Oh, good. What is it?"

But the modiste waved her hand impatiently. "No questions! First I must sketch and plan. I will send the finished items to mademoiselle, who will swoon with joy to see them. Mademoiselle must trust me."

Tamsin wasn't in the habit of trusting anyone, but she had little choice in the matter.

After the modiste left, Tamsin had to do something even more unpleasant than a dress fitting. She had to steal from her employer.

She hated herself for it, especially after Royce had so kindly decided to shower her in yet more gifts. It was savage of Tamsin to take advantage of him in this way, and yet, what else could she do?

If she refused to give Hector the money, he'd tell Royce her real identity, and all about their relationship, and surely Royce's opinion of her would plummet. It was too much to hope otherwise—Tamsin had learned to distrust hope. And then Tamsin would lose the tenuous position she had. Though Royce would doubtless pay her wages, unlike Hector, the result would still leave Tamsin on the streets again, without even the network of associates in Catchpenny Lane—they'd rat her out to Coaker in a heartbeat.

And anyway, she had to stay with Royce until the matter of the Viper was resolved. "Perhaps I can pay him back someday," Tamsin told herself, then laughed in derision. One hundred pounds was her annual wage, and she'd worked for Royce for less than a month.

In Royce's study, she looked around to make sure she was utterly alone, and then closed the door. Hector suggested stealing the house's silver, which was a stupid notion. Missing silver would be noticed instantly—and blamed on the servants. However, as Royce's secretary, Tamsin had access to something that was far more valuable.

She stood at Royce's desk and pulled out a few items. Bending down, she grabbed a pen, studied Royce's signature one more time (though after weeks of sorting his correspondence, she could sign his name in her sleep). Then she wrote out a few short words and ripped the paper out of its book.

"Dear God, forgive me," she prayed, tucking the paper into the pocket tied beneath her gown. As if what she was doing could ever be forgiven. Royce literally saved her life, and she was responding with this cowardly, selfish, stupid act. For the thousandth time in her life, she wished she'd never met Hector Englefield. But wishes were for other people.

The instructions for meeting Hector appeared in Wednesday's edition of the *Pall Mall Advertiser*. God, but the man was bold, abusing his knowledge of her position to tell her where to meet and participate in his humiliation of her.

"I should bring a knife," she muttered.

"What do you need a knife for?"

Tamsin jumped, whirling around to see Royce standing there. She hadn't even heard a footstep.

"Oh, my God, I should bell you! Why are you so quiet?" she demanded, more scared than angry.

He smiled briefly, but then stepped up to her. "Why a knife, Tamsin? And where are you bringing it?"

"I was just talking to myself," she said hurriedly. "I'm not going anywhere."

"You know I don't believe you. You're a terrible liar," he said, putting his hands on her shoulders. "If you've got plans, you should let me know. I can help you."

"You cannot help me. I mean…I don't need help, because I'm not doing anything."

His expression tightened. "Your lies are getting worse by the minute."

"I wanted to get out," she gasped. "I'm getting cooped up and I was thinking of the park but I thought I ought to have a knife and yes I know that's foolish but it was what I was thinking—"

Royce's mouth came down on hers, and Tamsin ceased thinking of anything besides how shockingly good it felt to be held in his arms, and taste his lips like this. She opened her mouth, wanting more, and getting it. His kisses grew deeper, drowning out all rational protests she ought to have made.

The silk of his tongue against hers made her moan with need.

And that was when he broke off the kiss, stepping back and staring at her.

"I'm sorry," she whispered. "I don't know what came over me."

Royce said nothing. He just turned and walked away. Tamsin stood there, feeling the raw desire heating her body, and a spread of shame in her heart. At least the moment of passion distracted him from his earlier questions. Even if he was angry with her for tempting him into a kiss, he was no longer thinking about Tamsin's secret plans.

When she left the house that afternoon, out a side door, she was confident that Royce didn't see her and he certainly wouldn't follow.

Hidden under a bonnet that concealed all her features, Tamsin hurried to the meeting spot designated by Hector. Fortunately, the scoundrel chose a location fairly close by. It was a small park with a stream running through it, and several little footbridges to allow walkers to cross. On this cold and cloudy day, however, the park was scarcely populated. Tamsin walked to the bridge he'd specified, shivering in the breeze.

He was there before her, standing on the far side of the bridge, forcing her to walk over to meet him. A subtle way to prove that she was not in control of the situation.

"You kept me waiting," he complained the moment she reached him.

She ignored that, and presented him with the vital piece of paper. "Here."

"What is this?" he asked, not taking it.

"It's a banknote from my employer's bank."

He looked annoyed. "A cheque? I was expecting cash."

"Oh, well I can rip this up, then." Tamsin pinched her fingers, about to do so, but Hector plucked the banknote out of her hands.

"I'll take it."

"I hope you take the money to a tavern and drink yourself to death with it." Tamsin wore gloves, but still felt sullied by her proximity to Hector. "So. That's settled. A hundred pounds you don't deserve. I will not wish you good day, since I hope you'll drop dead."

"Don't you dare leave, Thomasina. We are not done yet."

"You can't mean to ask for more," she said aghast. "Once I may get away with, but any more than that and he'll notice, you fool. And I will be gone from his house soon enough, before he can notice that theft."

"Do you know where your father is?" Hector asked, far too casually. "Because I do."

Tamsin stopped cold. "What?"

"Your father got out of debtor's prison. He worked off most of what he owed, Lord knows how. He lives in London. And you can save him."

"Save?"

"I've thought about it, Thomasina. The Earl of Pelham doesn't care about you. If I reveal your past to him, he'll get a laugh, you'll be sent from the house, London will get a juicy story for a month, and that will be that. No, I think we need to raise the stakes."

"Raise them to what?"

"As I said, your father managed to get out of debtor's prison, but I can put him right back inside."

"How?"

"Remember, he borrowed money from me too. That's why I laughed so much when you thought you'd be paid to work as governess. He owes me a rather large amount, and I doubt he can repay it should I press the matter."

"Why didn't you present it before, along with all the other creditors?"

"What's the point of squeezing water from a stone? I decided to keep the IOU and see what other benefits I'd get from your family. And I got you, didn't I?"

Tamsin turned her head away. "You disgust me. And I don't understand why you're bringing up old history."

"It's not old at all. The IOU can be brought up at any time—your father still owes me."

"Then ask him for the money."

"I'd rather ask you. And if you refuse, not only will I present the contract, I'll also tell your *father* exactly what occurred between us while you were governess. How shamefully you behaved, how lusty and naughty, how you got yourself with child but then never gave birth to that child. Curious! I've been thinking about that. One wonders if you paid a doctor to take your troubles away."

"I told you that I miscarried," Tamsin said harshly, remembering the horror and pain of the night it happened, and her mingled relief and regret—relief for herself, regret for a child lost, and for all the decisions that led to that moment.

"What is the word of a slut worth? I can press for payment from your father, which will land him back at Number Nine Fleet Market, and I can bring charges of abortion against you, which will get you in prison…or the gallows, depending on what the doctor says."

"What doctor?"

"The doctor I pay to tell the tale. Or you can pay me two hundred pounds to keep silent."

"Is this how you live?" Tamsin hissed. "By blackmailing people?"

He shrugged. "I press the advantages I have. That's how one succeeds in the world."

"You're a liar and a cheat and I hate you."

"Two hundred pounds, Thomasina. Do be sure to read *Pall Mall Advertiser* daily."

"I *despise* you," she spat.

He grinned. "I don't care what you think of me, Thomasina. You're nothing."

* * * *

Tamsin spent the next three days in an agony of waiting, reading the newspaper, wondering when Hector would contact her again. She snuck into Royce's study when he was out, and practiced his handwriting and signature. She hated herself all the while, but the fear of Hector's reprisals left her unable to refuse him. If it were true that her father was out of Fleet Prison, then Tamsin would do anything to keep him out.

Including stealing from the man she loved.

No, it's not love. Tamsin shied away from that word. Love was for innocent people. She liked and admired Royce. She was deeply grateful to him. She felt her breath snag every time he smiled. And the few times he'd forgotten himself and kissed her...

"Oh, Lord help me," she whispered. Why deny it? Tamsin was utterly in love with Royce. It was a stupid, useless love, but it was there all the same. She couldn't ever let him know how she felt. He was above her in station. He was her employer. He was working on the right side of the war, while she'd only helped the enemy.

So Tamsin tried to stick to her duties as a personal secretary, and not allow herself to fall deeper into the emotional pit she teetered on the edge of.

"Just stay till the Viper is captured," she told herself one day, while brooding in the library. "And then you'll collect your wages and leave this house."

"Miss Black, there you are."

She turned in her seat to see Marlow there. He approached her and gave a little bow. "The man you were looking for is no longer in Fleet Prison, but he is in London. Here is his street direction." He handed her a slip of paper.

"Oh, my goodness." Tamsin's heart thumped once as she saw her father's name and location written so plainly. In the span of a week, Marlow had managed what she couldn't find out in over a year…and he didn't ask for a thing in payment. "You're certain of this?"

"Indeed, miss. My sources are very reliable." He paused. "Now that you have the information, what do you plan to do with it? Visit him? I can call for the lord's carriage."

"Oh, no!" She gasped. "Absolutely not. That would never do."

"Why not, miss?"

"Because I don't know if he'd even want to see me." Tamsin wondered what her father had already been told about her behavior. If he knew the facts of what happened at the Englefield home even without Hector announcing it (servant gossip being what it was), he'd be too ashamed of Tamsin to speak to her again. "He might prefer it if I were dead."

"Can't see anyone wishing that, miss." Marlow glanced at the clock. "You'll be wanting some tea this afternoon. I'll have Wendy bring you a tray."

"Thank you…and Marlow, please don't mention this to the earl."

He bowed and gave her a little smile.

Wendy came in a little while later, but she wasn't holding a tea tray. She was holding a large box. "Miss, your order came in from the dressmaker! I'll bring it up to your room, but I thought you'd want to see it right away."

Tamsin followed the maid upstairs, more amused by Wendy's excitement than out of real enthusiasm. After all, she'd told the modiste that a plain gown would do.

Wendy opened the box and pulled aside the wrapping muslin to reveal a pile of silky material in the brightest shade of red imaginable.

"There's been some mistake," Tamsin said immediately. "The wrong dress was sent here. We'll have to send it back.... Are those feathers?"

Wendy had pulled out what looked like *wings*.

"I don't understand," Tamsin said. "What is in this box?"

"It's your outfit for the party tonight." But it wasn't Wendy who spoke.

Tamsin turned to see Royce in the doorway. She echoed, "Party? Are you mad? I told you that I will not go anywhere, whether it's among Society or among the common people. I can't afford to be seen."

He smiled. "That's the best part. It's a masquerade. No one will hear your name and no one will see your face. I know you want to go out. You hate being all cooped up."

"I cannot. They'd never let me in."

"Anyone *I'm* with will go anywhere they like," Royce replied. His voice was cool—the voice of a true aristocrat who lived by a different set of rules than the rest of Society.

He turned to Wendy. "Make sure Miss Black doesn't run away before you can dress her. We leave at eight o'clock."

Before Tamsin could protest, Royce strolled away.

Of course, Tamsin did not run away, though her stomach threatened to leave her body several times. She'd never been so nervous.

But Wendy very capably took over and saw to it that Tamsin was bathed and oiled, her hair washed and dried and styled into a mass of auburn curls, and finally dressed in the creation of Madame Lucille.

Tamsin looked nervously at her reflection. "Oh, no." When she thought that the modiste was there to make her a simple evening gown, she'd requested one that was not too showy, something that would allow her to blend into the background, to be ignored.

For this costume, the modiste had made her a phoenix.

The gown was the color of fire, petals of sheer silk dyed in rich reds, oranges, ochres, even greens and blues. Thanks to a lacy, stiffly constructed underskirt, the gown belled out more than was typical for fashion, but it helped bolster the image of a bird being reborn from the ashes.

Tamsin turned to view the wings that had been made to slide over her shoulders: like angel wings, but again, colored like fire, all gold and blazing orange.

The mask was feathered as well, and covered all her face except for her mouth and chin. There was a little jar packed in with the mask, and a note: "While ladies of course never wear paints, you must apply this to your lips to complete the costume. Do not fail me."

She laughed, somewhat hysterically. Madame Lucille took her creations seriously.

When Wendy declared her ready, she went downstairs, wearing the mask and feeling distinctly awkward about the bright red color on her lips.

Royce stood at the bottom of the stairs. He was in costume as a pirate from the previous century, and he looked wonderfully debonair in the old-fashioned flared boots, formfitting pants, and a white shirt left untied at the neck, allowing a peek at his bare chest—a look that would otherwise never be permitted in a ballroom. He even had a black tricorn hat. He only had a simple black silk half mask, which left the lower half of his face exposed. Those who knew Royce would not be fooled, but then, he was not the person trying to hide.

He stared at her, his mask dangling from his hand. "You look…astonishing."

"I think everyone will stare at me."

"That's the idea, I'm sure. You're going to get a lot of attention."

"But what will I do?"

"Have fun. Be mysterious. Lie to people. That's essentially what a spy does."

"Oh, Royce. This is a bad idea. I'll stay home."

"No." He took her hand. "This is the one night that you can be yourself. Because no one will know who you are, and you can get away with nearly anything. Shall we go, Miss Black?" He offered his arm. "We can take the carriage, or I can steal a ship for you."

"That would make for a memorable entrance...but only if the party is taking place by the river."

"The carriage it is, then. Mind your wings." He helped her step into the carriage, and followed her. Then they were off.

♍

ROYCE HAD NEVER DREAMED TAMSIN would look so spectacular, and he couldn't wait to show her off, even if no one would know who she was.

The arrival of Lord Pelham made waves at the party. Though it was a masquerade, people still seemed to recognize him instantly, and they clearly expected him to perform some outlandish stunt like the ones he'd been known for before he became earl.

And indeed, he started the evening off with a bang, holding his old-fashioned firearm aloft at the top of the stairs.

"Ahoy!" he called, sweeping his hat off his head, bowing extravagantly. "I have returned from the roughest voyage on the seven seas with the greatest prize imaginable. I present to you the fabled phoenix!"

Cheers and laughter erupted below, as guests appreciated the spectacle of Tamsin's costume.

Under her mask, Tamsin glared at him. "What are you doing? They'll all see me now!"

"Curtsey, darling. Yes, they'll see you…as a phoenix who belongs to me. Your real identity is irrelevant now."

He escorted her down the stairs into the crush. Guests instinctively made space for her, perhaps due to the huge feathered wings springing from her back.

He leaned down and murmured, "You're the most

beautiful creature here, love. And the most mysterious. Enjoy yourself."

"I've never danced in wings," she muttered back.

"Then dance with me first."

Before the dancing, there was the chatting and the drinking and the endless speculation about who was who. Of course, several people knew who Royce was, but he enjoyed their guesses regarding Tamsin's identity.

"Even I don't know her name," he once said with wry truthfulness. "She is unknowable, and I'm just grateful she chose to grace me with her company tonight."

"Oh, a hint," one gentleman pleaded. "At least tell us if she's spoken for! For such a beauty, I would overlook a meager dowry."

"She is most certainly spoken for," Royce snapped back. Then he smiled, catching himself. "At least for the first dance!"

The music was just starting up and the floor cleared for the next portion of the evening. Royce secured his place beside Tamsin. And as it turned out, she danced perfectly well in wings, and there was no hint in her bearing that she'd missed the last several Seasons while hiding in Catchpenny Lane.

Partners changed several times, and by the end of the first set, Royce was at his quota for feminine companions not named Tamsin.

Fortunately, Tamsin's phoenix costume made it easy to sight her, even across the ballroom. He crossed the space as quickly as he could. "There's my beautiful prize," he said loudly enough for the onlookers to hear. He took her hand and kissed the backs of her fingers, just as he'd do if he were courting her.

Behind the mask, Tamsin's eyes widened, and he suddenly wished he could take that mask off...along with everything else she wore. He leaned over to her and whispered, "It's getting crowded in here. Come upstairs with me."

The party was certainly growing wilder than most he'd attended lately. The aspect of anonymity, plus the punch, lowered inhibitions for all the guests.

Still, to walk toward the bedrooms in the company of a man was step beyond for Tamsin, and she shook her head. "I can't do that!"

"Yes you can. I need you to forge something."

"Here? At a party?" she asked.

"Why else do you think I brought you, darling?" He smiled, hoping that his teasing tone hid his very real desire.

He told Tamsin to wait a moment, and then walk up the stairs and turn left to walk down the south gallery. "I'll meet you there."

Then he left her, moving through the crowd with a flamboyant air, pausing to compliment ladies and speak to gentlemen—he knew nearly everyone, or at least he was bold enough to act as if he did. His training as a spy helped him push away his normal feelings and playact as Royce Holmes, the fun-loving lord who never took anything seriously.

He glanced behind him once, happy to see that Tamsin was nowhere to be found. He was distracting attention from her, so she could slip toward the stairs and away.

A moment later, Royce wished he had someone to distract attention from him. A few young ladies angled subtly for a dance or an introduction. A few older ladies angled for a more intimate association, one even asking what sort of booty he was interested in. But he evaded them all and managed to escape.

Compared to the ballroom below, the south gallery

was cool and quiet. He breathed a sigh of relief, but then immediately felt exposed. If he or Tamsin were found up here, there would be questions. He proceeded down the hall to a spot where a sconce had gone out, leaving the area in shadow. Tamsin was hiding in an alcove there, her red gown dimmed to burgundy, her wings shadowed.

"Follow me," Royce said, keeping his voice low. "We've only got a little time."

She followed him wordlessly to a closed door. Royce pulled out a key and opened it swiftly.

"How do you have access to a room in this house?" she demanded.

"You don't want to know, darling."

"Whose room is this?" She looked around, seeing what was obviously a man's bedchamber.

"It belongs to a man named Pearson, a diplomat in contact with the Royal Court of Portugal in exile. He's a close personal friend of Lady Mathering. He often stays here while he's in town, though he spends most of his life abroad. He's very well connected throughout the courts of Europe."

"I begin to understand," Tamsin said. "So tonight was not merely a test of my comfort with social events."

"Alas, no." He thrust a piece of paper at her. "Sit at the desk. Study Pearson's handwriting and then write out this text in his style. Use a piece of the stationery marked with his crest. Should be in the top drawer of the desk."

Royce, with the guidance of the Zodiac, had drafted a false letter that suggested the Portuguese court would move back from Brazil in the next three months, specifically to show that Portugal was safe from Napoleon, and that naval forces would regroup closer to Lisbon as a precautionary move. He expected that the letter (coming from a supposedly unimpeachable source) would anger the Viper and force him into a more foolish action.

"Royce, I can't do this with so little time! I need to study and practice…"

"You've got less than half an hour, darling. Sit down and get to work. I'll keep watch at the door."

"What good will that do? By the time you see someone coming down the corridor, we won't have time to escape."

"Definitely not," he agreed. "But we will have time for me to throw you on the bed and make it look like our interest in this room is far different than it really is."

Tamsin's cheeks went red-hot at the suggestion, and she hurried to the desk.

He went to the door, keeping it cracked just enough that he could look down the corridor and see anyone approaching. He'd "borrowed" the key from Mr Pearson's pocket when they spoke earlier this evening, and he'd have to return it promptly. Tonight's deception depended on the man remaining unaware that his handwriting was being used for a forgery.

He glanced at Tamsin, noting that she sat frozen at the desk.

"Tamsin?" Royce whispered. "Are you all right?"

"No, I'm terrified!"

"There's nothing to be scared of, darling. Just do what you do best. I'm here."

Tamsin inhaled deeply, and shook herself. Royce wanted to be standing there with her, but he instead focused on the hallway.

Once a giggling couple appeared, trying door handles in their quest for a more private spot to conduct their tryst. Royce closed the door and twisted the key in the lock just moments before they reached it and rattled the knob.

It was nerve-racking, and he remained completely

still. Tamsin looked like a startled deer, and he held his finger to his lips.

Then the couple passed on, found an open door, and disappeared, though the sounds of their lovemaking filtered through to the hallway.

One cry of passion made him want to toss Tamsin on that bed. The image of her lying there, wearing nothing but red-feathered wings, nearly undid him.

He clenched his jaw and eased the door open again, watching for danger.

After what seemed like an hour, he asked. "Are you done?"

"No! Don't bother me!"

He bit his lip, and then heard a new sound…heavy footfalls.

"Hurry up," he urged. "Someone's coming."

"I need more time!"

He listened to the sounds outside, and felt his body preparing to fight when he recognized Pearson's voice.

"*Hurry*, Tamsin. It's him."

"I can't hurry," she protested.

"Then destroy it and get to the bed."

"Destroy it? I'm so close—"

"Hush!"

Pearson wasn't alone. He was chatting with another man, though Royce couldn't hear words.

Thirty feet.

Royce pulled the key out of the door, pocketing it. With luck, he could drop it somewhere, perhaps make Pearson think he'd lost it earlier.

Twenty feet. He pushed the door shut, blocking his sightline, but maintaining his hearing post by the keyhole.

Royce gestured for Tamsin to get up and move away from the desk. The desk was the one piece of furniture she couldn't be found near.

Ten feet. Pearson name was reaching for the key he no longer had. Time was up.

Then a lady's voice called, "My dear Mr Pearson! You must come and meet Lady Susan. She's just arrived and it's a crime you don't know each other! Come now!"

Pearson sighed and turned around, dragging his companion with him. "It'll keep, sir. But you should read the particulars…"

Royce let out a silent breath as the voices faded down the corridor. He glanced back.

Tamsin stood between the desk and the bed, holding a letter in her hands.

"It's done," she said.

He saw that she was shaking. He pulled the key out and locked the door once more before striding over to her.

"Fold it, and address it to…here." He indicated a street direction for a government building that the Viper had stolen items from before. "Then just put it on the tray there with his other letters. He won't even notice, and it will go out with the next post."

"And we hope Yves will snatch it soon after?"

"Precisely."

She nodded and quickly carried out his orders. Royce then escorted her from the room, locking the door behind.

"So the subterfuge with the bed wasn't necessary," she said, back in the ballroom.

"Alas," he murmured. Elation flooded through him. They'd accomplished everything Royce hoped to do at the party, and Tamsin even looked like she enjoyed herself, which he considered a bonus.

Then she froze. She stared at a merry, bellicose, and rather drunk Roman soldier across the room. "Oh, no," she whispered.

"What is it?" Royce asked.

"Let's go," she urged him. "It's very late."

"You just said you were having a good time. I wanted to dance with you again."

"Royce, please. I can't stay here." She glanced at the Roman soldier again, fear in her eyes. "I need to get out to here."

He regarded her for a moment, then nodded. "Whatever you say."

Royce took her by the elbow and escorted her out of the ballroom, toward the front hall. Tamsin was stiff as marble, her normally full lips pinched and her skin white.

Royce said nothing until they got into his carriage. Then he whipped the pirate hat off and leaned back. "What the hell happened to you in there? It was day and night."

"I saw someone."

That was all she said, and Royce didn't press her to tell more. Her breathing was erratic, too close to sobbing.

"I'm fine," she said preemptively.

"Liar."

Tamsin bit her lip. "Yes! I'm so sorry." She inhaled, with the sort of sound that heralded a flood of tears.

Royce moved beside her, pulling her into his arms. "Don't, Tamsin. You don't have to tell me anything. So you saw someone from your past that you'd rather not see again. The details don't matter now. You're out of there. He never saw you...not that he'd recognize you in your costume anyway."

"I didn't say it was a man."

"I guessed," he said dryly.

"Royce, I've done something terrible," she said. "I shouldn't tell you, but I have to, even though you'll hate me for it...."

But Royce didn't let her go on. "I've done terrible things too, love. And probably with less justification."

Tamsin looked up at him, her eyes haunted. "What I've done is unforgivable. It's—"

He kissed her, cutting off her confession.

She responded with a desperate fury, twining her arms around him and pushing her body against his. Or he grabbed her and pulled her to him…it was impossible to tell in the moment. All was a tangle of shadows and silk, masks and murmured promises.

They arrived home all too soon. Still in his piratical mood, Royce growled a simple order that he and Tamsin weren't to be disturbed that night. Then he slipped an arm around her waist and escorted her upstairs. He directed her to his room, and she went without a protest.

Inside, she said only, "This was bound to happen, wasn't it?"

"Inevitable," he agreed. "Get rid of the mask, Tamsin. I like you better without it."

She took it off, and stood there before him, as wary and as beautiful as the first night he'd seen her. "I've taken my mask off, my lord. Will you do me the same honor? I think I've earned it."

She'd more than earned it. He wanted to remove not just the mask, but everything he had on. He wanted Tamsin to see him. And he wanted to see her.

"Well, the masks are gone. What shall we remove next?"

♍

TAMSIN WAS ENSNARED BY THE expression on Royce's face, challenging and sensual.

"I...I can't get this gown off by myself," she whispered. And she'd be damned if she asked for help from Wendy, who would then know exactly what was going on!

"I'll help you," he murmured.

Tamsin turned to allow him to undo the costume. His hands were gentle, loosening the bodice until she had to hold it up with her arms to prevent the whole thing from sliding in a heap to the floor.

"You can step out of it," he told her, his voice a rasp.

She took a breath, and then did so, very carefully, mindful of the expense of the outfit. Underneath she wore the thin cotton chemise cut tight to keep the lines of the costume clean. That meant her body was obvious underneath the fabric, with no pleats or ruffles to obscure the view.

Royce inhaled at the sight. "Turn around," he said.

She put aside the costume, then did so. He took her face in his hands and kissed her, hard. Tamsin's knees almost buckled, she was so consumed with need for him. He urged her to open her mouth, to let him deepen the kiss.

She did, clinging to him like she was drowning. Only

when she broke off to take a desperately needed breath did she say, "Wait, Royce. You don't want to do this. You don't really know who or what I am—"

Suddenly, he pushed her back onto the desk, so she sat on the edge of it. He leaned over her and grabbed something, saying, "I'm done with this nonsense about how I don't know you."

He took the pen and held her arm steady, writing her name on the soft skin of her inner wrist. She felt the nib scraping over the skin, and enjoyed the near-pain it caused. Royce smiled. "There. Tamsin." Then he underlined the last half of her name. "Interesting. You can't spell Tamsin without *sin*."

She laughed despite herself. "You're indefatigable."

"Now there's a word." He handed her the pen. "If you can spell it, I dare you to write it."

Tamsin took the pen, and took the challenge as well. She wrote *indefatigable* along his arm, noting that somehow he'd rolled the sleeve up while she was distracted.

He took the pen back, then touched it to her cheek. "Hold still," he told her.

Tamsin held herself breathless, feeling the nib of the pen slide against her skin. Royce looked intent; his gaze never wavered as he wrote the word.

"What did you label me as now?" she asked when he finished.

"Lady."

She swallowed, unexpectedly moved by that simple declaration. But then she said, "You ought to cross it out. It's not true anymore."

"Would you like to retaliate?" He offered her the pen, but then took it back when she reached for it. "I'll let you write whatever you want…if you write it while we're on the bed."

Tamsin slid off the desk and snatched the pen out of his hand, walking past him to the bed. She kept her stride even, as if she were not trembling inside at the thought of what else was going to happen on the bed...and how much she wanted it to happen.

She sat on the edge of the bed, noting the softness of the covers. Then she looked back at Royce, and her jaw dropped.

He was naked. While she'd been strutting over to the bed, he'd taken the next step to ensure that she would not be changing her mind, because she now had the desire to write on every magnificent inch of him.

"That was fast," she said, her words breathy.

"I want you have your pick of where to write," he told her with a smile.

And then he was stretching himself onto the bed, lying down on his stomach, offering his body to her for a canvas. "Well?" he asked after a moment. "What word describes me now?"

Tamsin dipped the pen into the ink, then bent over Royce's shoulder. She wrote the word *chivalrous* on his back, enjoying the way his muscles reacted to the scratch of the pen nib.

"What did you write?" he asked.

She told him, and he laughed, delighted. "My turn again."

He rid her of the thin chemise, leaving her naked too. Then he had her lie down, writing something on her back...something much longer than a word.

"What are you doing?"

"Hush, Tamsin. Poetry is a serious business."

Poetry? He was suddenly scrawling love poetry on her body? Perhaps things were getting out of hand. *You're naked in the bed of an earl who's also a spy*, she reminded herself. *Things have been out of your hands for quite a while.*

"I'm done," he announced. "Shall I recite it?"

"Please."

So he recited, in a very serious, loving tone:

I know a young lady named Tamsin

Whose existence is as erotic as sin,

Her body stiffens my cock.

Is it the key to her lock?

When she screams my name, I'll know it fits in.

Tamsin bit her lip against laughing and closed her eyes. "Oh, a limerick. Such masterful poetry can only be the result of an Eton education."

"It could need revision. I'm not sure it scans quite right."

"You didn't really write *that* on me."

"Every word."

"Royce!"

"What? It's all true."

"Perhaps, but now I'm covered in bad poetry!"

"Oh, I've thought of another word." He made Tamsin sit up, and wrote across her thigh in huge letters: *siren.*

"You keep calling me that, yet not once have I enticed you to run aground on the shore where I'm singing."

"Can you sing?" he asked, looking curious.

"Not a note. I was the despair of the local music tutor."

Royce lifted the pen and drew the feathery end across her mouth. "I bet I can make you sing."

She smiled. "You don't know what you're asking."

He leaned forward, his lips replacing the feather. If it were possible to become drunk off a kiss, Tamsin now was. Her head swam as she responded greedily to him, her mouth to his. Their tongues tangled and then Tamsin gasped when she felt the teasing stroke of the feather drawn across her breasts. Her nipples tightened in response and she clutched at Royce's hip. She caught a glimpse of his expression, amused and hungry all at once.

"How long has it been for you?" she asked suddenly.

"I'm not choosing you out of desperation, Tamsin," he assured her. "I would not have pursued you this doggedly if all I wanted was a warm body in my bed for a night."

He flicked the feather toward her, this time aiming for her torso. Tamsin closed her eyes, feeling the delicate ends of the plume across her skin, teasing and soft. She smiled. "Keep going."

Royce inhaled, and the feather twirled across her stomach to her hips, and then along the sensitive flesh of her inner thigh.

"Oh," she moaned, instinctively parting her legs, allowing him access to more of her skin.

He made a sound of deep satisfaction, but said nothing. He only continued to tease her with the delicate plume, barely grazing her skin, making her concentrate on every little sensation, or be very surprised where the feather touched her next.

And then the feather brushed her somewhere very unexpected, and Tamsin let out a little cry of surprise and pleasure.

Royce's hand gripped her knee tightly, and she knew he was as aroused by this play as she was. The feather touching her most sensitive parts was maddening, the definition of teasing.

She thrust her hips in reaction, needing more than this too-light, too-soft feather could provide.

Then Royce shifted, bending down, and the dry tickle

of the feather was gone, replaced by— "Oh, *god*," she moaned.

His tongue. Where the feather teased, his tongue satisfied. He licked her without restraint, sending jolts of pure, shocking pleasure through her body. She cried out again, louder, his name forming on her lips.

Tamsin's back arched as her hands came down to the crown of his head, her fingers running through the thick, wavy hair.

Her toes curled, and she tensed up, her body overwrought by the wicked strokes of his tongue.

"Royce, finish me," she moaned, hardly knowing what she was saying.

His mouth came over the rigid, sensitive nub he'd been lapping at, and Tamsin inhaled as he sucked hard against her body. She twisted her head to the side to bury the short scream that erupted from her throat.

Heat burst through her, a damp, heady warmth that left her muscles pliant and her heart hammering. She took several ragged breaths before she realized that Royce had moved up and was pulling her into his arms. He kissed the top of her head, and she pressed her lips against his neck. She was too devastated to know what to say or do. No man had ever done such things to her before.

Royce wrapped his arms around her, cradling her.

"Did you like my tongue?" he asked softly. "Do you want me to do that again?"

She nodded, tears pricking her eyes. To feel that wonderful again…of course she wanted it.

"Have I finally rendered you speechless, Tamsin?" He pulled away enough to see her face. "Or are you just bored?"

"Definitely not bored," she promised. "It's been a night of firsts. First writing on skin lesson, first feather torture, first…time a man tasted me like that," she finished, embarrassed that she lacked the vocabulary to describe what happened.

Surprise crossed his features, but then he smiled slyly. "Not the last. You were meant to be pleasured. Listening to you is the only aphrodisiac I need."

Oh, lord. Tamsin realized that while she was flushed and sated, Royce was still very much aroused. His cock lay against her thigh, hard and thick.

She bit her lip. "It's time, isn't it? I mean, you do want to…um…" She trailed off.

Royce chuckled. "For a voluble, outspoken woman, you go silent at the most interesting times. And the answer is yes. I want to make you just as gorgeously undone as before, but with my cock inside you while you wrap your legs around me and beg me to finish you again."

"Oh." At his words, Tamsin felt her body stirring into excitement. How was that possible? She'd been shattered only moments ago. "I want that too."

"Are you sure?"

"You want a written invitation?" Tamsin suddenly twisted, sitting up to look for the errant pen. She found it, and lunged over Royce to dip the nib in the ink well.

She found a blank patch on his upper arm, and wrote her invitation, narrating as she did. "Tamsin cordially requests the presence of Royce in her body, on this night, to celebrate the discovery of her sinful, lustful nature. RSVP."

He took the pen out of her hand, and sat up to meet her gaze. "I am honored to accept your invitation," he murmured.

Tamsin's breath came out in a rush. "Good. I'd…I'd like to lie down."

"Of course."

He drew her down, pushing her back onto the soft sheets. He moved over her, dipping his head to kiss her deeply.

Tamsin reached up to touch him, reveling in the male beauty of his body, the taut muscles and the breadth of his chest.

They moved together quickly, both of them eager, too eager to be graceful about it. Tamsin shifted her body to accommodate his, and kept finding reasons to run her fingers through his hair, which she'd decided suited him perfectly.

Royce touched her gently between her legs, teased the moisture out of her, and then positioned himself to enter her.

She caught his gaze and nodded once. He pushed into her, and instead of the regret she feared she'd feel, all was wonder. Wonder that this man could fit her so perfectly, wonder that she was still so needy after the things he'd already done to her.

When he slid one hand to her bottom, lifting her up a little, she moaned at the sudden rush of heat she felt.

She gasped and clutched at his shoulders. "Royce, what are you doing?"

"Helping you find an angle you like. You think everyone has an angle. I want to find the angle that makes you come undone."

Tamsin's breath threatened to stop altogether. "Oh my, that's a perfect...angle."

He held her there as he drove into her. She'd never felt quite like this—touching herself brought relief, but this was entirely different. Because he was there, inside her and holding her to him, and needing her just as much as she needed him.

"Royce," she moaned, as her orgasm broke over her.

Tamsin's body seemed to blossom into pure light. She wanted him to feel that too.

But then he was withdrawing, pulling out and away from her. Before she could say anything, could ask why he stopped, she understood.

Royce bit his lip as he spent himself on the bedsheets, rather than in Tamsin's body. Then he rolled onto his back, his chest rising and falling as he recovered his breath.

"God damn, Tamsin. That...was not easy, leaving you."

"But you did it anyway," she said softly.

He looked at her and then reached one hand to touch her cheek. Tamsin blinked back tears, undone by the tenderness in that gesture. Why should that little move render her helpless?

"Are you crying?" He leaned on one elbow, his expression worried. "Did I hurt you?"

"No! Just the opposite. You're really far too nice to me."

"Should I be less considerate, then?" he asked, clearly confused. "I should have thought you'd be wanting some consideration."

"Oh, God, Royce. I want so much, and I just never thought I'd get any of it." Tamsin wiped a stray tear off her cheek. "Don't listen to me. I'm obviously addled after all that...um..."

He grinned. "Um? You define one of the best activities two humans can engage in, our first night in bed together, a session of lovemaking that included not one but two orgasms—not counting my own slightly lonely one—as *um?*"

"I should have just kept my mouth shut."

"I like your mouth open." He kissed her then, and as

his tongue teased hers, she had to agree she liked it too.

He drew her down to lie against him, kissing her all the while, running his hands over her back and hips as if he'd never get enough. Tamsin put her head on his chest, reveling in the sound of his breathing, and subtler sound of his heartbeat, solid and steady.

"Go to sleep," he told her, the words rumbling though her as her ear was pressed to his body. "We're both going to need it, because I am not done with you tonight."

♍

TAMSIN AWOKE IN DARKNESS. HER bare skin was wrapped in the finest bed linens she'd ever touched, and next to her, Royce lay asleep, his breathing deep and even.

She rolled over and reached to the bedside table to light a candle. Lord, she'd completely lost her head and given in to her most base desires—as stoked by the incredibly, sinfully attractive Royce.

The candle flame rose up and illuminated the bed. Tamsin gasped—the sheets were splotched with ink stains and ghosts of words. Royce's body was just as messy, the bold black ink in Tamsin's own handwriting covering him with praises. She looked down at her own skin, and traced the smudged letters *S-I-R-E-N* on her thigh. Royce had called her a siren that first night they met. She knew it was because she was so soaked with rain that she looked like she'd emerged from the sea. But perhaps it was also because he saw her in a way no one else did.

Oh, no, my girl, she warned herself. Falling for Royce was not an option. Last night was an aberration, a one-time failure to keep her distance, to keep their relationship impersonal.

She closed her eyes, remembering how he'd demolished all her barriers, removing her excuses along with her clothes. The way he'd teased her with the feather pen, and then how he'd ripped her heart open with the words he'd written on her body.

"Tamsin."

She looked over her shoulder to see Royce, awake and alert. He reached out one hand and touched her hip. The mere contact of his fingertips on her skin made her shiver with desire.

"You're cold," he said, mistaking the cause. "Come over here and warm up. It's not anywhere close to morning."

"I can't sleep."

He smiled. "We don't have to sleep."

"We've made a terrible mess," she said.

"It's just ink."

"Royce, I don't mean the sheets. Though the sheets are done for too. They won't be able to use them as rags —"

He kissed her, his lips brushing against hers until she gasped at the sensations running along her veins.

"You make a beautiful mess," he told her. "I'm going to remember this night until the day I die."

"You don't usually scrawl all over your lovers?"

"What lovers? You are unique, Tamsin. I haven't written a tenth of the words I think of when I see you."

She traced one of the words she'd written on him. "I can think of a few others as well."

"Come over here," he beseeched, pulling her on top of him.

She straddled his hips, noticing that he was growing aroused once more. Boldly, she ran her fingers over him. "You're insatiable, my lord."

"Call me *my lord* in this bed, and I'll make you regret it," he growled.

"How, exactly?"

With a sudden movement, he flipped her onto her back, covering her with his body as he pinned her arms above her head. "I'll think of something," he warned, though his expression held only desire, not danger. "I may keep you chained to the bed. How would you like that?"

"It doesn't sound much like a punishment," she purred. Indeed, when Royce said it, it sounded exciting... even erotic. "That is, if you visited me in bed."

"I don't see how I could stay away." He kissed her long and slow.

Tamsin moaned, wishing her hands were free so she could stroke him. "Let me go. I want to touch you."

"Hmm, not just yet. I like this, with you wrapping your pretty legs around me."

She hadn't realized until that moment that she'd done just that, eager to keep him close to her.

His cock pressed against her center, already grown hot and slick.

"Tamsin, are you ready for me again? I want to take you like this, pinned to the bed, with your hair wild."

In reply, Tamsin twined her legs tight around him, all but begging him to enter her right now.

When he did, she let out a huge sigh.

He thrust within her, drawing out moans from them both. "Tamsin, why do I need you so badly?"

"Not for my penmanship," she guessed, only to receive a biting kiss in response.

He thrust harder. "I find your penmanship exquisite. Just like your breasts and your hips and your legs and all the rest of you, beautiful."

Tamsin gasped as the pleasure built up within her. "Royce, more."

"Hell, yes, my love."

He moved steadily, driving into her with an almost

violent force, but never moving beyond pleasure into pain.

She welcomed the roughness of it, wanting to feel everything Royce was giving her. She came undone, locking her legs around him as her body seemed to contract. The sensations were exquisite, and she wanted to pull him even closer, to keep him with her for all of it.

But then Royce pushed her down roughly, causing her to cry out in confusion and hurt. He was withdrawing, his face taut with anger.

What had she done? Tamsin sat up, only to see Royce kneel and hunch over, his upper body not quite hiding his hand on his cock, gripping it hard as he came.

"Oh," she said, understanding and feeling idiotic that she didn't think of it before. Royce's violent move had been one of desperation. Her peak had forced his own, and he didn't want to spill inside her.

He gave a groan as he straightened up again. "Almost too late."

"I'm sorry," she said.

Royce shook his head, then lay beside her and held her close in an embrace. "God damn, Tamsin. You drive me to do things I never thought I'd do. I haven't lusted after a woman like this since I was a randy boy just out of school."

"I've never lusted after a man like this," she admitted. "It's like a curse. As soon as it's done, I want to begin again."

"Oh, sweetheart, you read my mind."

She held him tightly to her, loving the contact of his skin against hers, their flesh hot and slippery with sweat. After a few minutes, Tamsin said, "I wish I could have a bath. I'll never be able to get this ink off and explain it away to Wendy."

He smiled down at her. "That's a wish I can grant. Now stay here. I'll be back in a moment."

Tamsin protested as he left the bed, but then yawned and closed her eyes, her body thoroughly sated.

A second later, Royce leaned over. "Wake up, siren."

"I wasn't asleep!"

"Oh yes you were. But you've got to get up now and come with me. We don't want the water to get cold."

"The water?"

Tamsin allowed Royce to lead her to a room adjacent to his suite. It was tiled floor to ceiling, and looked like a roman bath. Instead of a metal tub, there was a tiled pool in the center, filled with steaming hot water. It was probably large enough to accommodate six people, but she had a hunch that Royce kept it for a solitary retreat...until now.

"An earl does live extravagantly," she said, amazed at the sight.

"This earl does." He pointed to one end. "There are three steps down. Walk carefully. I refuse to rescue you if you drown."

Tamsin descended into luxuriously hot water, sighing as the heat worked its way into her muscles. "This is heaven," she said.

"It is now," he agreed, suddenly standing beside her, his naked body temptingly close. "I had this room built so I could recover after assignments. Some of them left me half dead. But I've never had a beautiful woman with me before. I like it better."

Tamsin allowed him to pull her down into the water, up to their necks. She'd piled her hair on her head before going in, and Royce kissed her exposed neck over and over.

Then he washed her.

He ran the sponge over her body, the warm water sliding over her flesh in a silken caress. She inhaled the scent of whatever soap he used—something rich and spicy, of course. No pale florals for a man's bath. This smelled of clove and incense. Like him. Now she knew why she always thought of rare spices when she was near him.

"The ink will make the water dirty," she said, slashing at the surface.

"Then I'll draw another bath," he responded, a laugh in his tone. "As many as required."

"You're nothing if not thorough," she agreed.

Royce slipped his hand between her legs. "It's one of my strongest traits. I don't like to leave anything incomplete."

Tamsin gasped at his touch. "Oh, my lord. I...am complete, I assure you."

"Then let me see you completely undone again."

"Oh. You're supposed to be cleaning me...ohhhh." She gripped his shoulders as he teased her, his fingers stroking her center in a maddeningly intimate way.

"That's it," he said, watching her avidly. "Let yourself feel everything."

She kept her gaze locked on Royce's as he continued to touch and tease her. It became a sort of challenge, to face him head-on in such a torturous, devastating scenario.

"Royce," she murmured.

"Tell me what to do," he said. "You want it faster? Deeper?"

"Deeper. But slower. Oh, my go—" She lost her voice as he slipped his wicked fingers into her body, touching her like no man ever had. "Royce, why are you doing this?"

"Because we both want me too." He rubbed his palm

against her, pressing hard, rolling up and down until she threw her head back and gave herself up to the pleasure he offered.

The orgasm took Tamsin's breath away, and seemed to linger for a long moment while her whole body went soft against Royce's. She sighed, feeling utterly pampered and spoiled...not to mention thoroughly sinful.

"Turn around," he said. "Sit against me and the water will keep you warm."

As if she were in danger of cooling off after what he'd done to her blood. She rested against him, her back to his chest.

Royce ran his fingers along her body, under the water and above it, drawing lazy, shapeless loops over her skin. It felt lovely and soothing, and she never wanted to leave the bath.

"Tamsin," he murmured, his voice thrumming in her ear, sending a shiver of pleasure through her body.

"Mmmmm?" she asked, her eyes closed.

"You have to marry me."

♍

At his words, Tamsin's heart shuddered to a stop. "What?" she whispered.

"I want you to marry me," he replied.

Splashing water everywhere, she bolted upright. "That's not what you said! You said I *have* to marry you."

"And then I said I want you to." Royce reached out to prevent her from leaving the bath. "Surely you can't object?"

"Oh, yes I can! Marriage is a terrible idea."

"Why? It's got advantages. For one, you'll be a countess, and you can go to any event you wish to, not just the masquerades."

"Royce, are you mad? That is the one thing I can never do."

"You'd be perfectly safe, darling. Swigg would never dare touch you once it was known you were a countess."

"Swigg is the least of my worries. My own past is the reason you have to stay away from me."

Instead, he pulled her closer. "I've tried to stay away from you, and it doesn't work. And no matter what you think, Tamsin, you need me too. Especially now."

She felt a little sick to her stomach, thinking of the bluntest and most obvious reason for why she needed a husband. After the evening's escapades, even with his withdrawals, she could very well find herself pregnant.

Again.

Tamsin struggled against him. "I don't want to talk to you now. Let me go!"

"Not till you agree to a wedding date. How does to-morrow sound?"

"It sounds insane. Royce, do you think the world will forgive all my sins just because you marry me? You are perhaps unacquainted with the society in which we live. All that will happen is that your name and reputation will be sullied too. You'll be laughed at. I will never let that happen to you."

"You're protecting *me*?" he asked in amusement.

"Yes, since you don't have the sense to protect your-self."

She ignored the flash of pain and anger in his eyes, and climbed out of the bath. Though the room was warm, she started to shiver, but she blamed it on her damp skin and hair rather than the shock of his proposal.

Wrapping herself in a luxuriously soft towel, Tamsin tried to get her heartbeat back under control. It was not cooperating, instead jumping wildly around in her rib cage.

She looked over her shoulder. Royce remained in the bath, lounging with his eyes closed, looking as if he had no cares in the world. Before she could stop herself, her gaze traveled up and down the length of his body, which wasn't hidden in the slightest by the rippled water.

"Royce," she said, "it's very nice of you to offer to do the honorable thing. Truly. But it would hurt you far more than it would help me."

He didn't open his eyes, but after a long moment, he replied, "Fuck honor."

Tamsin winced at the crudity and the lack of emotion in his voice. Well, that was one way to retract an offer of marriage. Fearing what depths the conversation might fall to if it continued, Tamsin fled to her own room to dry off and prepare for bed. Her initial shock had now soured into a more general regret. Once again, she had ignored her better sense, succumbed to her desire, and the result was ruination.

True, she was already ruined, and therefore couldn't get *more* ruined. But she'd managed to ruin her tenuous hold on a better life. Surely, in the morning she'd learn that Royce would no longer employ her as secretary, meaning she'd also lose this wonderful safe haven to live in. And he didn't even need her to help him find the French spy, since she'd already told him all she knew and forged the document that would bring the spy out into the open. Tamsin was no longer useful to Royce in any way.

Lying in her cold bed, Tamsin wiped away a rogue tear. If only she had acted more sensibly. If only she hadn't fallen in love.

"Foolish, foolish girl," she muttered, curling up on her side. And then, because she could, she cried herself to sleep.

The next morning, she woke to find that Wendy had already been in the room and started the fire in the grate, keeping the worst of the autumn cold at bay. She also saw her phoenix costume carefully arranged on a padded chair, the wings cradled in the swaths of red and orange silk.

"Oh, Lord," Tamsin muttered. That meant Wendy had retrieved it from where it had fallen in Royce's bedroom and brought it up here. Tamsin hadn't even remembered that little detail in her mad dash back to her own room. So much for discretion.

She slid out of the bed and dressed, choosing the plainest gown she had. Her hands shook, and her head was still muddled with the memory of last night, from the excitement of the party to the raw sensuality of making love to Royce, to his sudden proposal.

What was he thinking? she asked herself sourly. Was his offer some sort of lordly amusement, asking random women to marry him, just to see what they'd say?

"I bet he did it just to get a rise out of me," she said, knowing that it wasn't true, and that whatever was behind the proposal, it was certainly not done as a joke. But her mind shrank away from the other possibilities, because they required her to examine her heart, and Tamsin didn't have the strength to do that at the moment.

Knowing that she couldn't delay the inevitable, Tamsin went downstairs to find some breakfast before Royce sacked her.

In the parlour, she was quietly chewing dry toast when Wendy entered.

"Good morning, miss," the maid said with her usual cheer.

Tamsin didn't trust herself to reply, or even to look into the young woman's face, where she'd see the judgment that surely lurked there.

"Cold out today," Wendy went on, pouring a cup of coffee and setting it beside Tamsin's place. "You'll want to stay near the fire, miss, while you work."

"If I have any more work," she muttered. Louder, she asked, "I don't suppose the earl is awake yet?" Tamsin might have a little time to pack her few belongings...although most of the items in her wardrobe were purchased by Royce, and therefore didn't actually belong to her. Packing wouldn't take much time at all.

"Actually, his lordship ordered the carriage at eight. Early for him," she added in passing.

Tamsin had no idea what could have motivated Royce

to leave at such an hour, but she could imagine the worst.

"Wendy," she said suddenly, "I don't expect I'll be here much longer, so I want to thank you."

"Thank me, miss?" Wendy asked, puzzled. "I've only done my duty."

"But you did it kindly, and that's not something I can say for everyone. You and your family have been very good to me. Better than I deserve."

Wendy paused in surprise, holding Tamsin's empty plate in her hand. After a moment, she said, "Well, my ma always told me that we all must hope to get better than we deserve. Ring if you need anything else, miss."

Tamsin went to the study after breakfast. She'd decided that the one thing she could do today was tidy the place up. At least her replacement would start fresh. The tidying, however, did not take long, since Tamsin was a naturally tidy person.

She picked up a book and began to read it, trying not to wonder what business took Royce away all day, and whether it had to do with her. It probably didn't—far more likely that he was off to do some spying, which would involve chasing hardened criminals through the streets or leaping off a building or something equally dangerous.

Tamsin realized that she desperately wanted Royce to come back home. His absence was killing her. She wanted to apologize, or ask forgiveness, or simply know if he despised her after last night. Men's opinions changed after they got what they were after, a fact Tamsin knew all too well.

It must have been hours later when she looked up from her book, and saw Royce in the doorway, watching her.

She jumped. "How long have you been standing there,

my lord?"

"Long enough to know that you're not reading a word of that book." He strode in and sat in the chair opposite her chaise.

She surveyed him, examining his clothing and hair for signs of clandestine struggles. But he looked as precise and put together as always.

"I thought you might have been chasing the Viper today," she said finally. "Part of me expected to find you wounded…or worse."

"No such luck. My struggles today were entirely bureaucratic." Royce leaned back in the chair. "Speaking of that, we need to talk."

She put down the book, preparing herself for a dismissal. "I can leave tomorrow, my lord. If you'll pay me the wages for the weeks I've worked so far…"

He frowned. "What the hell are you talking about?"

"It is utterly wrong to sleep with one's employer," she said flatly. "Last night was entirely my fault, and I apologize for doing what I did. So—"

"Tamsin, shut up." He said the words quietly, softening the effect of them. "You're so damnably clever most of the time that when you do act foolishly, it's almost funny."

She bit her lip, mindful of his order to shut up.

He leaned forward. "First off, I seduced you. Let's be entirely clear on that point. To think otherwise would be an insult to my station and my male pride."

The faint smile on his lips was the only clue that he wasn't entirely serious. Tamsin raised an eyebrow, but didn't reply.

"So," he went on. "We've agreed that you've done nothing wrong. As to your other point, that one ought not to sleep with one's employer, I agree. It was a mistake on my part, and I'll not do it again. It was short-sighted. And last night, you were absolutely correct when you said we couldn't publicly announce a marriage."

She sighed with relief, and some hidden regret. "I'm glad you realize that, my lord."

"So it will just have to remain secret for a while."

"What?" She was confused again.

"Our marriage. We won't announce it until later."

Tamsin held up her hand. "There is not going to be a marriage."

"Can't promise that, darling." Royce smiled at her, the maddening smile of a man who was used to getting everything he wanted. "We've already agreed that I can't take my secretary to my bed. So you'll have to forego the title of secretary and use the title of wife. Though you can still open the mail if you like. You seem to enjoy it."

Tamsin stood up, in the hopes that a new perspective would tilt the world back into its proper position. "You cannot marry me! What would you do, stash me in a carriage and drive off to Gretna Green?"

"Certainly not." He wrinkled his nose in distaste, then pulled an envelope from his inner pocket. "I've made other arrangements which you'll find far more convenient. Special license, which was a beast to secure in a discreet manner, so I'll be very put out if you don't let me use it."

Tamsin stared at the envelope. All she knew of special licenses was that they were horrifically expensive and so rarely issued that they were nearly mythical documents.

"Oh, and I picked out the church," he added. "We leave in a half hour, so if there's a particular gown you'd like to wear to your wedding, now is the time to put it on."

Tamsin thought about her meager wardrobe, and just

shrugged helplessly. Her outfits had been chosen with the goal of making her look presentable as a skilled employee, not to stun guests in a church. She looked down at the cotton gown she wore now, with blue block-printed flowers on the ivory fabric. She had on the black leather slippers, and a blue linen shawl lay draped across the chair. "I believe what I have on will suffice."

"It will more than suffice—you look lovely," he said. Then he stood up and abruptly pulled Tamsin into his arms, kissing her firmly on the mouth. "Actually, why wait a half hour? Let's go now."

They went. Errol drove the carriage.

Tamsin sat quietly, but her mind buzzed like a hive of wasps. *This is mad*, she told herself every ten seconds. But then a little voice said, *What if it isn't? What if this is exactly what should happen?* Tamsin so wanted to have a place in life, and what Royce was offering—a place as *his* wife—was like a dream. She felt a connection to him the first night they met, and it endured despite all the many things that had transpired since.

Just then Royce leaned over and took her hands in his. "You look nervous."

"Of course I'm nervous!" she squeaked out. But then she caught his gaze, and was captivated by the warmth there. Royce exuded confidence, and even hope.

"Trust me, Tamsin," he said, his tone filled with what sounded almost like excitement. "This is the right thing to do."

"Yes," she breathed, finally giving herself permission to believe.

When they arrived at the church, it was empty, except for the clergyman in front of the altar and a couple standing near the first pew. With a jolt, Tamsin recognized the two spymasters Royce had introduced her to when they first came to London, the man he'd called Julian Neville, codenamed Aries, and the woman named Miss Chattan.

"We need two witnesses," Royce told her, "and who better to keep the secret than professional secret-keepers?"

Both witnesses seemed surprised to be there, and Tamsin couldn't blame them. Miss Chattan gave her a brief nod as they approached, smiling a little.

"Hell bent on this, are you?" Aries murmured to Royce.

"'Fraid so," Royce said shortly, but with an edge of triumph. He was delighted to be doing this, Tamsin realized, and that made her giddy too. No wonder all the papers talked about Royce Holmes, who would dare to do *anything*. He was truly fearless.

"Oh, now don't be a grump," Miss Chattan said, drawing Aries away. "You must confess it's rather romantic."

"*Romantic* is another word for *mad*," the man said. Chattan's low laugh was the only response.

The marriage ceremony was brief, since it wasn't accompanied by any sort of homily or speech. The clergyman recited the bare text from his little book, and they dutifully repeated the phrases.

Finally, the clergyman asked, "Do you, Lord Pelham, take this woman to be your bride?"

"I do," said Royce, smiling.

"And do you, Miss…" The clergyman trailed off, for he didn't know Tamsin's name.

Royce was looking at her with a challenge in his eyes. "Go ahead and tell him, darling."

She swallowed, past the dryness in her throat. "Thomasina…Black."

"Do you, Miss Thomasina Black, take this man to be your husband?"

Tamsin paused, then closed her eyes. "I do," she whispered.

The clergyman pronounced them man and wife. Just like that.

Afterward, she bent down to sign her name to the certificate. She replaced the pen in its holder and looked over at Royce. He was staring at her signature, and Tamsin abruptly realized that no matter what name she might have scrawled on the paper, it didn't matter any longer, because that name was no longer her own.

She was now Lady Pelham.

And she couldn't tell anybody.

Moments later, they were back in the closed carriage, once again being driven by Errol, who'd not asked a single question about why he'd driven to a church, let the couple out there for twenty minutes, and then drove them directly back home. Errol, it must be said, was a disciplined young man.

Inside the carriage, Royce sat next to her, rather than across. Was that a husband's prerogative? She had no idea, and indeed, the word *husband* sent her mind into a spin like a wounded bird's. Intelligent thought was beyond her at the moment.

"So," Royce said quietly. "Tamsin is short for Thomasina."

"Yes. No one ever called me by my full name, which is for the best."

"You will always be Tamsin to me. I think that name suits you eminently well."

"Thank you, my lord."

"You don't have to do that, you know. We are married. A little familiarity is acceptable." His tone was teasing, and she gave in to the delicious kiss that followed.

When she ended it—even a countess had to breathe—

Royce said, "Isn't this better after all? Now you've got the full protection of my name and family behind you. And I can kiss you." He looked as if he were about to burst with joy.

Tamsin smiled helplessly, but said, "Royce...you cannot tell people that you married me. Not right now. You know that. There will be too many questions." She shuddered at the thought of her old circle seeing her name in the papers, and whispered in the front parlors of Society matrons. *Did you hear Lord Pelham got snared by the Latimer girl? What, the penniless one who ran away from her job as governess and disappeared?*

No, it would be a scandal that would be the talk of London for the next year. A rich, eligible earl who married a woman of shattered reputation? Tamsin would be locked out of all the homes of Society. Royce would have to endure mockery from other men, and what could he say in defense? *I married her because she might be pregnant and I don't want to deal with another bastard.*

But worse than that, she feared what Hector would do when he found out. Tamsin was under no illusions that he'd let her alone. No, he'd find a way to harass her, embarrass her, and ultimately ruin her. Again. Because that's the sort of man Hector was.

It was just a matter of time.

"I know, I know. It's not as if the papers will get ahold of it. But I've taken steps to ensure that those who do need to know about the union will be informed as necessary," Royce was saying.

"What does that mean?" she asked, alarmed.

"Never mind the details. Aries and Chattan will know what to do if something needs to be done." He leaned into her, saying in a different tone, "You're mine now. No one can ever hurt you again, Tamsin. You're safe."

His mouth sought hers, and she responded to the kiss with a raw tenderness she didn't know she was capable of.

Safe.

The word summoned a wonderful feeling within her, but was that the only gift Royce was giving her through this marriage? Safety?

They returned to the townhouse just as dusk was falling. Wendy opened the door and took their coats, showing a similar lack of interest in where they'd been.

"If anyone calls this evening, no one is at home," Royce instructed. Wendy bobbed her head in acknowledgment.

Royce escorted Tamsin up the stairs without further words, and she allowed herself to be swept along in his wake. Her mind was still spinning with the events of the last twenty-four hours. Attended a masquerade. Forged a document. Seduced by her employer. Fought with her lover. Dismissed by her employer. Married to an earl...

"I think I missed lunch," she murmured, the mundane fact making her giggle. Yes, she was dangerously close to hysteria.

But there was no time for her to fall further into such thoughts. Tamsin scarcely stepped past the bedroom doorway when Royce circled his arm around her waist, drawing her to him.

"I want a wedding night," he told her, his voice hot in her ear. "Tell me you do too."

In fact, she was aching for it. "Yes, Royce," she murmured, lifting her face for a kiss.

He crushed his mouth to hers, and within seconds, they were gasping for breath, shedding clothing with no regard for cost, pushing against each other with hands and lips.

Royce picked her up and walked to the giant bed, setting her down on the edge.

"I don't need to write anything on your body anymore," he said, pulling at her shift, the last thing she still wore. "I know you now. My Tamsin."

"Royce," she said, her breath catching with sudden emotion. "Do you truly mean to do this? It's not a marriage until it's consummated…"

"Be difficult to prove you a virgin at this point," he pointed out.

The words stung, though she was certain he didn't mean them like that.

"Tamsin," he said, cupping her face in his hands. "I only meant we've lain together already—as far as I'm concerned, it's till death do us part."

"A moment that's a long way away for us both, I hope," she said shakily.

"You've nothing to worry about," he said. "You'll be taken care of." He kissed her then, and desire replaced the questions that had been welling up in her mind.

♍

ROYCE AWOKE IN THE MORNING to a most unusual situation. His wife sat in a chair near the bed, staring out of the window as she fidgeted absently with the tail of her long braid.

His *wife*.

Then he fully remembered all that had transpired the day before. His dash to ensure that he could marry Tamsin, his fear that she'd run away long before he got through the tangle of official nonsense to get the license in his hands, and then the actual wedding. Everything had been crystal clear: he needed Tamsin, and she needed him.

However, she currently did not look like she needed him, because she'd chosen to leave the bed, and was now nestled in the chair, looking quite solitary and content to remain so.

"How long have you been up?" he asked.

Tamsin looked over her shoulder, her eyes cool and calm. "An hour or two. I was restless."

He sat up against the pillows, wondering if there was any way to entice Tamsin back to the bed, short of ordering her there. Something told him that giving her an order wouldn't end well, even if she was his wife.

Then, out of the blue, Tamsin said, "Tell me about Laurent's mother."

Royce thought a moment, not expecting the question.

"There's little to tell. Dominique Suchet was an actress on the London stage when I was a very young man. I saw her and became infatuated. She was a spectacular beauty and a remarkable actress too, with eyes that could melt or freeze you from across the theater. She had dozens of admirers who came to every performance and showered her with gifts and flowers and I am sure more promises than I did. But there was something between us, and we began an affair."

"How long did it last?"

"Mmm, several months? A year? She finally left for the Continent because she had got a role at a major theater in Paris—the opportunity of a lifetime, and she cared for her career far more than my bed. I let her go, because I wasn't an idiot. There was no such thing as a quiet moment with Dominique. She was always on stage, even in the bedroom, even when there should have been no pretense. She couldn't help it—she was born that way. Always performing, always seeking the drama in every moment."

Tamsin stood up and walked toward the bed, perching on the side. "It sounds exhausting," she commented.

"That's exactly what it was, in the end. Exhilarating for a while, but ultimately unlivable. I can't tell you how many times I hurled myself out of her door, vowing to never see her again. But I went back, and back, and back. She made me feel alive." Or, as Tamsin had described it on another night, it got his blood up. Royce had always needed to find the next challenge, the next fight, the next cliff. With Dominique, he found all three.

"But when she left you," Tamsin went on, "did she know she was carrying your baby?"

He shook his head. "I doubt it. She couldn't have avoided making a scene if she had known! No, I heard nothing from her again. I assumed she'd forgotten me, and in truth, I'd more or less…well, not forgotten. Dominique isn't the sort of woman one forgets. But I'd moved on."

"Moved on to another mistress?"

He frowned at her. "No. I never had a mistress after that, actually. Not in the sense most gentlemen keep mistresses. It seemed like I'd spent all that fire and emotion on her, and when she left, the madness did too…for a while. I was grateful. It let me focus on other things."

"Such as spying."

"Yes, in short. I was recruited not very long after that. At the time I was just a reckless third son, and no one expected me to do anything, let alone something useful. In a way, all the antics with Dominique probably helped draw the Zodiac's attention. I was not exactly circumspect when I was younger."

"Is marrying your secretary by special license considered circumspect?"

"No, but it happened," he said with a little smile, "so you'll have to get used to it, Tamsin."

She looked back to the window. "You want to know something ridiculous?"

He nodded. He wanted to know everything on her mind.

"I already miss my work." She put her head in her hands and then laughed, her head coming back up with a sad smile. "You spoke of being useful, and as a scrivener and then as a secretary I *did* feel useful. And what do I do now?"

"Well, you can still do that work, if you like," he said slowly. "I mean, we've agreed not to announce the marriage for a while, and Lord knows I'm in need of the help. So you could still be Miss Black by day…"

Her smile grew, and joy sparkled in her eyes. "Do you mean it?"

"Yes…if you'll agree to be my wife by night." Royce leaned forward, catching Tamsin's face in his hands. "At least give me half of you."

Her eyes widened, and then she moved to kiss him. Royce was pushed back onto the bed by the force of her sudden affection, and he couldn't complain.

Not surprisingly, they didn't leave the bedroom until midmorning. Tamsin asked him not to treat her any differently in the presence of any others. "I just can't face having everyone call me *my lady*, not yet."

He agreed that a change in address would be confusing for her at this point. Secretly, he looked forward to the fun of seeing Miss Black by day, and the Countess of Pelham by night. It was a game he'd never played before, and his interest was piqued.

After Tamsin slipped out to go to her own room, Marlow appeared to help Royce get ready and dress. Royce suddenly felt the need to get moving, and he could barely sit still to be shaved.

"Do be calm, sir," Marlow warned him. "I'd prefer to not slice your throat open."

"I appreciate that," he returned. "Because I have a busy day ahead, and death would only get in the way."

And then, because he didn't want people to be totally at sea, he informed Marlow about the wedding, as well as Tamsin's wish to be addressed by her usual name until the marriage was public. "It was a bit sudden," Royce conceded, "and she is still adjusting."

Marlow's response was typically sanguine. "Congratulations, my lord. I'll tell the others. We certainly wouldn't want to upset Miss Black."

Soon after, Royce headed out to call on his family's

solicitors. The business of being an earl could never be put aside entirely, and he did have a duty to his mother and his tenants and all the people who relied on Pelham for their livelihood. He was in an uncommonly good mood today though, and when he met gentlemen he knew along the way, he greeted them with a cheerful grin that edged into mania. As for the ladies, Royce was now beyond their grasp, and this secret knowledge made him even happier. He bowed to matrons, was introduced to various daughters, and he flirted with nearly everyone wearing a skirt. The rumor mills around the *ton* would be grinding today...and for all the wrong reasons. Royce laughed to himself, enjoying the chaos he'd leave in his wake. *Let them talk*, he thought, *I've got Tamsin*. His countess.

He returned home briefly, but was handed a note from Marlow and knew he'd be leaving again immediately.

"Rook sent word," Marlow said. "He says you need to come to the lookout."

"Yes!" Royce closed his eyes in relief. The Disreputables' information network came through once more.

As part of his plan to catch the Viper, Royce had set one of the Disreputables to linger near the Mathering house, where the masquerade had occurred. The young man, nicknamed Rook, had worked for the Zodiac in a similar capacity before. He had an innocent face and sharp eyes that seemed to see around corners. Rook's job was simple: keep watch on the house and, in particular, the comings and goings of Mr Pearson. Royce had a hunch that the false letter Tamsin wrote in his name would spark some reaction from the man once he learned of its existence. If he left the house, Rook would follow. If he entertained a guest, Rook would find out who it was.

Royce told Errol where to drive, and he lost no time

locating a skinny lad loitering near a flower vendor's cart.

Once Royce got there, he said in a low voice, "Rook."

"G'day, sir. The gentleman you asked me to watch made a scene early this morning. He called for a cab. He was in a tizzy, and could barely wait for the cab to stop rolling. Told the driver to go to the corner of Gill and Harestock Streets, and hurry."

"Were you able to follow?"

"'Course," Rook said. "I hopped on the back of the carriage." It was a common trick of boys in the city to leap onto the back kickboard of a carriage and ride along until they reached their destination or until the coachman kicked them off. Such a move would not look odd.

"And what happened when the gentleman got out of the cab?"

"He walked a few blocks to a red brick building with a yellow door. It's on Gill Street, I'll point it out to you, if you want to go now."

"Then who will watch this house?" Royce asked.

Rook merely winked. "Buy some flowers, sir. Mrs Carter there is a good sort."

He chose white carnations, and the old lady took his coin with a broad smile. "Thank you kindly, m'lord. Do come again...I'm always here when I'm needed." She grinned at Rook.

A minute later, they were in the carriage again, Rook clearly enjoying the ride from the inside of the coach. "If these seats was any softer, I'd fall asleep!" he said in awe. Royce laughed, because just then the wheels rattled over a series of potholes that rattled his teeth.

Once they reached Gill Street, Rook led him to a local resident who also lived in the building, and who saw everyone who entered and left each day.

"Oh, aye. I know just who you mean. That swell met

him more than once." The informant gave his account of who he'd seen, and it fit very well with the physical description Tamsin had offered earlier. There were thousands of men in London who might match the features of Yves, but Royce felt in his gut that this was the man he'd been hunting for so long. And Mr Pearson knew him! Everything was coming together.

Rook added, "I asked the woman who cleans the rooms in this place, and she said he's lived here for almost a year now. Comes and goes a lot, very polite, but never friendly with the neighbors. Said that one time she tried to go in his rooms to clean them—this was early on before she knew better—and he nearly lost his head. He yelled at her, called her a thief, and told her if anyone but him unlocked his door, he'd kill them."

"That's all I need to hear," Royce murmured.

"What now, sir?"

"Now you're done, Rook. I don't want to risk my quarry seeing you too many times and getting suspicious. I want him to feel very secure in his nest on the third floor."

"You going to kill him?" Rook asked, with the eagerness of a street urchin.

"I'm going to neutralize him," Royce promised.

He grinned, because after so long, he was near the end of his hunt. Soon, it would all be over. The slow, frustrating chase was drawing to a close and only the direct, pure confrontation remained.

He could hardly wait.

♍

WITHIN MOMENTS AFTER ROYCE HAD left the house that morning, Tamsin hurried to the study. It was true that she felt the need to work—she had always liked to stay busy —but there was another reason she had to maintain her role as secretary. She needed to keep her access to Royce's financial documents.

That morning, Hector had posted in the *Pall Mall Advertiser* once again, demanding more money, another two hundred pounds.

"Oh, you should rot in hell," she grumbled as she read the infuriating words, the newspaper ink smearing under her thumb. In Royce's office, she walked to the desk and found the ledger and the book of blank cheques issued by the bank for clients wealthy enough to require such things.

She took a pen and dipped it in the pot of ink on Royce's desk. It was the only ink he used, and Tamsin considered the faintly rust-colored tinge of the blend to be just as integral to her forgery as the heavy rightward-lean of Royce's handwriting. She took only a moment at it, since by now she could practically write Royce's signature in her sleep.

Tamsin blotted it carefully and straighten up, only to jump when she saw Wendy enter the room.

"Oh, sorry, I just came in to clean, Miss…er…my

la…"

Wendy paused in confusion, and Tamsin seized the moment to cover the ledger and banknote book with the newspaper. Then she said, "Give me one moment to tidy up Lord Pelham's desk and then you may clean the room to your heart's content. I wanted to finish a few tasks before he returned." She kept her tone formal, both to cover her racing pulse and to deter Wendy from asking if her name had changed…clearly the servants all knew something was different now.

Thankfully, Wendy didn't seem to notice Tamsin's nervousness. She curtseyed and said she'd do the sitting room first, allowing Tamsin time to replace the ledger and slide the folded banknote into the pocket beneath her gown.

"I am so, so sorry," she whispered to the room. The guilt and shame from her actions were getting worse every day. "I will not do this again."

She wished she could believe herself.

Later in the day, Tamsin put on her pelisse and slipped out the side door of the townhouse. Errol was in the yard, but he was facing away from her, hammering away at something in the work shed. She was safe.

The walk to the park would have been quite pleasant if she didn't have to meet Hector at the end of it. The air was mild…one of the last mild days before winter swept in.

She made her way to the footbridge where she had arranged to meet Hector. He was there before her.

"Thomasina," he said, his voice positively dripping with contempt. "You look delicious this afternoon."

"I must remind you that we are not on a first name basis, sir," she replied, keeping her gaze on the park beyond. She'd never look at that pig again.

"We're a lot closer than that, as I recall. Have you got it?"

She slid an envelope from her pelisse and handed it to him, the action hidden from any spectators by the way they stood on the little footbridge. "Another banknote. The last one I'll ever give you, by the way. I cannot keep doing this. He'll find out what's happening."

"Oh, I've got more faith in you." He stepped closer, trapping Tamsin against the rail. Heat rushed through her body, the panic-heat of a gazelle on the savannah, knowing a predator has caught its scent. "Now you're playing secretary for Pelham, you've got a perfect cover."

Tamsin opened her fan and began to flick her wrist at a pace that would likely summon a hurricane if she kept at it. She wished she could conjure a breeze strong enough to send Hector over the rail. "I find this conversation tedious and unnecessary to continue—rather like our previous encounters. Please leave, Mr Englefield. Or stay here while I leave. It matters not which, so long as our proximity ends."

"Always the lady," he sneered. "Except I know you're not the lady you're playing. Good day, Miss Latimer—or whatever you're calling yourself now. But don't think that our acquaintance is at an end."

"We have no acquaintance. Good day, sir."

Hector left the way he'd come, and Tamsin stood alone on the little footbridge for a moment, contemplating the water below, which was barely more than a trickle, thanks to the ice at the edges of the streambed.

She was always running into men on bridges, she thought with grim humor. Turning, she started down the wooden span to reach the path she walked before. She moved as quickly as she could while still maintaining a ladylike gait. Tamsin wanted to return to the townhouse before anyone missed her.

But before she could even rejoin the main gravel road running through the park, she stopped short.

A tall gentleman in a wool greatcoat blocked her way, his expression cold.

It was Royce.

♍

ROYCE HAD CUT THROUGH THE park on his way home, choosing to walk despite the cold weather. He was excited by the developments in the assignment, and he needed to walk off his tension. He liked the park…you never knew who you might meet.

But he had not been expecting to meet Tamsin.

"What are you doing here?" she gasped, obviously upset.

"The better question is what you are doing here," he replied. "You've been adamant about not going out at all, and now I find you skipping off to meet some man."

"I was not!"

"I'm not blind, Tamsin." Royce took her elbow, steering her down the crushed gravel path. "Who was that man you were speaking with?"

"No one," she said shortly.

It must have been someone, or the conversation would not have lasted so long. Royce had seen Tamsin chatting with the man for several minutes. Unfortunately, from the distance he was at, Royce couldn't see anything of the man's face, and discerned only that he was blond and rather tall, probably close in age to Royce himself. All sorts of possibilities occurred to him, the first being direct betrayal.

"Who was it, Tamsin? One of your associates from the

dear old days in Catchpenny Lane? Was it your old boss Swigg?"

She shook her head. "Swigg would never meet in daylight."

"Or perhaps I've been a complete fool, and you still work for our mutual friend Yves. Is that it? Still creating masterpieces for the Viper? Do you do that when I'm not looking? Have you told him about me? Or the Zodiac?"

At that, Tamsin's skin went dead white, and she took a shaky step backward. "Oh, my God, Royce!" she whispered, horror in her voice. "How could you ever think that?"

Her reaction was enough to convince him that she meant it...and he never had a reason to suspect that Tamsin was playing both sides of this. But the alternative was also ugly. Jealousy was not a familiar emotion, and the green wave washing over him left him feeling distinctly chilled.

"Then who could it be? A friend from your old life?" he pressed.

Tamsin whipped her head around and glared at him. "There's no one from my old life that I'd want to speak to ever again."

They reached the street, and Royce signaled to one of the hired cabs waiting near the gates of the park.

Once seated in the carriage, Tamsin pulled the cape around her and let out a thin sigh. "I will never go out again," she announced. "This was such a mistake."

"Who was the man?"

"No one. He mistook me for someone else, and it was a very confusing conversation."

Royce didn't believe her for a moment, but he did believe that the distress lurking under her light words was a genuine problem. It was in her whole bearing—the pale skin, the rapid breath, the way her hands fluttered from place to place when Tamsin normally never fidgeted.

He leaned over to her and put his hand on her shoulder. "Tamsin, you do realize that I will find out one way or another. I'd prefer it to be—"

"He's got news about my father," she said in a rush.

It took him a moment to process that. "What?"

"My father was imprisoned because he couldn't pay his debts and I have not seen him since that day. My mother and sister are safe at a cousin's home in Somerset, but he was in prison! I want to locate him, and that man has a clue and the connections I need."

He frowned. Something was not right here. Aloud, he said, "Why didn't you ask *me*, Tamsin? I'm an agent for the Crown. I also have connections."

"He already knew my family," Tamsin mumbled, not looking at him.

"So that man *is* from your old life. Is he a friend?"

Tamsin's expression flashed into hate for a second, and Royce pulled her into his arms. "He's the one, isn't he? The man who ruined you?"

"Yes! Is that what you want to hear? He's the one."

"Don't you ever see him again," Royce told her harshly. "That's an order."

"You can't order me around."

"I just did, and you'll listen."

"Why?"

"Because if I have to track you down and I find him again, I'll kill him."

"Royce!" Tamsin's eyes went wide.

"Why shouldn't I? Or do you still fancy him?"

"I want to impale him with every knitting needle in London! But you, my lord, can't just go threatening members of the gentry as if they're common criminals.

Your spy games don't apply to ordinary people living ordinary lives…"

"What's ordinary about a secret meeting? If the man is in your life, he's in my life, and that means I can deal with him however I like."

She slouched into a corner of the carriage. "For someone who never wanted the title of earl, you certainly behave as if you were born to it."

He shrugged, unwilling to go into it. He watched his father and his older brothers as he grew up, and he knew how any proper gentleman was supposed to behave. Always in charge, always in control. Not once had he seen his father ask for something; he'd only laid down the law, totally confident that everyone would obey without question. When he gained the title, Royce could only imitate what he'd seen before. Even when it felt like playing a part.

They rode in silence until they reached Grosvenor Square. Then Royce said, "If you want help locating your family, or just speaking to them again…"

"Please don't," Tamsin said, stiff-backed and nearly in tears. "I know you mean well, but you cannot help me in this. And don't think that you can go behind my back and investigate," she added, glaring at him.

"Why shouldn't I?"

"Because you…can't. I lied about my name," she said hurriedly. "So you can't do a thing."

"Your birth name is Thomasina Latimer," he told her.

Tamsin's jaw dropped, and it would have been funny if he didn't care about her so damn much.

"How did you know that? How long have you known?"

"I didn't *know* until just now, because your reaction confirmed it. But I guessed. You once asked Marlow if he knew of any way to get word to a Thomas Latimer of Fleet Prison. It was logical to assume that as the firstborn child, you were named for your father."

She stared at him, aghast. "You knew all that and you never said!"

"It is literally my job to find out other people's secrets, and keep what I know hidden."

"I hate you!"

"I hope not, my lady," he said quietly, reminding Tamsin of her most recent name change and its significance. "How did you choose the name of Tess Black?"

"It fit." She lifted her right hand, showing the fingers which were perpetually stained with dark ink.

"All right, that works for the name of *Black*. But why Tess instead of Tamsin? Or why not just keep using Thomasina?"

She wrinkled her nose, reminding him that she didn't care for her given name. "I needed a break with my old life. Keeping either of my names would be unwise. I fell into Tess when I stuttered the first few times I had to introduce myself in London, and then I discovered that it worked far better as a moniker in the neighborhoods I was working. The working class doesn't name its daughters *Thomasina*. Only good solid, short names that you can yell across the street fit those girls. *Tessssssss*!" she cried, proving the point with a mock-howl.

He laughed at her rendition, then said, "Now that it's all settled, shall we go in?"

"Only if you promise not to meddle. Leave my personal history alone. Why relive the past when you can't change it?"

"I promise," he lied. Royce was relieved Tamsin had confirmed her real name, but he had no intention of remaining ignorant. Tamsin had often hinted at the tragic path her life had taken, but she'd consistently refused to give him the whole story.

Royce was not convinced that the past should be buried. Tamsin was born into a good family, and been given an excellent education, particularly for a girl. She'd been loved—he was quite sure of that. So what had happened? What turn took her away from the path of a well-bred lady of the gentry to a dangerous, secretive life in Catchpenny Lane?

Tamsin wanted to see her father again. And Royce would help her, whether she wanted him to or not. Most men would consent to a social call from an earl, even if they were angry at their daughter.

"Anyway," she said, when Errol opened the door of the carriage. "I don't want to pester you with anything when you've got far more important matters to occupy your mind."

As he helped Tamsin out, he couldn't help but smile. "As a matter of fact, there's been a development in that regard."

"Oh?" She looked at him warily.

"I know where the Viper makes his hideout," he admitted.

Tamsin's eyes widened. "Then you can capture him!"

"Yes. It will all be over soon."

Over the next few days, Royce left nothing to chance. On the night that he selected to pin down the Viper, he sent Rook and two other Disreputables to cover the exterior doors of the building while he entered alone, to keep things as quiet as possible. He was armed with a pistol, kept in a holster under his greatcoat. In addition, he had two knives: one in a sheath at his waist, and the smaller one he nearly always kept in his boot. (It was one of the many, many reasons he hated formal affairs that required shoes, as boots were not considered proper. Royce considered knives to be proper no matter how formal the occasion.)

He was in a good mood. He had to stop himself from whistling a tune as he walked through the hallways and climbed the narrow staircase to Yves's rented rooms above. Within an hour, perhaps less, he would capture and neutralize one of the most dangerous foreign agents working on the side of the French. It had been a long time coming, but now it was almost done. His heart already felt lighter.

After this, he could sort out whatever was dogging Tamsin. He knew she was still concealing something from him, something that troubled her far more than she let on. If only she would trust him, this would be solved...

Royce was so distracted by his worries about Tamsin he nearly missed the doorway to the fourth floor, where Yves's rooms were.

"Keep alert," he warned himself. He breathed deeply, once, twice, three times. His pulse pounded, but then it always did at a time like this, when he anticipated a fight.

Yves would resist him, of course. He'd fight back and try any dirty trick he could to escape. But Royce only had to call the signal to bring his Disreputables running, and then they'd drag Yves straight to the Zodiac.

He grinned savagely, eager for the battle.

Royce made his way down the narrow hall, moving in near silence. The floorboards were old and weak, threatening to creak at every step. But then, this was a residential building. Yves had to be used to the sounds of others moving about.

He got to Yves's door, and pulled out his set of lockpicks. He'd considered trying to trick Yves into opening the door himself, by pretending to be another agent or perhaps Mr Pearson but decided against it. Too risky.

He'd just let himself in.

Royce paused, hearing the sound of movement beyond the door. Rook had watched Yves enter the building twenty minutes prior, so they knew he was within. Someone would make the signal—a call like a nightbird—if by some chance Yves left through any other door.

Yes, he had to be inside.

Royce pulled out the lockpicks and eased the first one into the lock, angling it to find the tumbler within. These locks were not exactly the finest quality.

He heard a click and held his breath, praying Yves hadn't heard it too. After a moment, he drew the metal pick out. Then he straightened up and put one hand to the door knob, which turned smoothly.

He pushed the door inward…but nothing happened.

Royce suppressed a groan. Yves must have installed an extra bolt, though most landlords didn't permit tenants to do so.

Well, so much for subtlety. Royce backed up and then charged at the door, putting his considerable power into the move.

The door shuddered, but didn't open. Not yet.

Royce hurled himself at the door again, hearing a startled shout from within.

On the third try, the door gave way, sending Royce tumbling into the dark apartment, splinters of wood flying along with him.

Then another sharp crack shattered the night. A gunshot.

Royce ducked instinctively, feeling something whistle by far too close for comfort.

Another shot followed. Royce reached into his coat for his own gun, searching for where Yves's shot came from.

The darkness was a real hindrance, and Royce realized that Yves must have been much more suspicious than he let on, or he'd have lit a lamp when he came home.

Hearing the sound of a footstep, Royce aimed and squeezed the trigger.

A shout came from the opposite corner, but Royce doubted he hit his target.

Seconds later, someone rushed toward him, striking from the side and pitching Royce to the floor.

Both his instincts and his extensive training let him grab his opponent's arm without seeing it—Royce just knew where the other man was.

He followed up the grab with a swift punch, catching Yves in the jaw.

Yves grunted in pain and anger, but he wasn't going to give in easily.

The two men wrestled on the bare floor. Yves was not as big or strong as Royce, but he was slippery.

Royce opened his mouth to yell the signal to bring the Disreputables in for backup.

But then Yves fired his gun once more—how the hell did the man still have a gun in his grip? Royce saw the flash inches from his head, and it blinded him.

The sound also echoed in his brain…but he still had a brain inside his skull, so he must still be alive.

Yves scrambled up and was running toward the door when Royce roared the signal in a voice loud enough to carry to the end of the street. He jumped up and followed Yves out into the hallway.

The other man had a lead of fifty paces, which was enough to keep him just out of sight as the two of them pounded down stairs, down halls, past the cracked doors of fearful residents, and then out into the street.

Rook was watching the front door, and he sprang toward Yves with a stout club in his grip, ready to fight.

But Yves was ready too, and he flung the young Rook aside with vicious force, knocking the boy hard against the cobblestone surface of the street. He lay still.

Royce took this in and yelled for Yves to stop. The French agent merely laughed, running faster than ever now that he was in the open.

But Royce knew how to run too, and he kept up. He was dimly aware of shouting behind him, and the name of Rook being called in rage.

Yves ducked down short alleys and dodged around carts and carriages, in an attempt to lose Royce.

It didn't work. Royce was gaining. Forty paces behind now. Maybe less.

His quarry turned back, twisting halfway round to fling something back at Royce.

He avoided the little knife easily. In fact, he just grinned, because he saw the expression on Yves's face.

The other agent was furious. Royce knew he was getting the upper hand. Just a few steps more…

Then a horse galloped down the street, cutting between them. Royce had to skid to a halt and move around, cursing as he went.

He just caught sight of Yves turning aside into some fenced-in place. Without looking to either side, Royce plunged after him, and hurled himself into what seemed like a forest.

What the hell? He came to an abrupt stop, wondering where the city went. And where had Yves got to? The agent was clever, but he wasn't magical.

Royce checked his surroundings and realized he was in a graveyard. Nearby, an ancient church rose in the darkness, blocking out the sounds of the city from the other side. Here it was utterly quiet.

He held still, listening for the faintest sign from his quarry. A footstep, a kicked pebble.

I'll get you, you snake.

Then he did hear something, a faint scraping in the night, as if someone pushed a heavy stone against the ground.

He jumped into action, springing toward the sound, which came from the other end of the churchyard. He had to pass a huge willow tree with a trunk wide enough to conceal three men. But as he dove past it, he saw no one hiding there.

Out past the willow's shadow, he stopped just before tumbling into an open grave.

It must have been dug just that day, because the shovel was still there, jammed into a pile of freshly turned soil. Royce picked up the shovel to use as a weapon...and to stop Yves from doing the same.

He turned slowly, listening again. Yves was here, somewhere. Iron fencing at least eight feet high bordered the entire churchyard. The front gate was the only way in or out, unless Yves happened to have the key to the church itself.

Then a dark shape flew at him from the shadows. Yves was there for round two of the fight. Royce was more than happy to accommodate him.

He swung the shovel in an arc, hoping to smash Yves's head in.

Yves ducked just in time, and then kicked Royce hard in the chest, sending him back a step...which happed to be empty air.

Royce fell into the open grave, clutching his head in his hands to protect his skull. He slammed down on his back, groaning at the pain shooting through his whole body.

He shook his head once to make sure it was attached. It was. Bones broken? He didn't think any were. What angel kept him in one piece?

Perhaps an angel that wanted him alive to catch Yves.

Yves!

Royce tensed, expecting a dark form to drop on him from above. Yves was a killer—he'd want to finish the job.

A shadow loomed above, eclipsing the faintly blue tinge of the night sky.

Royce pulled out the knife out of his boot. "Come on," he growled. "I'm waiting."

Yves stared down for a long moment, not saying a word. Royce flexed his free hand, ready to punch the man's lights out before he stopped falling.

But then Yves's shadow vanished.

A single paper fluttered down to rest on Royce's chest. He heard a man's laugh fading into the distance. Royce grabbed the paper, shoving it into a pocket before he jumped to his feet. The grave was well-dug. The walls nearly vertical, the soil loose and loamy, crumbling under his hands.

But it was also just six feet deep, and Royce was slightly over six feet tall. He bent his legs to give him extra power, and then sprang upward, fueled by rage.

He jumped high enough to get his arms free, hooking his fingers into the ground and pulling himself up to the surface.

Royce rolled and got to his feet, expecting another attack.

But there was nothing. He was alone.

The paper. He pulled it out of his now-filthy coat, and unfolded it.

The words were written in a bold hand, with a flourish at the end.

Did you really think I did not see you coming?
Better luck next time.

Royce touched the ink, and found it still wet.

"God damn it." He crushed the paper in his hand. It was one thing to be a step behind another spy. It was quite another to be taunted for it.

And worse, Yves knew that his hideout was no longer a secret. He'd never return there. Royce lost the only true lead he'd got in months of searching.

It was over.

The fact was that Yves was a far better agent than Royce was. Aries should have chosen another member of the Zodiac for this assignment. Royce ought to resign. Let a new man take on the Sign of Virgo, someone who had the intelligence and skills to make a difference.

He stumbled out of the churchyard gate, startling an elderly woman who was walking by. She shrieked and made the sign of the cross to ward off Royce, who probably did look like something that just crawled from a grave.

"I need a drink," he muttered.

He might be a failure as a spy, but he did know where to find liquor in London.

♍

THE HOUR HAND HAD EDGED well past midnight, but Tamsin was still dressed in her evening gown. The day's newspaper lay on the lush carpet in the guest chamber of the townhouse. Tamsin was still reeling at the new coded message Hector placed in the personals column for her.

Three hundred at the bridge. Noon, Wednesday next.

Tamsin took a few deep breaths. This latest demand from Hector destroyed all her carefully constructed illusions. There was no way he'd ever stop bleeding her dry, and now Royce was involved, whether he knew it or not. Tamsin had to place her trust in Royce, and tell him the truth. She had to relate the full details of the scandal in her past, with names and dates, and then confess how she'd stolen from him to first try to cover up that shameful secret, and then to keep her father's future from being ruined too. Royce would be angry, certainly. But as Laurent once said, he always did the honorable thing. He'd help Tamsin through this mess because she was dependent on him.

Afterward, well, she'd accept whatever judgment he made.

It was time to admit to herself that she couldn't do anything in the face of Hector's threats. It was bad enough that he'd tell her family that she'd given up her virginity to him. Her mother would faint from shame, and her younger sister would be aghast. Georgina was six years younger than Tamsin, and she'd always been wide-eyed and impressionable. Tamsin hated to think how disgusted her little sister would be—she'd always looked up to Tamsin.

But holding her father's remaining debt in his hands, offering to ruin him all over again...that Tamsin couldn't endure. She'd take the shame she deserved, but she could not be responsible for hurting her family.

And now Royce was entangled in the mess too, all because she was too weak to refuse his offer of marriage as protection. But the potential damage was too great. Even if he paid Hector off for the rest of her life, it would inevitably come out that she had once been Hector's plaything, pregnant by him with no child to show for it. And now the world would think the same situation was going on with Lord Pelham. And then would be discovered eventually that Lord Pelham didn't just take her to his bed, but actually *married* her—a spoiled, fallen woman with the most dubious past. A mistress could be cast off. A wife was more difficult to dispose of. And Tamsin was the least suitable wife in London.

Tamsin walked downstairs to the parlour, so she'd know the moment Royce returned home. At least he'd be in a good mood to start. He was confident that he'd capture the Viper tonight, putting an end to his long-running assignment and the source of most of his distress over the past several months.

It will be a relief for me too, Tamsin thought, remembering the cold gaze of the French agent who made her work for a cause she despised. "The Viper under lock and key at last...how glorious."

She pictured it, and smiled, anticipating Royce's announcement. He'd be a little smug about it, she was sure…but then, he earned it.

"Royce, I have a confession," she whispered to the fireplace, practicing her speech again and again. She'd thought about writing it down…she much preferred writing to speaking. But who wanted to commit such shameful things to paper? She'd done enough damage with her pen.

There was a loud banging on the door. Errol opened it hastily, letting in a blast of chilled air and a disheveled figure.

"Dear God, sir," the footman burst out, forgetting all his training. "What happened to you?"

"London happened," Royce said, laughing oddly. "Get me some food, will you? And a drink. And maybe a bath… I'll be in here." He pointed to the parlour, and then blinked when he saw Tamsin. "I know you!"

She pulled him toward a couch, horrified at his appearance. "What's going on, Royce?"

"You look beautiful," he said, collapsing on the couch. "I ought to make you my mistress."

"Royce!" she hissed. "Are you well?"

"I'm right as rain, gorgeous." He grinned at her, and she smelled alcohol on his breath.

"You've been drinking."

"Dulls the pain." He gestured to a dark smear on his clothing. Blood.

"Oh, my God. You need a doctor."

"No, I need a spy."

"What?"

"I lost him."

"What?" she repeated, feeling like she too had drunk a bottle's worth of cheap gin. "You lost who?"

"The Viper. He's gone. He led me a merry chase and

left me for dead in a graveyard. I failed."

"Oh, Royce, no. You haven't. You can try again, once you're recovered…"

"Recovered from what?" His gaze narrowed, his lip curling into a sneer. "From being a failure?"

"Royce, you're not a failure in any way. You need to rest…we can talk in the morning…"

"No! Now! We're always dancing around the truth, always keeping things hidden. No more, Tamsin. Everyone needs to know the truth about me."

He lunged off the couch toward her. Tamsin barely caught him, his weight nearly bringing her down to the floor as well.

Just then, Errol opened the door to let Wendy in with a large tray, bearing a late night meal.

"Help me!" Tamsin said. "He can't keep his balance."

"Aye, 'cause he's three sheets to the wind. My lord," Errol said, in warning. "You ought to sit down."

"Don't tell me what to do," Royce snapped back. "This is my house."

"And you're drunk!" Tamsin yelled at him. "So listen to someone who isn't. Now sit down before you fall down. *Please.*"

"I've already fallen," he muttered. "I may as well just slit my own throat and get it over with."

Beside her, Wendy made a little sound of distress. "My lord, how could you say that!" She grasped Tamsin's arm.

Tamsin whispered, "As soon as you leave this room, go to the bedchamber and make sure to remove anything sharp. Scissors, shaving razor, anything."

"Yes, my lady." Wendy nodded.

At that moment, Marlow entered. He glanced over the scene, taking in at once what had happened. The older man sighed. "My lord, you're not yourself. Let's get you upstairs, shall we?"

"I'm exactly myself! That's the whole problem!"

"Sir…" Marlow said in a low voice. Mrs Marlow came in too, inexorably drawn by the unfolding disaster. "You are quite drunk, and you know how that doesn't help your moods. You need to get to your bed."

"I tried to tell him that," Tamsin said.

Her words brought Royce's attention back to her. "If you want me in bed, you know what to do, Tamsin."

She stared at him, open-mouthed. "Do not say another word," she warned him. All her worst fears suddenly manifested in the form of this man turning into someone she didn't know, with unpredictable reactions to the most basic requests. *If he talks like this about himself, what must he think of me?*

"Nothing matters anymore," he spat out, his head hanging so low his face was hidden from the others. He went on, mumbling, "I had responsibilities. I'd been tracking this man for months, and then he gets away like a ghost and there's nothing I can do…"

Silently, Mrs Marlow handed him a drink and he downed it in one go, his gaze still locked on Tamsin.

"…tell the Zodiac…" He paused, looking confused. Then he dropped the glass and promptly sagged to the couch, unconscious.

"Well, at least that blend works quickly," the cook murmured. She looked at Tamsin with a trace of apology in her expression. "When the lord's melancholy gets this bad, we find it best to let him sleep it off for a bit."

Wendy said anxiously, "Did he hurt you, my lady?"

Tamsin shook her head, overwhelmed. Had he hurt her? No, she'd hurt him. No matter what he said, this was her fault. She could have told Royce more about Yves, and sooner. Her fear became his undoing.

"I think, Mrs Marlow," she said quietly, "that I'd like a sip or two of your blend for myself."

* * * *

In the morning, Tamsin woke up in her bed, with little memory of how she got there. Wendy helped her upstairs, she recalled vaguely. The little maid spouted endless words meant to soothe and calm and reassure, but none of them worked. Tamsin had been a wreck, crying all over her gown and her night rail and the fine sheets that didn't belong to her.

But at least the drink had sent her into unconsciousness.

Now it was a new day, and she knew what she had to do.

Tamsin found Royce in his bedroom…though not in bed. Instead, he was slouched in the chair by the fire. His boots were off, but he wore the same outfit from last night, filthy from his midnight chase and rank with the smells of the city.

He opened his eyes when she approached, and sighed. "Tamsin. Whatever I said last night…I'm sorry."

"You don't remember?" she asked.

"Not the details." He rubbed his temples. "But I know that I said some vile things to you, and probably to Marlow and everyone else in my path."

"You were certainly not at your best," she allowed. "But you were very upset."

"I lost him, Tamsin," Royce said, more to himself than her. "Worse, I never *had* him. He was in control of the game the whole time, just playing with me to amuse himself. He staged the final chase just to stick the knife in."

"I told you he was a monster," said Tamsin. "For what it's worth, I think you were probably the only man likely to catch him. I should have helped you more, but *you* did your best."

"Clearly not," he growled.

"Royce, there's something I need to tell you," she said. "I'm leaving you."

He went still. "What?"

"I'm leaving you. I'm running away. I'd hoped meeting you would mark a fresh start for me, but things did not go as planned, which is the story of my life." She forced herself to sound nonchalant, even though she wanted to fling herself into his arms cry her heart out.

He straightened up in his chair, looking alarmed. "Tamsin, you can't."

"I certainly can. What happened last night…seeing you like that. It made things clear to me, and I am not the right woman for you." She couldn't tell him all the reasons why, but the more she thought about it, leaving Royce was the best way she could protect *him*, as well as herself.

"You can't listen to what I said when I was drunk."

"*In vino veritas*," she countered. "Royce, I can't live with you. I love you and I hope you'll eventually find someone you can love, but this is impossible. I'm never sure if I'm a secretary or a countess, I'm never sure if you'll smile or frown. I am a ruined woman who is somehow married to an earl. No one can live like this."

"But we *are* married," he said, seizing on that fact. "You can't leave."

She shook her head. "Tear up the evidence. Goodness, I didn't even use my real name."

"Still binding," he countered.

"Not if you don't press it. I vow that I shall never

come back as an inconvenient first wife. And then quash any rumors. Say it was a joke, one of your elaborate pranks. People will believe you—it's no more outrageous than anything else you've done."

"I need you."

"I don't want to be needed by you, Royce," she told him softly. "I can't be your pet chimaera, secretary by day, wife by night, there to take whatever mood you fling my way. I'm not a strong woman, and I'm not built for that."

"Tamsin, you're more than strong." He rose to his feet, then nearly stumbled, his legs and head not working in concert yet. She had to restrain herself from jumping forward to catch him and help him…her good intentions always hurt her in the end.

Royce cursed at his clumsiness, then said, "Don't you dare walk out of here. I forbid it."

"You did mean well, Royce. I'm sure you had the best intentions when you swept me off the streets in London and brought me home to save me. But saving someone is not so simple. Let's face it. I'm just another of your whims. And like all your whims, it's not durable."

"Tamsin."

"Trust me, you're better off without me. Goodbye, Royce."

Head held high, and her heart broken inside, she walked out.

♍

After Tamsin left the room, Royce didn't move for a long time. An observer who didn't know Royce might think he was unaffected. He didn't rant or rage or storm about. He was calm and quiet.

An observer who did know Royce would be chilled to the bone, because that quiet mien heralded the melancholy that so often plagued Royce, and once that pit yawned open in front of him, Royce would fall to the bottom and remain there for a long, long time. Days. Weeks. Months.

The specifics were uncertain.

Leave this house, a voice in his head warned him. The sooner he was away from the townhouse, the faster he could run from the feelings that were about to engulf him.

He ordered Marlow to pack his things and ordered Errol to call for the carriage to take him to Seabourne.

"You're leaving now, sir?" Errol asked, confused.

Royce shrugged. He stood at the window, staring at the slowly changing scene, wishing he could exchange lives with anyone he saw out there, whether it was a clerk hurrying down the street or the tramp slinking past the fence.

Anything was better than living inside his own body, his own muddied brain.

"Sir?" Errol prompted him.

"Never mind," Royce said then. "It's already too late."

Without saying more, he walked past Errol and went to his bedchamber, where he could lie down. Standing up was suddenly too much effort.

Sometime later, Royce was lying on the floor of his bedroom, arms flung out to his side, one leg straight and one leg bent. His pose reminded him of a tarot card a fortune-teller once showed him. He couldn't remember the name. Not that it mattered. Nothing mattered.

He was cold, despite being fully dressed except for his jacket, which hung on the rack where Marlow had put it earlier. Though Royce wasn't sure how much earlier. He meant to dress for dinner, but…it was a long time since he last ate. When was dinner anyway?

The effort to get up and put the jacket on, or to crawl to the bed and pull the covers over him, seemed far too great. So Royce just lay on the parquet floor and shivered.

Hour by hour, night by night, his thoughts swam through a dark blue world—Royce knew it well. It was the place he always came back to, no matter how he tried to evade it. The melancholy that afflicted him for years, ever since he was a very young man, had now grown into this blue morass of bad memories and miserable dreams.

The new part this time was Tamsin—briefly lighting up his life before leaving him, now in a darker place than ever before. It was somehow much more painful to endure these feelings after knowing that he *could* be happy. But he didn't blame her for walking away. Who would want to be near Royce when he was so weak and pathetic? He was terrible spy, a terrible earl, a terrible husband. Poor Tamsin. She'd be better off if he died. Then she could have all the benefits of being dowager countess of Pelham without having to deal with Royce.

Yes, he should kill himself for Tamsin. That would be

a good act, a final good act to counter a lifetime of bad acts.

How to do it, though? Once again, the sheer enormity of choosing how to die overwhelmed him. A shot to the brain would be quickest. But messy. And not worthy of the name of Pelham.

So, no bullets.

He could hang himself. Time-honored way to go, hanging. A bit fussy. He hated tying knots, and this would not be a time to get the details wrong.

Therefore, hanging was out.

Royce rolled his head to one side, catching sight of the dressing mirror on the wall.

"Broken glass," he said. Then, "No. Someone would have to sweep it up."

One by one, methods were discarded:

~~starvation~~ (too slow)

~~immolation~~ (too dramatic)

throw self off the cliff into the sea (too far to walk)

throw self off Charlesway Bridge (too repetitive)

The bedroom door squeaked open. Royce frowned, turning his head to see a figure in black.

"Who is it?" he asked, hoping it was Death.

Then the figure turned, and with an immense wave of disappointment, he noticed the crisp white starched apron.

"It's only Wendy, my lord. I'm here to light the fire." She skirted along the edge of the room, avoiding the area where he lay.

When Royce didn't say anything else, she knelt in front the fireplace and quickly cleaned it out before laying the new logs. By the time she lit the fire, the light from the windows had faded, leaving the sky the same deep, dark blue as his inner thoughts.

"What time is it?" he asked Wendy as she stood up.

"Nearly five o'clock, sir."

"Is it Tuesday?"

"Um, no sir. Friday."

Royce exhaled. Losing that much time wasn't good. "I don't remember when I last ate."

"You haven't touched the trays brought up to you, sir. Not since Miss Black left."

"Ah. So she's still gone, is she?"

"Yes, sir."

"You're certain?"

"Oh yes, sir."

"Bloody hell."

Wendy swallowed nervously. "Er, do you have any instructions, my lord? Or should I leave?"

He said, wearily, "I don't want to see anyone but Tamsin."

"But your meals…"

"Leave me alone!"

The maid fled, yanking the door shut behind her. Royce closed his eyes again. He shouldn't have snarled at the poor girl, but he could barely think, and could not bear to be questioned by some slip of a thing about whether he wanted dinner or not. Why would he want dinner? Tamsin left him forever. A dinner was not going to change that.

Time passed, while Royce alternately dreamed and woke, and hated both states. He didn't know how long it was until he was disturbed once more. This time, he opened his eyes to see a woman peering down at him, a quizzical look on her face. After a moment, he placed her. It was Chattan.

"I've sent several summons to you," she said.

"Didn't get them," he said shortly.

"Why not?"

"Don't care."

"I thought the erstwhile Miss Black handled your correspondence. Where is she?"

"Gone."

"Where has she gone?" Chattan asked with exaggerated patience.

"No idea."

"That's not very helpful."

"Ah, that could be the Pelham motto."

"I'm not here to see Pelham," the young lady said. "I'm here to see Virgo."

Royce twitched at the sound of the name...a name he had no right to use. "Get a new Virgo."

"Don't be ridiculous. You're the one who worked to get this far toward finding the Viper. We can't train a new person at this point."

Royce gestured to a chest in the corner. "Open it. There's a letter on the top. From the Viper. He's clearly far better than I am, and I've got no chance to catch him at anything."

Chattan retrieved the letter, read it, and folded it back up. "This is short, vague, unconvincing, and written by a man who's obviously driven by ego. He doesn't address you by your code name or your real name, he reveals no knowledge of your mission, and this letter offers absolutely no details. He might as well have left this for his landlord!"

Put that way, it made sense, but the only result was for Royce to feel as if he'd failed twice over. "All the more reason to get rid of me, if such a vague letter can work."

Chattan snapped, "It only works if you let it work! I am ordering you to get up off that floor and return to your duties, Virgo."

"Or what?"

"Or…I'll…"

"Get a new Virgo? I've already advised you to do that."

"We need *you*," she said, entreating this time.

"I am unworthy of the role. As evidenced by the fact that I am prone on my floor, unable to get to a standing position in the presence of my superior even when she is yelling at me to do so. Possibly a drink would help."

"I doubt that. The previous three bottles haven't helped." Chattan nudged a nearby empty bottle with her foot.

"Leave me alone, please. Tell Aries I've failed. Recruit a replacement. I'll find a way to end my life soon, so you'll not need to do it for me because you're worried about my lack of discretion."

She rolled her eyes. "We don't execute our retired Signs. Well, not often. And you can't kill yourself."

"I'm an earl. I can do whatever I like."

"Get up, sir. Present yourself at the Zodiac offices tonight at ten, or…else!"

Chattan stormed out, her ash-blonde hair flying out like banners signaling defeat.

The truth was that Chattan could offer nothing to persuade Royce to act, and she had surely realized that. Soon enough, Aries would make the decision to get a new Sign, and then Royce could die in peace.

♍

IMMEDIATELY AFTER LEAVING ROYCE'S TOWNHOUSE, Tamsin had spent an hour in an abject rage, until realizing that she had nowhere else to go. She was without friends or references.

But she did have some money.

She looked up the names of a few respectable boarding houses catering to ladies. At the third one, she found a proprietress who was quite willing to accept a few bank notes in lieu of references. Tamsin was shown to a room on the upper floor, plain but scrupulously clean. "Meals are taken in the parlour. You can make use of the sitting room in the morning and evening. Most of the women here are out during the day. Breakfast is served at six in the morning, dinner at six in the evening, and you do not pay less in rent if you skip meals."

Tamsin nodded, trailing after the woman as she swept along.

"No men are permitted in any part of the house," the woman warned her at the end of the tour.

"Good," said Tamsin. "The fewer men I meet, the happier I shall be."

The woman nodded. "Sensible girl, I see. What is your goal in London?"

"To leave it as soon as possible."

"*Very* sensible. Well, Miss Black, you may get settled.

Perhaps you'll be a voice of reason for some of the flightier young ladies here. Girls today seem to think that love is just around the corner, and a gentleman will solve all their problems. Where do they get such notions?"

From the whole world telling them that marriage is their only path to security, Tamsin thought. Aloud, she murmured, "They're reading the wrong sort of books, I expect."

"Undoubtedly," the woman agreed. "Myself, I do not read." She left then, which was for the best, since Tamsin wasn't sure how much longer she could conceal her disgust.

Out of sick compulsion, she continued to read the personal column in the *Pall Mall Advertiser*. Hector took four days to post his next message.

Quill—New home? Do tell, at bridge. 4pm Thursday

She knew what bridge he meant, though her mind flashed back to the Charlesway Bridge, where Royce first found her. Part of her wanted to retrace her steps there... hoping perhaps to step back in time and start over with Royce. She wouldn't make the same mistakes again. She wouldn't lose her heart and betray herself and him the way she'd done before.

On the appointed day, she walked to the wooden footbridge in the park where she last spoke to Hector.

He was there before her. "I've been waiting," he groused.

"Yes, that's typically what happens when someone arrives first to a meeting."

Hector ignored her sarcasm. "I wasn't sure you'd come, since you absconded from your old haunt."

"True," she said shortly. "I no longer reside there, nor do I have any dealings with anyone in the house."

"What of Lord Pelham?"

"What of him?" Tamsin asked carelessly, her heart aching at the mere mention of his name.

"Oh, confess. A lovers' spat? A falling out? Or did he find a younger and more luscious paramour?"

Tamsin did not reply.

"Did he learn of your clever accounting practices?" Hector asked, more concerned.

She shook her head at last. "No. At least, not at the time I left the house. He may have done since." In which case, she'd be sought by the city charleys, detained, and brought to a magistrate to learn her punishment…which would be transportation to a colony if she was lucky, or she'd simply be put to death. The amount of money she'd stolen from Royce suggested the latter possibility was more likely.

"Good," Hector breathed.

"What does it matter? I can't get more. As you know, I don't live there and am not welcome any longer."

"I think, Thomasina, you'll need to charm someone there into welcoming you for a little while. Long enough to write another banknote out to me."

"How greedy are you?" she snapped. "You have hundreds of pounds that you did not have before. Be content."

But evidently the one thing Hector could never be was content. He took Tamsin by the arm, squeezing tightly. "You never tell me what to do, woman. I was going to ask for two hundred again but you need a lesson in manners. This time, the payment will be five hundred."

"Five?" Tamsin gasped.

"In for a penny…" he said smugly.

She took a breath, then said in a shaky voice. "I'll get your five hundred, sir…in exchange for my father's IOU."

"What?" Hector laughed. "Never. It's worth more than five hundred. It's worth thousands!"

"Not if you'll never be able to collect on it," Tamsin countered. "My father may be alive and out of gaol, but he'll never be able to repay such debts. And you need the money now, to pay your own debts. Isn't that true?"

He grimaced, and she knew that was the heart of the matter. "A thousand," he declared.

Tamsin closed her eyes, but knew that it was useless to argue. After all, she was merely putting numbers on paper—it was no more difficult to write one thousand than it was five hundred. "Fine."

"You'll bring it here."

"No," she said instantly. "Pelham saw us last time, and he caught sight of you. If he's aware of what I've done, he'll track down all the places he knows we've been."

"Your new residence, then."

"Men are not permitted," she said, pleased to announce it.

"Mine, then."

"You must think me mad. It has to be a location we can both appear without arousing any suspicion," she continued, ignoring Hector's leer. "I have it. The Theatre Royal." That location would allow her enough light and space to view whatever document Hector brought, to ensure it was real. She wouldn't put it past Hector to try to trick her with a cheap copy, while Hector kept the original contract.

"Very well," Hector growled. "Meet me on Saturday at nine in the evening in the mezzanine. You'd better have the payment."

"And you'd better have the contract," she returned. She hurried away without a further word.

In the end, it was frightfully easy to return to Royce's

townhouse. She walked to the servants' entrance and knocked. Errol nearly pulled her inside by the arm.

"Oh, miss, thank goodness you've come back. His lordship hasn't been the same since you left, and now young master Laurent is here and we just don't know what to do—"

"Hold a moment, Errol!" She looked around, expecting to see the place on fire. "I am not really here. That is, I just forgot something and I need to find it upstairs. Then I'm leaving again, and it would be best if the earl never even knew I'd crossed the threshold."

He looked deflated. "You're not here because of his lordship's condition?"

Tamsin scarcely heard him, and certainly didn't register his words. "I only have a few moments. Please may I go upstairs? I left a…" She struggled to think of something innocuous. "A pen in the library. It's ivory and very important to me."

Errol merely nodded, not even listening to her now. "Go, then, miss."

"I won't disturb him," she promised.

"Small chance of that," the footman replied with a snort, leaving Tamsin to wonder exactly what was going on. However, her curiosity would have to wait.

She made her way up one floor to the library, which was dim and cold. It looked like the fire hadn't been lit in days, which made little sense, since Royce spent so much of his time in this room.

Still, it was lucky for Tamsin that he wasn't here now. Lighting a lamp, she hurried to the desk where Royce kept all the ledgers and forms she needed. She briefly checked the ledger to see if Royce had noted any discrepancies in the accounts. However, he'd made no notes at all. The last entry was one Tamsin herself had made the day before she stormed out. She sighed. Royce really was useless when it came to keeping his personal world organized.

Then she pulled out the little booklet where the blank cheques were stored. Trembling, she reached for a pen. Was she really going to steal a thousand pounds today? It was an unbelievable sum, more than she'd ever seen at one time in her whole life.

She wished she could tell Hector to go to hell. She wished that she could confide in Royce, and that he'd help her. But Hector held too many cards. He'd pull the IOU out, and ruin her father again, out of spite. He'd tarnish her whole family's name with the story of how she allowed him into her bed. He'd use the pregnancy to take Tamsin's freedom away—after all, she couldn't prove that she'd miscarried. In the eyes of a pious judge, she might as well be a murderess.

"It's the money, or it's everyone I love getting hurt," she told herself, trying to make herself believe it. "And this is the last time."

Suddenly, a howling sound echoed though the hallway outside, and Tamsin froze in fear, feeling as if some divine alarm had been set off by her shameful thoughts. What could be happening?

Then the door was pushed open and something streaked inside, heading directly for Tamsin.

She was nearly knocked off her feet by five stone of frantic dog, alternately licking her face and hands and then yelping happily.

"Jasper!" she said in surprise. "Oh, my lord, Jasper! How did you get here?"

Forgetting everything else for the moment, Tamsin hugged the dog close, then petted him and vigorously scratched his ears. "Who's my excellent boy?" she asked in a delighted confusion. "Who's so good to remember me? Jasper, you're so good! I hope you didn't run all the way from Seabourne to find me."

"He rode most of the way," a voice said from the doorway. "In a carriage. My father owns more than he needs."

Tamsin looked over to see Laurent, of all people. "You came to London? Did Royce send for you?"

"Certainly not, and even if he wanted to, he couldn't have."

"I don't understand."

"Oh, there's a lot I don't understand either," Laurent retorted. He looked both furious and frightened, and very much his tender age of sixteen. "What's your hold on my father?"

"My hold? I have none, I assure you." He let Tamsin walk straight out of the house, after all. He couldn't have been that enraptured.

"He keeps saying your name. Tamsin, Tamsin, my Tamsin. Whenever anyone tries to help him or reason with him or give him so much as a drink of water, he only wants you."

She frowned. Help Royce? Why would Royce need help?

"I am sorry. I can't imagine why he should be so fix-ated on me. We haven't known each other that long and I parted on very bad terms with him. I told him to forget me."

"He's not likely to forget his wife," Laurent snapped.

Tamsin sucked in a breath, her heart dropping to her feet. Beside her, Jasper whined in consternation.

"What?" she whispered.

Laurent gave her a thin smile. "My father's not the only one capable of skulking around and getting into trouble. I happened upon his will a few days ago. A new will that makes it clear that his *wife*, Lady Royce, the Countess of Pelham, nee Thomasina Latimer, also known as Tamsin Black, shall be well provided for."

"Oh, damn." She closed her eyes.

"Why does he have to hide a marriage?" Laurent went on. "Who are you hiding it from, and how long did either of you expect to get away with it?"

Her knees buckled.

Laurent caught her before she hit the floor. "Oh, no! Don't swoon on me, I beg you!"

He helped her to a chair, and she sank onto the cushion. Tears were flowing down her cheeks as she took gulping breaths. But it all happened silently. Tamsin had no words. Her mind was utterly blank.

Meanwhile, Laurent was staring at her in horror, unable to think of what to do with a fainting woman.

However, there is one action that a gentleman can always take in a time of crisis—regardless of what sort of crisis—and Laurent took it now.

He yanked the bell rope to summon help.

Wendy appeared a moment later. "Yes, sir?"

"I need tea! That is, the lady needs tea. Or smelling salts. Or something," Laurent said, slightly frantic. "And I need a drink."

Wendy rushed to comply with the conflicting orders, fetching smelling salts from her mother's own supply to bring Tamsin to a sitting position.

"Ugh, that's enough!" Tamsin said, pushing the bottle with its pungent aroma away. "I'm fine! I just had a turn."

"Tea, miss?" Wendy asked anxiously.

Tamsin said yes, mostly to give Wendy something to do. Meanwhile, Laurent made his way to a side table and poured himself a glass of brandy. He took one swig, coughed, and then refilled the glass.

Laurent sagged back in his chair. "I shouldn't have sprung that on you. It's just that everything is so damnably upended around here. Clearly, something is the matter—something serious. And yet I've got no clue what. Only that you play a role, Miss Black...or Miss Latimer. No, you're Lady Royce now. God damn. You see the problem!"

"Why not call me Tamsin," she said, still reeling. "And I shall call you Laurent. After all, we are technically family."

He nodded. "So, Tamsin. Can you tell me why he married you, and why neither of you made it public?"

She sighed. "It's fairly simple in the end. Certainly, I never intended to...um..."

"You slept with him," he supplied, with no trace of censure.

She nodded. "Afterward, Royce asked me to marry him, or rather told me to marry him. I said no, but he was very insistent, and Royce is a difficult man to oppose for long."

"Indeed," Laurent said.

"His argument may be more noble-sounding, but I am sure that he feared I would become pregnant with his child, and he did not want that child to be born a bastard..."

"...like me."

Tamsin nodded. "He saw the difficulty you endured, and he wanted to avoid that for another child."

"I suppose you are too well-born to be cast off. Whereas my mother was just a common actress."

"Oh, Laurent," she said, sensing his pain. "You told me once that Royce is very aware of his duty. If he'd known your mother was with child, he would have taken care of her and you from the first moment. He's not the type to refuse to do the right thing."

"Is that why he married you?" he asked.

Tamsin nodded. "I suspect that he saw marriage as the only way to handle the results of our affair honorably. I accepted his offer…well, because my heart wanted to believe it."

Laurent was quiet for a moment, frowning thoughtfully. Jasper helped by providing a soft, silky head for Laurent to pet while he thought. At last he said, "*Are* you carrying a child?"

"Not that I know of."

"So why jump into marriage? He's no fool, and it sounds as if you weren't angling for it. He could have waited."

"I wish he had. The wife of Lord Pelham is a very public role, and I would prefer to live anonymously. If Royce is talking to anyone, that person should talk him into an annulment. He must regret his choice."

"Who the hell knows what he's thinking," Laurent said. "I've been here three days and he's barely spoken to me."

Now Tamsin frowned. "So Royce really didn't ask for you to come. Why are you in London at all?"

"I was only intending to stay here one night," he said. "Just long enough to rest and get some, er, funds, before I boarded the ship to France."

"If you hate Royce so much, why are you still here? When does your ship sail?"

"Two days ago," Laurent growled. "I'll have to find another. But I couldn't just leave my father like he is."

"Like what?"

"You don't know?" Laurent blinked in confusion, until he realized that in fact there was no way Tamsin would know, since she'd been gone for over a week. "He's up-stairs, nearly catatonic. He hasn't eaten in days, apparent-ly."

"Oh, my Lord. I have to see him."

Upstairs, Wendy looked at her with a stricken expres-sion at odds with her usual cheer. "It's terrible, miss. He won't speak to anyone, and he barely eats. Aside from calling your name, he hardly ever makes a sound...it's like a tomb in there."

"Well, I shall try to find out what's going on. I owe him that." She owed him much more than that, but for now, she had to focus.

Wendy opened the door to the master suite, and Tam-sin slipped inside.

The curtains were drawn, the fireplace cold.

Royce lay on the floor, a blanket half wrapped around him. His eyes were open, and he was staring at the ceil-ing. She saw the rise and fall of his chest, but that was the only indication that he was alive.

She sank down beside him. "Royce?" she asked softly.

No response.

She reached out and took him by the shoulder, shaking him. His flesh was cold to the touch, and she pulled the blanket around him. "Royce, you're freezing here on the floor. Can't you get up?"

He reacted to her touch, flinching away slightly. But otherwise, there was no indication that he heard her or cared that she was in the room.

Tamsin frowned. Royce in a mood was one thing. This was entirely different, and far more serious than what she could have imagined. Still, what could she tell him except the truth?

"Royce, I need you to know that I didn't come here to speak to you. I didn't even know this was happening. You lying on the floor for a week, I mean. The truth is, I came here to steal your money."

She waited, but evidently that statement wasn't even enough to shock him out of his fugue state. "Royce, did you hear me? I stole a thousand pounds from you today! I've stolen from you before this too. I wrote cheques in your name. Honestly, it's too easy. You're lucky none of your former secretaries thought of it."

Tamsin reached for his hand. She gripped his fingers tightly, but got no answering squeeze, which made her heart break.

"The fact is," she explained, spurred on by the terrifying silence and eager to fill it in, "I'm being blackmailed. A man named Hector Englefield saw me at Seabourne, and he recognized me as Thomasina Latimer, the girl who worked as a governess in his house in Somerset. You probably already guessed what had happened to me. Years ago, I ran away to London to get away from him, and if I'd known he was anywhere near Norfolk, I never would have let you drag me there. I'd rather have run into Swigg or Yves at midnight! Hector said he'd tell my family that I got pregnant with his child and then tried to maneuver him into marriage, or some other horrible story."

She laughed hollowly. "As if I'd marry that hideous man. But he threatened to tell you, causing me to lose my position as secretary. So I paid Hector to keep his mouth shut. Thank God he doesn't know we actually got married. He'd have enjoyed destroying your reputation too. As it is, he threatened to produce a doctor who'd lie for him and claim that I aborted my own child. And what could I say to that? There's no way to prove or disprove such a claim, especially years later. The courts would side with a man, you know that, which would put me behind walls for the rest of my life. A simple lie for him, a prison sentence for me. I had no choice but to pay him, at least for as long as I wanted to remain free."

Tamsin rubbed her thumb against Royce's fingers, trying to bring some warmth and life back into them. "Oh, I wish you'd wake up. I wish you'd be angry at me. You should be. I'm a disaster of a woman. I let my family down, I let you down. I am utterly ruined and I ruin everyone else I come to care about." She leaned down and kissed his forehead.

"I'm leaving now. I have to go to the Theatre Royal tonight. I'm going to pay off Hector one final time, and then I'm leaving England. It's the safest thing to do. I plan to tell him that there will be no further way to get money from this scandal. And he still doesn't know about our secret marriage, so you'll be safe enough once I'm gone."

Tamsin took a few moments to relight the fire, feeding it with logs until the blaze warmed the bricks and sent heat into the room.

"My God, it's amazing that you haven't died yet. It's cold outside, you know that, Royce? You're not even wearing a shirt!"

He also looked rather hollow, his cheeks sunken under the growth of beard, and his stomach concave. She'd learned from Wendy that the servants tried to entice him to eat, and even tried to hand-feed him, all to no avail.

"I love you, Royce. I think there's never been a person on this earth who has done so much for me when there was nothing to gain by it. When you emerge from this melancholy, you'll probably not even remember me. So I'll not bother you again. I don't even know where I'm going, so I can't tell you if I'll end up in America or India or Canada. Who knows! But I'll never forget you, my love." She kissed him again, softly on his lips. Her eyes stung at the lack of response, but then again, why should she expect anything else?

Tamsin stood up and wiped tears away before they fell. "I wish I could stay, but I can't. If I don't meet Hector, this is all for nothing anyway. Look," she said desperately, "if you want, I'll come back tonight. I can sit with you! Would you like that?"

Nothing. *Nothing.*

Her heart broke a little more. "All right, then. I'll go. Goodbye, Royce."

She left the room, closing the door. Wendy was still there, patient and hopeful until Tamsin shook her head sadly.

"I couldn't get through to him. I tried everything. My advice is to call for a doctor, one who will actually know how to address this matter. It's clear that I am not up to the task."

Tamsin walked away from the house, and did not look back at the window in the left corner, where the curtains would be drawn anyway, hiding Royce from the world. This strange ordeal was over. She allowed herself to believe in an illusion—a happy life with a good man, free from scandals and suffering. But Tamsin brought suffering with her. Her past mistakes could never be erased, and she was a fool for thinking otherwise. Well, at least she was letting Royce go. She refused to drag him further into her tragedy of a life.

Meanwhile, back in the gloomy, grey stone house, in the dark bedroom where he lay, Royce blinked slowly. He'd heard everything she said, but his body was so frozen and sluggish, he hadn't been able to respond to anything. He couldn't even open his eyes while she was there, spilling her heart out to him.

And her words now hit him, though the details were still jumbled and frightening. She stole from him, she loved him, she was leaving again, she was going to meet the man who ruined her, an immoral beast of a man who was about to learn that his golden goose was going to be lost forever.

He knew what a man like that was capable of.

Royce sat up slowly, a fire kindling in his eyes.

♍

WHEN TAMSIN LEFT ROYCE, SHE felt utterly defeated by his lack of response, his lack of love for her. But now she had to hurry. She'd spent far longer inside than she expected, first talking with Laurent, then to Royce, then to Marlow and Wendy. After hurried discussions of consulting more doctors, or even the Zodiac (who, Tamsin was astonished to learn, Marlow was fully aware of), it was decided that they'd wait one more day, and then (as Marlow put it) "let the stars decide" what to do.

Sadly, she had to leave Jasper at the house too, though she would have adored bringing the dog to her appointment with Hector. She remembered how Jasper had behaved the last time they met, and how helpful the dog was at keeping Hector at bay.

But now, it was time to meet Hector in the mezzanine of the Theatre Royal in Drury Lane. She barely had time to stop at her rooms and change into her one suitable gown, so that she might fit in with the theatre's attendees. She was relieved that they'd be meeting at the theater, however. The setting would be so crowded that a quick conversion shouldn't attract attention, and so public that Hector couldn't raise his voice or manhandle Tamsin without her calling for help.

And this would be the final time. If he asked for any more money, he'd find there was no one to ask, because

Tamsin intended to leave England. If he revealed the story of their brief affair publicly to spite her, he'd be squandering the only value the story had, which was that it was a secret. Tamsin worried that some rumors would leak out to cause trouble for her sister or for Royce, but she reasoned that Gina was safe enough in Somerset, and Royce had his own ways of dealing with scandal, assuming he even cared.

The streets were clogged with traffic, so she alighted a block away and paid the coachman, then turned to walk the last part of the way to the theater entrance.

Along the same side of the street, a light-haired man in an opera cloak and black silk hat was walking toward her at a fast pace. He slowed upon reaching her, asking, "Excuse me, ma'am, but have you seen a little girl wearing green? Blonde hair in curls?"

"Why, no. I'm sorry." Instinctively, Tamsin looked around hoping to catch a glimpse of this missing child, and that was her undoing.

As she turned away from him, the man slipped an arm around her neck and jabbed something sharp into her lower back.

"Now, Miss Tess Black," he said in a low voice, "don't struggle or I shall accidentally puncture your kidney. There's a man who wants to see you. Come with me and don't make any fuss."

"What is this?" she gasped. "Hector too scared to meet me alone?" But no…Hector never knew her by that name…

The man started walking her away from the theater, and turned down a narrow passage before he replied, with a snort, "Whoever Hector may be, he will have to wait. How many men have you given the slip in this city? I ought to bind you."

Even as he said the words, Tamsin tried to escape, but he was too fast and strong for her. A moment later, he'd forced her into a painful position with her arm pinned behind her back. The man produced a length of thin rope from somewhere under his voluminous cloak, and bound Tamsin's hands. "There we are," he said, satisfied with his work. "I do like a biddable lady."

Then he marched her down the alley to another street where he hailed a hansom cab. He hustled her inside. There was no chance to scream or to signal the coachman—not that he looked very alert anyway. She was also acutely conscious of the sharp point of the knife in her side.

Did she have anything she could use as a weapon? She did have her little pen knife in her reticule…but the moment she thought of that, she realized she no longer had the reticule with her. She must have dropped it in the scuffle. Tamsin closed her eyes and moaned in despair when she remembered the other little item in that bag—the forged banknote. Oh, Lord.

Galvanized by desperation, Tamsin leaned toward the other door, but the man yanked her toward him the moment he noticed.

"Don't be clever, my girl. Just go along with me to Swigg, and you'll be safe and sound back home soon."

She sent him a scathing look. "You cannot be serious."

The man shrugged. "Well, it's no matter to me either way. As long as I deliver you alive, I get paid."

"Truly you are a paragon among men."

After that remark, he gagged her as well.

She spent the rest of the journey trying to breathe while biting down on the foul-tasting cloth, hoping to gnaw it apart. She only succeeded in making her mouth dry.

The coach stopped at the head of a depressingly familiar alleyway. This was the entrance to Swigg's little kingdom in St Giles. She was hauled out of the coach and marched down the alley, with no chance for escape.

Finally, they arrived in the big room where Swigg conducted his business. He sat in his customary chair, looking like a slovenly king in a cheap theatrical farce.

"Miss Tess Black, as requested." The man shoved her forward, still bound and gagged.

Swigg looked her up and down. "So it is. Very nicely garbed too. Whooo! Silk and fur. Our little Tess is moving up in the world. Heard you was some swell's bit, and I had one of my men watching the house you was seen at. Where was it? Grosvenor Square? Well done, Tess. Well done indeed."

Tamsin glared at him, unable to speak due to the gag.

Swigg made a cutting gesture, and the kidnapper removed the gag, then the rope at her wrists.

She rubbed life back into her hands, wishing that she could have a glass of water.

"Well, Tess? What have you got to say for yourself?" Swigg asked.

"Why am I here?" she demanded.

Swigg raised an eyebrow. "No sense getting testy, Tess. You're here because I own you."

"You most certainly do not. And you'll regret kidnapping me and bringing me here. You don't know anything about me!"

"I know you're awful slippery to catch. Where were you hiding for weeks, Tess?"

"A charming estate by the sea," she replied. "And then, as you apparently found out, a London townhouse in Grosvenor Square."

He laughed. "Should have stayed by the sea, Tess.

One of my pickpockets saw you in the park while he was working. Had to look three times to be sure it was you, he said. 'Twas that pretty hair that caught his eye. Not many ladies with hair like yours."

Tamsin wished she'd cut it all off.

"Enough of this." Yves stepped into the light, and Tamsin took an instinctive step back. Now that she fully understood who and what he was—the Viper, one of Napoleon's most lethal agents—she realized what danger she was in.

"The lady has a task," Yves went on. "I need one more document, and then her work will be finished."

Tamsin took a deep breath. "And after that?"

"Let's not get ahead of ourselves," Swigg cautioned. "Just do what the gentleman says and you'll come to no harm."

"That's probably the sort of order you give the prostitutes in your house on Mulberry Street," she retorted. "I doubt they believe you any more than I do."

"Tess, my girl, I don't want you to get hurt," Swigg said, his eyes flashing in some sort of warning. Then Swigg glanced at Yves, guilt written all over his face.

Tamsin knew he'd never help her. He already made a deal with this French agent. He cared more about his reputation among the underworld than about sparing Tamsin's life...or even his presumed loyalty to England.

Yves walked up to her and took her elbow, quite gently. "This way, mademoiselle. Swigg set aside a workroom just for you."

Oh, what a prize, Tamsin thought, as rising panic started to eat at her nerves.

Upstairs in the room set aside as her prison cell, Yves regarded her for a long moment, then said, "I wish you had not vanished, mademoiselle. It was rather inconvenient."

"I am so sorry that I did not take your schedule into account while I was fleeing for my life from Swigg's goon."

He rolled his eyes. "Swigg has his uses, but he is not subtle, yes? That man Coaker scared you when there was no need for it."

"I never want to see him again."

"You won't," Yves said in an offhand way. "I was very irritated when he brought back the news that you'd got away. I took out my irritation on him."

Tamsin went still. "You killed Coaker?"

He dropped a familiar-looking knife on the desk. "It was no great loss to society."

Coaker was several stone heavier than Yves, and anyone would have wagered that Coaker would come out ahead in a fight against the wiry French agent. Yves was even more vicious than she'd thought.

Taking the knife back, Yves placed two papers before her on the desk, one obviously an official document that had been stolen. The other was in Yves's own hand, a short block of text that Tamsin was meant to copy in the style of the stolen document.

"Practice this man's hand, and then copy out the text onto this page." He produced a blank sheet of exquisite stationery, the sort only the very rich could afford. "I have a few spare sheets, but I do not recommend sabotaging my efforts by sullying the papers."

"I have never done that in the past," she said stiffly.

"Ah, but that was the past."

Tamsin held up the stationery, admiring its quality. She saw the watermark, lit up by the glow of the candle behind the paper, and squinted. Then she gasped.

"That's the crest of General Wellesley! He must have

ordered it made just for him! Where did you get this?"

"Such special items are sent to the customer via courier. Alas, this courier had an unfortunate accident on the road, and died of his injuries. I could not have him alive to tell what happened, of course."

Tamsin was aghast. An innocent man was killed for blank paper? She ought to write her forgery in blood.

"But…someone would see the paper was missing."

"I only took a dozen sheets, and changed the listing on the inventory. I am careful, mademoiselle. To have taken the whole supply would be greedy and stupid. Swigg would have taken it all. That is why he's the petty strongman of a waterside slum, and I consort with kings."

She always guessed Yves had a high opinion of himself, but his ego was truly offensive.

He leaned over her and whispered in her ear. "I happen to like you, Mademoiselle Tess. Do this for me and I will keep you safe. Your skills would be quite valuable to the empire."

She nodded, but didn't believe him for a moment. She'd seen the coldness in his eyes—Yves was a killer. Tamsin's penmanship was not enough to save her life.

With no other choice, she turned her attention to the text Yves gave her. It was straightforward, conveying orders for troops to withdraw from the city of Faro in the south of Portugal on a certain date in December. Tamsin recalled an earlier document that she'd done for Yves. That had been about ship movements, but the date was very close.

"You're clearing the area around Lisbon and the south of the country," she said, enlightened. "The French need to take it, but the British forces are too strong now."

He gave her a thin smile. "Mademoiselle is a general now. Yes, the city of Lisbon, and indeed, the country of

Portugal, is a major prize. The Emperor means to have it."

"I thought he was such a good general himself. Why resort to trickery? Can't he just win on the battlefield?"

"Ah, that is very naive of you. But not surprising. That is the lie we are all told as children, that war takes place on battlefields, between two armies playing by rules we all agree on. Nonsense. War is constant. It happens on battlefields, in bedrooms, in bars. It's secrets stolen from those too stupid to keep them close. It's a well-placed word in the ear of an easily persuaded noble. It's a contract with a shipping firm that divides the owner's loyalty between countries."

"Spying isn't war."

"It's the heart of war," Yves corrected. "Information is far more valuable than raw strength. It's in the oldest stories. The Trojan horse! Just think if the Trojans had known what it contained. They would have never allowed it inside the city, they'd have burned it, along with the men inside. *That* is war."

Tamsin looked away. She didn't want to argue with this man any longer. She didn't agree with his cynical view that all means were justified to achieve victory. She was sure that Royce adhered to certain rules—would he kill an innocent civilian to get a few pieces of paper? She couldn't believe it. He'd find another way. Yves just liked to kill.

And she was his next target.

♍

IN THE GROSVENOR SQUARE TOWNHOUSE, Royce walked out of his room for the first time in nearly two weeks. "Marlow, get my coat."

"My lord?" The butler gazed at him in shock, which in retrospect Royce would have to concede was natural, since not a half hour previously, he'd been virtually co-matose on the floor upstairs.

But now he was awake, aware, and absolutely ready to chase Tamsin and her tormentor to the gates of hell. "My coat, Marlow! Now, if you please. I've got to go after Tamsin." In his state, the nicety of referring to her only as Miss Black was forgotten.

"Sir, she's already gone. Said she had to go to the the-ater tonight. And you should not go anywhere until you've been seen by a doctor. And taken a bath," Marlow added, with a meaningful wave of his hand past his nose.

Royce took a deep breath, ran his fingers over his chin in thought, and realized that a bath wasn't the only thing he needed to do before going out among polite society. When was the last time he shaved?

The butler sighed. "Not to worry, sir, we'll have it all sorted." He bellowed for his daughter to get the hot water ready for a bath, then turned back to Royce. "One hour, and you'll be fit for Almack's...not that you'd ever be seen there."

"Did she say which theater she was going to?" Royce asked intently. "She said, but I can't remember."

"The Theatre Royal."

He nodded. Tamsin was clever to choose a public spot for her meetings with her blackmailer. Royce could hardly wait to find the bastard.

An hour later, Royce was fed, bathed, shaved, and dressed. Errol got the carriage ready just in time for Royce to jump in and order him to drive for Drury Lane. Inside the cab, Royce drummed his fingers against the glass, eager to jump out as soon as Errol slowed down. He felt like he'd risen from the dead, given a final chance to redeem himself by extracting Tamsin from the clutches of this blackmailer.

Errol drove with extreme recklessness, to judge by the yelling that occurred at every cross street. At the Theatre Royal, Royce practically leapt out, calling for Errol to keep the carriage ready.

Inside the theater, the crowd was gossipy, glittery, somewhat tipsy, and mostly unaware that the play itself was actually in progress. The lobby and halls were still thronged with people, making Royce grateful that he'd taken Marlow's advice to make himself presentable. Everywhere, he looked for Tamsin. A few times, he spotted a woman with red hair, but each time he was bitterly disappointed when he saw a face that didn't belong to her.

"God damn it, Tamsin, where are you," he muttered as he pushed through a knot of gentlemen blathering about some actress debuting that night. He wanted to knock them all to the floor.

Then Royce drew himself up short. He was panicking. Never a good sign. He was an agent, he'd trained for this sort of thing—finding clues in a crowd. He deliberately stopped and moved to a wall, looking over the whole crowd, taking in the scene.

He breathed deeply. The calmer he was, the better chance he had to catch sight of Tamsin...or notice something else.

The crowd actually was moving, albeit slowly, into the auditorium proper. Those who held box seats passed through the individual doors to each one, while the bulk of the crowd entered the doors for the main seating.

Within about fifteen minutes, the mezzanine was much closer to empty. Royce examined the remaining people, and noticed one gentleman who impatiently checked his pocket watch every few moments. The man was blond, broad-shouldered, and probably close to Royce in age. He looked as impatient as Royce felt.

He's the one, Royce thought.

Rationally, there were a dozen reasons for a man to look at a watch in a theater lobby. But one thing Royce learned as a spy was to trust his gut.

He detached himself from his patch of wall and strolled directly toward the man. He recognized him when he was halfway across the space. He'd met him at a party some weeks ago. What was his name...Dingleman...Eagleford...Englefield!

To judge by Englefield's startled expression, he also recognized Royce.

"Lord Pelham!" he said, sounding anything but pleased.

"Where is she?" Royce returned, skipping all pretense.

Englefield's expression grew furtive. "I don't know who you mean."

"Don't lie to me. She said she intended to meet you here. So where is she?"

"Hell if I know!" Englefield snapped, suddenly revealing his anxiousness. "She was supposed to be here nearly an hour ago!"

Royce didn't like the sound of that. Tamsin was scrupulous in keeping her schedule, and she definitely wouldn't be late for an exchange like this, when her reputation hung in the balance.

If she wasn't here, something had gone wrong.

He walked toward the main doors without a further word. Englefield said something behind him, but Royce had already excised the man from his attention. Now all his concentration was aimed at finding Tamsin and all the possible things that could have prevented her from arriving safely.

Royce walked down Drury Lane, which was quite dark by now, lit only by occasional lamps from taverns or other businesses still open at this hour. He kept scanning the people he passed, but no one seemed out of the ordinary, and there was no hint to lead him to...

He stopped, seeing a tiny crumpled wad of fabric near the corner of a brick building leading to a narrow alley. The material wasn't remarkable, just the simple cotton of a lady's evening reticule. But the fact that it lay unattended on a London street was ominous. A lady did not drop her bag, and if by some chance she did, she'd raise a hue and cry immediately.

Before he consciously decided to do so, Royce had already pulled the ribbon off, letting the bag gape open. He dug out a few small coins, a piece of folded paper, and a small silver knife, the protective leather sheath stamped with ivy leaves.

He'd seen that knife many times, when Tamsin used it to sharpen the nib of whatever pen she was using. Royce took a breath, then moved on to the paper, hoping it would lead him to her somehow.

When he unfolded it, though, he was hit with a sense

of the uncanny. Here was a banknote for one thousand pounds with his signature on it...but he certainly never signed this!

"Hell, she is good," Royce muttered, staring at the curves and loops of letters painfully familiar to him. His very own penmanship, but not his at all.

A thousand pounds was an outlandish amount, and it reminded him of just how deep in trouble Tamsin was. But if she had been robbed, the person would have taken the reticule. Instead, it was the one thing left behind.

Royce closed his eyes, imagining the scene. Tamsin hurrying toward the theater in evening dress, focused on meeting her blackmailer. She passes an alleyway...a man steps out...a scuffle, and the reticule falls to the ground in the chaos as the two figures disappear into the alley....

The picture might not be perfect, but it made sense. Tamsin hadn't been robbed. She'd been kidnapped.

Englefield had no reason to kidnap her. But there was a man in London who doubtless put the word out that if Miss Tess Black were spotted on the streets, a hefty reward awaited whoever brought her in.

Swigg.

Instinct now took over Royce's actions. He identified his quarry; all that was left was to hunt him down. But he wasn't an animal, he was a civilized man.

So instead of prowling the streets in search of a scene, Royce turned back to his carriage. He asked Errol, "Where's the best place to find a Disreputable who will know where to find the leader of St Giles's criminal lot? Marlow mentioned hearing about Swigg...I want to find out where he lives."

Errol nodded. "I know who will know, but he might not be willing to talk."

"I'll convince him," Royce muttered, cracking the

knuckles of his right hand without noticing he did it.

Errol drove the carriage to a neighborhood considerably poorer than the one where the Theatre Royal sat. Royce looked out at sagging houses and rubbish-strewn streets when Errol brought the carriage to a halt.

Royce got out, hearing Errol say, "See that building, with the white window trim? Go in there and ask for Dr Cutter."

"A doctor?" Royce asked in surprise.

"Just ask for him. He's often helped the Disreputables when one of us gets into a scrape and can't go for help where awkward questions would be asked."

He nodded and headed for the building. Inside, the place was as clean as the streets were dirty. A skinny girl carrying a mop and bucket stopped in surprise on seeing a well-dressed gentleman step in.

"I need to speak to Cutter," he told her. "And I can't wait. A woman's life is in danger."

She said nothing, but after a moment, she jerked her head to indicate that he should follow her down the hallway, up a narrow staircase, and into a whitewashed room lit by a dozen oil lamps, blazingly bright compared to the rest of the building. A prone body lay stretched on a narrow table, the torso exposed and bloody. A man in a thick canvas apron stood next to the table, holding a wickedly sharp implement in one hand.

"Sally! I'm operating. You know better—"

"I made her bring me to you," Royce interjected, stepping in behind her. "I was told you know where I can find Swigg."

"Lots of men named Swigg in London, I'll bet," the man said, looking at the inert patient instead of Royce. Dr Cutter, for that's who he had to be, was quite thin, with a crown of curly black hair and vividly alert dark eyes.

Royce got the sense that this was a very intelligent person.

"The Swigg I'm looking for lives in or near St Giles. You know exactly who I mean, and I need to find him *now*, or a woman I'm responsible for will very likely be killed."

The blood-spattered doctor now focused on Royce. "You look rather more well-born than my usual clientele. Who told you to come here?"

"Someone disreputable."

Cutter blinked, then said, "Ah. Well, in that case. I don't have to warn you to keep your source of information secret, do I? I provide my services to certain underworld figures so that I can do this kind of work"—he gestured to his patient—"for those who need it but can't pay. I can't afford to get caught up in some war of reprisal… that will lead to even more people dying."

"I know how to keep a secret," Royce assured him.

Cutter gave him precise directions to find where Swigg actually held court, in a well-fortified building filled with a small army of guards, trained dogs, and other protections. "Good luck. Bring a gun. And your own army."

Royce didn't intend to bring either of those things, but he nodded, laid a few silver coins on a chair by the door, and strode out.

"Sally," he heard Cutter say behind him, "bring up more hot water, will you? This one's bleeding all over the floor."

♍

IN THE SMALL ROOM IN Swigg's headquarters, Tamsin kept her gaze locked on the papers on the desk, too afraid to look anywhere else. She'd been left alone in the room, because she could not possibly escape from it. A burly man stood guard outside the door. The single window was barred on the outside. There were no other doors. Above her, the cracked plaster of the ceiling showed huge mildew stains, but no escape route. She could occasionally hear the scratching of rats in the attic, and envied their freedom. The heavy, dark-stained floorboards were just as solid.

She was trapped.

Just then, the door opened, and Yves walked in, humming to himself. Behind him, the guard pulled the door shut once more, leaving them alone.

"How are you progressing, Mademoiselle Tess?" he asked. He persisted in using the name she lived by in Catchpenny Lane. It didn't occur to Tamsin to correct him.

"I am not progressing," Tamsin replied. The pages lay before her, as blank as they'd been two hours ago.

He frowned. "What's the matter? I gave you all the information and material you needed."

"None of that matters. What you're telling me to do is wrong," she said. "People will die."

"People will die regardless. That's what happens in a war." He looked truly confused at her argument, unable to understand simple morality. "You forged many documents before this, and it did not prick your conscience then."

"It did, but I told myself to ignore it." She stood up, to better face him on the same level. "I valued my one life above others. I know better now."

Yves's fists clenched, and in the silence, the skittering of the rats above was all the more loud. Finally, he said in a very calm voice, "Mademoiselle Tess, don't be a fool. It is one letter. After this, no more. You can go about your life."

"You're going to kill me after this anyway. Don't try to deny it."

"If you will do this tonight, I will let you live. My hand to God, Tess."

"I don't believe you."

His eyes flashed in anger. "You stubborn mule! What must I do to convince you?"

"You can't. That's what I'm saying."

Yves paced the room, once, twice. Then he looked past her and smiled. A very cold smile. "You're resigned, yes? You're ready for death."

No, she wasn't. But she was ready to do the right thing. "I am willing to die so others won't," she said, trying to keep her voice—and her knees—steady.

"Admirable. Stupid, but admirable."

He drew out a thin loop of wire from his waistcoat pocket. Her eyes widened as she saw him pull it taut. She swallowed, already feeling her throat constrict in anticipation, because he intended to kill her with a garrote.

"It will be quieter this way," he said soothingly.

Tamsin disagreed. She grabbed the chair she'd been sitting in and held it up to fend him off. And she screamed.

She screamed so all the rats in London would hear her. She screamed every curse she knew, in English, French, and then in English again for good measure.

Yves rushed at her, and grunted as she warded him off by jabbing the chair legs into his stomach.

The door opened and the guard leaned in. "What the hell is going on?" he barked.

"This man is trying to kill me, you idiot!" Tamsin shot back, her voice already raw.

The guard showed his valor by wrenching the door shut again, abandoning her to her fate. Tamsin howled a few more curses at him.

Yves recovered from Tamsin's first assault and came for her again. She whipped the chair in a circle, but he ducked and evaded the blow. He reached out, grabbing one chair leg and wrenching the whole thing away from her. He flung it aside, his eyes blazing.

He said something in a dialect of French that Tamsin never learned, but she knew enough to know it was filthy. Yves snapped the garrote wire taut again.

"Did you know, mademoiselle, that this wire will cut to the bone?"

Voices shouted somewhere below. The guard hurrying to tell Swigg that the Viper had gone crazy…not that anyone would come to Tamsin's rescue.

Yves rushed at her, his weight shoving her several feet backward against the wall. He grinned savagely as he raised his arms and looped the wire around her. She gasped as she reached up to hook her fingers around the wire, trying to stop it from touching her neck.

Pain arced through her fingers—the thin wire sliced into her flesh. She'd never fight him off this way.

Tamsin screamed again, right in Yves's face. He grimaced. "The sooner I silence you, the better, woman."

Woman.

With a flash of inspiration, Tamsin did the most feminine thing she could imagine. She fell to the floor in a faint. The garrote wire was just loose enough to let her head through, though her hair snagged and pulled and was cut as she slid downward.

She heard a loud crash and assumed it was her own body, though it sounded further away.

Perhaps my ear got cut off, she thought.

She winced at the new sources of pain, but scrabbled away from Yves, heading for the door. No matter who Swigg put on guard throughout this building, she had a better chance dealing with them than with the Viper.

Behind her, he cursed and lunged upward, intent on catching her before she could open the door. As Yves stood, he lurched and hit the desk, knocking the lamp over. The room plunged into near darkness.

Tamsin rushed to the door, her memory leading her to the knob without faltering. She turned it…and nothing happened.

The door had been locked.

"No," she moaned, rattling the knob, hitting the wooden panel, losing her mind. "No, no, no, no!"

Yves laughed, the sound of his voice terrifyingly close. Tamsin turned, sensing him about to attack again.

She moved sideways, only to get pinned against the door by the solid weight of Yves. He hissed in triumph, and grabbed her neck in his hands. Tamsin began to scream again, only to hear her own voice choke off into a gurgle.

"I told you, be qu—" Yves broke off, and suddenly pulled away from her.

No, he was *being* pulled away from her.

Tamsin watched as a shadowy form wrestled Yves further into the center of the room. She had to been hallucinating, the strangulation making her dream. Someone else was in the room? How could that be?

"Stay out of the way, Tamsin," the shadow told her, in a tone that sounded just like Royce.

I am dying, she thought. *There's no other explanation.*

The two figures tangled in the middle of the room, with the murk hiding the detail of what was happening. She heard only grunts and the rough, violent sound of fists hitting flesh. Yves shouted in that dialect again, the words barely coherent. But he was not going to die easily, and he had weapons that the shadow could not possibly know about.

"Garrote," Tamsin tried to shout, only to find the word burn in her throat before it could come out of her mouth. "Viper has a garrote," she said again, forcing out the warning. "And a knife!"

The shadow did not reply, but a moment later Yves seemed to fly across the room toward the coal-burning grate, the only source of light left. He crashed against the far wall, moaning.

Before she could do anything, the shadow chased after Yves, trapping him in the corner. The French agent fought like a man possessed, but who can fight a shadow? Especially a shadow trained to hit like that...

She winced at every punch, thankful she couldn't see the details. But at last, one hit knocked Yves into the wall, where he went still, then slid slowly down to the floor.

Silence reigned at last.

Tamsin moved to the desk. The lamp was smashed on the floor, but she had seen a candle in the drawer. With trembling hands, she grabbed for it, then stumbled to the grate, thrusting the wick into the coals. After a second, it flared into light. She pulled it back and looked toward the shadow, seeing Royce's eyes staring back.

"Oh, my God," she whispered, nearly dropping the candle.

Royce moved to her, catching her hand before the candle tumbled to the floor. "I'm here, Tamsin. I found you."

"How…" she murmured, then saw that what looked like a pile of snow on the floor was actually shards of plaster. Above, the ceiling gaped with a single large hole. Royce had made his entrance through the attic.

"I thought it was rats," she whispered.

"There were plenty of those," he assured her. "I knew I couldn't fight my way in from the ground floor. So I climbed up the outside and crawled through the attic. When I overheard your voice, I knew exactly which room's ceiling to chop through. Unfortunately, I don't think we can go back that way."

"The Viper…is he…" she whispered, terrified the calm would be shattered again.

He moved swiftly to the prone figure of Yves, bending down to hold a hand to the man's neck.

"Dead," Royce said after a moment. He stood, then walked back to Tamsin, looking her over anxiously.

"You're bleeding," he said.

She tipped her head to Yves. "His doing. He had Swigg's people kidnap me, and when I wouldn't create the final forgery, he decided to kill me." She held up her blood-streaked hands. "I never knew how sharp a wire could be."

"Dear God, Tamsin. I've got to get you out of here."

"We're locked in. Unless…" Tamsin bent down by Yves's corpse, searching for a key. He'd never let a petty bodyguard trap *him* in a room, would he?

A moment later, she pulled a small brass key into the light. "Here."

"Genius," Royce told her, taking the key.

They moved quietly to the door. Royce leaned against it, listening. Then he eased the key into the lock and turned it. The audible click nearly made Tamsin weep with relief.

He opened the door, and looked out. "Clear," he muttered, pulling Tamsin with him.

"A guard knew Yves was attacking me," she said. "He fled downstairs. Everyone will be on alert."

Royce smiled. "You might be surprised."

They found the stairs and descended. Every moment, Tamsin expected one of Swigg's guards to emerge, or for Swigg himself to appear and shout for Tamsin to stop.

But there was no one.

"What's happening?" she whispered, more on edge than ever. "Where is everyone?"

"It helps to have allies in low places," Royce said. "I am honored to have some contacts among the less-law-abiding parts of society, though they themselves are now quite reformed. One of them dropped a helpful hint to Swigg's crew that a whole brigade of charleys were on the way, eager to arrest every criminal they could find here."

"So Swigg's people fled."

"Like rats deserting a sinking ship. Leaving us a clear path."

"But what about the charleys?" she asked, not wishing to be arrested herself.

"Oh, we didn't bother with that part," Royce said. "After all, I was in a hurry."

By that point, he had walked her through the back of the building to a small door near a foul-smelling kitchen. "This goes through a short passage, with a carriage waiting beyond it," he told Tamsin.

"And then?" she asked.

"And then you get in the carriage and you're free," he said, opening the door.

The air beyond was fetid with rotting food and garbage, but to Tamsin, it smelled as fresh as sunshine. She stepped outside, with Royce next to her.

"A man and a woman often come in together," she murmured, thinking back to the first time she met Royce, and the barkeeper's cynical words. "I don't see them leaving together quite as often."

But once again, she and Royce were doing exactly that.

♍

"YOU DID WHAT?" ARIES ASKED.

"I killed the Viper," Royce repeated, for the third time.

Both he and Tamsin sat in the discreet offices of the Zodiac, prepared to give an accounting of what had happened that evening. They'd agreed that despite everything, despite wanting to do nothing else but rest, it was necessary. Tamsin quietly confessed that she wouldn't be able to sleep until they were able to tell the whole story.

"That way," she'd said, in the aftermath of the vicious battle in Swigg's headquarters, "I can tell myself that it ended. Understand?"

He did, and he couldn't wait to let Aries and Miss Chattan and the Astronomer himself, whoever he might be, hear the news. Let them deal with it from now on. Royce was done.

But at the moment, Aries seemed to not understand what Royce was telling him. "You killed the Viper? Before, you couldn't even find him. According to the most recent report, he got away and you had no idea how else to trace him."

Royce nodded. "True. But the idiot couldn't leave well enough alone. He wanted Tamsin to forge that last document, the capstone to his plan to weaken Portugal and thus allow Bonaparte to take over the country completely."

"It's a compliment, in a way," Tamsin said. She sounded distant and tired, as if none of this really had to do with her anymore. "He thought highly enough of my forgery skills that he risked contacting Swigg, and having me kidnapped, just to get it done properly."

"But he didn't count on Tamsin refusing to do it, even at the cost of her own life," Royce reported. He was proud of her for that, and he always would be.

Then Royce explained it all, from the moment he snapped out of his fugue state earlier that day. He told how he followed Tamsin's path to the theater, and then to the streets, and then using the Disreputables' leads to reach Swigg's headquarters, where the Viper happened to be.

"He was an excellent agent, but he made the mistake of staying in one place too long. I was able to corner him and fight him head-on."

"And you do like to fight head-on," Aries murmured.

Royce grinned, inadvertently hurting his split lip. There was nothing like a pure bout of bareknuckle boxing to clear the air…and it was even better when his opponent deserved justice.

"So it sounds as if the Viper's plan to weaken Portugal's ruling system enough to give the Emperor an opening is done. At least that part of the war will not concern us for a while."

"If needed," Tamsin said suddenly, "I could create a few documents that would help the British government to smooth over any ruffled feathers. I'm sure the Zodiac can procure the materials I'd have to look at to copy someone else's handwriting."

Royce reached over and squeezed her shoulder. It was generous in the extreme for Tamsin to offer, especially when she'd been forced to use her skills inappropriately for so long.

"Something to keep in mind," Miss Chattan said with a little, secret smile. "But I'd guess that for now, the last thing you'd want to do is pick up a pen."

"Very true." Tamsin tried to cover a yawn with her now-bandaged hands, and only partially succeeded.

Chattan took her by the arm and helped her up. "Come with me," the blonde woman instructed. "I've got a pot of tea brewing in the outer office, and I know Aries has some more to discuss with Virgo."

Then it was just Royce and Julian at the desk, and Royce knew the time had come to reveal everything. Not just about this assignment, but his own struggles with his worth and his self-doubt about being an agent over the past years, especially since assuming his father's title.

Royce spoke quietly, and Julian didn't interrupt once.

"I didn't know," Julian said when Royce finished at last. He looked chagrined. "When you said that you simply did enough, or that any agent could have managed it, I thought you were being modest."

"There were assignments that I failed to complete."

"Virgo, do you understand that *no* agent has a perfect record? The sort of work we do here is nearly impossible by definition. We work with little information, limited time, in the face of great opposition from the enemy, and to top it off, we need to keep everything secret. In fact, you've got one of the highest success rates of any Sign actively working now. That's why you've been entrusted with the most challenging tasks. We rely on you to get them done, and get them done well."

"I think you'll feel differently now that you know the truth."

"Truth," said Julian. "What is that?" He shrugged philosophically, and then rubbed his temples. "God, what time is it? We should all get some rest."

Royce stood up, swaying slightly as he did so. Well, that at least was a truth they could all agree on.

He found Tamsin in a chair near Miss Chattan's desk in the large outer office, dozing while Chattan flipped idly through her notes. Royce nudged Tamsin's shoulder. "Wake up."

She blinked. "I wasn't asleep!"

"Of course you weren't."

Tamsin stood up, thanking Chattan for the tea, just as if she were finishing an afternoon call.

Chattan nodded, then said, "Oh, by the way, what happened to Swigg?"

Royce answered, "I let him scurry into the shadows with the rest of the rats. It's not worth it to kill him. In that part of the city, another criminal will simply take over. At least we know who and what Swigg is."

Chattan nodded in satisfaction, making a note in her little book. "We can pass the information on to the relevant parties in the city watch and among the magistrates. They'll have their own ways to rein in Swigg."

"What now?" Royce asked, utterly drained. Aries hadn't yet told him to get out of the Zodiac offices, no longer being a Sign, and Royce wondered why he was drawing it out.

"Well, I'd suggest taking your wife home, bathing—both of you are rather worse for wear—and then sleeping for the next few days. With this Viper business concluded, you've more than earned a holiday."

"A holiday?" he echoed.

"Yes. You didn't truly think I would let you go, did you?"

"I'm still a Sign?"

"As long as I'm in charge, yes. Use your time well,"

Aries counseled. "Because the Zodiac will need you again."

"Always," Chattan added with a little smile. "Now, for the love of God, go home!"

It was good advice, and he followed it, taking Tamsin downstairs and outside, where Errol was still patiently waiting with the carriage.

"Home," Royce instructed. He helped Tamsin in and climbed in after her, sitting opposite so he could watch her. He never wanted to let her out of his sight again.

The carriage rattled down the otherwise empty streets. Tamsin put her head back against the cushioned seat, and sighed.

"Home," she echoed. "Such a small word for such an important idea."

"Small words are all I can manage just now," Royce replied. "*Home. Sleep. Wife.*"

She frowned, the word evidently not soothing her in the way it soothed him. "About that. We'll have to arrange an annulment sooner rather than later. Laurent knows about the marriage, by the way, but he'll not talk. However, we've got to deal with it soon."

Royce shook his head. "No."

"I'm not pregnant," she said, in what he assumed was meant to be a reassuring statement. "I found that out today. You're quite safe on that front."

"Tamsin, you obstinate woman. I didn't marry you to avoid raising a bastard child. I married you because I love you and wanted to keep you safe in the best way I knew how."

Her eyes widened. "That's not what you said then."

"I did say that! I told you that the name of Pelham would protect you."

"No, I mean you never said you *loved* me."

"Yes, I did."

"No, you didn't."

"Well, I thought it, very loudly," he said.

A tiny smile twitched at the corner of her mouth. "Ah, so it's my fault for not reading your mind, like some sort of traveling sideshow magician?"

"You read my mind very well in other situations." He moved to her side of the carriage, sliding his arms around her.

"Royce, you can't…" Though she protested with her voice, her body reacted with openness, meeting his.

"Tamsin, I love you," he said. "I know it's quite unfashionable to love one's wife, but I've never been a typical nobleman."

"That's true enough." She still looked rather stunned at his words.

"Please give me a chance, Tamsin," Royce said suddenly. "I know that I'm not the man you thought you were marrying. My soul is a wreck and you've seen me at my worst—you've seen me in a way no one else on earth has. And I can't promise that I won't fall into a depth like that again. But for you, I'll try to climb out. I'm not asking you to rescue me. I'm just asking that you show patience with me."

"Oh, Royce. You know I won't leave you."

"But if you're only staying out of a sense of duty, then it will be worse than if you leave entirely."

"I'm staying because I love you too," she retorted. "You're not like any other person I've ever known. You're maddening, and difficult, and I want to slap you sometimes. But you've shown me more love and care than any man on earth. And despite all your faults and mine, I want to live my life with you…" She trailed off, leaving something unsaid.

But Royce heard all he needed. "We're together, Tamsin. Now, tonight, tomorrow, always."

Her eyes, inexplicably, filled with tears, but then she kissed him, and all other questions faded from his mind.

♍

A LETTER FROM HECTOR ARRIVED the next morning, and Tamsin nearly lost it. "He can't give me a moment's peace!" she said under her breath. But then, the insufferable Hector Englefield didn't know what transpired the previous night. All he knew was that Tamsin never arrived to hand over the money at the theater, forcing him to increase his threats.

My Dear Miss Latimer,

I was most concerned at your absence yesterday evening. I trust that you have not taken some foolish notion that I am not serious about my intentions. For the love of your family and your own interests, I will offer once more. Ask for me at the Daracott Hotel at seven o'clock this evening.

She grimaced. The language was carefully phrased, and the average person might mistake the missive for a request to propose. Tamsin crumpled the note up and tossed it into the fire, wishing that she could burn Hector himself.

"Who's writing to you, love?"

She turned to see Royce in the doorway. He looked hollow-cheeked and tired, but much better than he did the previous day.

"You should be sleeping!" Tamsin said, hoping to put him off. "You're not fully recovered."

Royce strolled toward her and took her in his arms. "I assure you I'm up for anything."

"That is not true, my lord. Rest, food, and more rest. That is what any doctor would say."

"I'll go directly to bed if you join me," he said in a low voice. "But I don't want to rest."

She pushed him away, smiling as she did. "Don't be silly. We are not going to do that today."

"Why not, wife?"

"Royce, please." She looked around in alarm, as if there might be someone lurking in a corner to overhear the term.

"Inside this house, it's not a secret," he said, looking pleased. In fact, Laurent had stood watch until Royce and Tamsin returned last night, and uncharacteristically embraced his father when he saw him.

"But the news cannot be bandied about," Tamsin protested. "At least not yet."

"We'll have a second wedding for show, then. Will that suffice?"

"Let's talk about it later," she said, still thinking of how much damage Hector could do if she didn't retrieve her father's IOU from him. Thankfully, Royce seemed to have no memory of what she'd told him while he was unresponsive on his floor. At least, he hadn't said anything regarding her theft and forgery of the cheques.

"Why do I get the feeling you're hiding something from me, wife?" His voice was teasing, but his expression was not.

"Spies see secrets everywhere," Tamsin returned, keeping her tone playful. "Now, come upstairs and I'll see that you get a tray for lunch once you're in bed. Then you must rest. You've been through so much."

Royce acquiesced without further protest, which should have made Tamsin suspicious. However, she was so happy that he hadn't asked her anything more about the note she burned that she didn't question her luck.

The afternoon passed quietly, and all too quickly.

Tamsin dressed in a dark gown and a black velvet pelisse with a hood to conceal her features from prying eyes. She called for the carriage at six, leaving plenty of time. Sitting alone on the seat, she gripped her spare reticule tightly, thinking of the newly forged banknote inside.

"The last thing I shall ever forge!" she vowed to herself. No matter what happened tonight, that part of her life was over.

The Daracott Hotel was a respectable establishment catering to wealthier guests, and Tamsin was shown to a discreet sitting room to wait for Hector to come down.

Hector looked smugly at Tamsin when he entered the sitting room, but faltered for a moment when he saw the bandages she wore.

"What the hell happened to you?" he asked.

"A misadventure with some criminals, while I was on my way to meet you, as it happens."

"I suppose you're here to tell me that they took all your money and you need more time to pay me."

"No."

Tamsin offered nothing more, and indeed enjoyed the march of changing expressions on Hector's face.

Finally, he shrugged. "Let's go upstairs."

"I don't think the hotel condones female guests going upstairs."

"They'll condone what I pay for them to condone," he snapped back. Tamsin realized anew that Hector truly believed that everything and everyone could be bought. "Now, come along if you want to see the contract."

He led her upstairs via the servants' stairs, and showed her into his suite.

"Well, then?" he demanded. "Have you got the money? If you hold out on me, I'll go directly to a woman I know who's one of the biggest gossips in London. She'll have your tale talked about in every tearoom by the end of the week."

"I will produce the payment when you hand over the contract that you claim you have. My father's IOU."

Hector sneered, but went to the desk drawer and pulled out a piece of paper. "Look then, Miss Latimer. Look at your father's idiocy."

Tamsin walked to the desk and reached over to take the IOU. She surveyed it carefully, with a professional detachment that surprised even her. The language was standard enough. Tamsin knew it well because Swigg collected dozens and dozens of IOUs in the course of his business, most of them quite legitimate.

She paused on seeing the date. "June 14th," she said aloud. "Interesting. Where did my father sign this contract?"

"My home in Somerset. He'd come to ask for money."

"Because in June of that year, the whole family went to visit Mama's cousins in the Lake District. My father came as well. There's no way he could have signed it at your house in Somerset. This is a forgery."

"You'll never prove it."

"I just have, you idiot. This will not stand in court."

"It doesn't have to. Remember, Thomasina, all I need to do is tell the world about you. Try to challenge this contract now, and all the money you paid before will be wasted. I'll ruin you all over again. I'll do it in a heartbeat. I'm a respected member of the gentry and you're a ruined slut who spread her legs without protest. You can't fight me and win, Thomasina."

"She's already won," a new voice said.

Tamsin turned to see Royce enter the room. "What are you doing here?"

"I'm following you."

Hector's jaw dropped. "Lord Pelham…you came here?"

"Indeed. And I must insist that you not refer to this lady as a ruined slut. It's quite rude."

Hector was obviously flummoxed at the sudden appearance of a six-foot-tall, angry earl, but he suddenly pointed to Tamsin and said, "This is all her fault! This woman has clearly tricked you into hiring her as personal secretary to cover the fact that she was your mistress. She snuck in and stole cheques, forging your signature so the bank would accept them!"

"And you cashed them anyway?" Royce asked. "That's a crime, to knowingly benefit from false documents."

"Don't look at me! You should have that cow of a mistress arrested for stealing from you."

"She's not my mistress. She's my wife."

Hector blinked. "What?"

"The woman you've been calling a slut and a cow and a thief is in fact the Countess of Pelham."

"That's impossible," Hector said. "She's ruined. Unmarriageable."

"She was quite marriageable. I know because I married her." Royce used Hector's momentary shock to reach over and pluck the IOU from his grip.

He handed it to Tamsin. "Here, darling. What would you like to do with that? We could rip it up, and your father wouldn't have to worry about returning to debtor's prison."

"Oh, I'd prefer to keep it as insurance, so that Mr Englefield here doesn't get any ideas about spreading rumors involving my name or yours." Tamsin folded the contract and slid it into her reticule. "If he dares, we can make this forged document public and bring a case against him in court."

"Well reasoned, darling. I suppose I should take this banknote and destroy it. Although there's a certain poetry in a forged banknote being offered in payment for you to keep this forged contract hidden."

Royce waved the banknote in front of Hector before holding it to the flame of the lamp, where it caught fire. "Too bad. That could have been a thousand pounds. Now it's ash."

"Shall we go, Royce?" Tamsin said. "We've stayed here quite long enough, and Mr Englefield is not looking at all well. Goodbye, Mr Englefield. I expect to never see you or hear from you again."

She turned and walked to the door, but looked back when Royce didn't follow.

"Go on, darling. Wait for me in the carriage. I just want a final word with Mr Englefield, man to man."

Hector's face paled.

Tamsin smiled. "Of course, my lord."

She walked out, closing the door firmly behind her. She strolled down the steps to the foyer, feeling light as air. The truth that she feared telling Royce was out fully, and it was far less terrible than she imagined it would be. Why were monsters always more frightening when half hidden? Sunlight was stronger than darkness, she told herself. She'd have to work to remember that.

So the great burden of her life for the last several

years was now finally gone. It was funny how something as immaterial as guilt and fear could have such weight. But now the fear was defeated, and Tamsin held her head higher.

She left the house and walked to Royce's waiting carriage. The hotel's footman helped her in. "We will wait just a few moments," she instructed Errol. "Lord Pelham will be out directly, and then we shall go home."

The footman shut the door to keep out the cold, and Tamsin arranged the woolen throw over her lap, grateful for extra warmth.

Less than five minutes later, Royce emerged from the hotel and strode down the walk. He waved the footman off, opening the door himself and climbing in to sit opposite Tamsin. It was all very proper.

He looked every inch the earl, in fact. His clothing was immaculate, his hair slightly—and rather attractively—mussed. There was only one thing that didn't match. Tamsin noted how he flexed his hands, and the new cuts on his knuckles, the sort of cuts that only come from the most primal kind of fighting.

"I didn't want you to see what I had to do," he said quietly.

"That was very thoughtful," Tamsin replied, touched. "It seems like the lesson you imparted to him did not take long."

"No. Englefield is a coward and a sniveling wretch and put up no fight whatsoever. I told him that if anyone I know sees or hears from him, he'll regret it."

"I hope he listens."

"In fact, I'm not going to wait to take some corrective measures. Englefield will soon find that many doors are closed to him. He won't be able to borrow money from any reputable bank, he won't find admittance to any clubs of note, and many of his friends will reconsider how close their friendship really is."

"That sounds rather appropriate," Tamsin said, considering how much pain Hector had caused her over the years, how many doors he'd closed to her through his selfishness and vindictiveness.

"You don't think it's too much?"

"Oh, no. You do always get me the nicest gifts." She smiled at him, then leaned over to kiss him, softly at first, and then with more passion. "But you are the nicest gift of all."

♍

IT WAS THE LAST DAY of the year. Outside the walls of Seabourne, a cold wind howled past, carrying an army of snowflakes to pile upon the frozen ground and to gather softly around the fenceposts and evergreens planted along the walkways.

Inside, however, the Countess of Pelham lay warm and snug underneath an eider-stuffed quilt and absurdly soft linen sheets. When Tamsin had gone to bed, she also wore a silk chemise…but that had been quickly discarded by her husband, who warmed her tenfold in exchange.

She thought back to the small but pretty wedding ceremony conducted two weeks prior, in Seabourne's library. Royce's mother had come all the way from Bath to attend, and Laurent held Jasper's leash during the service. On the other side of the aisle, Tamsin's sister, Georgina, beamed at her, and her parents looked as if they'd gone to heaven.

Several weeks prior, Tamsin had finally contacted her family—after all the trouble was over—and she was astonished by their reaction. She anticipated a somewhat chilly reception, but instead her mother wept with joy the moment she saw Tamsin in person. As it turned out, Hector had told her mother that Tamsin ran off with a footman…and he had the temerity to suggest that Georgina be the new governess! Thankfully, Gina was already living elsewhere. Mrs. Latimer was suspicious of Hector's story from the start ("As if my Tamsin would ever disgrace the family name like that!"), but was unable to find out more information. Gina wept for days when she heard the news, declaring it all a sham. After months of silence, they feared that Tamsin had died, whether by accident or illness. Her father wore a black band around his arm for six months, and her mother and sister wore only black and grey for a year.

"We despaired of ever seeing you again in this life. And all of a sudden, you reemerge, and on the arm of an earl!" Her mother made no secret of how impressed she was by Lord Pelham.

So would they like to come to Tamsin's wedding?

Wild horses could not keep them away.

The essential family members and friends were invited to Seabourne for the ceremony,

which took place just before Christmas. Perhaps to make up for the year of mourning, Mrs. Latimer and Gina wore gowns in bright blue and deepest red, respectively.

Royce and Tamsin were already married, of course, but they went through it again for propriety, and so others could witness the happy event. Tamsin made sure to sign her actual name this time.

The wedding breakfast afterward was probably the largest gathering at Seabourne since the passing of the old earl. Following the wedding day, most of the guests stayed on through Yuletide, travel being difficult this time of year.

Laurent even decided to appoint himself Master of Jollity, conducting snowy walks (with Jasper leading), musical evenings, and snowball fights. When Royce had recovered from the worst of his recent melancholy, he asked Laurent to his room. Father and son locked themselves away for the whole afternoon. Tamsin never asked what they talked about, but when the two men emerged, the old enmity and tension was gone. Laurent was clearly going to remain with Royce and Tamsin for the long-term, a fact that pleased Tamsin enormously.

Thus, Seabourne turned from silent to lively within the space of a few weeks.

Fortunately, even the onslaught of family and friends did not completely fill Seabourne's forty-seven rooms, and the inhabitants were merry without feeling cramped.

All in all, Tamsin thought things were going quite well. "Is it morning yet?" she murmured to Royce, who stirred beside her.

"Mmm, I fear so. But as my countess, you do not need to obey the whims of time. Stay in bed all day, won't you?"

She laughed. "We cannot, silly. We've got house-guests! And remember, we invited all the neighbors for a New Year's Day celebration."

"Un-invite them," Royce suggested. "We're doing something much more important."

"Oh, and what is that?"

"Ensuring the continuation of the line of Pelham."

"So that's all I am to you," she said with a false pout. "A mere vessel to carry your heirs."

"Tamsin, you're the world to me." He kissed her deeply, and Tamsin responded with such eagerness that they did, in fact, try their very best to ensure the continuation of the Pelham line that morning.

Afterward, Tamsin curled up against Royce, running her fingers along his chest and shoulder. "I love you," she said.

"That's lucky, since you're my wife." He kissed the top of her head. "I adore you, though, so it'll turn out all right in the end."

"You make light of a serious matter, my lord. Love is not a joke."

"Of course not. It's a reason for living. And as it's a new year, I thought I would make a resolution to tell you that I love every single day."

"Oh, I like that." Tamsin snuggled closer, enjoying this intimate moment, free of spying or blackmail or scandal or muddy dogs. She yawned. "Should I make a resolution as well?"

"If you like. You could resolve to make no resolutions."

"Is that not a tautology? Or at the very least nonsensical." She smiled, thinking. "Perhaps I shall resolve to learn a new type of calligraphy. I once saw some very beautiful Chinese calligraphy, done with brushes instead of pen. I should like to do that."

"Then you shall. I'll find an instructor in the city to teach you. Oh, by the way, I got you a present."

"A New Year's present? What is it?"

"Two presents, actually. Hold on while I make the tremendous sacrifice of leaving your exquisite body all alone for five minutes."

He slid out of bed and walked across the room to the clothespress, giving Tamsin a magnificent view. "Was that one of the presents?" she asked slyly.

He cast a look back that made her heart pound. But he returned from the opened press with two boxes that had been hidden there.

Sitting on the bed, he offered her the top box, which was the smaller of the two. "Start with this, love."

It was wrapped with care in gorgeous marbleized paper in swirls of blue and white, not unlike a snowstorm, she thought. She lifted the lid to find a long and extremely plush white ostrich feather pen, and three bottles of ink in red, blue, and purple. The memory of the night they finally gave in to their passion for each other caused Tamsin's cheeks to warm.

"You know me so well, my lord," she murmured.

Royce leaned over and kissed her. "Just think of what you'll write next."

"I already am." And before he could stand up, she caught his face in her hands and kissed

him back. She intended to make immediate and thorough use of her present. As indeed she did.

The other gift, which wasn't opened till much later, contained a new set of bedsheets.

ABOUT THE AUTHOR

Elizabeth Cole is a romance writer with a penchant for history. Her stories draw upon her deep affection for the British Isles, action movies, medieval fantasies, and even science fiction. She now lives in a small house in a big city with a cat, a snake, and a rather charming gentleman. When not writing, she is usually curled in a corner reading...or watching costume dramas or things that explode. And yes, she believes in love at first sight.